OPPOSITE OF ALWAYS

OPPOSITE
OF
ALWAYS

justin a. reynolds

KATHERINE TEGEN BOOKS
An Imprint of HarperCollins Publishers

Katherine Tegen Books is an imprint of HarperCollins Publishers.

Opposite of Always
Copyright © 2019 by This Just In LLC
All rights reserved. Printed in the United States of America.
No part of this book may be used or reproduced in any manner whatsoever
without written permission except in the case of brief quotations
embodied in critical articles and reviews. For information address
HarperCollins Children's Books, a division of HarperCollins Publishers,
195 Broadway, New York, NY 10007.
www.epicreads.com

Library of Congress Control Number: 2018946216
ISBN 978-0-06-293515-1 (special edition)

Typography by Erin Fitzsimmons
19 20 21 22 23 PC/LSCH 10 9 8 7 6 5 4 3 2 1

First Edition

to k and b,
with all the love my heart holds
and for the loves we've lost

So.

You know that saying "Time is undefeated"?

This is a story about the time that Time lost.

HOW TO SAVE NO ONE

My face is mashed sideways against the trunk of a police cruiser when Kate dies for the third time. The box meant to save her life is smushed near my feet.

I've learned a few lessons along the way.

For instance: *don't waste time on clothes.*

It's cold out, easily sweater weather. I'm in short sleeves, plaid pajama shorts, and a pair of beat-up Chucks I wear to mow the lawn. The insides are damp, and there's a clump of grass in my right shoe scratching my toes, but there wasn't time for socks. Socks, and weather-appropriate attire, are a luxury. They take time. And I can't waste any.

Not tonight.

Not ever.

Because big lesson number one is this: *all the time travel in the world can't save the people you love.*

3

45 MINUTES EARLIER

The police are already here.

A marked car, idling beside the emergency room entrance. There's a chance they're here for me, but there's no turning back. Split seconds matter. I grab the small package sitting on the passenger seat and hop out of my car. I rip open the box, jam its contents into my sneaker. I pick up my pace.

I should've left earlier.

Should've done a hundred things differently this time around.

I push open the door, thinking, *Get to the elevator, make it to the fourth floor*, and then I run face-first into a concrete wall. Also known as colliding into three hundred pounds of beef and nightstick.

Ah, this must be the driver.

I nearly crumple onto the wet floor, except the officer snares me by my T-shirt.

"I got him," he mumbles into the walkie holstered on his shoulder. "Back outside," he orders me, pushing open the door, his other hand hugging his gun grip. "Come on, kid. Let's go." All sorts of things run through my mind—acts of valor, courage. I think about pushing past the officer and bolting for the stairs or slipping inside the elevator before it closes. But in the end my legs are spread apart, my hands cuffed behind my back.

Part of me thinks, wonders, hopes: maybe this is it. This is the solution. I'm not supposed to be there. If I'm not there, she'll live.

They rattle off my crimes, and after breaking and entering, I stop listening. I don't bother trying to explain, because how do you explain you're from the future?

". . . you understand your rights," they say more than ask.

I nod, the aluminum trunk cool and sticky against my cheek.

"You have anything on you? Weapon, drugs, or the like?" the large officer asks.

"No," I lie. Because I can't tell the truth. Not now. Rough hands slide up and down my body. My keys jingle as he fishes them out of my pocket. Then he removes my wallet.

"Nothing interesting," the large officer says to his female partner.

"Have him take off his shoes?" she suggests.

And my knees nearly buckle.

"Please," I plead, "just let me go inside. My girlfriend's dying. Check with the doctors, her nurses. Please. Just *five* minutes. Please. A heart, have a heart. Just let me see her for five minutes and then you can haul me away to prison, throw away the key, whatever. Please. Think of your kids. Do you have kids? If they were dying, would you want them to be alone? Please. *Please.*"

I try dropping to my knees to beg, but it's tricky when you're being physically restrained. The officer who put the cuffs on me looks over to the other one, a dirty-blond-haired woman with bloodshot eyes, and she sighs in that studied way that all mothers must learn on the first day of Mom School. But then she nods her head. And the cuffs come off.

Which is beyond crazy.

"Don't be stupid, kid," he says in a voice that makes me think *he thinks* I'm going to do something stupid.

"Five minutes," she says. "That's it."

They walk on either side of me, assuring me as we march the greasy linoleum floors and ride the we're-trying-to-hide-the-piss-smell-with-bleach elevator to the fourth floor that if I try anything funny they will not hesitate to lay my stupid ass out. But I'm not going to run. I check my watch again. There's a chance.

Except the elevator door hesitates for twenty seconds before finally hiccuping open. And then we're forced to detour down another hallway because a maintenance man is mopping the floors and apparently takes his floor-mopping very seriously, because he starts shouting and jumping up and down. The

6

officers mumble apologies, but the man just points angrily toward an alternative route, also known as The World's Longest Possible Way Around.

I try to explain that we don't have time for detours, for tired elevators, for wet floor signs. But no one listens. And when we get there it's nearly too late.

Kate's almost gone.

"Well, look who it is," she says, her eyes blinking open. In the corner, the chair her mom normally occupies is empty. A crumpled blanket on the floor beside it. A lipsticked Styrofoam cup on the windowsill.

"Hey," I say. For a second I'm taken aback at how small she looks. The room is quiet, except for the hiss of oxygen pumping into her nose, the drone of IV fluids chugging into her arm.

"What time is it?" she asks, squinting. Even at three in the morning, confined to a hospital bed, she's beautiful.

"We don't have a lot of time left."

Her face twists in confusion. "What are you talking about?" She leans forward in her bed, glances over my shoulder, wincing. "And this time, you brought the police with you. Interesting move. You really know how to make an entrance, Jack King."

I look back at the officers. "I'm sorry about them."

"You're crazy, you know that?"

"I can see how you'd come to that conclusion, yes," I say, smiling.

"*Five*," the female officer reminds me.

Kate shakes her head. "Jack, why are you here? I don't get it,

7

man. What, you have some morbid fascination with hospitals, is that it? Or do sick girls turn you on?"

"I came here to tell you . . ." My voice trails off because I haven't really come to *say* anything.

"What, Jack?"

"I think I know what I'm supposed to do now. I think I've figured it out. Finally."

"Okaaaay," she says, her eyebrows sliding up. Clearly, I'm only confusing her. Of course I am. Because none of this makes any sense.

"You're going to be okay, Kate. Everything's going to be okay."

She turns away. "Everyone keeps saying that, but they're lying. Don't be a liar, Jack. Not like—" She stops when she sees what's in my hand.

Because for the last twenty seconds I've carefully worked my fingers into my shoe. And now I have it.

"Jack," she says, her voice rising. "Jack, what the hell—?"

But before she can finish I yank back her blankets and fire the syringe into her thigh. She lunges forward, like I've hit her with a million electrical bolts.

The police tackle me to the ground, shouting curses into my ear, into the room. "*What the*—! What the hell did you just do, kid? What the hell was that?"

"Someone help," the lady officer screams, running out in the hall. "We need a doctor in here! We need a doctor!"

The man officer presses my face so hard against the linoleum it's a wonder my brain doesn't rupture out of my eye sockets. Legs and feet come rushing into the room. Lots of shouting and screaming, and people keep shaking me and asking me what I injected her with, what drug was it, and the truth is I wouldn't know exactly how to explain it even if I wanted to. But I don't want to. Because this is the only thing that I could do. This is the only way.

While the doctors scramble to save her life, the officers drag me across the wet floor, across the lobby, back out into the night.

I know that if I make the tiniest move, if I even breathe too hard, they'll probably shoot me. Or at least knock me out cold. But it doesn't matter. Because I got a peek at the clock on my way out of Kate's room. And if things happen like before, then either Kate lives, or any second now it starts again.

The male officer has a thing for smushing my face, because now my cheek is back against the cruiser. I'm guessing he intends to search me more thoroughly this time.

"If that girl dies, I'm going to—"

But I feel it hit me before he can finish. I close my eyes. The air already peeling, gravity ripping away from me like a pulled parachute. The tremors are nastier this time, too. I can barely stand. My body one long violent vibration.

"Kid, are you okay?" He barks an order to his partner, tells her to go inside for help, and she darts off at full speed, but it doesn't matter. She won't make it in time. If I could talk, I'd tell them not to worry. That I'm not dying. I'm merely buffering.

That I was trying to save her. Not that they'd understand. Not that I understand. The first time it happened, I thought I was a goner. But now.

I don't know how to describe it except that it's like my body's preparing for launch. You know, if my body was a highly evolved space shuttle and space shuttles traveled through time instead of just into space.

"Kid, listen to me, talk to me! I think he's having a seizure. Kid! Kid!"

Oh yeah, lesson number two:

Time travel hurts.

the
BEGINNING
beginning

THE EXPERIENCE OF HAVING ZERO EXPERIENCES

People love to say, "There's someone for everyone."

It's one of those "feel better" things your mom tells you after your relationship has crashed and burned, or your normally noncommunicative dad mumbles as he slaps you between your shoulder blades, then announces "good talk." But it's mostly true. If you consider how many people are walking around this planet, there has to be someone you could fit perfectly with, right? The person who makes your heart say super-crazy things like "I'll love you forever" and "I can't wait to meet your parents" and "Oh, sure, let's definitely get each other's names tattooed on our necks." The problem is we spend most of our puny lives chasing someone else's someone, and, if we're lucky, we end up with only a third of the time we could've spent with the person truly meant for us. That is, if we don't wind up missing them altogether.

Take me, for instance.

I'm an expert on *just missing out*—on the girl of my dreams, on class valedictorian, on making it onto any sort of sports team. (I've tried them all. In one desperate moment I auditioned for mascot. Turns out "Hairy" Larry Koviak executes a far superior somersault.) And the extracurricular clubs? Yep, tried those, too, only to narrowly miss the cut. Which is funny because I'd always thought that anyone could just join a school club (add that to the Things Jack Has Been Utterly and Unequivocally Wrong About list). Point is, you name it, I've found a way to miss my chance, often by the slimmest of margins. By now I'm an authority on Almost, with nearly eighteen years of working experience on my résumé.

Need more proof, just walk with me through our attic. It's a virtual shrine to Nice Try, or as I like to call it, "Jack's Stupefying Museum of Almost Was but Never Will Be." There's a skateboard in mint condition, from the summer that I almost became a semipro skateboarder. There's a sewing machine that I used to tell everyone was my mom's but was actually mine from that time I was really into *Project Runway* for a few seasons. There's the Frisbee golf set, the antique marble collection, a crate full of tiny unfinished circuits, a box with every Super Nintendo game ever created, a coffin-size container that was my first (and only) attempt at a time machine (don't ask!), and a never-used set of noncollectible ninja stars (seriously, don't ask!).

Almost, almost, almost, almost, almo—

You get it.

I joke that my parents were prophets when they named me Jack Ellison King.

Jack of all. King of none.

Except my mom's always reminding me that I was named for Jackie Robinson, who broke through the pro sports color barrier, and Ralph Ellison, writer and scholar, best known for his seminal work *Invisible Man*.

I'm an only child. My parents had me rather late in life, after trying hard for years, and, well, just as they'd abandoned all hope—I swam along. Mom wanted to name me Miracle, but Dad (not usually the voice of reason, but willing to make an exception here) intervened—*is it your dream to have Miracle get his ass kicked every day, honey?*

And so Jackie Ellison it was.

Which I can't help but think is a prime example of the Best and Worst of Parenting.

Because on one hand, it's awesome knowing that my namesakes were these incredible men. An honor. A privilege.

But on the flip side, it's possible that my parents did not comprehend the ridiculous amount of PRESSURE they were placing upon my freakishly narrow shoulders.

So, yeah, there's that, too.

* * *

Anyway.

I'm Jack King. The guy sporting a five o'clock shadow and an old flannel jacket at a party full of people, sitting near the bottom of the living room stairs, holding an empty glass, semi-watching a basketball game playing on the TV, but mostly staring out into the kitchen, looking at—

It's always the same girl.

Jillian.

When we signed up for this college visit, I pictured Jillian and me finally getting time alone. That we'd spend the weekend together and she'd at long last see just how (sorta) charming and (semi-) cool and (relatively) interesting I was. That I'm more than just Friendship Material Jack, you know?

But instead, I've been sitting here for thirty minutes, alone, although in fairness, I'm not *completely* alone; there are quite a few people who keep bumping into me walking up and down the stairs. I swear I'm not normally this awkward, this antisocial.

Let me explain.

A BRIEF HISTORY OF STRONG LIKE

Jillian and I are best friends. We met freshman year in high school, literally bumping into each other (how horribly cliché, right?), our backpacks spilling their guts all over the hallway. I helped her gather her books and we avoided that whole bumping-heads thing as we stood up, only for idiot me to step on her backpack strap and send her crashing back onto her ass. If there was an embarrassment gun, we'd bypassed Stun and switched right to Kill. A few kids paused to gawk and laugh, and there I was, rapid-firing apology after apology Jillian's way.

But she'd simply hopped to her feet, barked at our spectators to "keep it moving," and introduced herself.

"Jack and Jill," I said, putting it together.

"Ha." She smiled. "Guess this was meant to be."

"Sorry I didn't come tumbling after." I was far too giddy

with my clever reply only to realize hours later that it was actually Jill who tumbled after Jack.

But Jillian didn't seem vexed by my mistake. "We can always try again," she said. Her smile upping its wattage, she added, "The tumbling part, that is."

I knew then we had a chance at something amazing. But in keeping with my long-standing theme of *almost*, we had neither. Which is to say, three weeks later Jillian had a boyfriend.

Now maybe you're thinking—who cares if she has a boyfriend, Jack? Tell her how you feel. Let her decide. Except the whole *I have a boyfriend* thing seemed an impregnable defense. I'm talking snipers on the roof, motion-activated lasers, trained attack dinosaurs, and a moat boiling with molten lava—impenetrable.

Because, major plot twist: Jillian's boyfriend, Francisco "Franny" Hogan, is my *other* best friend.

I know, *I know*.

And I wish I could tell you this is a story about a horrible boyfriend (Franny) who doesn't appreciate what he's got, who treats his girlfriend (Jillian) like crap, who doesn't deserve her. Or that he'd viciously stabbed me in the back going after the girl of my heart. Except Franny didn't even know I liked her.

The truth is, Franny's a good guy—hell, a *great* guy. Were I to pick someone other than myself to be with Jillian—like if Jillian and I were together and were playing that game where you pick one of your friends to take your place in the event of your untimely demise—I'd pick Franny for Jillian, every time.

He'd take care of her. He'd love her. (That's sort of a sick game, right? Let's not play that again.)

Anyway, they're a couple. An awesome couple. And I'm happy for them. I would never consider doing anything to jeopardize their relationship. No, I'm here for the Jillian-Franny love connection. The ultimate third wheel, the undervalued eleventh toe, the superfluous third nipple.

Until tonight.

Possibly.

Maybe.

Probably not.

Never.

THE THING ABOUT STAIRS IS THAT THEY'RE UP AND DOWN

"Excuse me, man, but you're sort of damming up the steps," a voice behind me says.

"What?" I swivel around.

It's a girl with bright eyes and shoulder-length curly hair. She's wearing one of those sweater-dress things—except I think it's just an oversize sweater that she's cinched around her waist with a skinny belt. I recognize her from earlier, our student center tour guide.

"You're blocking the stairs. You're a very proficient human dam."

"Sorry," I mumble.

I scoot over and she applauds. "Oooh, he's a motorized dam. Brilliant."

"Surprise, surprise," I say.

I wait for her to complete her trek down the stairs, but she doesn't move. "If you like her so much, you should try talking to her."

"Huh?"

"I hear that *talking to people* usually alerts them to our existence. You know, as opposed to just staring at them like a deranged serial killer."

"As opposed to a *non*deranged serial killer," I say over my shoulder.

She snaps her fingers. "Bingo."

I frown. "I don't know what you're talking about." Of course, I know exactly what she's talking about, but I'm offended that I'm so transparent.

"You were clinging to her during the entire tour, man."

"I was?"

"Dude, you reached barnacle status."

"Gee, thanks."

She grins. "I'm saying, get in that kitchen and talk to the girl."

"I don't need to. I talk to her all the time. She's my best friend."

"Wow, so you guys are best friends but she has no idea you're in love with her?"

This girl is awfully loud. I realize we're at a party, but her voice is set to *Evacuate Immediately*. I almost shush her, except not being shushed is an unalienable right, right there with pursuit of happiness.

I whisper, *"I'm not in love with her, okay."*

She leans in closer. "What?"

"I'm not in love with her," I repeat.

"I can't hear you. Why are you whispering?"

I resume normal volume. "I said I'm not in love with her. She's really nice, is all."

"That's obviously your problem. You're *too* nice. You're, what, waiting for the perfect opportunity to tell this girl how you feel and you've already waited for . . ." She pauses for me to fill in the blank.

"Three years."

She palms her forehead. "Whoa, it's been *three years* and she has *no* clue you want to jump her bones?"

"I like to take things slow."

"Yeah, you do. At this rate, you'll have to hope they find a way to freeze our bodies so that they can defrost you in two hundred years and you can ask her to go steady. You know, right after you do that whole fake yawn-and-stretch thing and slip your arm around her shoulders. Smooth move, by the way. Spoiler alert, she *never* sees it coming."

"Hahaha. Listen, I appreciate the pep talk, but if you don't mind—"

It is at this point that this girl, rather than proceeding down the steps, instead slides in beside me. Now, by our powers combined, we are officially damming all second-floor access. No one is going to pee on our watch.

22

"I'm Kate," she says, extending her hand. Which is awkward because it's a tight squeeze on the stairs, and I can't turn my arm to meet hers.

"Jack," I say, managing to give her The Wimpiest Handshake in Recorded History. "Jack King."

"Do you always give people your full name when you meet them?"

"Nope. I only hand out full-name intros to cool tour guides."

"Ha." She grins. "Well, it's nice to meet you, Jack King."

"It's nice to meet you . . ."

"Kate."

"*Just* Kate, huh?"

"For now."

"Ouch."

"Gotta keep the mystery alive, right?"

"I don't know. I sorta hate mysteries. I'm more of an all-cards-on-the-table guy."

"So, *Jack* and *King*, that's different."

"'Cause I'm just looking for my queeeeeeeen," I say with instant regret.

She bursts into laughter.

My cheeks are ablaze. "I promise I've never said that before."

She shakes her head. "It came out of your mouth pretty quickly, so . . ."

"I'm serious."

"I'm not sure if I believe you, Jack."

"Cool. Only fifteen minutes in and we've already introduced

distrust into our relationship. I normally like to reserve that for the second time I talk to someone, but."

She snickers. "So, look, Jack King, I'm not trying to bust your balls, okay? But I think you could use help from someone who understands the female species."

"And you can put me in touch with this someone?"

"Hey!" Kate punches me in the shoulder. It stings, but I pretend to shrug it off.

"Okay then, Ms. Love Doctor, what do you suggest?"

Kate laughs again. "Honestly, I haven't the slightest. I'm still only in my Love Doctor residency, so."

"Well, I haven't told you the best part yet," I say. By this point, I'm laughing too—partly because it took a stranger to validate what I already knew (that it *is* too complicated for Jillian and me), and because if I don't laugh, I'll probably cry.

"What's the best part?" Kate asks. She clasps her hands together.

"She's dating our mutual best friend."

Kate erupts in laughter and mock-horror. "You giant douchebag!"

"I know, right? I am The World's Giantest Douchebag."

"Easy, boy, don't give yourself too much credit. I'm guessing you're an average giant douchebag at best."

"That's sort of my MO."

"What is?"

And I don't mean to say it but I'm on a sad roll, so. "Average at best."

Her mouth opens but she says nothing, and for this minor miracle, I'm grateful.

We watch a kid sporting the plungiest V-neck sweater murder a pop song while a girl with a Hello Kitty tat on her neck accompanies him on the piano. Kate's lips are moving, faintly singing the melody. My phone buzzes.

A text from Franny.

FRANNY: Hope you're having fun, man! I know I don't have to say this but watch out for Jillian. Keep those drunk frat-goons away from her!!

ME: I got you

I redeposit my phone. Kate stops singing. I try to think of something to say because I don't want her to stop talking. "Is it just me or do these steps smell pretty awful? I'm thinking numerous people have puked and peed up and down them."

She nods. "So us sitting here, it's like we're participating in ancient party history."

I laugh. "I like the way you think."

She smiles an awesome crooked smile.

Maybe it's her smile that emboldens me.

Maybe the jittery party lights are doing weird things to my brain.

Or maybe it's that there's suddenly guitar strumming from the speakers. Me, forever a sucker for acoustic.

Maybe it's that, for the first time in three years, I feel like it's okay that Jillian and I will never be. That after a few minutes on some crusty stairs I can suddenly see a different future. An alternate ending, or two.

Maybe it's because everything around us is now an unrecognizable swirl, Kate the only thing in perfect focus. Portrait mode IRL.

I gulp, which I don't think I've ever done before. "Can I ask you something, Kate?"

Kate smiles, and in a very formal-sounding voice says, "Yes, Jack, you may ask me your question."

"It's a tough one, though. Fair warning."

"Consider me warned."

I clear my throat, a habit when I'm uncomfortable, and/or when I'm about to say/do something stupid. "So how would you suggest a guy transition from talking about a girl he has a crush on but has no chance of being with to another very attractive girl—okay—to hitting on *that* very attractive girl even though he, at this point, also has zero chance of being with her, either?"

"Ooooh, that *is* a tough one."

"See, I told you."

"I'm fairly certain that such a maneuver is entirely impossible," she says.

"I figured."

"But were I to suggest a strategy . . ." She grins, as if she is about to divulge a top-secret tactic.

I lean in. "I'm listening."

"I'd say, start with getting *that* girl a drink, and when you come back she can tell you she's not looking for anything serious because she has a million commitment issues that she's currently not at all interested in sorting, and also because she is only just escaping a disaster of a relationship and essentially hates all human beings at the moment."

"Right, so *definitely* hold *that* thought because I'm definitely gonna go get *that* girl a drink, okay?"

She smiles. "Okay."

"Don't go anywhere. You must guard these steps with your life."

"I'll slay anyone who tries to scale these here steps, sire," she says.

"What was that voice just then?"

She cringes, covering her face as she laughs. "My attempt at sounding Scottish."

"Oh, is that what that was? Hmm," I say, smiling hard. "Yeah, maybe work on that. Or maybe just don't do it again. Like ever."

"Was it that bad?"

I shrug, playfully. "The worst."

She nods. "I'm a big fan of failing miserably, so I feel pretty good about it."

"Oh, well, in that case, mission accomplished. Glad I could be here for that."

"Me too," she agrees.

"Sooo . . ."

"So," she repeats, smiling. "Perhaps you get the drinks and we reconvene this epic pity party on the back porch?"

I stare at her a beat. "Maybe you should just make all of my decisions for me from now on."

27

Kate extends her hand to me, this time with far better results. "Deal, Jack."

I squeeze and sidestep my way into the kitchen, the alcohol scattered across the long countertop. I feel a tap on my shoulder. "Hey."

It's Jillian.

"Having fun?" she asks.

I shrug. "You?"

"It's okay. Was considering leaving soon actually."

"Yeah?"

"Maybe grab a burger."

"Oh," I say. "Yeah, we could do that . . . um . . . I was just gonna . . ."

She nods to the bottle of wine in my hand. "Where you going with that?"

"Oh, uh, nowhere, um."

"Nowhere?"

"Well, not nowhere. That would be silly. No, I was gonna go to the porch. The, uh, back porch."

"You shouldn't drink alone, Jack," she says, smiling.

"I wasn't planning to," I say, clearing my throat. "I've, uh, made a friend, I guess."

Her face flashes something I can't compute, but it's gone before I can consider it. "Oh, I see," she says, her smile now somehow different. "Jack's made a new *friend*."

"It's not a big deal."

"No, I'm happy for you, J," she says.

"Thanks, J," I reply. A thing we do. "We can totally get

28

a burger, though, like I'm down for whatever . . . just let me, um . . ."

"No." She shakes her head, already backing away. "You go do your thing. I'm gonna probably head back to the dorm anyway. Gotta call Franny, so."

"Oh, yeah, okay, cool."

"Cool." She nods. "So, have fun, man."

"You too. Tell Franny hey," I say, because what else can I say. Because for maybe the first time the words aren't easy between us.

*   *   *

Five minutes later Kate and I are drinking from a disgusting bottle of red wine and splitting real estate on the warped porch steps. Already we have Our Thing. *Steps.* Only this time we don't budge the rest of the night. Not even when the party's over, not even when the only lights still on are for security, not even when the moon's a whisper against brightening sky.

"I think we're the only people still awake at this house," Kate says.

"Damn, what time is it?" I say, not actually concerned with the time.

"Who gives a damn about time, right?" Kate says, stifling a yawn.

We move for nothing and no one.

"Tell me about your family," I say.

"What about them?"

"Anything," I tell her. "Everything."

She's quiet. Crosses her legs, then uncrosses them. She passes

29

me the wine, and I take a sip. It's still not very good, but somehow less not very good than before.

"My parents are basically professional arguers these days, and it's mainly because of me."

"Oh."

"It's odd, you know, seeing people who you remember sharing so much love, who once couldn't get enough of each other, and then one morning you're lying in bed wondering how soon before they start fighting."

"You said they argue because of you?"

"Yep."

"How come?"

She shrugs. "They can't agree on how to take care of me."

"That sucks. I'm sorry, Kate."

"Why are you sorry?" she asks. She bites her lip, reaches for the bottle, and puts it to her mouth, but she doesn't drink. Brings it back down, lets it rest between her knees. "If anything, I'm the one who should be sorry."

I'm not sure if I should ask what she means, although I want to, so I settle on silence, leaving her space to continue if she wants.

"I don't know. Maybe they'll stick it out, if only because starting over is scary and complicated and messy. And who wants that when you're old? Hell, who wants that when you're young?" She takes a sip, holds the bottle out for me, and our fingers brush, and I don't know, it's like a zillion bolts flow into me.

"Yeah," I say, her touch still stunning me.

"So, what about you? What's your family like?"

"Well, I'm an only child, for one thing."

She nods. "That explains everything."

"Hey now!"

"Just saying."

"Let me guess, you're a middle kid."

She turns to look at me, which is not without difficulty considering how close we're sitting, and our faces nearly touch. "What makes you say that?"

I shrug.

"Whatever, Jack. But you're right. I have an older sister. Kira. She's a stylist. And I don't know exactly how she's done it, but she has like a million YouTube subscribers. Like, people *clamor* for her videos. It's weird, but it's cool she's doing her thing."

"Maybe she could style me," I say. I smooth the front of my shirt. "I could use some help."

"I don't know," she says. She taps my collar with her finger. "You're doing okay."

"Thanks." I've never been happier with *doing okay* in my life. "So, your younger sister or . . ."

"Brother. The terror."

"Oh, wow."

"No, he's all right. Just hyper."

"Oh, sometimes I have trouble focusing, too."

"No, like hypervigilant. He's forever in everyone's business, but he specializes in mine."

I laugh. "Sometimes I wish I had more family. Even if they were annoying, just knowing they were there. I mean, my parents are pretty great. I'm lucky that way. And they're still crazy for each other in a way that almost seems sick. But sometimes it's like they want so much for me, they're planning on me doing all these cool things, and I don't know, like, I worry about letting them down. I mean, they've funneled so much of their energy and love into me, while doing their best not to seriously screw me up, but sometimes I still feel like I'm just a screwup waiting to happen. Uh, wow, I can't believe I just shared all that."

"I'm glad you did. And that screwup feeling, Jack? I think that's called youth."

"Yeah, maybe."

"The fact that you care so much, that's good, though. That means you're gonna try hard to not mess up. But you also gotta leave room for your hopes, your dreams, too."

"What do you hope for, dream about?"

"Man, I just want to live."

"Like, live life to the fullest?"

"That too, yeah." She hesitates.

"What else?"

"I want to be an architect."

"What made you choose that?"

She smiles. "You're gonna think it's really corny."

"No way."

"No, you will. And you'll be right, because *it is* corny.

32

But . . . I don't know. Something about the idea of designing something that will be there, still standing, even when you're long gone. Like, this thing that came from your brain just keeps on being for years and years, for decades, maybe longer, like, somehow that just does it for me."

"Okay, that's literally the *least* corny thing you've said all night. I don't think you understand what corny means. Like at all."

She laughs, leans into me with her shoulder. "Stop."

"I'm serious. You're officially banned from the word."

"You can't ban me."

"Okay, maybe not ban, but we definitely have to impose a moratorium."

"Oh, do we?"

"Yep, for like two weeks. You can't use the word *corny*."

"Hmm. We'll see about that."

"I'm sorry, but the Word Committee has spoken."

"Well, I'm filing my appeal."

"Noted. The committee will take it under advisement."

"Why do I get the feeling this is a committee of one?"

"The committee does not comment on its membership."

"Huh, why am I not surprised?"

"Strict policy." I hunch my shoulders, bring the bottle to my lips, but it's empty.

"You killed that," she says.

"I had help."

She shakes her head. "Okay, your turn now."

"For?"

"What are Jack's hopes and dreams?"

"Uh-uh, no possible way I can follow after hearing yours."

"Just try."

"Okay, uh, let me think." I clear my throat, clasp my hands. "Let's see . . . uh, I sorta want to write a book, or several books, I guess." I laugh because hearing the idea out loud sounds preposterous. Like, if the walls could talk they'd be echoing *nevergonnahappen nevergonnahappen*.

Except Kate doesn't flinch. "What kind of books?"

"Uh, fiction, I guess. Maybe young adult books."

"Why young adult?"

"I'll tell you, but remember, you can't say *corny*, so . . ."

"Just tell me."

"Uh, okay, well, I've always loved reading. But there aren't a lot of books about kids like me. And I just think every kid deserves a book that looks like them. So . . . you can laugh now."

"Why would I laugh? You think about lots of things, don't you?"

"I tend to overanalyze, yes."

"Ha. Me too. I've had a lot of time to do nothing but think and think and think."

"Lucky thoughts," I say.

"Lucky thoughts?"

"They get to spend all that time with you."

Kate shakes her head. "Okay, so *that* was corny," she says. Except she stares at me in such a way that, for a moment, I think she might kiss me. I imagine how that would feel—Kate's lips against mine. And I must've zoned out because Kate's snapping her fingers in front of my face. "Earth to Jack, Earth to Jack," she's saying.

"Huh? Yeah? What?"

Kate smiles. "I was asking you, I know it's a little late now but your friend, she got home safe last night, right?"

"My friend," I repeat.

"Your best friend who you were drooling over only hours ago? The one true love of your young adult life?"

I look up at the sky—have we really talked the entire night?—I barely remember the moon's being there, and now the sun's already punched in, a smudge of campfire orange stoked above our heads.

"Yeah. She went back to the dorm to talk to Franny."

"Franny's the boyfriend?"

I nod.

"Your *other* best friend?"

I nod again.

She claps her hands together. "Okay, one last 'are Kate and Jack even semicompatible as friends' question, okay?"

"Shoot," I say, twisting my body toward her in preparation.

"Which *Godfather* movie is your absolute fave?"

"Uh, that's a tough one."

"It's not tough at all."

"No, it is, because, uh, I haven't actually seen . . ."

"Which one haven't you seen?"

"Any. Of. Them."

You would've thought I said I didn't believe in the moon, the way her jaw drops.

"You're kidding, right? We're watching them ASAP, Jack Attack," she promises.

"You name the time and place," I say.

"I'm not sure when," she says. "But sometime in the future, my place."

The future can't come soon enough.

* * *

Behind us, there's rustling inside the house, signs of life dragging themselves into the kitchen, chairs scooting, cabinets shutting, glassware handled.

"Come on," Kate says, standing up.

"You know these people?" I ask.

"Just come on."

I follow her inside to the kitchen. Last night's party remnants—plastic cups, stomped-on cheese curls, random wrappers—are strewn everywhere. A girl is slumped in a chair, her blue-blond hair untamed, a bowl of cereal on the table in front of her. A lanky kid with plastic black specs has his face almost inside his bowl. They look up at us.

"Who are you?" the girl asks, midslurp, not like she's alarmed, but amused.

"We're starving," Kate says, reaching for the box of cereal. "It's cool?"

"It's cool," the lanky kid says, wiping away a milk mustache. "Cap'n Crunch for all."

Two bowls and two spoons magically appear before us, and I think to myself, *Where did this Kate come from? And how can I keep her around?*

* * *

After our cereal, we wind up in a car that Kate says belongs to her roommate. Only we don't actually drive anywhere. Instead, we sit in the lot, taking turns playing music from our phones' playlists. She thinks my obsession with nineties hip-hop is cute, and she plays me a lot of stuff that I've never heard of. That I'm guessing no one has ever heard of. But I love almost all of it.

"You're weird," she says.

"Uh, thanks," I say, laughing. "Appreciate that."

"In a good way, silly. You're likably weird."

"Likable is good."

"Likable is very good, Jack Attack."

And somehow, suddenly, the music is even better.

"So, where do you see yourself in ten years?" I ask her, watching her scroll up and down for the next track. "Like, where do you want to be, and what do you want to be doing?"

"Man, you're obsessed with the future," she says.

"Lemme guess, you're one of those people who hates planning? You'd rather live all spontaneous and mysteriously?"

I say this jokingly, in the same spirit that she and I have batted jokes back and forth all night, only this one never makes it over the net.

Kate turns off the car, tugs her door handle. "I need some air."

"Hey, I didn't mean to . . ." But she's already outside, sitting on the rear bumper. I join her. "You okay?"

"It's wild, right? How we're breathing the same air as every human who's ever lived? The Queen of Sheba, Anne Frank, Rosa Parks. We come and go, but the air stays the same."

I realize she's purposely ignoring whatever just happened. But I let it go. "Yeah, it's pretty wild."

We walk across campus and it's quiet. Shadows and old stone buildings stretching across a mile of green grass.

Kate yawns. One of those fully loaded yawns, equipped with intense arm-stretching and growling.

"Well, it's been fun, Jack Attack," she says. I like that she's given me a nickname, because it means . . . okay, maybe it means nothing—*yet*.

It's time for us to go our separate ways. Only I'm not ready.

"What, you're turning in already?" I challenge with a smile.

Kate looks at her watch. I also like that she wears an actual watch, rather than just relying on her phone to keep time.

"It's only been nine hours, Kate," I say. "Where's your stamina?"

She massages her jaw. "What'd you have in mind?"

I shrug. "How about I make you an offer you can't refuse?"

"You definitely haven't seen *Godfather*," she says, laughing.

"That bad?" I say, feeling my face warm.

"Worse," she says.

"I can do better," I assure her. "Kate, howz about I make you . . . howz 'bout I make you . . . Okay, I can't do better."

She laughs harder. "Gosh, how does a lady say no to that?"

"She doesn't . . . I hope."

Kate smiles through her laughter.

And all I can think is, *God, Jack, please, please, please, don't screw this up.* And then, knowing myself, knowing good things always leave me, *At least don't screw it up so quickly. Hold on, Jack. For as long as you can, hold on.*

"I should really turn in." She glances at her watch again. "I have a big paper due in less than twenty-four hours, and I haven't even finished the reading. Plus, don't you have to get back to . . ."

"Elytown," I say. "Elytown Township, technically." Because I'm nothing if not technical.

"Right. The township," she says. She clearly has no idea where that is. "You probably have class, too. And parents?"

I laugh, wishing I could come off cool and aloof, but knowing I don't stand a chance. "It's just high school. No big deal. And my parents are totally cool. Very liberal. Plus, it's only Sunday morning. We head back this afternoon."

"Okay," she says, grinning. "Well, it was nice to meet you, Jack King. I wish you all the best during your senior year. Enjoy it, okay?" She offers her hand and I take it into mine, in immediate hindsight shaking it a bit too enthusiastically, like I'm a used car salesman closing a deal.

"I'll do my best, Kate."

"I know you will." She lets my hand go, turns to walk away. But she stops and swivels partially back to me, her hair cascading over her cheeks. "And Jack?"

39

"Yeah?"

"Don't be afraid. Take chances. And when those don't work out, take more."

I wonder if she means now. As in, *Jack, take a chance on me, on this moment.* But I don't budge. Not a muscle, not an eyelash; somewhere a mime is murderous with envy. Instead, Kate walks into her dorm building, into the glass foyer, and it hits me.

I pound on the glass and a startled Kate whirls around, her face making a *what the hell* look. "How do I get in touch with you?" I yell, my lips pressed against the pane, a condensation cloud blooming against the glass.

She smiles. "Don't worry. We'll see each other again."

Then, like that, she's gone.

And there's a feeling I can't shake—

This isn't the last time I'll watch her go.

SUNDAY FUNDAY

My plan is to sneak into the dorm I'm staying in, except I can't remember the code to the front door, so I have to buzz the intercom and wake up my host, Albert, who has to drag himself out of bed and walk down three flights of cold stairs. He doesn't even look at me, only cracks the front door enough for me to wedge my foot inside while mumbling something about a *massive headache* and *responsibility*.

I slink back to the room behind him, as he stuffs himself into a three-layer blanket burrito, before collapsing onto my own sleeping bag.

Except I'm not sleepy. At all.

My mind a speedway of competing thoughts.

I nearly call out to Albert, because I want to ask him if he knows Kate—

And if he does, how much does he know about her?

Do I have a chance? The slightest?

I'd be happy with the slightest.

I'm not picky. Slightest hope is still hope.

But I hear a thin wheeze coming from deep within the burrito, so I keep my questions to myself. My pocket hums, a text message, and for a second I imagine it's Kate, that she wants to see me right now, that she's waiting outside this dorm, homework and a good night's rest be damned. But of course it's not her; she doesn't have my number.

> JILLIAN: Hey, are you asleep?
>
> ME: Nope. You?
>
> JILLIAN: Obviously not LOL what are you doing?
>
> ME: Not sleeping mostly. And thinking.
>
> JILLIAN: About what? Lemme guess. The person you shared that wine with!!!
>
> ME: You think you know me or something 😑
>
> JILLIAN: What's her name anyway???

I hesitate before replying.

> ME: Kate.
>
> JILLIAN: Jack loves Kate, Jack loves Kate
>
> ME: What grade are we in again?
>
> ME: Kindergarten?
>
> JILLIAN: Ha! Just admit you're in love!
>
> ME: Did you have fun last night?
>
> JILLIAN: Yeah, but I wished you and I got to spend more time together.

ME: You were the belle of the ball.

JILLIAN: Hardly! I kept looking over at you, thinking we should go for a walk or something. When I was about to finally break free from the kitchen, you were preparing to disappear, Houdini.

ME: You know I suck at parties. I'm sorry.

JILLIAN: Don't be. I'm glad you had a good time.

JILLIAN: And you don't suck at parties! 😜

ME: You talk to Franny?

JILLIAN: He's bummed he couldn't come here with us.

ME: Yeah. He texted me like twenty times. LOL

JILLIAN: Only 20? LOL

ME: A conservative estimate

JILLIAN: Very conservative, I'm sure. Well, I'm getting sleepy now. Thanks for chatting.

ME: Anytime.

JILLIAN: Get some shut-eye, lover boy!! We leave in a few hours!!

ME: Night, J.

JILLIAN: Night, J.

I nearly turn my screen off but instead I tap a blue icon. I hit search, typing in *Kate*.

Kate *what*, though? The cursor blinks at me, impatiently. I don't remember Kate's last name. Or if I ever knew it in the first place. I search for "Kate" anyway, adding "Whittier University" to narrow the results, but the Facebook gods are not smiling this morning. Kate remains a mystery.

The cherry on top? Albert's only mildly annoying wheeze turns into a full-on death rattle, and I know that his snoring combined with my worsening case of Kate-on-the-brain, I'm not likely to sleep. I stare at the ceiling, and then out the window, wondering if it's possible that Kate's doing the same, looking up at a similarly brown-stained popcorn ceiling, eyeing the same sky and early morning sun, thinking about me.

And I'm not sure when I finally close my eyes.

I'm not sure about anything.

*　*　*

"Wake up," someone is chanting over me. I attempt to crack open an eyelid, but my eye muscles aren't cooperating. They want more sleep, too.

"Come on, Jack," Jillian says. She unzips my sleeping bag. "We've got to get on the road. You know my mom is weird about me driving in the dark."

"What time is it?" I ask, eyes still closed.

"Two."

"In the freaking morning?" As soon as I ask I realize it doesn't make sense, but I'm suffering from just-woke-up disorientation.

"Uh, try the afternoon. Ha, I don't think you even left the party before two."

"Where's Albert?" I glance over at the avalanche of blankets on the floor beside his bed.

"Probably somewhere being a functioning human being."

"Ugh, my body hurts everywhere."

"As it should, lover boy. Listen, jump in the shower, because you smell like a boy, plus you need to wake up. If we hurry we'll have time to grab food from the student center and gas up before we hit the highway for home."

My vision is still blurry around the edges, Jillian hovering over me like a midafternoon angel, her necklace pendant swinging back and forth just above my chin, a silver palm tree I got her for her birthday last year. *No one loves the beach more than you. Now you'll always have it with you*, I'd said, watching her unwrap the slender box. She'd made a weird face. A face I hadn't seen before, which was strange because I was certain that I'd seen all her faces. *Total cheesiness, right*, I'd said, embarrassed and unable to meet her eyes. But she'd planted the softest kiss on my cheek. *The exact opposite of cheesy*, she'd said.

"But we can't leave yet. I have something I need to do."

"Sorry, Charlie. No time."

"I promise I'll be quick."

Jillian grins with her entire face. "Jack, us girls don't like *that* sorta thing quick."

"You're sick," I say. I swing my pillow at her, but she ducks, and it sails harmlessly across the room.

"Shower, Jack," she barks, hopping to her feet. "And maybe, just maybe, we have a few minutes to stalk your new girlfriend."

I've never showered quicker in my life.

Okay, maybe that's not true.

But I've never showered *with purpose* quicker in my life.

*   *   *

"So how do we even find this Kate person?" Jillian says. We're standing in the quad—at least I think this is the quad. In any case, we're standing in a busy part of campus. Which seems odd for a Sunday. But what do I know about end-of-the-weekend college life?

Kids blanket the lawn, reading on tablets, a few holding actual books, a handful talking into their phones. A Frisbee's whipping back and forth between two guys. A girl effortlessly executes a series of somersaults, and her friends eagerly applaud.

"I know the building if I see it," I tell Jillian. "It has glass and stone. Oh, and a front door."

Jillian slaps her head. "I thought you walked her home."

"I did."

"And you don't remember her dorm?"

"I had other things on my mind."

"Oh yeah? Like what?"

I shrug.

She winks. "So, *what* then?"

"I was not thinking about . . . *that*!"

"You can't even say the word. Oh my God, Jack! I can't believe you didn't at least get her number."

"Preaching to the choir," I say. And then it hits me. "Hawthorne."

"What?"

"That's the name of her dorm . . . I think."

Jillian studies the campus trifold map. "Sorry, kid, but there's no Hawthorne."

"Damn it," I say, just as the Frisbee zips astray and lands at my feet. The Frisbee-ers yell for me to toss it back. I fling it with as much finesse as I can conjure, and then watch as it sails a good twenty yards over their heads.

"Gee, thanks, man," one of the guys says.

But even my Frisbee ineptitude matters not, because all I want is to see Kate.

Jillian wraps her arm around my shoulders. "But there is a *Hawk*thorne."

"You're screwing with me, right? Please tell me you're not screwing with me."

"I do love to give you a hard time," she says, grinning. "But that would be the worst joke ever."

"I love you." I kiss her on her cheek. "I love you so hard." I snatch the map from her hands and sprint across what I think is the quad.

"Hey," Jillian calls after me. "Maybe don't leave your ride behind!"

But I'm already tearing toward Hawkthorne dormitory.

Naturally, when I get there, Kate's nowhere to be found. "Out for the day studying," her roommate informs me.

"Any idea where?" I ask.

She's already replacing her headphones. "No clue."

But then I hear my name.

"Jack, what are you doing here?" It's Kate. Beautiful, radiant Kate. Her black hair is pulled back, a few curls dangle near her temples. She's perfect.

My throat clenches. "Looking—looking for you," I stammer.

"Figured you'd be back in the township by now," she says, smiling.

"I wanted to say goodbye. To you. And. To. Tell you. How. Much. I. Last night was . . . super. Uh, great, I mean. It was super and great. It was super great. And I wanted to give you my info. If that's okay?"

She walks into her room, returns with pen and paper.

"I could just text it to you. If you give me your number."

Kate grins. "Pretty smooth, Jack. I bet the township ladies love you."

I laugh. "Pretty much the opposite."

"Well, I prefer pen and paper. Something about words on actual paper. There's a romance to it."

I nod, because I like paper too. Especially the kind that makes Kate say *romance*. "Keeping it old-school, I likey," I say for no apparent reason other than to make myself look stupid. She laughs, and I have to assume *at* me.

I scribble my number and email.

She takes it and smiles. "Well, I'm glad you stopped by. It'll be cool to see you next year around campus. Maybe we'll grab some more random cereal."

"I'd like that."

"Me too."

And I must make a face, because she adds, "What are you thinking?"

"Honestly?"

"Honestly."

"Next year's far away."

For a few seconds we're silent until Kate's roommate, head-phones out and draped around her neck, giggles. And then Kate's giggling, and I figure that's my cue to leave. I wave weakly and turn for the exit, wishing I had some cool parting wisdom for her. Something like *remember, Kate, don't be afraid to take chances*. But I've got nothing, and then it dawns on me that I didn't write my name on the paper. What if she forgets whose info she has and throws it away? What if she wants to call me, or email me, but decides against it because she can't remember my name? (Okay, I admit the second of those questions is less plausible, but still.)

I pivot slowly. "Hey, I think I forgot to write my name—"

But Kate holds up her notebook. She's already written my name and even doodled a marquee around it. My name, in one-dimensional flashing lights. On Kate's notebook. In Kate's hands. Which incidentally are, in this moment, inches from her heart.

She leans against her door. "Drive safe, Jack Attack."

My cheeks warm, I nod, and then dedicate every ounce of my concentration to walking away without tripping.

Jillian's parked in front of Hawkthorne. I slip into the pas-senger seat, but she stops my hand before I can fasten my seat belt.

"No way," she says. "After deserting me, at least tell me it was worth it."

But it's like I'm in a trance. Or a powerful tractor beam that has my lips hermetically sealed and there's nothing anyone can do about it.

"Hello, paging Jack King," Jillian says. "How'd it go, man?"

I'm buzzing. Were I standing on the coastline, ships could use me to avoid running into rocks, that's how bright I feel.

"It went," I answer. "It definitely went."

Doesn't even matter where.

*   *   *

On the ride home Jillian is all about Whittier—

How she can't wait for high school to end and for us to start our new college lives.

How she knows we're about to embark on the most important chapter. *Our formative years*, she keeps saying.

How she's so happy that we're going there together.

How she can't imagine going with anyone else. I almost ask, *What about your boyfriend, and my best friend, Franny*? But I'm caught up in the Whittier euphoria too, so I let her continue on her passionate discourse, uninterrupted.

But then Franny comes up anyway.

"I feel sorry for him. That he didn't make it in," Jillian says. "Ever since he transferred to Elytown with us, he's worked so hard to get his grades up. He deserves a shot."

And she's right. Sometimes I forget how hard Franny has worked. *Is* still working. Before Jillian started picking him up, he spent forty minutes on the city bus, one way, just to get to school. It's crazy how you can live less than ten miles apart, and everything—the schools, the houses, even the grocery stores—can be different worlds. For the past four years, Franny has moved between both.

"It sucks. I mean, there's still a chance he gets in, though."

"A small chance."

"Well, State is still a good school. Plus, they have a far superior sports program, which I know he's geeked about. Not to mention we'll be living within ten miles of each other, so our trio lives on."

"Right," Jillian says. But I sense something else is bothering her.

"You okay?" I ask.

"Things are changing fast, I guess. I mean, look at you this weekend. Hooking up with a college girl already."

"We didn't hook up."

"It's just strange. Like, what else is going to be different? It's crazy how all the things you think you know, the things you think are certain, turn out to be not so much."

"Uh, what are we talking about here? Specifically?"

Jillian fiddles with buttons on the steering wheel. "So, are you going to call her later?"

"Call who?" I say.

Jillian shoots me a look.

"I don't exactly have her number." I glance out the window in time to see a family of deer flash out of a patch of trees. "Besides, even if I did, I don't want to seem desperate."

Jillian laughs. "Aren't you?"

51

"Hey!"

"I'm teasing. You don't realize it, but there are plenty of girls at Elytown who would pay to jump your bones."

I laugh. "Unless you mean literally jump over my rotting bones, you're right. I don't realize it."

But her face doesn't crack and she keeps staring straight ahead at the road. "Well, it's true. You just never gave them a chance."

And I don't know what to say to this, because Jillian knows that that's not true. She knows this more than anyone. She knows because I've told her, because she's had a front-row seat to Jack's Heartbreak for the last three years. Heck, she's had a backstage pass, too. How many times have I confessed to her how lonely I've felt—and now she's pretending that I'm Casanova in disguise. What gives? Sure, I've had a couple of girlfriends, but nothing that lasted. I was too busy wanting someone who I couldn't have. Who never wanted me back.

"It's like you don't realize how great you are, Jack. Because you are. You're smart and funny and corny, but in a non-annoying, mostly endearing way."

"'Endearing'? That sounds like a great-grandmother compliment. *Gee, Jack, you're so mostly endearing.*"

"I'm being serious here. Can't you ever just be serious for one goddamn minute?"

"Whoa," I say. I throw up my hands in surrender. "What's happening right now?"

She reaches up to adjust her rearview mirror. "Nothing,"

52

Jillian says. "Nothing at all."

"Is this about Kate?"

She scoffs. "Do you even know her last name?"

She turns up the radio. I almost turn it back down, but I stop myself, because I'm not sure why she's upset, how the conversation turned so quickly. One moment we're planning our collegiate lives together, and the next she can't even look at me. And for a split second I let my mind drift *there*—

But I sweep the thought aside, because if a planet where Jillian likes Jack like *that* exists, humans have yet to set foot on it.

I lean into my seat, try to lose myself in the music, in the road streaming by. Jillian's foot is heavier than usual, and we make great time.

I retrieve my bag from the back seat. "See you in the morning," I say.

"Right," she says. She already has the car in reverse before I can shut the door. "Back to our fabulous high school lives."

"Text me and let me know you made it home safely."

She nods and backs out of the driveway.

I barely have my key in the door before my parents yank me into the house and blister me with questions. When I've finally satisfied them, and munched on Mom's dinner, I settle into my bed and unlock my phone. There's a message from Franny— *Welcome back, man*—but no one else.

Thanks, bro, I reply. *Good to be back.*

A part of me feels bad for Franny, maybe even guilty, and I don't entirely understand those feelings because I haven't done anything wrong. Not exactly, anyway. Maybe I had been contemplating it. You know, the whole *confess my undying love to Jillian* thing. But I hadn't followed through. And lack of bad-idea-follow-through counts for something, right?

I open my text string with Jillian and start typing.

ME: Hey, you made it home okay, J??

A second later I see those three dots like she's typing me a message back, but in the end, nothing. She never replies.

And who knows—maybe her silence says everything.

OVERTHINKING OVERTHINKING

I spend the next three days waiting for a text, an email, a call from Kate, anything. I refresh my email (just junk), send a few test texts to make sure my phone is working (it is), check the ancient house phone caller ID even though there's no way Kate has our house number (I don't even know it), but nothing. Whoever said silence is deafening must've been waiting for Kate to contact him, too.

And the extra layer of icing spread thick atop my Loser City cake?

Jillian's award-winning, one-woman *I'm super annoyed with Jack* show is still playing in theaters everywhere. And there appears to be no end in sight.

I turn to Franny for insight. But he's no help. "She's been strange ever since you guys got back. Did something happen up there?"

The worst part is Jillian is everywhere I turn. We have four classes together plus study hall. She gives Franny and me a ride to and from school. Which means I get to fully absorb the depths of her silent treatment. It's easily the loudest nonaudible sound I've ever heard.

I beg her to talk to me. But not a peep.

When she pulls curbside at my house, I thank her over and over again for the ride, and I make sure to stuff a healthy wad of gas money in her ashtray, only to later find those same crumpled bills stuffed in the front zippered pocket of my backpack.

Most of my texts to her go unanswered. And the ones that don't are measly monosyllabic replies. The usual *stop texting me, you asshole* suspects:

Yes.

IDK.

Maybe.

Nope.

Finally, I show up to her house with her favorite triple chocolate chunk cookies and our mutual guilty pleasure flick, *Adventures in Babysitting.*

Jillian opens the door just wide enough to poke her head out. She looks anything but happy to see me.

"What are you doing here?"

"I just wanted to see you," I say. When she doesn't budge, I hold up the cookies. "I come in peace."

"It's not a good time, man," she says, moving to close the door.

"Jack, is that you?" a voice from within the house says. "Jillian, let Jack inside."

"*Mom*," Jillian protests.

The door swings open, and there's nothing but darkness inside the house, until Ms. Anderson steps into the frame, wearing a teal robe, her dark hair pulled up, the flicker of a burning candle in her hand. "I don't think Jack's afraid of the dark, are you, Jack?"

I shake my head, not quite following. The truth is, I'd go along with almost anything Ms. Anderson says because 1) her Italian accent is mesmerizing and 2) she's one of the most genuine people I've ever met.

"Come in, come in," Ms. Anderson says, using her lit candle to light another, handing it to me. I follow her and Jillian into the kitchen, our candles held in front of us like mini torches, polygonal shadows creeping along the walls.

"Your power went out," I ask.

Jillian doesn't answer. Even in the dimness, I can see she's upset.

"Oh, the electric company thinks I didn't pay the bill, but I did," Ms. Anderson says. She sighs. Puts a hand to her head. "I've just had so many things on my brain. I mean, it's possible I paid a little late, but not so late that . . ." Her voice drops off.

I nod, as if I understand. "It happens."

"It's nice, though," Ms. Anderson says, almost absentmindedly. "Not to have internet or TV or—"

"Hot water, a fridge, a stove," Jillian interrupts.

"I was gonna say *distractions*, Jillian. And the power company said it was gonna be back on by six tonight."

"Well, it's almost eight. You sure you called?"

"What do you mean am I sure? I told you I called."

"Right. Okay," Jillian says.

Suddenly I feel as though I shouldn't be here. It occurs to me that maybe Jillian hasn't been mad at me at all. That she has bigger concerns. And I haven't been paying attention.

Ms. Anderson frowns. "What's that supposed to mean? I called and . . ."

"Okay, Mom."

"Everyone makes mistakes, Jillian," Ms. Anderson says, her voice caving in on itself.

"Mom."

"Even you."

"*Mom.*"

"I'm just saying, I know I'm not perfect. But I'm trying. I'm trying my best, Jillian."

And Jillian's voice softens. "I know you are. Okay? I know."

The two of them stare at each other across the candlelit kitchen, until Ms. Anderson breaks the silence. "I picked up the cutest soaps from your mom's store the other day, Jack. How are your parents doing?"

But before I can answer, the darkness flickers, and all around us lights blink to life and machines hum sharply. "You see, my love," Ms. Anderson says, pointing at the ceiling light, then running her fingers through Jillian's hair. "I told you I'll always take care of you."

"So, uh, how's your mom doing?" I ask, leaning against the kitchen counter, Ms. Anderson having long retreated upstairs.

Jillian hands me a large bowl, dumps freshly microwaved popcorn into it.

"Same. She has her days."

"Yeah." I give the bowl a shake, even the popcorn out. "How are *you* doing?"

Jillian looks at me like I'm a stranger, like she's only just met me but she's already not sure she likes me. "I don't have a choice, Jack. I don't get to have bad days."

And I feel stupid, because I know this. Because I want to fix this for Jillian, except I barely know what *this* is, and even if I did know, I'm fairly certain I lack the required tools.

"I'm sorry, J." I clear my throat. "So, your dad's still, uh . . ."

She plunks ice cubes into our glasses. "I thought you came over to watch a movie."

"I did, but . . . I mean . . . if—"

"So, let's watch." She disappears into the den.

We're about halfway through the movie, sitting on either end of her family-room sofa, when I hit Pause.

"Not another bathroom break, King."

She only uses my last name when she's upset.

"You have to talk to me, J."

She crosses her arms. "I *am*."

"No, you're talking through me and sometimes at me, but not to me. Whatever I did, please know that I'm eternally sorry."

We sit silent for a beat, and then another, until Jillian sighs and crams half a cookie into her mouth. She chews and chews, and when she's swallowed, she looks over at me.

"I guess I was Alfred," she says, the last word snapping off in a mumble.

"You were *Alfred*? I don't get it."

She sighs. "Afraid, Jack," she says, softly but clearly. "I was afraid, okay?"

"Afraid how?"

"Everything's changing."

"What things?"

"All the things." She takes a deep breath. "First with my family. And now, it seems, with us. The other day on our drive home from Whittier, it was the first time it occurred to me I might not have you forever."

I'm speechless. Because I thought those were things that only I ever considered. Jillian always seems so supremely confident in herself, in her feelings, it's hard to imagine her struggling with any insecurities. But here she is, reminding me of how human she is, how human we all are.

"It's stupid," she says, "I know. I mean, you're my best friend. Always will be. But I guess I had all these expectations about what our last couple of months of high school would be like. That we'd be even more inseparable, that we'd do all the senior stuff together, like prom and senior luncheon and all those other cheesy things we're supposed to do but have always made fun of. And then we'd graduate and celebrate and leave all this crap behind, and we'd ride off into our college future together. We'd turn the page. Finally, you know, turn it for good. And then you—something about the way you were so excited about Kate, about spending time with her. You passed up burgers with your best friend for her." She tries to laugh, but it's strained. "I mean, you were going crazy at even just the *possibility* of talking to her. I can't remember ever seeing you like that. Like ever."

And I nearly say, *If only you'd noticed the way I acted around you, how excited and happy I always am even to be in the same room with you.* But I don't interrupt.

"I guess it made me feel . . . less. Like I was less to you. And that sucked so bad because you're so . . . more to me."

I scoot across the couch, closing the sofa distance between us, nearly spilling the cookie tray in the process. "J, you're my best friend because you're the best person I know. Nothing will change that."

Her eyes are moist, soft. This is a side to Jillian I'm not sure I've seen—it's as if she's nervous around me, uncertain.

"Really?" she says. "You promise?"

"Hope to die."

We hold each other's gaze and it's easy to remember why I fell for Jillian in the first place (as if I could ever truly forget).

"Jack?"

"Yeah?"

"You're the best person I know, too."

We unpause the movie and we sit there, sharing a single sofa cushion, her head against my chest. I can feel the soft, warm tremor of her breathing. And I don't pay attention to a single scene. I think about that day nearly four years ago, the day I bumped into Jillian in the hall, the day she offered me, a goofy, nerdy kid from Elytown, a chance for her heart—

Sorry I didn't come tumbling after, I'd said.

She'd smiled. *We can always try again.*

But then there's a knock at the front door. We don't move until the knock happens again, and then Jillian unravels herself from me to answer it. When she comes back, she's not alone.

"Not this movie again," Franny groans. "I didn't catch two transfers over here to watch some cheesy movie." He flops onto the sofa, in the exact spot formerly occupied by half of Jillian and half of me. Jillian sits beside him, and he pulls her in for a big hug. He laughs. "Hey, do I smell triple chocolate cookies?"

And at the precise moment Franny manages to wedge two entire cookies between his jaws, my jeans vibrate. I fish out my phone.

Hey, sorry I took so long. By the way, it's me, Kate.

For half a second I consider waiting to reply. I don't want to seem too eager, too attached. Except I can't wait a second longer to talk to her.

Don't be sorry, I assure her. *Your timing is perfect.*

"Who's texting you?" Franny says. He pries the phone from my hands with his oversize fingers. "Whoever it is has got you seriously cheesing."

I reach for it in vain. "Give it back, man."

It's too late. He jumps up from the couch, nearly spilling

my milk. He grins, studying the screen. "I told you she'd come around."

Jillian's eyebrows rise. "That's Kate."

"It is indeed," Franny confirms.

"Nice," she says. She turns to me, forces a smile. "Now everyone's happy."

Franny tosses my phone back. "Well," he says. "What are you waiting for? Shoot your shot."

THE THING ABOUT
SHOOTING ONE'S SHOT

The thing is I suck at all things move-making. I'm more of the *wait to be moved* type.

YOU: And how is that working out for you, Jack?

ME: Admittedly, not well.

Which is why I decide to try something different with Kate.

Take action.

Screw passivity.

Screw inertia.

To hell with the path of least resistance.

So shoot your shot already, Jack, you say.

Consider it shotted, my friends.

I pick up my phone and hover over Kate's empty photo circle, my thumb just above the generic, gender-neutral silhouette.

I hover.

And I hover some more.

Because the question that has dogged me ever since my first kindergarten crush still torments me a decade-plus later: *What in the world am I supposed to say?*

I think, *Just be yourself, Jack. At least you can be you somewhat believably.*

I type: *Hey, I'm sorta in your neck of the woods. Wanna grab some cereal?*

SILLY RABBITS, TRICKS ARE FOR (BIG) KIDS

I have to borrow Mom's car because my car is doing this billowing smoke thing, which probably isn't good.

"And where are you and my car going?" Mom inquires.

"Out," I say. I can't control my face, and apparently it wants to grin ear to ear. "For cereal."

Mom gives me a *what's wrong with my kid* look but tosses me her keys and says, "We're out of milk, too."

I probably should've mentioned that this particular cereal is ninety minutes east. But this way, when Dad asks how much she knew, she'll have what our government likes to call *plausible deniability*.

Anyway, to the metal I put the pedal, and I speed past a state highway patrol car idling in the center median, but either he's on break or he understands that I am a man on an important mission, because he doesn't even blink.

Then *I* blink and the next thing I know I'm pulling into a long driveway. I text Kate, *Hey, I'm here.*

My heart is shoving itself into a missile-shaped carton, lighting its wick, and exploding in my chest, a million and one fireworks erupting within my rib cage.

And I haven't even seen Kate yet.

Just the thought of her fires up my sweat glands, makes me sink into the front seat, and I wonder if it's too late to turn around. To go home. Yes, I want to see her. Badly. But also I don't want to screw this up.

Only there are signs everywhere prohibiting U-turns.

Plus, there's a tap at my window—

And it's her—beautiful, brown, super-tight-curls Kate. She leans into my window frame, making that *roll your window down* motion. And I try, except I have to turn the car back on since Mom's ride has power everything. I attempt to turn the ignition just enough to engage battery power without actually restarting the car, but it's not working, so I turn on the car, only to fumble with the window buttons because Mom keeps the child lock on—apparently she doesn't trust me or Dad to exercise good window-lowering judgment—and Kate is rolling in laughter.

Finally, I just open the door.

Kate shakes her head. "Uh, are you okay, man?" she asks.

The answer is no.

And the answer is absolutely.

* * *

We fill our arms with bowls and spoons, milk and cereal. She takes me to her favorite place. A quiet spot down in the gorges, where she goes to read and draw. "I do my best thinking here," she confides. "Or at least that's what I tell myself to justify the exorbitant amount of time I spend here."

We navigate the narrow trail, a wall of crimson rock on either side of us. We watch the water curl around smooth stones, flowing to wherever, taking its time.

And it's like she could lecture on pizza crusts for ten hours and I'd never stop listening, I'd never be bored. But we don't discuss crusts, except to agree that neither of us is a big fan of cheese-stuffed crust, that we're pizza crust purists, *why mess with a great thing.* We talk about where we grew up (she's originally from a suburb near Pittsburgh), and our favorite movies (I confess *Adventures in Babysitting*, which was introduced to me, ironically, by my sixty-year-old former babysitter, also known as my maw-maw; Kate loves a flick she stumbled onto called *Raising Victor Vargas*, which I've never seen).

"I challenge you to watch it and not craugh," she says.

"Craugh?"

She smiles. "Craughing is a simultaneous mix of crying and laughing that is triggered by only the absolute best things in life."

"So, what else has made you craugh?"

"That's for me to know, and for you . . ." She slurps up the leftover milk in her bowl and emerges with the most awesome fruity-loops-milk mustache ever, and she's not at all embarrassed or self-conscious and she doesn't flinch when I wipe it away.

And cereal is my new favorite food.

Probably why bowls and spoons were invented.

TRUTH & CONSEQUENCES

Naturally, when I make it back from my cereal expedition, my parents are less than thrilled to learn how far I traveled for a bowl of artificially flavored milk.

"You missed dinner, Jackie. What were you even doing all the way out there?" Mom asks.

"Something about the milk out that way, it's . . ." I shrug. "More organic-y?"

"Jack, come on," my dad says, in his understanding-yet-stern dad voice.

"I went to see someone," I blurt. "A friend."

Mom and Dad exchange looks.

"Okay, do we know this friend?" Dad asks.

"No. We, uh, only just met."

"Why didn't you just tell us that?" Mom asks, shaking her head.

I tell them the truth, which is: I have no idea.

And so we discuss what it means to be trustworthy.

Rather, my parents discuss and I listen, nodding my agreement when so called upon.

Because my dad is an English major at heart, his part of the lecture consists of breaking down the semantics—*do you understand what trustworthy really means, Jackie? It means that you must be* worthy *of one's* trust. *Hence, TRUST . . . WORTHY*—repeatedly, until even Mom seems bored.

"So, what's her name?" Mom interjects.

"Huh?" I say.

"Don't play with me," Mom says in her *I'm not messing around* voice. If Dad is the Lecturer, Mom is the Interrogator. "This new friend of yours."

"Kate," I say.

"And," Mom says.

"And what?"

"Tell me about *Kate*. Who is she? How do you know her? What's her criminal record?"

"No criminal activity that I know of. She's a freshman at Whittier. I met her during the campus visit."

"An older woman," Dad says, cheesing approvingly. "Apple don't fall far . . ."

Mom freezes Dad with a death stare and he retreats. "Jackie, Dad and I aren't upset because you took the car to Whittier. Or even because you like this Kate. It's that you were intentionally misleading. That's not like you." Her forehead creases in a way that spells concern.

I understand. Parents live in constant dread, forever worried that their kid's slightest transgression is an invisible step toward a life of crime, or at the very least, eternal dysfunction. For instance, what if the fact that I borrowed my mom's car and drove it ninety minutes away gradually morphs into grand theft auto when I'm twenty-three, culminating in a highway police chase whereby I drive into a giant sewer drain, living out my days as a smelly rat king? Or what if missing curfew leads to my inability to be gainfully employed well into my thirties and I live in my parents' attic with my invisible friend Otis?

I get it.

"So, as punishment, your mom and I have decided to . . ." Dad looks at Mom for crime-to-punishment value assignment.

"Put you on probation," Mom says.

"Right, probation," Dad confirms. "Otherwise known as thin ice. You slip up again in the next few weeks, and it's no cell phone, no parties, no . . ."

"Life," I finish. "I understand. And thank you. For the suspended sentence."

"Don't thank us yet. It comes with community service, too," Dad says.

I suppress a groan.

Dad and Mom look at each other again, I suppose to reestablish their parental telepathy. "That's right," Mom says, still studying Dad's face. "You'll be cutting Ms. Nolan's grass for the next month . . ."

"Which includes picking up after her dogs," Dad adds.

This time I groan. Ms. Nolan is a pleasant woman, but she

doesn't believe in pooper scoopers. Her yard is more crap than grass. "C'mon, guys. She has like forty-three dogs over there."

"You made your bed, mister," Mom says.

I sigh.

"You know you can always invite your friends here, Jack. We want to know the people in your life," Mom says.

"I know. I don't know what I was thinking."

"I hope you got your money's worth," they say, eyebrows raised.

Which to answer would be the equivalent of sprinting in dress socks through a field of black ice that's also encrusted with land mines. So, I keep my head low and cultivate a look that I hope conveys my sincere remorse.

"I'm sorry, guys," I say for the dozenth time. "Disappointing you really sucks."

"Well, as long as you learn from this experience," Mom says. I wag my head as she wraps me in a hug and Dad pats my head, and I keep wagging as they shuffle out, until Dad pauses in my doorway.

"Jackie, so, did you or did you not purchase milk for the family?"

Crap, I'd forgotten to stop by the store on my way home. "Negatory, Dad. Sorry."

"Right," Dad says. "Suddenly, I'd like cereal, too."

* * *

FRANNY: Hey, man, how was your big date?

I fall backward into my bed and I close my eyes and I'm back in the gorges, except the sun, clouds, and river rock are all puffy, pastel marshmallows, the sky twinkling with sugar grains, and silver spoon trees swaying in the frosted sugar breeze and singing about love, about happiness. Kate and I in the middle of it all, drifting lazily down a milk river, our butts flopped in giant Froot Loops. We're holding hands and partly singing along, partly laughing, because what's going to happen when our cereal tubes get soggy?

But it doesn't matter.

When we're together, how could anything else matter?

ME: Worth every penny.

FRANNY: Knew it would be.

FRANNY: So . . . I have big news.

ME: All the Wentworth players contracted encephalitis so you win the state championship by default?

FRANNY: The Coupon's coming home.

ME: Are you kidding me?!?

FRANNY: I'd joke about this?

ME: So he got out? Just like that? They let him go??

FRANNY: End of the month.

ME: WTF?!

FRANNY: Right. TF.

THE COUPON'S A-COMING

The Coupon is Franny's nickname for his dad. Coined back in fifth grade, when his dad, yet again, cut out on him, this time on the eve of his first ever game. Which especially sucks, watching your best friend's heart repeatedly smashed to smithereens, since Franny is the most loyal person I know.

It's true. No exaggeration.

Franny and I date back to—as so many friendships do—the playground. For most kids, the playground is a magical place of shiny aluminum slides and rusty chain swings. A place to make friends and run free.

For me, it was a place to get my ass kicked. Recurrently.

Enter Franny.

Even as a kid, he was intimidating. Hell, he towered over most of the parents, and his voice, at seven years old, was already deeper than most dads', mine included. On more than one occasion he saved me from imminent doom. Which I couldn't understand. I mean, what could I do for him, other than split my red Popsicles and single-leggedly lose every three-legged race for us?

Winning games is easy for me, he'd said one day after hitting our baseball so deep we spent all of daylight trying to find it. *But that's why I like you. You don't care about winning.*

Naturally, he was wrong. I did care. I just realized *winning* wasn't a particular strength of mine, and so I gradually grew accustomed to its antonym.

But that's Franny. Give him rain, he's pointing out the rainbow. Which is useful, because he's had more rain than anyone I know.

*　　*　　*

"Guess I thought this day would never come," Franny says, leaning against my back-porch post. He flings a rock over the fence and into the old cornfield. We used to ride our bikes back there, racing along the furrowed rows, jumping over the mounds of dirt, motocross stars in the making. I listen for the rock, but I don't hear it hit ground.

"It's been, what, six years?"

"Eight," Franny says. He casts another rock. "I barely remember him. And what I do remember, none of it's good."

"What's Abuela saying?"

Franny shrugs. "It's her son, you know, so she's all sorts of conflicted. She told me that she won't let him live with us if I don't want him to."

"What do you want?"

"I don't know. She's happy that he's coming back. But she's sad, too, because she thinks I haven't forgiven him. I know what she wants me to do. I mean, you know how she is, always talking, *Francisco, be the bigger person.* Which is bull. He's had a lot more time on this earth to figure things out, but because he's blown every opportunity, has ruined every good thing in his life, *I* have to be bigger. Where's the goddamn sense in that?"

He slumps onto the stairs. "But I tell him to stay away and *I'm* the bad guy. I let him back in and I start the countdown until he messes up again. I'm screwed no matter what. Story of my life, right?" Franny says, smiling. Except I know his real smile. His happy smile. This isn't that. This is his *I have to be tough, I can't let anything faze me* smile. This is the smile that I see most.

"You can't worry about what anyone else thinks," I tell him. "You have to do what's right for you." Which I realize is easier said, but it's true, even if it sounds like *Afterschool Special* Soup.

"I just have a bad feeling."

"What do you mean?"

He chews on his lip. "I don't know. Like, something bad might happen."

"Then maybe you should tell Abuela no. That you don't want him in the house."

Franny nods. "Will you come over still? You know, if he's around?"

I put my hand on his shoulder. "Since when do we let The Coupon decide anything for us?"

"You're right! The Coupon can kiss my ass." He laughs. "Sometimes I forget that about you, man."

"What?"

"That you're the toughest nerdy guy I know."

It's my turn to laugh. "Thanks, I think."

He stands back up, his shadow stretching out deep across the yard, throws a rock so hard, so far, I'm pretty sure it's still climbing long after we walk away. "It's definitely thanks, bro," he says, looking away from me. "It's definitely thanks."

I shove my hands into my pockets. "So, I'm on probation for the foreseeable future. And apparently, I'm also a dog wrangler now."

"That'll teach you to steal your mom's car."

"Hey, I asked!"

Franny grins. "Jillian says Kate's pretty hot. You really like this girl?"

"Think so, yeah," I say, playing it cool.

"Yeah, well, you're a good kid. Mostly," he says, tousling my hair in that big-brother way that he sometimes assumes, even though technically I'm older by four months. "I'm sure your folks will let you off early for good behavior."

"They were pretty disappointed."

"Disappointment's their job, man. As long as you can still practice, we're all good."

"Right," I say. "The band."

SOME JOY FOR YOUR TOY

You might not know from looking at us. If there's a mold for this sort of thing, we probably don't fit it. But the three of us are in band. No, not in *a* band (at least until just recently). In band. As in *at school*. You have Jillian on the big bad bass; Franny doing his thing on drums; and me holding down the trumpet. I won't kid you, though. We mostly suck. Well, to be fair, *I* suck. Jillian is pretty good and Franny holds his own. But it's not fair because Jillian comes from a musically inclined family, and Franny is one of those Good at Everything people.

That said, what I lack in natural talent (a considerable deficit), I make up for in (near) tireless effort. And for the last three months, we've been practicing harder than ever. Because in just a couple months our own newly formed band, JoyToy, will have its world premiere performance.

At my parents' thirtieth anniversary party.

Okay, so a limited world premiere.

And with a yard full of fifty-year-olds, not necessarily our target demographic.

But still.

A hundred and twenty-five people are a hundred and twenty-five people, right?

We're pretty amped.

But *shhhh*, whatever you do, don't tell my parents that we've formed a three-piece band, that we've been practicing nonstop for months, and that it's our way of saying thank you to two of the most awesome people this universe has ever produced.

It's a surprise.

COMPOSITIONS

I consider texting Kate, but I remember something my mom once said, that my dad had "wooed her with long handwritten letters." But my handwriting's terrible, and I'd like Kate to get my messages sometime this year, so.

I toss my laptop onto my bed. Click Compose.

Heeeey Kate . . .

Too informal.
Delete.

Wut up Kate,

Nope. Trying too hard to be cool.

Delete.

Dear Kate,

Classic, right?

Dear Kate,

How do you feel about student dances? Particularly *high school* student dances. And if you are not vehemently opposed to the idea, would you perhaps entertain the idea of attending one, say, with me? I promise you this will not be like in the movies where the high school loser shows up to the dance with some college knockout and is the envy of all his tormenters while simultaneously the king of the *Soul Train* dance line—where all of the cute, previously unavailable high school girls ooh and aah and wonder aloud when did Jack King become such a stud, while his best friends cheer him on, knowing that he had it in him all along.

I am not popular, but I am not unpopular. I am squarely in the middle. Meaning, your attendance will draw little to no fanfare, because people rarely notice me. I am largely obscure.

In case any of the above was unclear, what I am attempting to say is: Will you go to prom with me, Kate?

Please (print out and) circle: YES/NO/MAYBE

Best,
JK

PS While this will no doubt further remind you of my high-school-dom, aka *I still live at home with my parents and as such am forced to abide by their rules*, I would like to inform you that I am currently sentenced to community service. The community is my neighbor. The service is dog doody. And sadly, that's no typo. Yes, doody, not duty. I'll explain when I see you.

Anyway.

Please email me back soon, though, because otherwise I may die.

That is all.

* * *

Dear Jack,

I (mostly) like to follow instructions. Therefore, as you might imagine, I was super stoked to print out your last email, circle my decision, and then—

Well, that was the part where things went south. You see, I do not have your mailing address.

Sooooooo—

My only choice was to save your email as a PDF file, open a PDF editor, circle my answer using one of their highlighter options, save the file again, upload it to my email, and then send it back to you. Hence, the attachment. I know, I know, we're taught to be mistrustful of attachments. But please do not be afraid to open it, as it does not contain any malware and/or explosions. To my knowledge. At least at the time of me sending you this email. I cannot be held responsible for any alterations that might've happened after I hit Send.

I will tell you this. I am not overtly opposed to dances, even the high school variety. But I am opposed to dancing. Rather, my body is. Contrary to stereotype, not all black people are born with incredible rhythm and timing. Most of what I do on the dance floor is a sad variation of the two-step, and even then I lose count. So, please keep this in mind when (and if) you extend any future invitations involving you, me, and music.

Also, it sucks about your community service. But perhaps you can use this time to reflect on what led you down this criminal path (I'm guessing it has something to do with visiting me in your mom's car??) and how you can regain your footing as a doody-ful citizen. I feel as though that would be a constructive use of your time, considering your propensity for breaking the rules. The car thing *plus* your reckless abandon of cereal-eating etiquette—you totally finished the last of the milk, dude!

Okay, I have to end this because as I am writing you I am not studying, and not studying, while fun, is grade cyanide.

All Best,
Kate

PS Did you know your initials spell JK? I bet you didn't. (JK!)

[File attached: YesNoMaybe.pdf—scanned with no viruses detected]

I download Kate's attachment and this is what I find:

In case any of the above was unclear, what I am attempting to say is: Will you go to prom with me, Kate?

Please (print out and) circle: YES/NO/MAYBE

HOW NOT TO BE SO ALONE
IN THIS WORLD

Although my parents are disappointed in me (*no, not **in you**, honey—in your **actions**. We love **you**, Jackie Bear*) and despite my well-documented probationary status, they still let Franny sleep over on Friday. No, this is not the *mixed signals* mistake that parents sometimes make—when they tell you one thing but then almost immediately contradict themselves—rather, it's because Franny's grandma works nights every other weekend, and for the last few years, whenever he's wanted, Mom and Dad have let him crash at our house, no questions asked. This weekend is no exception. And I'm grateful for his company.

Probation isn't terrible (cut grass, scoop poop, stay out of trouble), but add the fact that I have a terrible case of Kate-on-the-brain, and that I can't shake her MAYBE and all of its possible meanings from my head, and, well, any distraction is welcome.

As always, Franny insists we eat dinner with my parents. In the dining room.

"You know how I feel about eating in kitchens," Franny says.

"I know, I know. But eating in the kitchen is, like, convenient. You know, because the food is already there."

"Kitchens are cool, man, but it's called the dining room for a reason. It's begging for us to dine in it."

I've heard this argument before. But I think the real reason Franny's infatuated with the dining room is because his abuela refuses to let anyone within a hundred feet of theirs, the table and chairs literally zipped in protective plastic.

I know when I'm beat. "Fine, man. Whatever. Dining room it is."

Franny smiles. "I knew you'd see it my way." He sniffs the air. "Bro, you need a shower. Like, bad."

I groan. "I had to clean up Ms. Nolan's yard today. I've never seen so much dog crap in my life."

"Do the crime, pay the time, bro."

"Whatever. How's Abuela?"

Franny shrugs. "Working her ass off, as usual."

"Yeah."

"I worry about her. She's healthy and all that, but I wish I could do more, you know?" Abuela's raised him since he was nine. *I'm lucky, though*, he's always saying. *A lot of kids in my hood don't even have one person they can count on.*

Franny's abuela is the definition of *count on*. At any one time she's working two jobs to make ends meet. Plus, she's forever taking on side jobs, hunched over her sewing machine altering suits, christening gowns, and probably every wedding dress ever worn in Ohio. Franny pitches in, bagging groceries at the Dollar Den and spraying deodorizer into beat-up shoes at the bowling alley.

"I saw your mom's commercial," Franny says, grinning.

"Don't even say it, man."

"I love your mom, you know that, but."

"Franny, I'm warning you, man."

"She's just so beautiful, man. Like, I don't know how you can stand it."

"Uh, she's my *mom*, that's pretty much how."

My parents love Franny. Most parents do. His parental charms aren't surprising, though. He is all kinds of *trustworthy*. If my parents are ever on the fence about letting me do *fill in the blank*, just mentioning that Franny will also be doing *fill in the blank* almost always tips the scales *yes*.

Plus, it doesn't hurt that Franny is the superathlete son my mom didn't get biologically. Mom played college ball, and was pretty good. *A lady in the streets, but a beast on the court,* she enjoys saying. (Side point: the way Mom behaves at sporting events—arguing with the refs, shouting out plays to the coaches, razzing the opponent's mascot—is a handy reminder that "fan" is short for *fanatic*.)

Anyway, Mom and I (and usually Dad) go to all of Franny's games (basketball, football, baseball, track meets), saving a seat for Abuela because her jobs keep her running late. *Brown-people time*, Franny always says, shrugging his shoulders and laughing as Abuela shows up huffing and puffing at the end of the first quarter.

"So, how's your lady friend, young squire?" Franny asks. He drops his overnight bag onto my bedroom floor.

Instantly, I'm all teeth and cheeks.

What does it mean that just the mention of Kate makes me cheese stupidly?

"Helloooooo? Jack?" Franny calls. He tosses a rolled-up sock at me, but I'm unfazed. I'm elsewhere, soaring above the hills of Kateland.

"And you say I'm whipped? Damn, kid, what's gonna happen when you've known her for a few months?" Franny says.

"She's pretty cool, man. I think you'll like her."

Franny walks over to my bedroom door. "If you like her, I already do. Mind if I get the lights?"

I nod my consent. He hits the switch, throwing us into darkness.

Franny's silhouette crosses the room, digs out his phone, and plugs it into the wall. He scrolls through his Favorites; his finger hovers above Jillian's face, her face cropped in a perfect circle, and I think of the times I've done the same—my finger not a centimeter from her face. Only my finger never moved, my brain too afraid. Not Franny—he taps Jillian's crooked smile, her scrunched-up cheeks.

"Hey, baby. I miss you, too," he says into the phone. He buries his face in his blankets, and he's all whispers and Franny-Jillian inside jokes and serious *I want you forever* voice.

And me—

I start reading, but I can't stop thinking about Kate. Soon, I'm trading my book for Instagram, and there's Kate's profile. I scroll through pictures of her laughing with friends, her being silly with family. No matter the place, or the people, Kate's always smiling.

After a while, Franny stops whispering. Rips the blankets from his head and looks up, his hair flopping over his eyes.

"Now what are you smiling about?" he whisper-shouts. "Go to sleep!"

"Mind your business."

"Hey," he says. His long arm extends like a crane, drops his phone onto my desk. "Seriously, though. Thanks for letting me crash. I needed this. Things at home have been . . . well, you know."

I lower my phone, reach for the nightstand light. "Yeah, man. Me too. And anytime, you know that."

Because, between friends, there are times when just knowing what you mean to each other isn't enough.

When you should really say the words.

"Hey, Jack," he says after a few minutes. His voice is faint, like he doesn't want to wake me if I'm already asleep, as if he's uncertain he wants to say what he's thinking.

"Yeah?"

He's lying on his back, hands behind his head, his eyes studying the ceiling with an intensity ceilings don't deserve. "When he gets out, Abuela's making this crazy dinner. All of his favorite foods, apparently."

"Oh yeah?"

"Know what's strange? Turns out he and I both really dig smothered pork chops. Small world, right?"

"Very," I agree. Although *I* also love smothered pork chops, as I am certain does most of the world.

"Anyway, I was thinking . . . I was wondering . . . if you might—you know. Be there. At the house. When he comes home. I don't know, I just think it would be cool to have someone else there. Like backup or a buffer or something. And I thought about Jill. I mean, she's awesome, and she's been crazy supportive, but I don't know if I'm ready for my dad and my girl in the same room yet. So. I was thinking you'd . . . maybe . . . it's probably weird, right? I sound like the biggest baby right now. Damn. Forget it, okay? It's stupid. I'm buggin'."

"Franny, I'll be there."

"Yeah?"

"Absolutely. And if he gets crazy, don't worry, we'll kick his ass. Or at least I'll jump on his back and try to steer him into a wall while you kick his ass."

"The Coupon won't know what hit him."

"He'll wish he was still locked up."

"Right," Franny says. He rolls onto his side, facing the wall.

And for a moment I imagine Franny's dad, wrapped in a blanket, staring at a similar blank wall—but I can't imagine what he's thinking.

"He'll wish," Franny says, his voice trailing off into nothing.

STATUS UNCLEAR

KATE: Jack, can we talk? Can I call you?

Which is sorta scary. *Can we talk* can absolutely be a good thing, a happy thing, but for me, its needle has firmly leaned *bad*. Granted, my sample size is awfully small, but still.

ME: That's cool.

"Hey," Kate says on her end of the phone.

"Hey," I echo.

"So."

"So."

"Before I agree to go to prom with you, there's something you should know."

"You're from another planet and the window for your homeland return coincides with the middle of prom?"

She laughs. "No, my return window expired years ago."

"Oh, so you're stuck here."

"I prefer to think I'm a permanent alien delegate," Kate says.

"And that makes you feel better about being stuck?"

"Well, it did, until this Earth boy ruined it."

"Typical Earth boy."

"I'd say atypical."

I don't know if atypical is good here, but it doesn't feel bad. Makes my heart do cartwheels across my chest.

"So, what do I need to know before we can go to prom?"

She sighs. "I told you I was recently out of a relationship?"

The cartwheels cease. "Yeah. I remember."

"I don't think I'm all the way out, Jack."

"What does that mean?"

"It's hard to explain. There's a lot of components to it. But." She pauses. "Essentially, he's been with me through some pretty crazy times. It's hard to completely extract someone who's always been your go-to."

"Are you saying you still wanna date your ex?"

"No. I don't think so."

"I don't understand."

"I'm saying, he's still around. We're not together, but we're not yet separate entities, either."

"So your status would be *it's complicated*?"

"Nope. We're status-less."

"So, where does this leave us?"

"Going to prom, also status-less? Maybe status-pending?"

"Hmmm." Because of course I want to go to prom with

Kate, but I'm naturally clumsy and these attached strings are trip hazards.

"I just wanted to be honest with you. All of this is new and confusing for me. I think you're a cool guy, Jack. And I'd love to be your prom date, if you'll still have me?"

And before my brain can spit out the cost-risk analysis, my heart chimes in. "We'll have you."

Kate laughs. "We?"

"I mean, me. Me'll have you."

I can feel her smile through the phone. "Oh, I can't wait to be awkward with you in person, Jack."

"The feeling's all the way mutual."

I'LL BUILD A MIGHTY MOAT AROUND YOUR LOVE

Kate and I decide she should probably meet the people we're tag-teaming prom with. My parents are out for the evening, so the four of us end up at my house.

"Guys, this is Kate," I say. "Kate, the guys."

Jillian laughs. "In addition to being one of the guys, I also play a girl. Hi, I'm Jillian. It's nice to meet you."

"Nice to meet you, too. I've heard a lot about you," Kate says. And then adds, "About you both."

"That's an awesome shirt," Franny says, pointing at Kate. "Don't tell me you've seen Mighty Moat live."

"Okay," Kate says. "I also won't tell you that the drummer is my sister's current beau."

"Get out of here. You serious?"

"I don't joke about Mighty Moat," Kate says.

"Oh my God. You have to get us tickets. Can you get us tickets?"

"Babe, relax," Jillian intercedes. "Can you at least let her take off her coat before you ask her to fly you to the moon?"

"It's okay," Kate says. "I can absolutely get us tickets. What are you doing two weeks from Friday? And would you be down for a road trip to Detroit?"

"Are you kidding!" he shouts. He hops onto a kitchen table chair, pumping his fists like a maniac. "This is a joke, right? You put her up to this, Jack?"

"Don't look at me," I say.

Kate smiles. "I promise you, I don't joke about things of this magnitude."

"Oh my God, we're going to Detroit to see Mighty Moat, babe, are you hearing this?" Franny is jumping up and down on the chair now.

Jillian reaches out to calm him down. "Please excuse my boyfriend. I water him whenever I remember, but he doesn't get much sun."

Kate and I laugh.

Then Jillian asks, "So, my dear Kate, in your honor, tonight we've pulled out all the stops. We have *shrimp*-flavored ramen."

"For me?" Kate says, laughing. "I'm okay with original flavor."

But Jillian won't hear of it. "No, no," she says. "Only the best for our esteemed guest."

Kate beams. "Well, thank you."

"Natch," Jillian says. She rips the ramen package open, drops the loaf of noodles into the water boiling on the stove.

"Can I help?" Kate asks.

Jillian grins, hand on her hip. "You've had ramen before, right? I don't even need *my* help to make it."

"How about I set the table?"

"I usually make the boys do that, but . . ." Jillian points to a cabinet. "Bowls are in there."

"Sweet," Kate says.

I look over at Jillian and then back to Kate. The only two women I've ever had real feelings for in the same room, about to eat shrimp à la ramen together, out of my crappy childhood bowls?

It's odd, right?

And yet it feels oddly right.

*   *   *

Two hours later, Franny's in vintage Franny Storytelling Mode, and our asses, if not laughed off entirely, are barely hanging on.

"So, then Jack's standing there with his pants around his ankles and Mrs. Calloway's face is on fire, and she's coming at us with one of those big-ass push brooms you use to clean a stadium. Except she's trying to decapitate us."

"Stoooppp," Kate says. She nearly spits out her Kool-Aid. "What did you guys do?"

Franny eyes me. "We did what young gentlemen do. We hauled ass, and hoped to God she didn't call our moms."

"Oh my God," Kate says, cracking up.

Franny shakes his head. "Seriously, Jack didn't even get his pants all the way up, but you should've seen his legs pumping. He ran like he needed exorcism."

"The first and only time I'll ever beat Franny in a footrace," I add.

"To good times," Franny says. He holds his cup out toward the center of the table.

"The best times," I agree, tapping my cup against his, the girls following suit.

I disappear into the garage to scavenge for ice cream in the storage freezer, but when I return victorious (Double Choco Fudge Fantastic *and* Buckeye Bite Bonanza), Franny and Jillian exchange looks. Franny shakes his head, scoots his stool back from the kitchen island.

"Actually, Jack-O, we're gonna take off," Franny declares. "Seems I have a history paper to write."

"Aww, no way," Kate protests. "When's it due?"

Franny winks. "Tomorrow. Morning. At, er, eight a.m."

"Yet you're the picture of calm," Kate says, laughing.

"You don't know this yet, Kate, but our friend Franny here is Lord of the Procrastinators," I say.

"Only *Lord*? You're really selling Franny short," Jillian adds. She gathers the dishes from the table, and I load them into the dishwasher.

"Guys, we all know I work better under pressure."

Jillian closes the dishwasher with her hip. "Well, considering that's the only way you ever work, it's hard to disprove."

"Ouch, that's cold," Franny says.

"Awww, my poor baby," Jillian says. She wraps her arms around his waist.

"Baby, love you," Franny says. He leans into her and she nuzzles her nose into his chest.

"Gross," I yell. "We *eat* in here!"

"Get a room already," Kate says.

But it's hard to imagine anything better than my two best friends in love. Hard to envision a world where they aren't perfect together.

On their way out, Franny calls over his shoulder, "You kids have *fuuuuun*."

Jillian turns back, offers an apologetic smile as she ushers him down the driveway.

I lock the door, then rest my back against it. "So," I say.

I squint, presenting Kate with The Jack King Eye of Irresistible Seduction. A look that, to date, has netted me exactly zero dividends.

"So," Kate repeats. "What should we do now?" Except Kate's voice implies she may have a few ideas.

"Video games," I suggest, probably too earnestly. "Or maybe TV? Do you like college basketball, because March Madness just started. Also, I could whip us up some milkshakes, or I think Mom has frozen cookie dough we could . . ."

"Jack." She brings her slightly crooked index finger to my lips. "You had me at video games."

And I'm not saying she wouldn't have beaten me anyway, but I can barely concentrate. I keep staring at her from the corner of my eye, afraid she might be an illusion.

She annihilates me eight games straight. "You okay? It feels like you're miles from here."

"Guess I'm just thinking."

"About?"

"The truth?"

She laughs. "Honesty's cool, yeah."

"I want to kiss you."

"Oh," she says. Only I can't decipher her tone.

Which means I've probably blown it. Too fast, too soon, Jack.

"So, how come you haven't?" she asks. Her question bounces into me like sonar, reverberating down into my darkest depths. *Why haven't you, Jack? Why haven't you? Why haven't—*

But before I can answer, she lifts my chin, takes my face in her hands, and her lips press into mine.

Her lips might as well be keys, because damn if they don't instantly have me wide open.

And—

And—

Fireworks, guys.

Freaking fireworks.

MALL TALK

Three days before prom I'm at the mall trying on formal wear. But my primary functions are Jillian's Chief Purse Guardian while she rifles through dress racks, and Franny's Heckler as he models *every* suit in his exhaustive search of The One Suit Worthy of His Body.

"Kate's not meeting us?" Jillian asks. We've just exited our two hundredth store, and Franny's still empty-handed save for a pizza pretzel. *You can't shop on an empty stomach, Jack*, he'd said. *If you're hungry, you make rash decisions.*

I shake my head. "She has an appointment she couldn't get out of."

Franny slaps at my department-store bag, laughing. "Probably for the best. Otherwise she'd discover just how color-blind you are!"

102

"Leave him alone," Jillian says.

"Thank you, Jillian," I say.

"Personally, I think it's cute that Jackie hasn't learned his colors," Jillian says.

"Wow. I really hate both of you," I say.

And maybe I wasn't excited about prom before—because, you know, it involves dancing and girls and maybe dancing *with* girls—but thanks to Kate, I'm starting to come around.

ORCHID

I know little* about flowers.

*Nothing.

So, I ask Mom to help me pick Kate's corsage—because 1) it'll make Mom happy and 2) where do you even buy corsages?

We walk up and down the greenhouse rows.

Finally, Mom stops. "This is the one," she says. She holds the brightest yellow flower I've ever seen.

"Perfect," I say.

Ten minutes later, we're driving home, the orchid balanced in a clear box on my lap.

Mom glances at me across the seat. "Jackie?"

"Yeah, Mom?"

Her hand leaves the steering wheel and she wipes her eyes.

I smile at her. "Mom, what's wrong? Don't tell me you're

having orchid remorse. We can go back and get the tiger lily. It's not too late."

"You're a fool," she says. She laughs through her tears. "Nothing's wrong." She ruffles my hair with her fingers, and I think about all the times she sat on the floor beside my bed, her fingers running across my scalp—nights I'd begged her to stay until I fell asleep. "I'm proud of you, Jackie. Of who you're becoming. Who you already are."

And I just nod—say a soft "I love you, Mom"—because what else do you say to the woman who made you you?

"Kate'll love your orchid, but it has nothing to do with the flower."

"I love you, Mom," I say again. This time not soft at all.

EXITS

Dad's in full paparazzi mode.

Shadowing me, taking pictures while I shave, brush my teeth, while I rifle through my sock drawer looking for my favorite pair.

"Jack, just look this way for a minute."

"Dad, c'mon," I beg. "When Kate gets here, this has to stop, okay?"

"I make no promises," Dad says, winking. "Okay, now turn your head a touch to the right. Nope, nope, that's too much. Go back a little. There, there. Now hold it. Keep holding . . . hold it."

"My neck is in danger of breaking if I hold this any longer, Dad."

Mom slides her arms around Dad's waist. "You know your

father lives for these moments, Jackie. Let him have his fun."

I break pose. "I don't want to infringe on Dad's fun. I just don't want it to be at my fun's expense. You guys know I hate pictures."

"But you're so handsome," Mom says. She steps away from Dad to pinch my cheeks.

I sidestep her reach. "Maybe I'll just meet Kate out on the front porch."

"Ha ha ha," Dad says, feigning laughter. "I still don't understand why you aren't picking her up."

"I told you, she's staying at her folks' house this weekend, and she said it didn't make sense for me to drive all the way out there only to drive back this way. I tried convincing her, but she insisted."

"Hmph," Dad snorts. "Back in my day . . ."

"You didn't have a car and it was the worst snowstorm the earth's ever seen even though it was April, and you trudged thirty-seven miles without a decent coat. And you still picked Mom up for prom."

"And he *still* showed up looking *so* sexy," Mom adds.

Dad beams. "My suit was so wet and wrinkled. Remember your mom made me hang my jacket over the radiator before she'd let us leave?"

Mom laughs. "The look on your face when Dad said you had to ride up front with him while he drove us."

"The man was *completely* unreasonable. Talking about 'no funny business on my watch.' Little did he know what was really going down on his watch . . ."

Dad pulls Mom into him, smushes a kiss onto her cheek. Mom laughs, slaps at his hands. "Don't give your son any ideas," she says. "Bad enough he has your genes working against him." Mom turns to me, a look of concern on her face. "Jackie, you'll be *careful*, won't you?"

I know this conversation's destination, and I'd rather not make the trip. "Mom, please."

"Don't take any chances. Better to be prepared than . . ."

"Mom," I say firmly.

"Listen to your mother," Dad insists. "We're too young and vibrant for grandparenthood right now."

This is the blessing of being an only child: you have your parents' undivided attention.

This is the curse of being an only child: you have your parents' undivided attention.

"Everything's covered, guys. Thanks for your incredible amount of uncomfortable concern." I pull out my phone. Kate's fifteen minutes late.

Dad reads my mind. "Maybe she needed gas."

"I'm sure she's on her way," Mom chimes.

Fifteen minutes later, I shoot Kate a text.

ME: Hey, just making sure you're okay. Hopefully you're just working on CP time. LOL

Another ten minutes and nothing.

Mom calls from the kitchen. "Maybe eat a little dinner before you go, Jackie? Take your mind off things."

"I'm okay, thanks."

I dial Kate's number and get her voice mail.

I call again, same result.

I take off my suit coat, drape it over the living room ottoman. No sense in letting it wrinkle. Take a seat beside Dad on the couch. He squeezes my shoulders, grunts his support. I grunt my appreciation back.

I hear a car pull into the driveway. I hop off the couch, pull the curtain away from the front window, only to see the car reverse and zoom away.

"False alarm," I announce.

"Maybe call her house," he suggests.

I shrug. "I only have her cell number."

"You could try the phone book?"

I smile. "What's a phone book?"

I call Kate and this time I leave a voice mail.

Thunder rattles the living room, rain falling in sheets outside.

My phone chimes. But it's only Franny.

FRANNY: TIme to turn up!! You ready to make some history, bro?!?!

I don't reply.

I text Kate again.

Mom comes out of the kitchen balancing two dinner plates, sets them down in front of us, kisses my forehead, then Dad's.

"Thank you, baby," Dad says.

"Thanks," I manage.

Dad spears a broccoli head. "Son, maybe you should go find her. Maybe you—"

But before he can finish I'm throwing on my jacket, slipping on shoes.

Mom materializes at the front door, the yellow orchid in one hand, her car keys dangling in the other. "Be safe, Jackie."

"Thanks, Mom," I say. I take the keys, the flower, and rush outside, forgetting that it's raining elephants.

"Jackie, umbrella," Mom calls after me.

But there's no turning back now.

I'm soaked before I make it into the car.

And then I'm speeding past cookie-cutter blocks of cookie-cutter houses and cookie-cutter yards. I merge onto the highway, rain slapping the windshield, puddles spitting away from my tires.

My phone beeps.

> **JILLIAN: Where are you, man?! You're supposed to hook up AFTER prom is over!!! LOL** 😊 **Hurry your ass!!**

I lean into the gas.

I nearly miss the exit, swerving Mom's car over two lanes, fishtailing along the median. But I make it. Still, part of me wonders, *What are you doing, Jack?*

What do you think is gonna happen?

You show up to her door and she answers—and then what?

Then what, Jack?

I don't have an answer.

GPS on my phone screen, her address plugged in, I still pass her house. I turn around in a neighbor's driveway.

There's an opaque window on Kate's front door; it's mostly dark inside. It's quiet, too.

My phone rings.

"Jack, I'm so so sorry," Kate says into my wet ear.

"Are you okay? Where are you?"

A long pause. "I can't go to prom. And I know this is sooo messed up, but I promise you if I could . . ."

"Did I do something, Kate? I don't understand."

"You did nothing wrong. I don't know how to explain."

"Just try. Try to explain."

"I just wanted you to know . . . I'm so very sorry."

"You're sorry?"

"Yes."

"That's it?"

"I don't know what to say."

"Say *something*, Kate. Because so far you haven't said anything."

"Jack . . ."

"Prom started two hours ago. I've been waiting for you."

"So, you didn't go?"

"We were supposed to go together, Kate. We were supposed to . . . where are you? Are you in your house?"

"No. Look, it's a long story . . ."

"As it happens, I have a lot of time on my hands."

"I have to go, Jack. I'm so sorry."

"Yeah, you said that."

"Goodbye, Jack."

"Wait, Kate—"

But she's gone.

The curse of Almost strikes again. I lean against her front door and my legs give, my feet sliding forward. And I sit slumped against her door, wrinkled, confused, wet.

I prop the world's brightest orchid against Kate's door.

And as soon as I'm back in the car, the rain stops.

Because, of course.

HOW TO GET OVER SOMEONE (HOW TO RE-SOLIDIFY YOUR HEART WHEN IT'S THE BAD KIND OF MUSHY)

If you want to know how to get over someone, I'm the last one to ask.

I can, however, tell you what not to do.

I'm exceptional at what not to do.

Do not: refuse to shower. By the time you realize how awful you smell (do you have any idea how bad you smell when your own brain can no longer keep it from you?), you're already too late.

Do not: devour entire boxes of cookies in one miserable, self-loathing sitting.

Do not: snot into your pillow. Or shirt. Or blanket. I actually did not cry, but I could see how tears might happen. It's an emotional time. In fact, cry if you want to.

But just so we're clear, *I* did *not* cry.

I had something in my eye.

Mom switched fabric softener and my allergies flared.

Dad made me be his sous-chef, and I had to chop onions.

I'm just saying there are a million perfectly good reasons for what you think you saw on my face.

* * *

My friends seem to think band practice heals broken hearts.

Which explains why they've dragged me from my bed into Jillian's garage.

"You can't sleep away the pain," Jillian says.

"Says who," I argue.

"You'll feel better once we get into the music. Which song should we start with?" Franny asks.

"Not a love song," I mumble.

"Well, that's gonna be hard considering our set list is for an anniversary party," Jillian says.

I shrug. "Whatever."

Franny and Jillian trade looks. "How about the Stevie Wonder," Franny suggests. Normally, this would be a great starting point. One of my parents' all-time favorite songs—one of mine, too—but today hearing Stevie croon about falling in love just hurts.

"Do we have to?" I ask.

But Jillian's already counting us down.

Thirty seconds in, I screw up the notes. I stop playing.

"Don't stop," Jillian says.

"Catch back up," Franny encourages me.

And I try, but it's no use, I sound even worse than usual. Which is hard to do.

"Next song," Franny suggests.

Jillian counts again.

This time I manage to reach the refrain before self-destructing.

"Crap," I shout, nearly throwing my horn down.

"Let's take ten," Jillian says.

"Let's take forever," I say. I pull out my phone and start browsing.

"What are you looking at, Jack?" Jillian asks.

"Nothing," I say, scrolling up.

"He's on her IG," Franny says, groaning. He snatches my phone.

"Hey," I protest.

"You need an intervention, bro," Franny says. "It's for your own good."

And then my phone starts ringing. I try to reach around Franny but he boxes me out. "Give me my phone back, Franny. I'm not playing."

"Relax, man. It's not even your phone. *My* phone is ringing. It's Coach. I gotta take this." Franny tosses my phone to Jillian. "Make sure he stays away from social media, will you?" He steps outside. "Hey, Coach, what's up?"

I hit Jillian with my best pleading face.

"Uh-uh, don't even try it," she says. "That face isn't gonna work."

I stick out my bottom lip. "What about the pouty lip?" I ask.

"I'm immune to your ways," she says. She slips my phone into her jeans, crosses her arms.

"Fine then."

"Jack, how are you really doing? Like, how concerned should I be?"

"Mild to medium? I don't know."

She smiles. "I can do medium."

"What about you?" I ask.

"What about me?"

"How are you doing?"

She shrugs. "I'm doing."

"Your mom?"

She sighs. "She was actually having a pretty decent week. And then he called."

"Your dad?"

Jillian nods.

"Where is he?"

"Headed home."

"Home? Like here?"

"No, *home* home. As in Côte d'Ivoire."

This is a turn I did not expect. "Oh. Wow."

"Yeah. Wow." Jillian flops onto the garage sofa. "I mean, he'll be back. He's just going to visit family. 'Clear his head,' he said."

"That's a long drive to clear your head."

"Guess that's why Franny and I get along so much. We both have dads who love themselves the most."

I join her on the sofa. "C'mon. Your dad loves you."

She snickers. "Parents assure you that they're only running away from each other, that they're not leaving *you*. They swear nothing will change. But eventually everything does."

"I don't get love," I confess. "Like when it's good, it's this amazing thing. Except it never stays good."

"Not never. I mean, some people figure it out, right? Your parents did."

"I guess. I mean, they've had their ups and downs too."

"That's life, though. You have problems. But you keep trying. You fight for the things you love."

"But what if those things don't love you back?"

"Well, then you're screwed," Jillian says with a mini laugh.

"So, maybe it's not how something ends that matters. Maybe it's about having something good, even for a little while."

"Maybe."

"What did I miss?" Franny asks, leaping back into the garage.

"Nothing," I say.

"Everything," Jillian says.

"Okayyyy." Franny looks at me, then at Jillian, and we laugh.

I hop to my feet, pick up my horn. "You guys ready to jam, or what?"

And it's not the best I've ever played. But it's not the worst.

NO-SHOW CITY DOESN'T HAVE TO BE A SAD PLACE

The Elytown High Panthers lose in the second round of the playoffs 62–57, despite Superman-like heroics from Franny. Jillian and I wait for him in the parking lot.

As soon as we see him, Jillian throws her arms around him, and he stoops down to hug her back.

"You played awesome," we take turns telling him.

"Thanks," he says. "Too bad it wasn't enough."

Jillian shakes her head. "Depends who you ask."

I climb into the back seat, Jillian at the wheel, Franny shotgun.

"I know it's crazy stupid, but I thought he might show up today," Franny says. "I mean, he's been out for a couple of weeks and no one's heard from him. Even if he doesn't want anything to do with me, he could still check on his mom. You know, the woman who put money she didn't have onto your commissary card. Who humped over to Winston Hills three hours round-trip to see your tired, orange-jumpsuit-wearing ass. Least you could do is call. Let her know you're okay. And then you have the nerve to refuse to come over for dinner, even though your mom practically begs your ass, has got her heart set on cooking you your favorite meal. Honestly, I don't know why I even thought for a minute that he'd changed."

Jillian takes one hand off the wheel, brushes Franny's cheek. Suddenly there's a fist-size lump in my throat, and it burns, too large to swallow, too sticky to cough up. It's stuck there, on fire.

My phone buzzes, and my mind goes to Kate. It's been nearly two weeks since we last talked.

But it's a text from Mom: *Tell Franny we love him!*

"His loss, Franny," Jillian says. She says this so softly that maybe she actually said *he's lost* instead. Either way, she's right.

"Hell with that cornball," Franny says.

"Franny, maybe he's—" I start. But Franny's already on to the next.

"Oooooh, turn this up," Franny says. He turns up the volume button, his shoulders bopping with the bass.

Jillian touches the car ceiling and the moonroof slides back, letting in patchy moonlight and whistling wind.

"Yo, can you believe we graduate in a week," I shout, standing up to lean out the roof.

"The world is ours," Franny screams.

We spend the rest of the night driving around, picking up fast food, popping our heads out of the car to howl at people, at the three-quarter moon, at our disappointments. And no, maybe it's not the same thing as your dad finally showing up and telling you he loves you. Maybe it's not your parents deciding they're still in love, to give it another go. Maybe it's not a phone call from the girl you're super into, admitting that she hasn't stopped thinking about you.

IRL, there are no video-game power-ups for broken hearts.

But this is something.

It's not nothing.

PARTY OF THE YEAR

JoyToy isn't about to win a Grammy for best live performance, but we put on a good show for my parents' thirtieth. Mom's all happy tears, and Dad's a grinning maniac, both hugging me tight enough to crack ribs.

All in all, the party's a success.

After everyone's left, our backyard a ghost town of gently blowing streamers and glittering globe lights, my parents pour red wine for all of us—Franny and Jillian included.

"You guys were so good," Dad says.

"Our pleasure, Mr. King," Franny says. "Least we could do."

"And you're sure you taped it, Jack? You didn't miss anything?" Mom asks.

"Yaaaaasss, Mom," I say.

Dad reaches for Mom's hand. "Well, me and Mom are going

to enjoy our wine upstairs on the balcony, so."

Franny winks. "You kids have fun."

"Uh, gross," I interject.

"Probably time we talk to Jack about the birds and bees, what do you guys think?" Franny says. "He old enough yet?"

"Not even close," Mom says. "Maybe if . . ."

"Night, gang," Dad says, leading Mom out of the kitchen. "Jillian and Franny, you should probably crash on the couch."

Mom pokes her head back into the kitchen. "Separate couches!"

Dad pulls her back again.

We're in the basement watching the video of our performance when my phone rings. Absentmindedly, I nearly accept the call before I register the name, the face.

Everything stops.

Everything's black.

Like someone's shoved a vacuum down my throat and is slurping up my vital organs.

Jillian looks up at me from her seat on the floor. "Who is it?"

I decide to let it ring.

It's obviously a mistake. An unfortunate butt dial. Someone's playing with her phone. She's accidentally called the wrong Jack.

A thousand reasons why it's not her calling me.

A hundred thousand why I shouldn't answer.

Only there's not enough willpower on this planet to hold back my finger.

"Hello? Jack?"

Her voice obliterates the freestyle world record, swimming three laps around my body in seconds.

"Jack, it's me . . . it's . . ."

I don't answer. I can't. My mouth a knotty jumble of feels.

"Are you there, Jack?"

My tongue doesn't budge.

"I understand why you don't want to talk. Why you're mad. And maybe confused. And hurt. I'm sorry that I made you anything but happy. I'm sorry that . . . I'm all of those things, too, Jack. Mad, confused, hurting. But at myself. Because I'm to blame. And I'm sorry. For all of it. I was afraid, Jack. Of what would happen when you found out the truth. About me. That you'd leave. It's too much to ask of anyone, to stay. Jack . . . have you ever been so afraid of losing someone that you think maybe it's better to just get it over with?

". . . And I swear I'm not calling you because I feel guilty. I'm calling you because I just feel like all these things . . . Jack, it's like you've hot-wired my brain. And I want to spend my last hours with you. Does that count as an apology? That out of everyone in the world, I can't think of a single person I'd rather spend my literal dying moments with than you. And I know, it's weird. I don't even know you, right? You don't know me. Not really. Except I know what I know, Jack. And I don't care if no one else knows it. I know you know, Jack. I know that . . ."

My nose needs a tissue. Or two. Or three.

"Jack? Please? Just say something. Tell me to piss off. That

123

I have the wrong number. To leave you the hell alone. Tell me anything."

"Kate?"

"Yeah?"

"Stop talking."

"I tried that already. And I lost you."

". . ."

"Jack?"

"Where are you right now?"

* * *

"Jack, where are you going?" Jillian asks, springing up from the carpet.

"I'll call you later," I say, already halfway up the basement stairs.

"Jack," Franny calls behind me. "Jack!"

AS A TIME OF DAY

There's not a traffic law I don't break on my way to her.

I nearly drive my car right through the wooden security arm, the guard taking her sweet time letting me into the parking garage. I run down five hundred identical hallways, stopping for directions twice, until I'm finally there.

Room 443.

I nearly tackle a nurse coming out of the room.

"I'm so sorry," I say. I look past her into the room. There's a curtain blocking the bed, the room dim, save for buttery moonlight.

But the nurse isn't interested in my apology. "Are you family?" she asks.

"Yes," I lie. Because I don't want her to turn me away. But then, in an effort to be honest, I revise, "No, I mean. I'm her . . . I think I'm—"

"He's with us, Linda," a woman's voice says from inside the room. The nurse moves aside.

"You must be Jack," the woman says. She extends her arms and I walk straight into them. I'm assuming this is Kate's mom, though I've never met her. And it doesn't feel odd, embracing her this way. Plus, she smells like the best kind of mom. The kind with a comprehensive supply of Band-Aids and smiles.

"I'm Kate's mom," she confirms.

"It's nice to meet you, Mrs. Edwards. I mean, well, I wish it could be, you know, uh, under better circumstances," I choke out.

She wipes her eyes. "Call me Regina."

"I'd better stick with Mrs. Edwards. My mom would kill me if she heard me call you Regina."

Her laughter sounds like she's underwater. "Fair enough, Jack."

"Kate's going to be okay, right?"

Mrs. Edwards shakes her head. "We don't know much yet. She's not . . . God . . ."

Without thinking I hug her again, her body a sputter of mini convulsions. After a moment, I turn toward the curtain.

"Go ahead," she says.

I step around the curtain slowly. There are pumps swishing, lights blinking, machines humming. And at the center of it all, Kate.

"Hey," I say.

"Hi," she says. She winces, like it hurts to talk. "I didn't think you'd want to see me."

I walk over to the foot of the bed. "I don't and I do."

"You look good," she says.

"You too," I say.

"Liar."

But I'm *not* lying.

She motions for me to come closer. "I won't bite," she says. "Not this time, anyway." She tries to smile, but grimaces.

I step closer, navigating the stream of cords running along the floor.

"Are you okay?" I ask. A stupid question. I could make a living raising and selling all-organic, free-range stupid questions.

She wince-laughs. "Oh, I'm great. This hospital just has the best chocolate shakes, so I decided to check in."

"I'm an idiot."

"You're not." She bites her lip. "I'm glad you came."

Mrs. Edwards clears her throat. "I'm just going to . . . coffee . . . at the cafeteria. Can I get anyone anything?" I'd forgotten she was there.

"I'm good, thanks, Mom," Kate says.

"Me too," I say.

Mrs. Edwards nods, squeezes Kate's feet. "I'll be right back," she says. She walks into the hall, the nurse calling after her. The nurse speaks quietly but animatedly. Kate's mom does a lot of nodding, and then they hug.

"I'm sorry about prom, Jack."

"Looks like you had a pretty good reason," I say. "And if

you're going to be sorry about anything, let it be that you didn't just tell me the truth."

"'I'm genetically unwell' is a turnoff to most people."

Genetically unwell? What does that even mean? A wheel of possibilities spins in my brain.

"Good thing my name isn't Most People then. So, are you going to tell me what's wrong? Why are you here?"

"Yes." Kate nods. But then she shakes her head. "No, actually."

"Kate."

"I owe you an explanation, I know. And I promise it's coming, but not right now. Right now all I want is to enjoy a moment with you where I'm not the sick girl. Where you look at me the way you did when I wasn't wearing oxygen. Like when we first met. When we sat in a random kitchen and shared cereal."

I start to protest, because of course I want to know what's wrong, why Kate's in the hospital, but I want her to be happy more. I want her to feel safe with me. The way she makes me feel safe.

"Okay, not right now," I say. "But later."

"Later, I promise," she says. Her face brighter, like a bulb's been replaced in her eyes.

"So." I hold up a plastic grocery bag. "I know it's not exactly Froot Loops, but I come bearing gifts."

"My hero!"

"It's just leftovers from the party."

"Oh my God! Your parents' party! Damn. I feel awful. You

should be with your family. Not here."

"Don't feel awful. The party's over, anyway." I rifle through the bag. "Nothing too fancy. Some modestly tasty sweet-potato casserole. And, uh, spinach lasagna. I hope you don't mind it's a middle piece. It's pretty good, but I'm not sure about the cheese blend, so, yeah. Oh, and some fairly awesome anniversary cake. Which, you know, pairs perfectly with chocolate hospital shake."

"Oh, Jack. You are scoring lots of points right now, kid."

"It's an end piece, too."

She claps her hands together. "You brought me an end piece? Extra icing?"

"Extra icing," I say. "You think I'd show up if I didn't have extra icing for you?"

We sit there, silent. Not because we don't have anything to talk about. Because we have everything to talk about.

Kate tries to smile, tries to discreetly brush away the tears pooling between her nose and eyes. "Talk about terrible timing. Gosh, I'm such a loser. Your parents' special day, you shouldn't be stuck here."

"I'm not stuck." I lift my feet off the ground, one at a time, high enough for her to see over the bed rail. "My feet work fine. See?" I spin in a small circle.

"Well, whaddya know? They do."

I set a folding chair beside her bed. "So, what do you want to talk about? The upcoming election? FEMA? Should I tell you a story?"

129

"No. No. And depends. What kind of story?"

"I'm thinking boring, run of the mill, garden variety, happy ending."

She pulls her blanket up. I fix her pillow. She looks small in this bed, pale brown against the stark white sheets.

"I like boring," she says. "Boring's good."

"Well, good, because you're looking at *the* most boring storyteller ever."

"My lucky day."

I take her hand; her fingers are cold. I hear the hiss of oxygen rushing into her nose. I smell the bitterness of alcohol swabs. I smile at her. *Everything's going to be okay*, I tell myself.

"I had the craziest dream last night," she says.

"Oh yeah?"

"Yep, you were this great novelist, no surprise there. And one of your books was turned into a play. And I don't think you were expecting me to be there, so I sat in the crowd by myself, and I was so happy though. Just being there. Watching something you'd made. And when it was over, I waited for you outside. And then you came out and you were walking toward a group of friends, and I said, 'Psst. Hey, Jack Attack.' And I could tell just by the way your head moved, even with your back to me, that you knew it was me. And you turned and smiled. And you walked over to me, our eyes locked, and . . ."

She stops.

"Then what happened?"

"And then the dream completely shifted and suddenly I was turning into a car. Like a transformer. It was awesome. I was a

130

fire-engine-red car with tinted windows and a roll cage."

I bust out laughing. "You're the real writer in this relationship."

She shakes her head. "I wanted to apply for the position of *muse*. If the job's still open?"

"It is," I say. I squeeze her hand. She squeezes back. Our own Morse code.

"Where did I find you?" I ask her.

"On some crappy, piss-stained stairs."

"Best stairs ever."

"Best stairs ever," she repeats. She breaks our gaze, looks toward the curtain. It's dense. But she looks at it as if she can see through it. Maybe she can. Maybe she's been at this place, at places like this, enough times to know what's on the other side.

"Jack?"

"Yeah?"

"If something happens, I want you to remember me—"

I cut her off. "Don't. Nothing's going to happen."

"Stop." She squeezes my hand again. "Listen to me."

I nod, because if I talk my voice will break.

"I want you to remember me . . . not as a sick black girl with chicken legs from some no-name suburbs. I want you to remember me like this, right now. The moonlight over your shoulder, stretching against the night, the stars fluttering. Remember me like this. The rain slanting, the fog rolling. The street-lights flickering on. Every time you feel or see another evening like this, I want you to think of me smiling, laughing at you. Remember me, remember us, as a time of day."

I start to speak, but nothing comes out. Just the faint pucker of my lips opening and then closing.

The nurse enters, offers Kate IV pain medication, warns me that it'll make her sleepy, that the best thing I can do for her is to let her rest.

And I want to do all the best things for Kate.

Except the only thing I know is that I don't know what's best for Kate. My mind revs a thousand revolutions a minute, but I'm getting nowhere.

So I sit quietly, watch Kate's eyelids flutter until she drifts to sleep.

"Jack," she says, just before her eyes close for good.

"I'm here."

"Tell Franny I'm sorry about Mighty Moat. I owe him a concert."

I take her hand. "I think he'll live."

And her lips curl upward into something not quite a smile, but close.

When her mom comes back and hands me a coffee, I sip it, and it doesn't matter that it tastes like it came from a pot made days ago; it's just something to do while Kate rests. While I sit, waiting for what's next.

When the coffee's gone, her mom squeezes my shoulder. "Jack, go home. I'll have her call you when she wakes up."

"Are you okay?" I ask her.

She nods. "Mr. Edwards is on his way up here. We'll be fine."

I start to argue. But I hug her instead, the way I should hug my own mother more. Then I hover over Kate, hesitating before pressing my lips to her forehead. She doesn't move. "Good night, my favorite time of day," I say.

*   *   *

I cut the headlights. My house is dark and still, deflating balloons twirl against our mailbox. In a few hours it'll be daylight. It's odd—you put so much time and energy into something, and then it's over, a new thing already forming in its place.

Inside I trip over my trumpet case. So much for sneaking into bed.

But it doesn't matter, because my parents are waiting for me in the kitchen.

"Jack," Mom whispers, like she's afraid I'll combust if she uses one decibel more than necessary. She studies my eyes. "How is she?"

"She's going to be okay," I tell them.

"What happened? What's wrong with her?" Dad asks.

"I'm not sure. She wouldn't tell me."

"Well, glad she's okay. That's what matters. You should call Jillian and Franny," Mom says. "They're worried."

"They left?" I ask.

"I drove them home a bit ago," Dad says.

I nod. "I'm sorry I cut out so quick without telling you."

But they're all head-shaking and tsking.

"Don't be sorry," they tell me. "You did the right thing, Jack."

Upstairs, I shoot Franny a text to let him know all is well, that I'll see him in the morning. Jillian calls me as I'm climbing into bed and we make plans to go to the hospital together tomorrow.

I pull my flannel sheets up, thinking about everyone in my life, my family, my friends; I think about Kate snug in her hospital bed, and yes, I'm absolutely afraid—of the future, of the unknown, life's nasty twists and unexpected turns—but also I realize that I'm incredibly lucky, to have so many, and so much. I wonder how I got to be so lucky.

I fall asleep trying to figure it out.

* * *

Kate's ringtone wakes me up from dead sleep.

I reach for the phone. It's 3:37 in the morning. I clear my throat before I answer. "Hey, you, how was your nap?"

"Jack, I'm so sorry to call you so late."

The voice sounds like her, but it's not Kate. And I know something's wrong.

"Jack, are you there?" her mom says. "She's gone, Jack. Kate's gone." And I don't hang up. I don't even move the phone away from my lips. But I don't talk either. What is there to say, except why did everyone lie to me? Kate's mom. The nurse. Kate.

She just needs rest. You just need rest, they said.

Why are all of them liars?

And I think, she must've known. *If something happens*, she'd said.

And I hate the moon.

I hate the stars. I hate the darkening sky. And rain and fog. I hate hospitals. And beds with sheets. And every machine ever made. And nurses and doctors. Keep her alive, that was the one thing they had to do. That was the one thing I had to do. And I hate myself most of all. My terrible lies. *You're going to be okay,*

I told her. I had no right. I wasn't right. I was the worst wrong.

"I'm on my way," I finally say. But I'm not even sure Kate's mom is still there. I stumble out of bed, slip on jogging pants, wedge my feet into old sneakers, and race for the stairs. But my head is foggy, and the landing is dark, and I miss the first step.

I slip headfirst down the stairs. My hands lash out at the wall, at the railing, but my fingers slip away and I can't stop my fall. Nothing slows me. My body snaps against every stair. And I tumble. And I thud. Until it finally stops. I can't breathe. The air knocked from my chest. I can't think. Thoughts rattle in my head.

"Jack, are you okay? Jack? Jack!"

Someone is screaming at the top of the stairs. But I don't recognize the voice. Maybe Mom. Maybe Dad. It could be God for all I know. The hall light snaps on, and my instinct is to shield my eyes except I can't move my arms. I can't even wiggle my fingers. And I hear wood creaking. And panicked voices. "Call an ambulance! Call 9-1-1! Jack! Jack!"

And then the worst pain ever.

Like my head's an ice cream carton, and someone's attempting to scoop out my brain, one thinly curled spoonful at a time.

And then a shrill of feedback blasts between my ears and I know this is the end.

Good night, evening. Good night, world.

Good night, Jack. Good night.

so sequels
usually suck
but . . .

DO YOU BELIEVE IN LIFE AFTER LOVE?

Death isn't like I'd expect.

My life isn't zooming past my eyes. Maybe whoever's running the projector decided to spare me the boredom.

There's no vast sea of inescapable blackness.

I don't feel weightless: like I'm drifting but going nowhere.

Death, it turns out, feels a lot like waking up.

Which, considering that a moment ago I was asteroiding down a flight of stairs, coming to a stop only because my brain smacked against the landing, waking up at all (even in the deathly sense) feels like a major win.

Still, I suppose heaven wouldn't be the worst *welcome back to consciousness, Jack, we missed you* present. But I figure a hospital bed is more probable. So, when I open my eyes, I'm not sure what awaits.

Sterile, white walls, maybe.

Crisp, artificial light illuminating me.

My parents draped over my bed.

But that's the thing about expectation. Most times it's just a setup.

Because instead I get peeling, yellowed wallpaper.

Cheesy disco lights.

And loud music.

Only it's not a choir of beautiful angels strumming harps.

This is sticky, thumping bass.

There are voices, too. Except it's not my parents.

Or someone directing me to *walk toward the light*.

These voices are young, carefree, celebratory. These voices careen around the room with abandon, with energy.

Someone is complaining that no one makes real music anymore. And whoever he's talking to agrees. *Hell yes*, she shouts.

I touch my head. Although I just played wall-seeking human torpedo, I'm not bleeding.

All my senses appear intact. I think I'm alive.

I'm alive.

My eyes are blurry, but it's clear that I'm sitting on stairs.

Only this isn't my house. And these aren't my stairs.

Certainly not the ones I kamikazed down.

But I know this house. This horrible wallpaper. These warped stairs. I've been here, in this exact spot. Once. Months ago. Except this is impossible. I hit my head harder than I thought. I must be in a coma.

Or maybe I got it wrong. Am I . . . the opposite of alive?

I touch my chest, my legs. Everything's solid.

I slap my face. It stings.

But it doesn't make sense. Maybe this house is a processing station, a place to hang out while God or whoever reviews my paperwork?

But if this place is even remotely associated with heaven—and I don't mean to sound ungrateful if it is—it's wholly underwhelming. The music and lights, how many curse words I've heard in the last forty seconds—doesn't scream *heavenly abode*. Not that I've given much thought to heaven. Or dying, for that matter.

In fact, the only mention of God comes from a kid shouting at the TV across the room.

"Oh my God, get a damn rebound. They're getting destroyed on the glass," he says to the taller kid standing beside him.

The announcer has zero chill. "This would be the UPSET OF THE YEAR!"

The taller kid shakes his head. "They're not going to have any momentum heading into the tourney."

Wait, I know this game. I've *seen* this game. State goes on a frantic late run and wins with an off-balance three at the buzzer. I remember because Franny talked about it for days afterward.

I scan the room again. I've seen these people.

Plunging V-Neck Sweater Guy.

Hello Kitty Tat Girl.

It's exactly the same as four months ago.

And even before I look into the kitchen, I know who's there. Leaning against the counter, surrounded by a swarm of people, my best friend.

Jillian.

We meet eyes and she waves. Without thinking, I raise my cup to her, tilt my head. She smiles and I feel it, a thunderbolt to the brain, like always. She motions for me to join her. But before I can get my feet under me, I hear the one voice I was sure I'd never hear again. I look back, and the owner of the voice is shaking her head like every second that she's forced to wait for me to move out of her way is another second of night-ruining agony, and she says those magical *I'll never forget them* first words:

"Excuse me, man, but you're sort of damming up the steps."

*　*　*

I officially understand the meaning of *stunning*.

This is *stunning*. I am *stunned*.

Except, surprisingly, my gross motor skills are largely functioning. I rocket to my feet.

"What are you doing here?" I exclaim. My body already leaning in for the World's All-Time Tightest and Most Meaningful Embrace.

Only she jerks away, makes an *eww gross* face. The same face I've seen her make at twelve-legged, eight-eyed bugs. "What the hell, man?"

I laugh. "What, do I smell like death?" I raise my arms for a quick pit check.

Kate looks beyond confused. Bewildered, even. But she sniffs anyway. "Maybe, but in general, I don't make it a practice to go around hugging strange boys."

"Strange boys? I'm hardly—have you been drinking the punch, because I'm pretty sure it's spi—"

But then it hits me.

Hello Kitty girl.

The basketball game.

You're damming up the steps.

She's not pretending. She genuinely has no clue who I am.

We haven't exchanged emails.

She hasn't stood me up for prom.

My parents' party hasn't happened.

We haven't even shared a bowl of cereal.

We are, in every way, history-less.

This is the *beginning* beginning.

We are, once more, perfect strangers.

Well, not exactly perfect. I still know her. I still almost-love her.

But she doesn't know me. And judging by the face she's giving me, she's a million miles from love, even the almost kind.

We stand there, awkwardly, until she clears her throat and I realize that the only reason she's still in front of me is because I'm impeding her descent.

I squish myself against the grimy, floral wallpaper. "Oh, I'm sorry!"

"Nice to meet you, Sorry."

"No, my name isn't sorry. . . ."

She laughs. "Is this your first human-to-human interaction? Or are you always this uneasy?"

And I want to touch her. If only to be sure she's real. "Only when the other human is special."

She smiles. "So, I must be *really* special then?"

"The specialest."

She bats her eyes. "I bet you say that to all the other humans." She takes another step down. "Well, I'll see you around, Sorry."

"Cool," I say. I wave inexplicably hard at her, like I'm her mom watching her climb onto the school bus for the first time. "It was nice to meet you." *Again*, I think to myself.

"Yeah, you, too." She grins. "I think."

"Hey, wait," I call after her. But my voice is swallowed by the festivities.

And then she's gone, absorbed by the mass of partygoers.

As for me, I'm stationary on the stairs, which, incidentally, don't smell so pissy anymore.

And you could've told me you've solved global warming.

Or that you'd actually found Park Place and won the McDonald's Monopoly grand prize.

And I wouldn't have heard you.

Because Kate. She's alive.

*   *   *

Jillian is at my side. She pops a chip into her mouth. "Hey, J. Having fun?"

How did she get to the stairs so quickly? But then I

144

realize I've apparently abandoned the stairs and floated into the kitchen. I'm using *floated* loosely here, which I feel the need to explain since somehow I've traveled back in time, and so I couldn't blame you for interpreting *floating* as me being a ghost or whatever.

"Yeah, this party is . . . awesome," I say. I scan the crowd for Kate. "You enjoying yourself?"

Jillian shrugs. "I was sorta hoping you and I would just hang out. Like without anyone else. And just talk or whatever."

I pause my Kate search and look at Jillian. "Is everything okay?"

"Everything is fine. It just feels like lately we're never alone. Between school and jobs and family stuff, we're always so busy."

"I hear you," I say, my search unpaused.

"What are you looking for?"

"Nothing."

"Liar. Is it a girl? Did you meet someone, Jackie?"

I smirk. "Me? Meet someone? Yeah, right."

"Oh my God!" She jabs me in the shoulder. "Where is she? I wanna meet this girl."

"It's nothing," I say. "We just . . . I don't want to make it into something it's not, but . . ."

"I'll help you find her. What does she look like?"

"Umm, let's see. Well, she's black. With dark hair. Brown eyes."

Jillian shakes her head. "Okay, so you've narrowed it down to half the party. Anything else? What is she *wearing*, Romeo?"

"A sweater-dress thingie. With like a belt cinching it."

Jillian snaps her fingers. "Oh, I saw that girl. She got some punch and then left, I think. Or at least she went outside. Maybe she—"

But I don't wait for Jillian to finish. I'm already diving out the front door.

REMIND ME HOW I KNOW YOU

I race around the house, dodging smokers and drinkers, until I spot her against the side of the house. She's holding a cup and staring into her phone.

Sensing my approach, she glances up. "Are you following me, Sorry?"

"Who, me?" I ask.

"No, the weird kid behind you."

I resist the urge to look behind me. "Just to be sure, there is no weird kid behind me, right?"

She grins. "Only when there's a mirror behind you."

"You're funny," I say. It's sort of nostalgic, recalling how she always made me laugh.

"Said no one ever," she replies. "But thanks, man." She sips from her cup. "So what do you study here?"

"Huh?"

"I know, I know. Totally weak pickup line, right? *Hey, man, what's your major.* But I have a tendency to be weak, so bear with me."

"I don't go to school here."

"No?" Her face twists into wonder. "You go to State then?"

"I'm just visiting Whittier. For the weekend."

"For the weekend? You have friends that go here?"

"Not yet," I say sheepishly. "I'm here for a visit."

"Like a campus visit? As in you're still in high school?"

"I'm a senior," I say. I attempt to subtly bassify my voice. "You actually led our tour at the student center."

She points at me like her finger shoots lightning bolts. "Quiet kid in the back!"

"Yep. That was me," I say quietly but still extra bass-y.

She laughs. "You're a big, bad senior," she says, mimicking my quiet-bass. "So, what, you thought you'd come up here this weekend? Land yourself some college ass?"

I retreat into my normal *there's a g-g-girl in front of me* stammer. "No, uh, not at all, I was actually just, I mean, I wouldn't do that, like ever, anyone who knows me knows that I'm not like that, in fact, I—"

"Relax, man. I'm messing with you."

"Right. I knew that."

"Of course you did. You're a senior." She balances her cup on the porch banister. "So, Sorry, you hungry?"

And the truth is, I'm not sure what's happening to me. Why I'm here. Again.

148

If I'm even here.

If any minute I'll wake up having been in a coma all along, or having dreamed the entire thing, or some other cringe-worthy plot device.

But just the possibility of another chance with Kate has me reinvigorated.

I bounce on my soles, like I've just discovered I can fly.

Like I'm about to lift off for the first time.

"Yeah," I say. "I could eat."

* * *

She guides the longest fry ever into her mouth. "I'm Kate, by the way."

"I'm Jack."

She gestures at my mostly intact burger. "Thought you were hungry."

I take a small bite. "I am." I'm not. How can I eat when I'm still trying to digest the fact that I've time-traveled?

When I'm trying to figure out *why* I'm here.

At *this* particular time.

With *Kate*.

She frowns. "Are you one of those super-agreeable people who always says yes to everything?"

"No," I say, chewing. "I'm just in a particularly agreeable mood tonight, I guess."

Her eyebrows lift. "Oh yeah?"

"What can I say? It's sorta feeling like one of those *once in a million years* type nights."

"You're a confident kid. I like it. I bet you're a heartbreaker."

"This may come as a shock to you, but nerdy doesn't play all that well in high school."

She chomps on another fry. "Don't worry. Nerdy plays well when you need a job. Besides, the best thing about college is that it's a chance to remake yourself."

"So, who did you used to be?"

"Me? I'm still working on my transformation."

"Well, don't change too much. Otherwise, how will I recognize you?"

She cleans her mouth with a napkin. "Jack, do I know you from somewhere?"

I shake my head. "Why would you ask that?"

She stares at me, and I stare back, and we sail right past the point where most people would've broken off their gaze, when most would've felt uncomfortable.

"That," she says. "Because of that."

"What's that?"

"The way you look at me. Like you've been doing it our whole lives."

* * *

"What do you want to do now?" I ask.

We're outside the diner, and it feels twenty degrees colder.

Kate pulls her sleeves down, burying her hands inside her sweater. "I think I'm gonna turn in for the night. I've got a paper to write and I haven't even finished the reading."

"Oh," I say. I rack my brain for a reason to extend our night. "Besides, won't your friend worry about you?"

150

"My friend?"

"You said you came here with a friend from home."

"Oh. Right. Jillian. No, she's not the worrying type."

Kate gazes upward, the moon staring down at us. "That's a good way to live. Worrying is for the birds."

"So, let's not worry tonight. Let's do something fun. If you could go anywhere right now, where would you go?"

"Anywhere," she repeats. She taps her chin. "Venice."

"Okay," I say, laughing. "Anywhere within driving distance."

"Well, there is one place, but it's in the middle of nowhere." She hesitates. "You're not a serial killer, right?"

"Not *serial* yet," I assure her. "But ya gotta start somewhere."

"Sicko." She smiles. "There's something about you, Jack. I can't quite put my finger on it. But I'm working on it."

"Good. Keep working."

*　*　*

"It is sort of beautiful."

"Sort of?" Kate twirls on her heels. "Look around, Jack. There's nothing *sort of* about the gorges. This is the best place on earth, in case you didn't know."

"I didn't. But I do now."

"Damn right you do." She balances on a log. Walks it in precise but graceful steps.

"Are you a dancer?"

She looks at me over her shoulder. "In a past life."

"Why'd you stop?"

She stares down at the water. Juts her hand into it and

emerges with a smooth stone, studies it in her palm. "The world had other plans for me."

"You don't strike me as a person who'd let anything dictate her plans, the world included."

"Yeah, well." She drops the stone back into the water. "I guess you don't know me, do you?"

"Hey, I'm sorry," I say. "I didn't mean it like that. I was just saying—"

"I know what you meant. Don't apologize." She steps deeper into the gorge. "You want to see something really cool?"

We walk through the riverbed for another hundred yards before I realize where we are. Where she's taken me. We're standing in the exact spot—where we shared cereal together and talked about what our futures might look like. Before I knew she was sick. Before I knew her. When we were still only *in like*.

She points skyward. "The stars are popping tonight."

"It's like they're competing. *I'm the brightest! No, I'm the brightest,*" I say in my best high-pitched star voice.

She grins. "You have an interesting point of view."

"That's not the first time I've been told that. I'm developing a complex."

"No. Interesting is good. Interesting is very good."

And I can't wait anymore. I can't. "Kate, can I ask you a question?"

She looks away, eyes back on the sky. "Uh, sure, I guess."

"It's going to come across as odd and definitely premature. Fair warning."

"Okay, you're scaring me now. You're not going to ask me to kiss you or something, are you?"

"Not yet, but maybe we'll get there, one day. I mean, if you play your cards right."

She laughs, and I feel it, her laughter, travel through my bones. Like old times. "So, what is it then?"

"Remember, I warned you."

"Okay, okay. Get to it already."

"How do you feel about high school proms?"

CEREAL KILLERS

Somehow we end up at the $ave-Mart.

In the cereal aisle.

And the aisle is daunting. There's so much cereal to choose from. Like, even as we stand at the top of the aisle, the boxes are multiplying right before our eyes.

Kate and I stand shoulder to shoulder. "So, what's your poison?"

She shrugs. "What's *your* fave?"

I shrug. "I pretty much just like cereal."

"Yeah, but you've got to have a favorite."

"What's yours?"

She laughs. "Froot Loops all the way."

I look down at the handbasket I'm holding. "I think we're gonna need a cart."

She grins. "Race you?"

"On your mark, get set . . ."

But she's already gone.

I chase after her, and then we're running down the cereal aisle, swiping boxes into our cart. We show zero partiality. Fruity cereal, nutty cereal, thousand-grain cereal, it doesn't matter. If it floats in milk, it's in our cart.

And I can't stop laughing.

And then Kate's chasing me with the cart, nipping at my heels, threatening that annoying, semipainful collision when someone crashes the cart into the back of your ankle, and you swear and cry and one-foot hop. But fortunately for my ankles, I'm just quick enough to avert Kate's cart-pushing danger. Up and down the multicultural foods aisle we sprint, and then down the fruits and veggies, and finally we halt our cereal caravan in the tundra.

Also known as the dairy section.

Kate giggles. "We're gonna need a lot of milk."

"You think they sell cows here?" I ask.

You should see the look on the cashier's face when it's our turn to check out. "Umm, so, did you find everything you were looking for?" she asks us, as we load box after box onto the conveyor belt.

I turn to Kate and nod. "I can't think of anything else I need."

Kate shakes her head, like *this guy is so cheesy*. But then she slips her fingers into mine and everything fades until it's just me, Kate, and a never-ending conveyor belt of cereal. And the world makes sense.

We drag our bounty up Kate's dorm stairs and proceed to gorge ourselves until we're a few spoonfuls from frosted combustion.

Kate's floor is covered in partially consumed cereal boxes and their cheesy-but-adorable cereal-box prizes. We're both already sporting the temporary tats we found at the bottom of the Wheat-O's; Kate, a flame-spewing dragon on her forearm, me with what we've decided is a friendly wombat applied to my shoulder.

Kate scratches her head. "People are going to think we're high."

"So," I say. "What should we do with our remaining treasure trove of whole-grain wheat and artificial flavors?"

Kate holds up her finger. "I have an idea." She gathers an armful of boxes.

I push aside my empty bowl. "Wait, what are you doing?"

"C'mon! Cereal for the people," she declares. She walks to the door.

I pop up and open it for her.

"Are you going to tell me what you're doing?"

"What are you waiting for? Get an armload, Jack Attack."

And then we're knocking on every dorm room, tossing random boxes of cereal into the hands of surprised—yet appreciative—dorm occupants. Because everyone needs a Silly Rabbit, or a Cap'n, or even a chocolate-loving Count in their lives.

Everyone deserves to taste magic.

CLOSE ENCOUNTERS OF THE FRIEND KIND

Before Jillian even says a word I know this isn't going to be a pleasant conversation. She's leaning against the car, her body language invoking rather lovely vocabulary, such as:

Irked.

Exasperated.

Aggravated assault.

"Where have you been?" Jillian demands.

"I'm sorry," I say, holding up my hands. "I'm really, really sorry."

"You don't know how to answer your phone? I was worried something happened to you."

"I lost track of time and I didn't realize . . . I'm sorry, J."

She puts her hands on either hip. "This have anything to do with sweater-dress girl?"

I nod.

"I figured as much." Her face relaxes the tiniest bit. "You have a good night?"

I slip my hands into my pockets, rock on my sneaker heels. "It was cool, yeah."

"Well, lover boy, now we've gotta haul ass back home. Where's your stuff?"

"Um, about that. The thing is, I was sorta hoping to, uhh . . . stick around until later tonight."

"But you know I have to get home and study for my French test tomorrow. I'm sorry, Jack, but your girlfriend isn't going anywhere."

"I was thinking . . . maybe . . . you should . . . head back without me?"

"What are you talking about? How are you going to get home?"

"Bus," I say softly. I dig a gravel-hole with my shoe.

"I'm an idiot, right? Because I was under the impression we were going to hang out this weekend. But then we go to a party and you're a ghost the rest of the night. I think to myself, *It's okay, we'll meet for breakfast like we'd planned*, but then you don't show up . . ."

Damn. I totally forgot about our breakfast plans.

"And then you send your phone straight to voice mail all morning, only to finally show up at my car and tell me you're gonna find your own way home."

"J, it's not like that. I'm sorry. I really meant . . . something crazy has happened."

"Something crazy is *still* happening, Jack," she says. "I hope you have a great time, really. Give Sweater Dress my regards."

"J, I just . . . don't be that way, please. You don't understand."

She flings open her car door. "Nope, I have an excellent handle on things. Maybe I'll see you back home. You know, if you remember how to work a phone. Later, Jack."

She pulls out onto the road. I wave at her.

And this is what feeling happy and crappy at the same time looks like.

*　*　*

Kate and I find a quiet spot in the library; she spends her time studying economics, while I spend my time studying how cute she is. My primary study method consists of staring at her and then quickly averting my eyes when she notices.

"What, do I have something on my face?" she asks, looking up from her book.

"No," I assure her. "But my lips are up for the job."

She groans loudly. "Just when I thought humankind couldn't be any cornier . . ."

"I came along." I finish the sentence for her.

She rolls her eyes, but she smiles, too.

"Kate, can I ask you something?"

"What, you thought of another school dance?"

"Are you feeling okay? Like, how do you feel, like, uh, physically?"

"Why would you ask me that?"

"I don't know." I lie, because *why* would I ask her that.

"You're a little pale?"

She studies my face. "I feel fine, Jack. Thanks."

"Cool," I say. "Good."

"Actually, I may have slightly overdone it the last twenty-four hours."

I nod. "We've been running all over the place." And I feel bad, because I don't want to be the reason Kate's not well. But also I'm not sure what to do about it. "Maybe we cut back on our grocery store marathons," I suggest.

She smiles. "Cereal aisle sprints are more my speed."

HIGH OFF LIFE 2.0

I catch the midnight bus home, which my parents are less than thrilled about.

> MOM on the phone: Crazy people take the bus late at night.
>
> ME: I'm pretty sure crazy people aren't as strict with their bus-riding schedule as you think.
>
> DAD: Don't be sharp with your mother. She's worried about you.
>
> MOM: Your father grilled steaks.
>
> ME: I'm sorry, guys. Really.
>
> DAD: There's not much we can do now.
>
> MOM: Maybe we should come pick you up.
>
> ME: I don't think that's . . .
>
> DAD: That's not necessary.

ME: *I agree with Dad.*

DAD: *But we will have a talk about being trustworthy, Jack-O.*

ME: **sigh* Okay.*

DAD presumably speaking OFF-PHONE to MOM: *Guess you and I will be dining alone tonight, baby. I say we bypass the main course and skip straight to dessert.*

MOM presumably speaking OFF-PHONE to DAD: *Two or three desserts, if you think you can handle it.*

DAD: *Oh, I'm feeling extra hungry, baby girl . . .*

ME: *Uh, guys, maybe hold the phone farther away from your mouths the next time you want to engage in what sounds like a private conversation, or you know, there's also this rather cool thing called the mute button.*

DAD: *See you in the morning, Jackie.*

MOM: *Be safe! Call us when you're on your way!*

ME: *Okay, I'll probably just walk from the bus stop, since you know it's only like two blo—*

DAD: *Excellent! Nighty-night!*

Click.

Love you guys too.

So.

With stops, it's a two-point-five-hour ride.

I decide I should get some shut-eye.

Which means, of course, I can't sleep.

And it's not even that the bus smells like a dirty-diaper factory. Or that there's more duct tape than vinyl on my "seat."

It's more like, I may never sleep again. How can I?

Because if this really is ~~the past~~ ~~The Past~~ THE PAST!, why am I here?

I mean, out of all the places for God, the cosmos, whomever, whatever, to plunk me down in the stream of time, why *here*—on a set of decrepit steps, with the girl that I almost-love, the girl who died, now alive and well and annoyed with me for blocking her staircase descent? A girl with zero memory of me or the last four months.

Am I supposed to do something different? Change something this time around?

I mean, it can't be a coincidence that I respawned (too video-gamey?) right after Kate died.

Maybe somehow I'm supposed to help her not die.

Because Kate's future wasn't supposed to end.

Maybe everyone replays parts of their lives. But it's so unbelievable that no one talks about it.

When I get home, Dad's snoring on the sofa, so I decide to test my theory on Mom.

"Uh, what's up, Mom?"

"Just thought I'd catch up on some canning."

"It's three in the morning, Mom."

"Well, we can't all take midnight bus rides for fun."

"You got me."

"Mm-hmm, I know."

"I'm so sorry. I didn't mean to worry you."

To which Mom responds with a championship-caliber eye roll. "There better not be any court dates in your near future, Jackie Ellison."

I kiss her cheek, and she shakes her head, stirs her peaches.

"Mom, can I ask you something?"

"Oh, Lord."

"At any point in your life, have you blacked out, suffered through an agonizing pain and wondered if you were about to explode into human confetti, only to wake up several months back into the past?"

Mom sets down the ladle, cleans her hands on a dish towel. "Jackie, are you high?"

*   *   *

Since sleep is still elusive AF, I invest my time elsewhere. Wake my laptop. Compose new message.

Dear Kate,

When you saw this in your inbox, I know what you thought. So, let's just deal with the elephant in the email first, shall we?

This email is *not, in any way*, a follow-up to the question I asked you the other night in the gorges, the question that you told me you'd think on and get back to me ("in a reasonable amount of

164

time"—your words). So please, please, please, whatever you do, do *not* feel any pressure to reply with an answer to that question. Because that is *not* what this email is about, okay?

If you'd like to reply to that question with your answer, please do so on your own time. Because this particular email is all booked up, okay?

Good.

I'm glad we got that out of the way.

Now we can move on to the actual business of this email. Namely, to mom you. Because who doesn't like to be mom'd every now and then, especially via email from a mostly complete stranger, right?

So, are you eating okay? Getting enough fruits and veggies, because they're easy to forget. My mom likes to sneak them onto my plate. Sometimes she disguises them as meat. She's incredibly crafty. She'll carve an eggplant into the shape of a T-bone. And she's forever preaching this body-to-soul connection—*the health of your body, Jack, reflects the condition of your mind*—I know, absurd, right? 😊

Stop reading me like that, Kate. You see right through this, don't you?

Okay, so maybe I stretched the truth a *bit*.

And I know, I know—dishonesty is so *not* the way to kick off a relationship (friendship or otherwise). But I'm nervous. TBH, I'm petrified.

I admit it, this email is sort of (solely) about my question the other night in the gorges. Because I want you to say yes.

So here's some info about me that I'm hopeful may sway you, should you happen to still be mulling over your decision.

I am 5'9 . . . in (very high) high-tops. This information may prove beneficial should we engage in any high-top-appropriate activity.

My favorite food (other than cereal) is pork belly. Mainly because people are less judgmental about pork belly than bacon, although they're basically the same.

I (inexplicably, if you ask my best friends Jillian and

Franny) love popcorn-flavored jelly beans. I also
dig reading books in actual book form (the smell
of paper does it for me), and like everyone else in
the world, I love love *love* long walks on the beach.
I distrust Siri, but I heart Google. I want a chocolate
Lab, but my dad pretends like he's allergic to dogs
when in reality he's just afraid; so for now I get my
fix watching chocolate Lab puppies doing adorable
things online.

I'm mostly opposed to school dances, prom
included.

But I'd make an exception for you.

No pressure.

With tons of pressure even though I concluded the
email with *no pressure*, but really I'll understand if
you can't make it, or if you just don't want to go,
I mean it's a high school dance, so of course you
don't *want* to go, but you know if you were willing,
that would be cool, too, anyway, totally *no pressure*
either way,
Jack

WAY MORE THAN 100%

I text Jillian to ask if she's still giving me a ride to school tomorrow, but she never replies. She's turned off read receipts on her phone, so I can't tell if she's simply ignoring me.

That's why I'm surprised when she shows up at our usual table in the cafeteria.

Which is a relief because 1) Franny's skipping lunch to work out and 2) I was faced with the unwelcome decision to either eat by my lonesome or disturb the finely tuned cafeteria ecology by joining another table mid-school year, an impossible feat.

"Hey," I say.

"Where's Franny?"

"Pumping iron," I say. I flex my nonexistent bicep.

"Oh," she mutters. Which I take to mean that she probably wouldn't have shown up had she known it was just us.

Uncomfortable silence ensues.

Which I break with strategically disarming small talk. "So, can you believe Mrs. Holstein canceled that quiz? I mean, like, WTF, right? I mean, who does that?"

But Jillian stares intently at her phone, as if any minute now POTUS is going to call her for advice on overseas troop deployment.

"Can I ask you a question, J?"

She mumbles something I choose to interpret as *certainly*.

"How long are you going to be mad at me?"

"Depends. How long are you going to be an asshole?"

I glance at my watch. "Uh, I think I'm done right about now."

She breaks her phone trance, glares at me. "You sure about that?"

"One hundred and twenty percent," I offer.

She groans. "I hate when people do that."

"Do what?"

"Say more than 100 percent, as if that's really a thing. Plus, if you really wanna emphasize your commitment, why not go all in on the hyperbole? Why not say 900 percent or 5,383 percent? I mean, at least be creative with your terrible math."

"Jillian?"

"Yeah?"

"I'm 1,234,424 percent sure I'm done being an asshole."

"Good." She smiles. "Now I'm only 72 percent away from believing you."

"Nice, I'm further along than I thought."

"Yeah, yeah," she says. She settles into her normal seat. I offer her a peanut butter cracker; it disappears into her mouth.

"J, is something else wrong?"

She sighs. "You want the entire rundown?"

"Of course."

"We didn't have power this morning because Mom forgot to pay the bill. I found a stack of unopened past-due notices. Lately, it's like she's on another planet."

"Wow."

"I had an awesome candlelit cold shower this morning, though."

"That sounds incredible."

"It was, believe me."

"Any word from your dad?"

"The same word. He just keeps saying the same stuff over and over. I told him he picked a fantastic time for a midlife crisis."

"Damn. Even still, to go back to Côte d'Ivoire is wild."

Jillian's face knots. "Wait. How'd you know he was going back there?"

Crap. "Huh? You must've mentioned it."

"No, I definitely didn't, Jack."

"I mean, uh." Backpedal, Jack. Backpedal. "I just assumed, you know, if I was having an existential crisis, I'd probably go back to, uh, where I grew up, you know, for answers. Yeah."

She studies my face and isn't buying my explanation, but at

the same time, what other explanation is there, short of time travel?

She looks away, fiddles with her necklace. "When you're a kid, you think your parents have it all together. That they know what they're doing. And then one day you realize they're just as screwed up as you. They're just old and screwed up."

"So, you're saying we're all doomed?"

She snags another cracker from my package. "Pretty much."

I GOT THREADS ON
THREADS ON THREADS

In the throes of a mind-numbingly boring fifth-period study hall, this pops up:

Dear Jack,

I must admit that as I read your email I was starting to feel pressure but then, because you told me *no pressure* at least a dozen times, all the pressure totally went away. It was awesome. And completely unexpected. So thank you! 😳

The truth is I'm leaning toward no to your proposal. Here are my reasons, in bullet points:

Prom Scares Kate Because . . .

- Dancing scares me. I'm afraid I don't have the stereotypical *black girl* rhythm. I'm afraid I don't even have *inebriated white people at a party* rhythm. Seriously, two left feet would be a step up for me.
- Party streamers make me nervous. I think because they remind me of thin and crimped, multicolored paper snakes.
- I'm a punch-bowl pusher-over. Don't ask me how, but it's true. No matter the setting, if there is a punch bowl present, I'll find a way to knock it over. Carpet doesn't stand a chance against me!
- I hate dresses. How come they don't make parties where you can show up in your jogging pants, and with your hair tied up in an old (non-chic) bandanna, without people thinking you're a charlatan? Or at least, a spinster in the making? And who doesn't love jogging pants?
- I am an octopus. Okay, this one's not true. I blame Mrs. Nielson, my ninth-grade English teacher who felt arguments should always, ALWAYS be composed in sets of five. Although she also called cell phones *transponders*, so.

Anyway, hopefully you now have a better understanding of what you're dealing with—or rather at least *who*. Perhaps you wish to withdraw your invitation?

But if not, Jack, I do have a serious question for you. Actually two questions. I know—Kate being serious is like [insert some absurdity here].

But here goes—and please, pardon me for the severe cheesiness of what I'm about to say next— probably 4.5 out of 5 cheese wheels—but 1) how is it that I feel like I know you already, Jack?

And 2) why did I write an entire email explaining to you why I can't go to prom with you when I already know that I'm going to go to prom with you?

That is, if you'll still have me, because by now it's abundantly clear to you that I'm crazy myself, you know, if that wasn't already clear before, so if you don't want to go to prom with me anymore (or anywhere else for that matter) I completely understand, okay,
Kate

PS And Jack?
PPS No pressure! 😊

I immediately reply:

Dear Kate,

Speaking of crazy, what if we knew each other in a past life.

All I know is I want to know you well in *this* one.

ASAP, as a matter of fact.

So, what do you say?

Me, you, and a tragically awkward public dancing session (otherwise known as prom)?

Jack

* * *

And then in sixth period, I get a response. (Which is awesome—Kate's Ultra-Rapid Reply Speed—because sometimes it feels like we're all so caught up in appearing cool and aloof that we'd rather wait some randomly imposed time before replying, rather than be true to our feelings. You know, those so uncool feelings like *excited* and *happy*. But not Kate. Kate replies thirty-eight minutes later.)

Dear Jack,

Officially, all the way, yes.

But I owe you fair warning. I'm recently out of a relationship; a couple of months now. But (and I probably shouldn't tell you this) I'm not certain I'm over him just yet. Probably because it seems like he's always around. Probably because he is always around. I broke up with him, because in my head I know we're not good for each other. But that damn, blasted heart of mine—treacherous, naive, and generally idiotic . . .

I don't know, Jack, it's just one of those unknowable things, you know (ha!)? Sort of like whatever you're pretending is not going on with you and your friend from the party—Jill, if I recall correctly?

Okay, so I actually know it's *Jillian* but I'll be honest with you, there was some strange tugging happening inside of me that wanted to pretend as though I'd forgotten her name . . . I know, so *maniacally* petty . . . but at least I own my issues, right? Any credit for ownership? 😋

And don't even try and deny it, either.

I saw how you looked at her. Like there'd been an arrow shot into your narrow ass. I was asking you to move from the stairs for like two minutes before you even realized I was standing behind you. There were singing baby bluebirds flying loops around your head, too, so there's that. ☺

But don't worry, it doesn't bother me. I mean, even though it feels like we do, the truth is we barely know each other, right? Except for the time we spent together in our previous lifetime, of course.

I just don't want to screw things up, Jack. That should've been my fifth bullet point earlier—that I have a habit of destroying good things. Especially right as they're about to reach their full potential, here I come, the human wrecking ball. Maybe that's my talent, messing things up. Perhaps instead of denying it, I need only embrace it.

So, consider yourself warned, man.

Me <————— Big. Random. Stupid. Trouble.

I can't even write an email without being weird, see, Kate

*   *   *

Dear Kate,

Great minds think alike, I guess—

Thank you for your honesty. About your situation. I
totally get the *mind and heart not on the same page*
thing. All too well sometimes.

But you're only half right about Jillian. There was
a time when I wanted to be with her, a time when
there were few things I wanted more. But she and
I are meant to be friends—best friends actually—
and I'm happy to have her. The other day she told
me she's basically my bodyguard, that her job is
to protect me from getting hurt. When I asked her
what hurt she was protecting me from, she said
everything. I guess I'm lucky to have someone like
that, who cares about me so much. Her boyfriend,
Franny, is also my best friend. The three of us are
best friends, in fact. So you can imagine how weird/
awkward/difficult it was to have/hide my feelings
for her. Once upon a time there was a moment, at
a party very much like the one you and I met at,
where I nearly told her the truth. But something
(fate/kismet/chance/divine orchestration) made
me hold back. Whatever it was, I don't regret it.
Especially now. 😳

Anyway, I don't want to rush off, but I sort of have a band, and I'm supposed to meet Franny, so I have to go. For now. If you happen to hear something that sounds like a moose crying in a wind tunnel, don't worry. That's just our band warming up. Okay, I'm lying. That's us attempting to play songs.

No moose was harmed during the playing of these songs,
Jack

PS Tell me something you've never told anyone. (<— You probably didn't think I was capable of this level of cheesiness, but SURPRISE! I am!)

THE IRONY OF PRISON SENTENCES

Still buzzing from Kate's emails, I meet Franny at his locker, the same way I do every day before band class. "Hey, man, you ready to rock out?" I ask as I pretend to strum my trumpet case as if it's a guitar.

But Franny slams his locker shut. "Not going."

I laugh. "What, you got something better to do?"

"Not really feeling like hanging out with Nerds 'R' Us today, that's all," he mumbles, then turns to walk away. "But please give my regards."

I grab him by his backpack to stop him. "First you skip lunch and now you're trying to bail on band, too? Yo, what's up, man?"

"Everything's kosher, bro. Enjoy *band*, okay," he says, like *band* is a dirty word. Or like instead of *band* he means *enjoy your sweet-ass, trouble-free life, okay?*

"Yeah, okay. You don't think I know when you're lying? What's really going on?"

I finally get a good look at his eyes, and it makes immediate sense why he doesn't want to look at me. Bloodshot would be putting it nicely. "Damn, Franny, have you been drinking?"

"'Gee golly, Fran, have you been drinking?'" he parrots.

"Really, Franny? That's how you wanna play this? You've worked so hard. If a teacher sees . . ."

His eyes darken, his brow tightens. "What are you, my guidance counselor now? Next you gonna lecture me about how I'm throwing away my opportunities? Get the hell outta here, man."

He sidesteps me, but I grab him again, this time more forcefully. "Franny, we've been friends since . . . I can't even remember not being friends. If something's happened, or . . . you can tell me anything. The fact that I even have to—"

But he interrupts me. "Just stop," he yells, his voice sharp, hard. A couple of kids in the hallway halt whatever it is they're doing to look over. But Franny gives them the eye and they keep it trucking. He turns back to me, his voice still edgy, but lower now. "What do you want from me, Jack?"

I want you to tell me that your dad is getting out of prison. "How about the truth?"

"And just when I think you can't possibly be any cornier," he says. He bites his lip, gives me a forced grin. His red eyes are moist. His pupils bottle up the overhead halogen, giving them a dirty-white shine. "You're going to be late."

"What's wrong, Franny?"

The late bell rings.

"See?" I point skyward. "Too late. Now you gotta talk to me. I was tardy for you. You know how I *detest* tardiness."

"Something's seriously wrong with you." Franny nearly laughs, but catches himself. "They're letting The Coupon out early for good behavior, kid. The irony, right? Only time anyone's ever put him and *good* in the same sentence."

* * *

The news of The Coupon's release, although not new information, makes me contemplate The Big Picture.

Namely, I'd assumed that I was back here to help keep Kate from dying.

But maybe I'm back for Franny, too.

Maybe I can be here for everyone.

Dear Jack,

Now that you mention it, yesterday afternoon I did hear a moose crying. And I kept thinking, *I wish someone would cheer the poor thing up*, but it just kept right on playing, ahem, *crying*. Soooooo— when were you going to tell me that you're in a band? And how would you feel about playing for an audience of one? (The one would be me, if that wasn't clear enough. 😊)

With regard to Jillian and Franny, I think the fact that you have friends who are willing to protect you from *everything* means you have the best kind of friends. Usually you have a friend who's good at *this* and another friend that specializes in *that*, but to have friends who do *everything* is super rare. Of course, I'm sure you already know that.

One thing no one else knows, huh?

When I was a kid, I ate spiders. Not because I thought they were fascinating*, or particularly tasty**, but because I wanted to spin silk from my stomach and create beautiful webs of my own.

But as it turns out, the only thing I got was nausea.

I can hear you laughing your ass off.

Okay, so I'm pretty sure that's not at all what you had in mind, but it's 100 percent true and you're the only one I've ever told, clearly for good reason. So, your turn, Jack. Tell me something.

Eagerly anticipating something juicy or at least thoroughly embarrassing so that I'm not so alone in my arachnid-eating humiliation,
Kate 😊

*although I did

**they weren't

* * *

Dear Silk-Slinging Kate,

I'm actually from the future. Well, if you can call four months the future. I mean technically it is the future, and honestly you'd be surprised how much can change in only four months—literally the entire world. So I guess I shouldn't sound unappreciative, because it's quite the opposite. It means everything to be back here. Everything.

So there you have it, something I've never told anyone. I trust you'll keep it in strictest confidence.

[Do you wish to delete this email or save it for later?]

Save.

[Your email has been saved.]

Compose new message.

Dear Silk-Slinging Kate,

Only I don't get a chance to write another email because Dad calls me down for dinner, and then Franny shows up to eat with us, and I spend the rest of the evening figuring out how to bring up The Coupon's parole to my parents, but in a way that Franny won't want to reach across the table and stab me.

But I can't think of a good way, so instead I spend my time warding off Franny's forked attempts to poach Mom's homemade ravioli from my plate.

I only pretend to put up a fight.

*   *   *

"So, Fran, about this whole Coupon homecoming thing," I say.

My parents have retreated for bed, and we're in the basement, the two of us illuminated by the glow of *Metal Brigade IV*, analog sticks rumbling beneath our thumbs as we narrowly avoid enemy cannon fire.

"What about it?" Franny asks. He activates his super power-up just in time to light up the opposing squad's best player.

I shrug. "I just think you should be prepared . . . like, you know his track record isn't exactly impeccable. I just want you to be okay if . . . you know . . . he's not . . . if he doesn't . . ."

"Do we need to talk about this now? Like, we're in the middle of some serious kick-ass here."

"Guess I've just been thinking."

"Well, you can stop wasting your time thinking about *that* stuff, okay?"

"Yeah, okay, Fran. Sorry."

And I wonder if I've messed things up. If I've said too much. I sneak a look at Franny. Only I can't read him. His eyes laser-focused on the screen, lips pinched tight, forehead creased in concentration. And we sit there, still and quiet except for the snap of our fingers, the wails of our enemies falling all around us.

DRIFTING, DRIFTING

I convince myself that the best way not to lose Kate is to not let her out of my sight.

Or at least stay as close to her as I can.

And so:

We pull epic near-all-nighters together, which basically consist of her studying and me pretending to study but mainly just watching her study, and then acting super studious whenever she looks over at me, shaking her head disapprovingly at my upside-down textbooks.

We eat lots of bad-for-you food together. There's this taco truck that stays open late that becomes our go-to. Best guac EVER!

We spend hours in the gorges, talking about anything and everything. One afternoon she tries her best to convince me

187

that the new Star Wars trilogy is better than the original. I ask her if she's even seen *Empire Strikes Back*.

She tries to catch me up on all the cool indie movies that have somehow escaped my viewership. Which turns out to be almost ALL THE COOL INDIE MOVIES. Shout-out to *Raising Victor Vargas* and *Short Term 12*!

We have random we-both-stink-at-dancing dance parties in the middle of her dorm room, much to her roommate's dismay.

And we kiss during our study breaks. And we kiss doing our taco truck visits. And we kiss in the gorges, and during our movie marathons.

"Do you think you'll ever get tired of kissing?" Kate asks me.

"Kissing you? Never," I assure her.

"You're sure?"

"Hmm," I say. "Maybe we should conduct an experiment?"

Kate's eyebrows rise. "You think?"

I scoot closer to her. We're in the middle of the library stacks. Alone except for a girl a few tables away.

"It feels like the only way to really know," I say.

She smiles, places her hand on the back of my head in this way that makes me feel melty, and kisses my nose, and then my cheek, and then my lips.

She pulls away, looks at me. "In the name of science, right?"

I slide closer still. "I love science," I say in between kisses.

I lose myself in Kate's eyes, in her lips, in the irregular rhythm of her breaths.

And it's simple math, really: the more time I spend with her, the more time I want with her.

I might be a Kate addict.

And there doesn't seem to be a cure for my addiction, and even if there were an antidote, I don't think I'd want it.

I know I wouldn't want it.

I'd refuse treatment, check myself out of the hospital against medical advice, wouldn't even bother changing out of my gown, or those one-size-fits-all hospital skid-proof socks.

Jack, you need to stay here. It's for your own good, they'd plead.

But I'd wave them all off.

Because I'm happy, addiction be damned.

THE FLIP SIDE TO HAPPY

But there's a flip side to Jack Can't Get Enough of Kate.

I turn on the kitchen light and nearly have a heart attack.

"Dad, what are you doing lurking in the kitchen?"

"I'm not lurking. You can't lurk in your own house. I couldn't sleep. And I'm waiting for you, I suppose."

"Everything okay?" I walk over to the cabinet, pull out a glass, take the grape juice from the fridge.

"Funny. I was going to ask you the same."

The grape juice tastes sweeter than usual. "I'm good. Why?"

"Well, I just wondered what happened to you tonight."

"I went out."

"So you forgot about helping me clean out the shed so we can get the new lawn mower inside?"

"I'm sorry, Dad. It slipped my mind."

"Your mom was counting on getting it done today. Because

if we can't get the lawn mower inside the shed, we won't be able to get the party chairs and tables she ordered into the garage."

"I said I'm sorry."

"I heard you."

"Look, I'll move some things around and we'll do it tomorrow after school."

"It's already done, Jack."

My eyebrows rise. "Already done? There's no way you moved everything by yourself."

"You're right. That's why your mom pitched in. And Franny came over and helped. Jillian, too. I couldn't have done it without them."

"What's really going on here?"

"How's that?"

"You're waiting in the dark for me to come home. You're clearly pissed off . . ."

"Not pissed off, Jack. Disappointed," Dad says. He sips from his water. "And concerned."

"Concerned about what?"

"This feels like a pattern. Your behavior lately."

"My behavior," I say. "I forgot to come home and help you move things. You could've just called me."

"I did," he says.

I pull my phone out of my pants pocket and realize my phone is off. Either I accidentally turned it off or the battery died. "Crap, my fault, Dad. I didn't even realize my phone—"

"That's sort of the problem, Jack. You've been doing a lot of forgetting, a lot of not realizing, and it's starting to catch up to you."

"It was one thing, Dad."

"So you didn't also forget about family dinner tonight? That your friends were coming for your mom's chili?"

He's right. I *had* forgotten. Two things in one night was a bit much.

"I'll call Franny and Jillian. They'll understand. We'll do family dinner this weekend."

"We already had family dinner, Jackie."

"You can't have *family* dinner without all the family."

Dad shrugs. "Your mom and I made a lot of food. We didn't want it to go to waste."

I cross my arms. "Well, it sounds more like you were just trying to prove a point."

"And what would that point be?"

"You tell me."

"Jackie, it's one thing to be wrapped up in this girl—"

"Kate. Her name is Kate."

"—but not at the expense of the people who love you, who've been here for you . . ."

And I nearly say, *She's here for me, too. And we make each other happy. And that should make you happy, too. And I can't screw this up, this chance to make things right, not again. Not when there's so much to lose. Because* almost *won't cut it. Because I'm not the guy who gets second chances, let alone at love.*

But I can't explain any of this to him. How astronomically

high the stakes are. No one, not even my dad, who would want to believe me, could actually believe me.

"Of all people, Dad, I thought you would understand."

"What'd you think I'd understand, Jack?"

"That sometimes good things happen in your life that you didn't count on, that you can't completely account for, but once they do, life is about embracing those things, about expanding your world, about . . . doing something bigger than yourself. I mean, look at what you and Mom have, what Franny and Jillian have. Why can't I have that, too?"

"You can. And you will. But right now, you and Franny and Jillian are barely out of high school. You have your whole life to live, to find what truly makes you happy. There's no rush—"

"Who says I'm rushing? Why can't I have the real thing now? What if Kate's the one? People act as though you have to wait for everything good in life. Sometimes good things happen earlier than you expected. Sometimes you don't have to wait."

"If you feel that strongly about her, how come you haven't brought her here? Introduced her to your mother and me?"

Because I don't want to share her. Because there's only so much time. "What do you want me to say?"

"Jackie, we all love you. And believe me, we're happy you're happy. And we all agree Kate sounds like a great young woman, but . . . maybe things are moving a bit too quickly. Maybe . . ."

I polish off my grape juice, set my glass inside the dishwasher, and head for the stairs, not wanting to hear the rest of whatever he's trying to say. Because it's a refrain I've heard before. People always say they're happy you're happy until they're afraid that maybe your happiness is affecting their happiness and then they're not so happy about you being so happy.

Okay, that was unnecessarily confusing. Still, I think you probably get it.

"Like I said, I'm sorry I wasn't here, I am. But I'm really tired. I'm gonna go upstairs and crash."

"Right," Dad says, softly. "Night, Jackie."

TO FRANNY, JILLIAN: Hey guys, sorry about tonight. I totally got my days mixed up and I thought dinner was next week. Please forgive me?

FRANNY: Bro, you owe us BIG time!!!

JILLIAN: I'm sorry, who is this???

ME: I do! And I promise to pay you back WITH interest!!

ME: Ouch, J. That hurts!!

JILLIAN: Well, this number used to belong to our best friend, Jack, but he's been MIA and we assumed he'd been vaporized from the planet, so . . .

ME: Actually, he has. And you've unwittingly exposed our alien plot to take over Earth. So now the two of you are number 3 and 4 on our To Vaporize List . . .

FRANNY: WTF? Who's numbers 1 and 2??

JILLIAN: He's going to say the president.

ME: The president.

ME: Hey! Stop acting like I'm predictable!!

JILLIAN: Believe me, I'm not ACTING. 😊

FRANNY: So, who's the other vaporizee?

ME: That's for me to know and you NOT to know. Ever!

JILLIAN: It's clearly Kate!!!

ME: Yep. Kate stumbled onto our plot, too. But dang! Am I really that transparent?

JILLIAN: Do you really want me to answer that??

FRANNY: Bros over hos, man! Bros over hos!

ME: No offense, Jillian^^^^

JILLIAN: None taken. I'm a bro in the spiritual sense, duh!

FRANNY: Exactly!! J's more of a bro than you these days, Jack.

ME: I am sorry, guys. My dad sorta pointed out how douchey I've been lately and I'm sorry I've been THAT GUY.

FRANNY: Well, clearly, Kate can give you things Jillian and I can't, sooooo . . . hahahaha

JILLIAN: You have been pretty sucky lately. Like there's no reason you can't be with Kate and still be good to your friends. I mean you've blown off band practice that we're having for YOUR parents even. Like, really??

ME: I know. You're right. There's no reason.

ME: I'm sorry. I've just felt this simultaneous push and pull, I guess. Like, where I have to find a balance between my friends and my girl, and it's harder than I thought.

195

FRANNY: Oh, it's hard all right!! LMAO that's the prob, man! Just stop thinking with your junk and you'll be cool.

ME: Sage advice as usual, Franny.

ME: I guess I wanna say, thanks for not hating me.

FRANNY: Sometimes you're such a mushy idiot.

JILLIAN: Shut up, Jack! Seriously! Just stop!

ME: I love you guys, too. <3 <3

And I know you'd think that tonight would've been enough to jar me back into reality—disappointing my parents, letting down my friends.

Only you'd be wrong.

You'd be so gloriously wrong.

*　*　*

Because less than a week later . . .

TO FRANNY, JILLIAN: Hey guys, sooooo . . . it's looking like I'm not going to be able to make practice today. Something has come up.

JILLIAN: Are you serious?! The party is six weeks away and we're nowhere near ready, Jack! Whatever SOMETHING is, SHE can wait!

FRANNY: Bro, this is like the fifth time you've flaked already. Like, if this isn't important to you anymore, just say the word. But you know, it was YOUR idea. And it is YOUR rents' 30th.

ME: I know, I know. You guys know I wouldn't cancel unless I had a really good reason.

FRANNY: Do you, bro.

Thirty minutes later . . .

FROM JILLIAN: Are you okay, man? Like, really, what's going on with you these days?

ME: I'm great, actually. Like, really happy.

JILLIAN: Glad one of us is.

ME: Wait, what happened??

JILLIAN: I got a B- on my last French paper.

ME: 😞 There must be some mistake!!

JILLIAN: Nope. I got what I deserved.

ME: You deserve the best.

JILLIAN: I remember when my friend Jack used to help me practice, but lately he's been busy doing other THINGS. LOL

ME: Nothing's changed, J.

JILLIAN: Everything's changing, J.

ME: How do you mean??

JILLIAN: Forget it. It's cool.

ME: I can't just forget it.

JILLIAN: I'm pretty sure you can.

ME: Hey, I'm sorry, J. Really.

JILLIAN: I gotta go.

JILLIAN: BTW, you should really talk to Franny, too.

ME: He okay?

JILLIAN: I think the possibility of seeing The Coupon soon is really starting to get to him. He's just all over the place lately. Which is understandable. I worry about him, you know. He hates talking about this stuff. He could really use you, Jack.

ME: I'll talk to him.

JILLIAN: Good luck with that.

JILLIAN: Okay, I gotta go 4 real now!

ME: Parle plus tard?

JILLIAN: Nous verrons.

5 minutes later . . .

ME to FRANNY: Hey, man, just wanted to say how sorry I am again about missing practice.

ME (after waiting to no avail for a reply): And I guess I wanted to let you know that I'm here, y'know. For you. Should you ever need to talk or not talk, or whatever, okay?

ME: I'm sorry I've been MIA lately. I guess this whole having a girlfriend thing is time-consuming. I finally get why you and Jillian are always so busy. LOL ☺

ME: So, uh, yeah, I guess hit me back whenever.

ME: Love you, bro.

ME: promptly erasing that last text, swapping it for this:

ME: 😎

90 minutes after that . . .

FRANNY: I'm good, man. No worries, with your awkward, guilt-feeling ass! LOL

ME: Hey now!

FRANNY: But there is one thing you can do for me, since you asked!

ME: What's up??

FRANNY: So, turns out Abuela invited The Coupon over for dinner tomorrow night. Know it's last min, but you still down for the cause?

ME: I'm there, man. Save me a good seat.

And I'm happy because I know in the end, Franny and I will always be there for each other.

Kate's face flashes on my phone.

"Hey, shouldn't you be in class?" I ask.

"I'm running late. But I'm walking at an uncomfortably rapid pace now."

"Ah, that explains why you sound as though you're standing on top of a skyscraper."

"Exactly. So, what are you doing?"

"Uh, studying," I say, quickly pausing *Rampage III* and tossing my controller onto the cushion beside me. "Why? What's up?"

"I was hoping to talk to you."

"I'm listening."

"I mean, like, where I can see your face and you can see mine."

"You mean *FaceTime*," I say, laughing.

Only she barely laughs back. "Seriously. Like I need to see you in person."

"Oh," I say, wondering what's wrong. Why suddenly things are so urgent. "Are you okay?"

"Yeah," she says, almost too quickly.

"Positive?"

"Yep."

"Okay, so when were you thinking?"

"I don't know. I have a paper due in the morning that I haven't started yet. And I'm supposed to go with my sister to some awards thing tonight, that she won't let me back out of despite my best attempts. I was hoping tomorrow?"

"Tomorrow," I repeat, already knowing that tomorrow isn't likely to work. That I can't double-book when I just promised Franny I'd be at his place. When Franny needs me.

But what if Kate wants to see me to tell me that she's sick—

What if this is the moment I discover why I'm back here?

How can I risk missing that?

I can't.

I have to do both.

Kate clears her throat. "If that doesn't work, I don't know, we can figure something else out."

"Well, what time were you thinking?"

"Any time. You tell me."

"Ummmm . . ."

Because I have school all day. And there's the travel time between here and Whittier to consider. But if I skipped last period, and managed to avoid any traffic, maybe I can be at both places, do both things. Be there for Franny *and* Kate. Which would be the best-case scenario. Win-win all around. And I know—maybe Kate would understand if I told her I couldn't make it, that I already had noncancelable plans. It's just that, well, this second time around—which is still hard to comprehend, that I have a second shot—I don't want to waste a fraction of a second. Because if there's one thing I've learned, it's that nothing's promised. That you have to treat second chances like an endangered species.

"Really, Jack, if it's too much . . ."

"No, no, I'll be there. Tomorrow afternoon."

"You're sure?"

"Couldn't be surer."

*   *   *

School is slow AF today. And tenth period can't come fast enough. I've already devised my exit strategy. All day I've been going out of my way to establish an emerging bout of stomach flu:

Asking for multiple bathroom visits.

Practically running out of each class in that hunched-over way you move when your stomach's churning.

A trip to the school nurse, who, after a quick consultation with my mom, doused me with antacids and fluids.

I even make sure to excuse myself from fifth-period study hall, which not so incidentally is the study hall overseen by Mrs. Randleman, who is also my AP History teacher.

"You don't look so well, Jack," Mrs. Randleman says, watching me rub my stomach counterclockwise, my body slightly compressed and forward-leaning, as if at any moment I might explode from all my orifices.

"I'm okay, Mrs. R. Thanks for your concern. My stomach is

just . . . well, it's not quite itself today."

"Hmm," Mrs. Randleman says, handing me a bathroom pass. "Maybe you should go home. Get some rest. The flu's going around right now."

"Maybe you're right," I agree. "But wait, what about our history exam?"

Mrs. Randleman nods her head, as if she's taking this situation under serious advisement. "Well, I suppose you could always make it up Friday. I have to be here for detention after school, anyway, so I guess . . ."

"Oh, thank you, thank you, Mrs. R. You're the best," I say.

"Be careful, Jack. I don't do well with vomit. If you throw up, I'll be right behind you."

"Right," I say. "Sorry, ma'am. So very sorry!"

And okay, does a part of me feel bad for deceiving poor ol' innocent Mrs. Randleman? Absolutely.

But I'm still taking the test. And now I get to be there for my girl *and* Franny. How is that not a fair trade?

QUICKIE MART QUICKSAND

I kiss Kate goodbye. Again and again and again. I can't stop kissing her goodbye.

She laughs, brings her lips to my cheek, and opens the car door for me. "You better get out of here, Jack Attack. Franny's waiting for you."

"Right," I say. But I don't want to leave her. I want to keep feeling her lips on mine at nearly any cost.

But she's right. I need to hit the highway ASAP.

"I hope it was worth it," she says. "You coming all the way out here? I hope you really like it," she adds, pointing to the box on the passenger seat.

I lean in. Kiss her again. "You're worth way more," I say. "And I love it, Kate. I do." And her face lights up in a way that I'd do anything to duplicate.

"You better go," she says.

I poke my head out the window and simultaneously back the car out. "I'll call you," I promise.

From my rearview mirror, I watch Kate get smaller and smaller, waving at me, until I can no longer make out her smile.

* * *

I make great time—for the first thirteen minutes. Then I run into an onslaught of rush-hour traffic. Horn-laying, middle-finger-waving, curse-word-screaming traffic. Apparently, none of these people care that I need to be in Elytown in less than thirty minutes.

Neither does my right tire.

Because when the roadblock of traffic finally begins to subside, I realize my car isn't picking up speed with its usual halfhearted gusto. It seems slow on the takeoff, even for its measly amount of horsepower.

And then I hear metal rubbing.

A woman in the lane beside me rolls down her passenger window and motions for me to roll down my own window—

"Flat," she yells across the freeway. "You got a flat!"

I pull over, wait for a crowd of cars to zip by, and hop out to confirm my worst fears.

Crap.

Super crap.

I kick a patch of gravel, and a rock ricochets off the flat tire and smacks me in the shin.

Because, you know, when it rains, it—

And then it actually pours.

A freaking deluge of rain from nowhere, as if mankind just won a championship and God decided to empty the Gatorade cooler over our heads.

Naturally, it takes me a good eight minutes to locate the tire iron, hidden neatly in a compartment in the trunk, only to discover it, along with the jack, is mostly corroded and barely usable.

So, as I struggle to change the tire, risking tetanus with every rust-ridden turn, traffic roaring past my head, all their nonflat tires shooting thick sheets of cool, dirty rain water into my face and clothes, already drenched from the never-stopping downpour, I realize something very important.

I'm going to be late.

Also, I suck.

* * *

I try to text Franny, but my crappy carrier's service isn't cooperating.

I push the gas pedal so that it's flat against the floor. I weave in and out of traffic, elicit my share of horn blares and middle fingers.

But they don't faze me.

I have somewhere to be.

* * *

I finally pull onto Franny's street and I know I've really screwed up.

1) Because I'm over an hour late. Closer to ninety minutes than sixty.

2) Because Franny is waiting on the porch stairs, his face buzzing with an anger I've never seen. Before I even throw the car into park he's already bounding for my car, fury in his stride.

My intestines twist into a French braid. I take a deep breath.

"Where the hell were you, man?" Franny shouts before I have both feet out of the car.

"Franny," I say, emerging with my hands up. "I'm sorry. I ran into traffic, and—"

He wags his head, a whooshing sound escaping from his lips like he's an oxygen tank that someone's cranked all the way open. "Traffic? It's a fifteen-minute drive across town, Jack. What are you talking about, traffic?"

I'm tempted to lie to him, if only to defuse the situation. But I can't bring myself to do it. Franny and I don't lie to each other. I could blame it on the flat tire, but that's not the whole truth either. "I wasn't home."

He's standing on the passenger's side of my car. I'm still on the driver's side, standing in the middle of the street, afraid of what might happen if I come any closer. Better to keep a barrier between us.

"So, where were you?" he demands.

"Franny, I . . ." but I can't say it.

"Wow. You chose ass over your best friend."

"That's not what happened, man. I—I went . . . there, yes,

but it's not what you think. I thought she needed to tell me something imp—"

"Important? Is that what you were about to say?" Now he's on the same side of the car as me. "Fuck you, Jack." Now his chest is at best two inches away from mine, except his chest is puffing, heaving, like if pushed he could blow a brick house down.

He could blow a continent right off the map.

He bumps into me, knocking me back. I instinctively raise my arms in defense. In all our years knowing each other, we've never physically fought. Probably because the consensus is that he'd pulverize me.

"Franny, listen, I'm here now. I'll go inside and I'll apologize to Abuela and to The Coupon and we'll still have a good dinner. Or I can run and get some ice cream and bring it back or . . ."

I lower my hands and finally look at Franny. Like, really look at him. His eyes are wet. And I smell beer. Not like *I had a drink or two*. More like, *I drank a case or two*.

"Ice cream," he repeats. "It's too late for all that."

"I can fix this. Just let me go inside and—"

"You're not hearing me."

"I know you're pissed at me, but if you just—"

"He's gone, man."

"What do you mean, *he's gone*? Gone where?"

Franny shrugs. "Probably back to prison."

"What are you talking about?"

Someone honks their horn at us and I remember that we're in the middle of the street. I try to get out of the car's way but Franny doesn't seem to care he's impeding traffic. The car honks again, and I try to pull Franny curbside, but he jerks his arm away and shoves me back. My leg clips the back of my car and I barely catch my balance.

"I'm sorry, but I don't understand what's happening, Franny."

"You should've been here. That's what *didn't* happen."

"I know. I know. And I'm sorry."

"You're sorry," he says to me, sneering. He turns back toward the car, which is maneuvering around him. "He's sorry," he says to the driver of the car, rapping his knuckles on the car's roof as it crawls by. "Yo, he's sorry," he yells toward the sky.

"What happened, Franny?"

"You wanna know? You really wanna know?"

"I do. Please."

"You were late, and I insisted we wait for you, because after all, my best friend knows how important tonight is, he's gotta be on his way, right? So, we're sitting there, Abuela, me, and The Coupon, awkward as hell. He's all trying to make small talk, only I'm not feeling it. I ask Abuela if she got enough ice cream for the cobbler, offer to run to the corner store. But then he says *I'll go.*"

Franny sits on the back bumper of my car. I stand beside him.

"Half hour passes and dude still isn't back."

I take a seat beside Franny on the bumper, half expecting him to move away. He doesn't.

"Abuela's worried. But he has one of those prepaid phones and we don't have the number. *Go look for him*, she says. In my head, I'm figuring this dude ran into some back-in-the-day girl he knows or whatever. But I get to the store and there's like three or four cop cars. Neighbor's kid says someone tried to rob the Quickie Mart. And now my head's spinning, because what if this dude got himself shot or something. I think *this might kill Abuela*."

Franny swallows hard. A car zooms by, heavy bass rattling its trunk.

"I try to get closer but an officer grabs me, says *back up*. But I sidestep him and keep walking. He snatches me from behind, and then I'm being slammed to the sidewalk. Which is when I see him. The Coupon. Sitting in the back of one of the cars. Our eyes meet, and he starts wigging out, mashing his face into the rear window, thumping on the glass, yelling, *Yo, yo, that's my son. Get the hell off my son!* And then I hear myself yelling, *That's my pop, man. That's my pop!* And the whole time it's happening, it's not real, you know. None of it's real."

"I don't know what to say," I say. Because I don't. I take a chance and drape my arm around his shoulders, and he bristles but doesn't move. "Let's drive down to the precinct, find out what the charges are. See if we can get him out."

"Abuela's already on her way. She called your parents. They're meeting her there."

209

And I know I'm responsible.

Franny's right.

If I show up on time, no one gets antsy.

No trip to the corner store.

No arrest.

No Franny hating my guts.

But I'm late.

"This dude can't even last seventy-two hours out in the real world. Like, who does that?"

"I'm sure it's a mistake, Franny."

"The only mistake is thinking he could change."

"I'm sorry I was late. If I hadn't been late, then . . ."

"If you're thinking I'm about to absolve you of your guilt, it's not the time, man."

"No." I nod. "I'm sorry."

"Besides," Franny says, standing up, smirking like he's some supervillain, a streetlamp casting a yellow haze behind him. "If anything, you did me a favor, man. He was bound to screw up sooner or later. You just saved us all the bullshit in between."

And then Franny walks up the sidewalk, and I don't have time to decide if I'm meant to follow before he disappears into the house, slamming the door behind him.

*   *   *

And here's the killer part.

You're probably wondering what was so important that Kate wanted to see me in person, right?

Like me, you probably figured it was about her illness. That she wanted to tell me face-to-face.

Like me, you figured wrong.

She wanted to see me because it was our three-month anniversary and she had a present for me. Which made me feel terrible because I hadn't gotten anything for her. And I felt worse when I saw how awesome her gift was.

A digital photo frame with carefully curated pictures of our times together.

Yep.

I get a thoughtful electronic keepsake that I don't even deserve, and Franny loses his dad, again, the same day he got him back.

*   *   *

Franny stops talking to me.

Jillian tells me I should probably find another way to school, *just until he cools off*, she assures me.

But I don't argue.

I deserve far worse.

Mom tries convincing me that I'm not to blame for Franny's dad, that he's a grown man who has to be accountable for himself, and while I appreciate her efforts to make me feel better, I know that's mostly Mom Talk.

"Where's Dad?" I ask one day after school.

"Uh," Mom says, intensely typing into her computer. I peek over her shoulder. She's typing on some spreadsheet for work. "I believe he's with Franny."

"Oh," I say. "What are they up to?"

"Shopping for a tux, I think. I guess Franny wanted help."

"I see."

"He'll be back for dinner. Did you need something?"

"No," I say. "Not really."

Mom slips her glasses off, but keeps them in her hand, which is something she does when she's about to say something important. "With all that Franny's going through, Dad and I thought it might be nice if Dad offered Franny help with prom stuff. Franny seemed really excited."

"I bet he did." I know I shouldn't be jealous. I mean, my parents have been asking me to spend more time with them, but I've spent most of my free time with Kate. That's not their fault, or Franny's, for that matter, but still—

"What does that mean, Jack?"

"Nothing."

She stares at me. "How's Kate?"

"She's good."

"Yeah? You two going strong?"

"Strong enough."

"Prom's coming up fast. You gonna be ready?"

"I was thinking you might wanna go with me to the florist? Help me pick out a corsage for her?"

"Aw, sweetie, I would love to," Mom says. "Only things are really tight right now with the store and planning this anniversary party and . . . I really want to help you. Franny asked me to go with him. We can all go together. It'll be fun."

I wave her off. "No, it's cool. You should probably just stick to your original plan. I don't wanna mess you guys up."

"Jackie, don't be like that. How about you and I . . ."

I manage a smile. "Don't sweat it, Mom. I totally understand. I should be able to pick out a silly flower by myself, anyway. No biggie." I kiss her cheek, then quickly turn away and pretend I'm busy looking for something in the cabinets, because something weird is happening to my eyes, to my nasal passages. They're getting wet.

"You sure something else isn't bothering you?" Mom asks.

"Yeah," I say. I discreetly wipe my eyes, my nose, before turning around to face her again. "I'm sure."

She opens her mouth to say something, but I'm already hurtling out the kitchen for upstairs.

So, let's recap: everything not named Kate has changed for the worse, and I'm to blame.

All this time I thought I was supposed to save Kate. Maybe it's me who needs saving.

*   *   *

Franny's dad gets ninety days in county for disturbing the peace.

Which is utter BS.

Evidently, the Quickie Mart store owner was under the impression that The Coupon had no intention of paying for his rocky road ice cream.

Told The Coupon he wasn't welcome in the store.

To which The Coupon did not take kindly.

The Coupon decided to take his time browsing, looking at stuff he had no intention of buying, because that was his right, same as anyone else's.

Finally set his ice cream atop the counter, waited for the man to ring him up.

The owner wasn't having it. Ordered him out.

What's your problem, The Coupon said.

You're the problem, and people like you, the owner shouted. *Now get out of my store!*

People like me, The Coupon repeated. *People. Like. Me.* Felt a whoop-ass rage bound through his body. He'd never been the Let Things Slide type. But he thought of his mom, his son, waiting for ice cream. Somewhat composed himself. Picked up the register scanner, aimed it at the barcode on the side of the carton, looked at the price, rounded up for tax. Tossed his money, snatched a plastic grocery bag from the counter, plunked his ice cream into it, and headed for the door.

Only he wouldn't get far.

The store owner's wife had already called the police.

And as luck would have it, there was a cruiser not a block away from the store.

And, well—

You've seen this scene before.

You write the rest if you want.

HOW TO COME HOME

What's scary is that you can drift and not realize it. The oncoming car feverishly flashing its lights, blaring its horn, as you float dangerously left of center. The thing you hope for is that when you finally open your eyes, it's not too late.

"Jackie, dinner," Mom calls up the stairs.

When I get to the table, there are two extra place settings, and Dad's ushering in Franny and Jillian.

I look at Mom and she nods, as if to say, *It's time, Jackie.*

Dinner is awkward at first. Namely, because Franny's playing Avoid Eye Contact with Jack at All Costs, and he's awesome at it.

"How's French?" I ask Jillian.

She laughs. "Hate to say it, but not the same without you."

My heart swells. "I hate that you hate to say it, but I totally

215

get it. I lost myself for a while."

"Yeah, you did," Franny agrees.

"Well, I'm sorry. You guys deserve better. Have always given me better. I owe everyone here an apology. I think it's just that I'd finally gotten what I'd always wanted, what I saw my two best friends have, and what my parents have, being so wonderfully intertwined with someone else, so cosmically tangled that you have no idea where they start and you end."

Jillian bites her lip. "That's beautiful, J. And that's what we've always wanted for you, too. Franny and I wanna see you happy. You deserve to feel loved, to be loved. Which is why we have tried to be understanding. Why we've tried to give you your space."

"I know," I say. "You guys have been awesome."

Mom squeezes my hand. "The thing is, you don't forfeit your whole world to prove your feelings to someone. You bring your worlds together. You get more world, not less."

* * *

"Hey," I say to Franny as we clear the kitchen table.

"Hey," he mumbles back.

"So, there isn't a good enough phrase to describe what I've done, but I'm really . . ."

But Franny shakes his head. "Save it, man. Soon as we get done with these dishes, I'm gonna get my payback."

"Uhhhhh," I gurgle.

"You're about to get the ass-whooping of your young life," he promises. "In *Metal Brigade*."

He pushes me in the shoulder.

Jillian *awwww*s behind us.

I push him back the same.

PROM-ISES

The night before prom I can't sleep.

I have Kate rattling around my head, of course. But it's more than that.

I think about my last prom.

The teeter-totter feeling—initially believing I'd been stood up by Kate, only to find out that, no, she was actually in the hospital.

What if tomorrow, it happens all over again?

What if Kate doesn't show? What if she's not well?

But Kate does show. And she's even more beautiful, which I didn't think was possible.

"How are you feeling?" I ask her as soon as I open the front door.

"Umm, nervous, actually," she says.

"That's it? Nothing else?"

She laughs. "Excited? I don't know what you want me to say."

I want to just ask her, *But do you feel healthy?* I study her, although I'm not sure what I'm looking for exactly, and I suppose she seems okay.

"Jack, aren't you going to introduce us to your date?" Mom asks behind me. "I swear he wasn't raised by wolves."

"Sorry," I say. "Mom, Dad, this is Kate. Kate, Mom and Dad."

"Nice to meet you, Kate," Dad says. "We've heard so many good things."

Kate grins. "I hope they're true."

Mom beams. "You two look so good together. Can I hug you, Kate? Is that weird to ask?"

"Mom," I protest.

But Kate laughs, holds out her arms. "I love hugs."

*   *   *

"Sooo." Kate nods. "This is what I missed out on when I didn't go to my own prom."

This year's prom theme is Mardi Gras, and there are possibly more beads in this room than in the rest of the world combined. "Yes," I say, taking in the scene. "All of . . . this."

"Should I flip my top up now or wait until later?"

"As tempting as *now* is, my vote is *later.*"

"Good call," she says, pulling me onto the dance floor. "First, let's get our nonrhythmic grooves on."

219

"Definitely," I say. I snap my fingers and I am not within ten miles of locating the beat. Fortunately, Kate is also very good at being dysrhythmic.

"Nice, horrendous moves," I say, as I perform a cross between the cha-cha and what I like to refer to as *cracked-out polar bear on wheels*.

"You're pretty awesomely terrible yourself." She flaps her arms so hard that either she is (invisibly) on fire and trying to put out the (invisible) flames or she is attempting to gather enough momentum to lift off, fly *Mary Poppins* style above our heads, before exiting this prom via the skylights.

"What do you call that move?" She steps back, presumably to get a better look at my killer routine.

"Isn't it obvious? Chicken trapped on an escalator," I say, not missing a beat, my arms flailing, my feet hopping up to the next invisible step.

And then she's twirling her arms in a circle and making a *whooshing* noise, and then she's spinning round and round. And I have to ask, "And what do you call that?"

"Cat on a windmill."

We spend most of the evening on the dance floor, thoroughly embarrassing ourselves. And it's electric.

"This punch would taste so much better if it was in a juice box," Kate shouts over the thumping bass.

"Juice boxes are the best," Jillian says.

"Juice boxes for president," Franny yells, raising his plastic cup in the air.

I raise my cup. "Juice boxes for czar!"

When our favorite Mighty Moat song comes on, our foursome erupts in our worst dancing yet.

"I didn't think anyone liked Mighty more than me," Franny says to Kate, impressed at her word-for-word recitation.

"Would I sound pretentious if I told you it's because I know the band?" Kate asks.

Franny stops dancing. "Get outta here."

"Okay, I'll get out," Kate says. "But I don't know how I'd invite you to their concert if I'm gone."

"Are you serious?" Franny says, jumping up and down.

"You have no idea what you've done," Jillian says, laughing.

"Jack, why have you kept Kate away from us?" Franny demands. Which seems to be a popular question.

On the last slow song, I mull over where I should put my hands, but Kate makes it easy for me—places my hands on her back centimeters above her ass. Her face rests on my shoulder. And there's no place I would choose over here.

But then I feel her body quiver.

"You okay?"

"Yeah," she says. "Just felt weird for a second. I think it's passed."

"You sure?"

"Let's just dance."

But the song's not over when Kate leads me out into the foyer.

The door still closing, she says, "I have to go, Jack. Like, right now."

"Go where?" I ask. "What's wrong?"

But she's already retreating down the corridor, her breath jagged, eyes anguished. "I'm sorry to do this to you."

"I don't understand. Where are you going?"

She jabs the elevator call button. "I'm sorry."

"Wait, tell me what's happening."

"This was a mistake. I can't be with you. Not the way you want. I'm sorry, Jack. I shouldn't have come. You should just forget me, okay? Just forget me."

The elevator chimes open. Kate steps inside and slips off her heels, squeezing them in the same hand as her clutch. And she's mashing the buttons as if the doors can't close fast enough, as though she can't be away from me soon enough.

"Kate, wait," I yell. "I can't forget you. I could never forget you." I wedge my arm between the doors.

"Please, Jack, just let me go," she snaps.

"Wait, just tell me one thing. Are you okay?"

"What are you talking about?"

Good question. "I don't know. Are you feeling sick or . . . unwell? I just . . ."

"I'm feeling like I shouldn't be here, Jack. Nothing else."

"But . . ."

"Please, let me go."

I step back from the elevator because what else is there to do? The doors close, Kate disappearing right before my eyes.

And it's like when you don't clean the chalkboard well enough, and you can still see the ghost of what was written before; I can't erase the last prom from my brain. I can't let Kate leave alone. I slap the elevator-down button but there's only two elevators and one hasn't budged off the tenth floor and the other is currently making its sweet descent to the lobby, where it will deposit Kate into the shiny night.

I push open the heavy stairwell door and I run, trip, and stumble down. I'm a speeding, heavily sweating torpedo, and I'm locked on my target. I explode into the gold-gilded lobby, my head on a pivot, sweat flinging left and right, and I possibly induce a heart attack in an old woman alarmed by my bluster, only I'm busy staring at Kate's empty elevator.

I burst through the brass front doors, cool night air invades my lungs, and there's Kate, standing beside a cab. Kate sees me as she slips in, pulls the door closed.

The cab's rear lights, two bright-red exclamation points stamping Kate's departure.

I collapse onto the concrete.

Like newly asphalted roadkill.

My heart raging.

And I can't breathe.

I can't do anything right. Not even breathe.

And then tires screech. I sit up in time to see the cab reverse violently into the hotel drive, kicking grass onto the sidewalk.

Kate came back.

The cabbie hops out, yells, "You're Jack?"

I stand. "That's me."

"Call 9-1-1!"

I scream into the lobby, "Call an ambulance! Call 9-1-1

now!" I race down the front hotel stairs, yank open the back-seat door.

Kate's lying there, chest heaving, her face clenched. "Kate, what's wrong? What's happening?"

The cab driver is muttering. "Does she need an inhaler or something? Please, God, help this child."

"Jack . . ."

"Kate, tell me what to do."

But she's barely there.

"Kate, talk to me."

"Jack," she says, feebly. "Stay with me."

"I'm never leaving." I crawl into the cab, gently lift her head from the seat, set it onto my lap.

Somewhere in the near distance, sirens shriek.

"Kate, you're going to be okay."

"I'm sorry," she says.

I don't know if I should try to keep her talking, or if I should tell her to conserve her energy. I don't know anything. Why don't I know anything?

"You don't have anything to be sorry for," I say, stroking her hair. "Just breathe, Kate. Nice and easy, okay. Nice and easy."

"Hey, what's happening, man?" It's Franny. "You guys okay?"

I shake my head. "Something's wrong with Kate."

"Oh my God," Jillian says, leaning into the doorframe. "Did someone call for help?"

"It's on its way," I say to my friends. "Help is on the way," I repeat near Kate's ear, wisps of her hair clinging to my cheek.

The siren is right on top of us.

I look through the rear window, only to see nearly our entire senior class standing on the hotel stairs, clasping their faces and each other.

A pair of paramedics appear and place an oxygen mask over Kate's face, and all I can see are her eyes, earthy and wet.

"Make a lane, people," the husky paramedic barks. They quickly deposit Kate onto a stretcher and hustle her toward their squad.

"Where are you taking her?" I hurry after them as they load Kate into the back.

"You family, kid?" the woman paramedic asks me.

"Yes," I say.

She knows I'm lying. "Hop in," she says.

"Just stay out of the way, man," the guy orders.

"Jack!" Jillian and Franny are on the curb. "We'll follow you."

I nod. The ambulance doors close. The siren squawks. I keep out of the way, only moving to take Kate's hand. She squeezes my fingers weakly, but I'll take it. I'll take it.

"She's going to be okay, right?" I ask the paramedic.

And I can tell she wants to say yes but she won't lie to me.

* * *

The hospital is a blur of moving bodies and glinting instruments.

Orders bellowed, machines stirring to life.

Get another IV in here stat!

Venturi mask now!

Yo, where's that IV? I needed that IV yesterday.

Her veins are crap on this arm. Lemme look over there. Move, move!

Why is this kid in my exam room?

Think he came in with her.

Well, he can't be in here. Yo, kid, you gotta get out. We got your friend covered. We'll come find you when she's cool.

Those fluids need to be up, Juan.

Saline?

Naw, give me some KCl.

We want blood gases?

Yeah, we need ABGs. CBC. BMP. The whole shebang, Tracy.

Kate. Kate. Listen to me. Look at me. I need you to breathe, nice and easy, honey. Just relax, okay.

Got it!

'Bout time.

Yo, why is this kid still standing here? This ain't a damn made-for-TV movie. Somebody get this kid to the waiting room already. How many times I gotta ask?

"Come on, kid, you gotta come with me. This way. Come on. It's okay. You sit here, okay? We just got cable, so there's probably something to watch if you try hard enough. You want something to drink, there's water there. Crappy coffee too, if you're desperate. That's a joke. Okay, no it isn't . . . listen, she's going to be fine. I'll come back out here when she's stable and I'll let you see her and you'll see how fine she is. Okay? . . . Okay?"

We love to say *everything's going to be okay*, but honestly there's no way to know. And *okay* can mean so many different things.

Such as:

This cereal is okay.

That movie, eh, it was okay.

I'm waiting for Dad to give me the okay about the road trip.

But applied to people it generally sounds terrible—

So, what do you think about the new kid?

Eh. He seems okay.

Yo, I heard about your mom. How's she holding up?

She's okay.

Hey, I heard you lost a kidney. How are you doing, man?

I'm okay.

Okay isn't as comforting as I think people intend it to be.

The nurse or doctor or ER tech or guardian angel, or whoever she is, sprints back down the hall, pushing through the doors marked Authorized Personnel Only. The doors rock back and forth, and I consider running after her, wedging my sneaker between the doors, rushing back to Kate. But the doors stop swinging, and there's a loud *clink*, a latching sound that seems better suited for a correctional facility, as they lock me and the other unauthorized away from the people we love.

From the people we need.

So that they can try to save them.

So that we're not there when they can't.

*　　*　　*

227

The same woman comes back forty-three minutes later. I've watched each minute tick. I can't tell you when Franny and Jillian arrived. Only that they're on either side of me.

The woman's smiling, which I interpret as GOOD.

"She's okay," she assures me. *Okay*, that word again. "Give it thirty minutes and you can see her."

"What happened?"

The woman wrings her hands. "I can't really discuss her health with anyone she hasn't authorized. I'm sorry."

I nod. "As long as she's all right."

"She is. Thirty minutes." She disappears behind the swinging doors.

"See," Franny says, sighing hard. "Everything's fine."

"Did you call her parents, Jack?" Jillian asks me, in a way that makes me think she's already asked me this, that maybe I'd been too lost in my trance to hear her earlier.

"They're on their way," I say.

"I wonder what happened," Jillian says.

"Me too," I say. "Me too."

"I'm just glad we were there," Franny says.

"Me too," I say. "Me too."

"You sure you're okay?" Jillian asks. "It's like you're somewhere else."

She's right.

I'm back on our first prom night, standing in the rain on Kate's parents' front porch, waiting for her to answer the door, for her to explain why suddenly she didn't want me anymore.

228

Except now I know that night was never about me.

Kate couldn't be at prom with me.

She was too busy fighting for her life.

*　*　*

When I go into her room, Kate smiles. But I don't believe her.

I know it's meant to assure me.

But I don't feel assured.

Not even almost.

I stand in the doorway.

"Hi," she says.

"Hi," I say.

She pulls the oxygen out of her nose, pushes it up onto her forehead. "Come here," she says, tapping on the bed.

I walk over. "Should you be doing that? Taking off your oxygen?"

"No," she admits. "But if I did everything only the way I should, what kind of life would I have?"

"Kate, what happened?"

"I got sick," she says.

"Sick how? What's wrong with you?"

"Nothing's wrong with *me*."

"I didn't mean it like that. I mean . . . please just talk to me, Kate. Whatever I can do, I'll do it."

"I'm not a machine, Jack. You don't get to fix me."

I follow her eyes out the window.

"That's not what I mean. I don't want to fix you. You're not broken, Kate. To me, the way you already are, you're—"

"I have a condition. But *I'm* not a condition."

"But what condition do you have? Why won't you just tell me? I don't understand why you're being so . . . so secretive. I mean, you're in the goddamn hospital and I just want to be helpful and understand you better and I'm trying to . . ."

But she slices through my words. Throws her hands up like a traffic cop, *Halt. Don't move.* "I don't like you, okay. Not like that."

"Like what?"

"I mean, I *can't* like you. I'm sorry, Jack. You're really awesome, and funny, and—"

My turn to interject. "Spare me the smoothing over, okay?"

"I can't do this."

"What can't you do?"

"This. A relationship."

"Who said anything about a relationship?"

"You don't know what the future holds, Jack. But I do. And trust me, this is the way it has to be."

And I nearly shout, *I know EXACTLY what the future holds! That's the problem!* But I stop myself. Instead, I say what I want to believe—

"Kate, the future can be anything we want."

She chews on her bottom lip. "Xander wants to try again."

"Who's Xander?" I ask, but as soon as I utter his name I know. "Oh."

"Yeah, oh," she says, like she wishes she could put the words back into her mouth.

"Xander. Of course his name is Xander." Even though I could not have guessed this name in a million-gazillion years, but that's what you say when confronted with the name of your newly appointed archnemesis. "I thought you said he was bad for you."

"I did. He probably is. He is . . . but sometimes you . . ."

"Sometimes you what?"

"It's complicated."

"Well, uncomplicate it for me, because I don't get it, Kate."

"I don't think you want to get it."

I shrug. She has a point. I don't want to get it. But answer me this, who would? Did Ponce de León *get it* that there was no goddamn fountain of youth hidden in the Florida Everglades? Did Mr. George Washington Carver *get it* when people sneered who in the hell would want to eat soup made from peanuts? It is my contention that *getting it* is seriously overrated.

"Okay," I say. "So, answer this, why are you here with me then? And not with Xander somewhere? Why did you come to a high school prom, of all places, when someone like you could be out doing way cooler things with way cooler people?"

She scrunches her nose, and I don't mean to reduce everything Kate does to a series of supercute gestures and expressions, but she is so beautiful, so utterly breathtaking, even when she's mad, even when she's frustrated, even when she's frustrated at *me*, that it takes all of my willpower *not* to melt into a sticky, gooey Jack-blob.

"Jack, I'm only a year removed from my own prom."

"I mean, you know I like you, Kate. It's obvious, right? How much I like you? And then you agree to go to prom. And then we're celebrating our three-month anniversary, and . . . I mean, am I crazy? I'm probably crazy. But am I crazy about this?"

She shakes her head in that *I don't want to say, don't make me say* way. I know I should stop, because this is the part where she breaks my heart. But I can't stop. Part of me knew this wouldn't last. That same part of me that wants to just get it over with.

But part of me also wants to put it off as long as possible. Suspend it indefinitely, and live with Kate in a vacuum of unhurtable feelings.

"Jack, you're going to be okay. I promise."

"There's no way you can know that."

"One day you'll forget all about me."

"Everyone says I have an excellent memory. Even elephants have told me."

"You should go," she says, reaching for her call light.

"Answer me this, what does Xander have that I don't? Why him and not me?"

"Don't do this, Jack. This is stupid."

I smile, stupidly, defiantly, because suddenly I feel brave. But not the good kind of brave. Not the kind where the hero runs brilliantly into the inferno because he knows he has to act, he knows that there are lives at stake, lives other than his own, and that he must be the one to save them. No. What I'm feeling is the kind of brave where a squirrel decides to squat in the middle of the highway and stop a semitruck with only his mind.

And, well—

Need I tell you how that ends?

"I want to know, Kate. Why him? Why not me?"

"Because Xander's been there. He was the first guy who stuck around when things got hard. Is he an asshole sometimes? Absolutely! But he's a known quantity. I know who he is. And I know if push comes to shove, he'll be there for me."

"I want to be there for you even when push isn't shoving, Kate."

"Stop being nice to me."

"I'm miles beyond that."

She shakes her head. "I'm sorry, but I can never love you, Jack. I just can't, and I never wanted to hur—"

But I'm already jumping off the bed. "Just stop," I say. It's too much. All of it. Everything.

I fling open the door, only narrowly avoid four people who all look like different versions of Kate, people I have to assume are her family.

"Excuse me," I say, brushing past them.

The girl in the group smiles at me. "Jack," she asks, saying my name like she's said it before. Like it's been said to her plenty of times.

"Yeah," I say.

"Hi. I'm Kira. Kate's sister."

"Nice to meet you," I manage to get out, tears welling up in places they don't belong, namely my eyes. "I'm sorry, but I have to go."

I don't wait for her to ask me *where* or *why*.

I run down the hallway, back into the waiting room.

"Let's get out of here," I say to Franny and Jillian.

"Wait, what's happening?" Jillian asks.

"Jack," Franny calls after me.

But I'm already outside.

I'm already sucking cool night air.

I'm already wiping stupid tears from my stupid eyes and telling my stupid heart to pull it together. *She's not for us*, I tell my stupid heart. *Get over her already.*

But I can tell it doesn't believe me.

LIFE AS WE KNOW IT

Naturally, thereafter, life sucks.

Everything is gray now. And not shiny chrome gray. Dull, monochromatic gray. I am the very image of the moping, love-angsted teenager. I wear the same jeans for several days as an outward symbol of my pain.

But no one bats an eye when you wear the same denim for a week.

So in a more obvious outward symbol of my pain I wear the same shirt.

And not just a flannel or solid-color shirt—those would be too easy to chalk up. Yes, you wore two red flannel shirts on back-to-back days, but maybe today's flannel has a white hatch that's slightly different from yesterday's eggshell hatch? No, to proclaim your heartache you must go all in—which is why I'm wearing a shirt that is unmistakably unique.

A white T-shirt with a giant decal smack-dab in the middle.

A birthday present from Grandma Charlie two years ago—featuring a giant bottlenose dolphin, who's smiling for no apparent reason, and who's spouting an impressive amount of water from his blowhole, a spiraling tower of water atop which a grinning yellow rubber ducky floats.

You heard right. Creepy dolphin, blowhole, scary rubber ducky. All on the same shirt. *Boo-yah!*

Like I said, there's no question whether I'm wearing the same shirt.

You *know* I am.

Boy does that get everyone's attention.

And yes, in the way you'd expect. Molly Hendricks stands up in art class and says, "Jesus, Jack, please tell me you own like fifteen of the same shirt. Or that your parents are getting a divorce and you're staying at your dad's crappy apartment and he didn't have quarters for the unit washing machine."

"Wow, Molly, that was a very rude yet decently composed joke," Ms. Haggerty, the art teacher, concedes. After class Ms. Haggerty pulls me aside.

"Jack, is everything okay at home?"

"Home is fine." *But my heart is another thing entirely.*

Even the JV basketball team gets in on the fun. "*Rubber ducky, you're the one, you make my bath time lots of fun, rubber ducky, I'm awfully fond of you . . . rub a dub dub . . . ,*" they croon while we stand in line for Mystery Meat Monday in the cafeteria.

At least the jokes are funny. I even laugh, especially at the *Sesame Street* serenade, although only for a second, because laughter goes against the broken heart melodrama that I am in the middle of suffering. My friends, on the other hand, fail to see the humor.

"Jack, you smell terrible, man," Franny says on the drive home.

Jillian doesn't pull her punches either. "If you show up outside in that shirt tomorrow, Jack, you'll have to find another ride."

But then she frowns and reaches across the car seat to pinch my cheek. There are times when Jillian is downright motherly; these are the times when I can see into her crystal ball and know that she will be an amazing environmental activist/doctor/Supreme Court judge, yes, but she will still find time to bake the best oatmeal chocolate chip cookies for her kids, and she will help them with their homework, even when it's *new math*, and she'll be front and center at their terrible, terrible choir concerts. And most importantly, when the entire world's chorus is singing in perfect harmony about how much they suck, she will be there to always remind them of her love, of their immeasurable worth.

"She doesn't deserve you, man," she says in a near whisper, like the ad-lib at the end of a love song. I appreciate Jillian's efforts, but the truth is this: I don't deserve Kate. I blew it.

"Seriously, dude, if you want her so bad, just go after her already," Franny says.

The three of us are lounging in my basement, Jillian finishing her history paper and me watching Franny play our favorite online shooter, *Imperials*. "But no matter what, this whole bleeding-heart thing has to stop. It's killing our vibe. And you seriously stink." He declares this in the middle of an amazing kill streak, demolishing the record I'd set weeks back, which I take as an omen.

I don't bother to tell him that I shouldn't stink anymore, because for the past two days I've been back to my regularly showered program.

But Franny is right about the other part.

Just go after her, Jack.

Drowning in your sorrows is no way to live.

I'd rather drown in love, or at least in a vat of "strong like." You know, if I have to drown, and if I'm allowed to choose my drowning-liquid preferences.

Later, Jillian texts me her take:

> JILLIAN: Will you just listen to me, you moron?!
>
> ME: Fine. All ears.
>
> JILLIAN: For some idiotic reason you think you don't deserve her, Jack. But the thing that really bugs me—that makes me want to slap you up and down the street—is that for some even more idiotic reason you

think you don't deserve to be happy. But you do, Jack.

JILLIAN: As much as anyone.

ME: But as my friend, you have to say that, right?

JILLIAN: No, believe me. I definitely do not.

JILLIAN: And when have you ever known me to say something that I didn't mean??

ME: Very good point.

JILLIAN: I thought so.

ME: I don't know what to say.

JILLIAN: There's nothing to say.

JILLIAN: Just go after her, Jack.

JILLIAN: Seriously! Stop wasting time talking to me and go get her back already!

ME: Thank you thank you thank you

JILLIAN: Go!

* * *

Only my car is in the shop.

And Mom needs her car for work.

And the last bus to Whittier left twenty minutes ago.

And Jillian has the late shift at Pizza Pauper, and I don't want to take her car and leave her stranded.

But then Jillian makes magic happen—tells her boss she has a personal emergency—and then Jillian's ordering me into her passenger seat and Franny war-yells, "ROAD TRIP" and flings himself into the back seat and we're floating down the highway, pushing time and orange-barreled roadwork behind us. Franny, on the fly, makes an awesome *get your love back* playlist, and he alternates between letting the songs play and serenading us with his own songs, most of which feature a surprise rapper guest appearance, the rappers being Jillian and me, which sounds awful, but whose awfulness cannot be done proper justice without actually hearing our *flow*.

"Okay, we've gotta pull over," Franny says in the middle of my freestyle.

"What? Why?" Jillian asks.

"I have to pee. Just pull over."

"No way. Do you realize how dangerous it is to pull over on the highway? You're practically asking to be decapitated by a speeding minivan."

"Well, I've gotta go bad."

"It's only nine miles to a rest stop."

"Only nine," Franny says sarcastically.

"Just don't think about waterfalls," I suggest.

"Or swimming in the ocean," Jillian adds.

"I hate you both," Franny says.

Nine miles later we pull into some creepy gas station.

"Please make sure you wash your hands thoroughly before returning to my vehicle," Jillian shouts out the window after Franny.

And Franny pauses near the entryway to moon us, although he manages only a half-moon because an elderly black woman walks out of the gas station, and Franny, clearly flustered, can't pull his pants up fast enough. The lady smiles, whistles the best whistle ever, and Franny laughs, takes a deep bow.

Jillian and I scribble numbers onto napkins, and when Franny walks back out, we lean out of our windows and hold up our napkins—and my napkin says "7.5" and Jillian's says "perfect 10," because love is knowing the bad is there but choosing to appreciate the good.

And if there are better friends than these two, you keep them. I don't believe you.

When we pull off the main road and pass under the Whittier arch, we all whoop and cheer and Franny leans into the front seat and rubs my shoulders, like I'm a boxer about to enter the ring.

I fly out of the car before Jillian has fully parked and I slip in the security door right as a red-haired kid exits and then I'm knocking on Kate's door.

I hear movement inside.

Suddenly I wish I'd detoured at a bathroom, or at least caught a glimpse of myself in a mirror. What if I look horrible? What if there's beef jerky wedged between my incisors? Should I pose? I reach out to lean one arm along the doorframe, but I misjudge the distance and stumble into the door, the sound of my collapse echoing down the corridor.

I pick myself up from the ground and consider leaving, but it's too late. The door opens.

"Can I help you?" a very good-looking guy asks with a smile.

I strain to look over his athletic shoulders, but the room is empty behind him. He looks back into the room, presumably to see what it is I'm staring at, and then he shakes his head.

"Kate's not here. Are you one of her kids from the center?"

I have no idea what he's talking about. One of her kids. But then I remember, Kate volunteers at the rec center. "No," I say, wondering who this guy is. "I'm a friend of hers, actually."

He smiles. "Well, friend of Kate's, I hope you didn't come a long way. Kate is gone until next Monday. Some family situation."

"Is everyone okay?"

He shrugs. "Hopefully, right?" But he says so in a way that I read as he, too, is in the dark about what *family situation* means.

And then he says, "Well, I was just going to head out. Kate asked me to drop something in the mail for her." He holds up a slender envelope with my name on it in swirly dark print. Below my name is my address.

"Hey, that's me."

The guy looks down at the envelope. "You're Jack King? Of Elytown?"

"Yep," I say, making a move for my wallet and whipping out my license.

He looks surprised, startled even, but then his smile returns, brighter, toothier. "Nice to meet you, Jack. I'm Xander."

* * *

"You didn't punch the guy?" Franny asks as we angle the car back out of the Whittier D Parking Lot. "I would've sent him into the next decade, happily."

"Franny, sometimes you're such a caveman," Jillian

242

announces, making eye contact with him through her rearview mirror.

"Why thank you," Franny says. "Me love Jilly."

"He was actually a pretty nice guy. Very attractive, too."

"So not only did you *not* punch the guy, you also want to date him?"

"He gave me this," I say, holding up the envelope. "From Kate."

"Well, open it already," Jillian says.

"It's really thin," I say. "If it was a love letter, wouldn't it be thicker?"

Franny sucks his teeth. "It's not a college rejection letter, man. Just open it."

"I don't know if—"

But Franny rips the envelope from my hands. And I undo my seat belt, lunging into the back seat like a man who has twenty seconds to disarm a bomb, but Franny transforms himself into the world's strongest human ball, his ass pointed at me and his broad, arched back acting as a force field.

"Boys, behave! You're gonna cause an accident," Jillian says.

"At least read it out loud," I plead with Franny.

"No way," Franny says a moment later. "No goddamn way!"

"What?" I ask, feeling very delirious. "Is it that bad? Is it a restraining order? She never wants to see me again, right?"

But Franny puts his heavy hand onto my shoulder and slaps me with the other, not hard, but firm enough to make me shut up.

"Get a grip, man. Otherwise, I'm going to have to find someone else to use your ticket," Franny says.

"What ticket?"

"These tickets," Franny says, holding up three Mighty Moat concert tickets. "She actually came through. Even though she hates your guts, Jack, she still came through. Too bad you blew it with her, she's actually really freaking awesome."

"Wait," Jillian says, studying us through the rearview. "Mighty Moat? She really got us tickets?"

"Yeah, her sister Kira's dating the drummer. I told you guys that."

"Uh, pretty sure I would've remembered," Jillian says.

"Who cares? We're going to Detroit," Franny screams.

The two of them launch into a lengthy *Detroit, Detroit* chant.

"Was there anything else in the envelope?" I ask, reaching out for it.

"Uh, just this," Franny says, holding out a pink Post-it note. "Whatever it means."

> *Have fun, Jack.*
> *The Eternal Cap'n to Your Crunch,*
> *Kate.*

* * *

Kate's "note" is an entire nine words, but I can't stop thinking about it. Dissecting it. Overanalyzing her choice in line breaks, squeezing each syllable for its drop of meaning, like that small amount of juice you get from squeezing a hundred lemons.

There's one word I keep going back to, and it's not *fun*.

You got it: *Eternal*.

As in, she wants to be my permanent, all-time cereal-eating partner.

So maybe there's still hope?

Not to mention the tickets themselves are a sign, no?

A peace offering, maybe.

An olive branch, extended.

But then Xander pops into my brain—Greek-God-Adonis-stunt-double-looking, easy-smile-having Xander—and all those hopeful feelings jump ship. Because why was he *there*? Out of all the people in the world, of all the thousands of students on campus, why did she ask Xander to go to her room while she was away? Why did she put Xander up to mailing my letter? Why is she still talking to Xander at all?

And then my favorite word *eternal* melds into Xander, so that every time I hear the word, every time I even think about it, Xander's face follows.

* * *

Mighty Moat is phenomenal. When the crowd refuses to leave, the band comes back out and performs half a dozen encore songs, including my all-time fave "Home Again." We're second-row center and it's a dreamscape, a horizon of stretching neon and electric bodies, rivers of smoke winding through the stadium. Franny and Jillian and I belt out each song at the top of our lungs, until our voices are gone, and even then we don't stop singing.

Jillian gets someone to buy us beer and we toast and drink up and the arena is one giant buzz; if you stand still long enough, you feel the hum, a tremble shuddering down your spine, rattling your feet.

But the entire show, I can't stop looking for Kate.

I keep waiting for her to sneak up on me, tap my shoulder, throw her arms around my waist. Cover my eyes with her hands and whisper *guess who*. But it never happens. There are times when I see her, somewhere in the crowd, but then I look harder, or blink, and she's gone, dissolved into the frenzy, morphed into the body of some other girl, some other girl mimicking the way Kate holds her head, copycatting the way she tilts her hips.

Hours later, Jillian pulls the car into my driveway, and I say good night to my best friends, and then I'm strolling to my front door. But I stop when I see something move. And I'm mentally preparing myself for a showdown with the next-door neighbor's crazy-ass German shepherd, Corky. But it's not Corky. A shadow sits on the front steps, its silhouette reaching across my front lawn. And then the shadow stands, steps just inside the white glow of streetlight, and it's her.

"How was the concert?" she asks, sliding her hands into her jeans pockets.

And it's her.

"What concert?" I ask, reaching out for her. I say it to be funny, but mainly because seeing her makes me forget everything that's happened up till now.

And it's her.

"I'm sorry," she says softly. "I shouldn't have—"

"No," I say. "*I'm* sorry. I don't care if we can only be friends. I mean, I do care. But if that's what it has to be for you to stay in my life, then I'll take it. Your friendship is like—every time, I'll take it, Kate."

She touches my arm, glides her fingers down to my hand. "There's so much we need to talk about. So much I need to tell you."

"And we will. And I'll listen. How'd you get here?"

"I walked."

"But that's like forty miles," I exclaim.

She laughs. "I took the bus, silly."

"Just to see me?"

"There's nothing *just* about seeing you, Jack."

And I don't know if the thumping I feel between us is her heart or mine, but I'd put big money on mine. And it feels right. Like it's about to happen, like we're finally going to come together—and then we hear whooping and clapping.

Also known as Franny.

Evidently, my friends are still in the driveway.

"Come on, guys," I say. "A little privacy."

Jillian pokes her head out the window, making kissing noises.

"Jackieeeeeeeee," Franny's yelling. "The kid's back!"

"The boy's so smooth, y'all," Jillian sings.

"You're going to wake up my parents," I say, waving them off.

But try as I may, I can't help but smile.

I'd forgotten my face knew how to.

* * *

We're sitting in my car, parked in the lot outside Kate's dorm, the engine running although Kate normally hates that, emissions and fumes poking holes into the ozone—but it's a brutally cold late-spring night, so she makes an exception.

She looks as amazing as always, sporting a new haircut. It's funny because I thought her previously very long hair was perfect for her face, but now that she's cut it, I realize she just looks perfect. Dad jokes that Mom could wear sackcloth and still be radiant. Maybe that's what this is—me caught in Kate's glow. And I'm good with that. *Caught* is cool.

"What," she says.

"*What* what," I say back.

She laughs. Touches her nose. "Do I have something on my face?"

"Why would you say that?"

"Because you're staring and you haven't blinked in like eight minutes."

"I guess I was just thinking."

"About what?"

About you. About whatever forces brought us together. Just kiss her already, Jack, I think to myself. "I don't know. This and that."

"Must be far more interesting than what I have to say."

I sit up in my car seat. "No way! Why would you say that?"

"Because I asked you a question just now and you didn't even notice."

I was too busy trying to figure out how to make my long-awaited, highly anticipated *go on and kiss the girl* move. "I'm sorry, Kate. What did you ask me?"

Her laughter vanishes and she frowns. Which sucks because I hate the idea that she's sad because of me. "Never mind. Just forget it." And the next thing I know she's jumping out of the car and heading toward her dorm building.

I hop out of the car after her. "What's happening here?"

She pauses on the sidewalk, her back to me. And it feels like something important is happening here, something of magnitude, the air charged between us.

Kate whirls around. "You're a giant douchebag sometimes, Jack, that's what's happening."

I jam my hands into my pockets. "I feel like we've had this conversation before."

"Nope. I would've remembered feeling like you were a douche and then calling you one."

I shrug. "Oh. Probably just a conversation I had with myself then."

"Probably," she concedes.

I take a few steps closer. "I'm sorry about not listening to you, Kate. About whatever it is you wanted to tell me."

"You don't have to pretend like you don't know, Jack." Her eyes are dark and intense, like they could absorb an entire constellation.

"Oh," I say softly, spreading some loose gravel around with my shoe. "Right. So should we talk about it now?"

"No," she says flatly. "You killed the *I'm going to die from my genetically inherited illness* vibe back in there."

"I hate when I do that," I say.

She cracks a grin, just barely. "I have sickle cell."

"Oh," I say because I'm an idiot. And because, while I've heard of it, I don't really know what sickle cell is. "I'm sorry," I say. Because what else can you give?

"Listen, I don't want you to act different with me now, okay?"

"Why would I do that?"

"Because everyone who knows does."

"I'm not everyone. I'm just one someone," I tell her. "Besides, I only know one way to act with you, Kate."

She raises her eyebrows in that sexy, inquisitive way she does. "And how's that?"

"Like I never want to be apart from you."

And she hits me with a *you're impossibly corny* groan, then walks back to my car, climbing into the driver's seat.

"Well, are you coming?" she asks.

I hop in before she can change her mind. "Where are we going?"

"Where the night takes us," she says, backing the car out of the driveway, narrowly dodging a pair of trash cans and a scraggly cat. "Or to Moe's for a big, fat, juicy burger and fries. Whatever happens first."

"Hey," I say. "Just one thing."

"What?" she says, tapping the brake just in time to avoid a slew of mailboxes.

"This," I say, leaning over and taking her face in my hands. Our lips pressed together, well, it's explosive. Like if you could somehow kiss a burning asteroid right before it smacked into Earth. You know, without being vaporized.

Except when I kiss Kate, I also hear trumpets.

And we're swallowed in blinking white light.

As if the love gods are saying, *Hey, you two, it's about damn time.*

Or maybe it's because the light we're sitting at has turned green and the cars behind us are flashing their headlights and honking their horns to get us to move.

Nope. It was the kiss.

*   *   *

When we finally release each other from lip-lock captivity, Kate drives us to the gorges. Tonight the sky's so low, and we sit there, a canopy of stars exhaling above us, and Kate tells me what it's like knowing you're going to die.

"I'm dying, Jack. And not in the *we're all going to die eventually* way. It's not a question of *when*, just *how soon*." She shrugs. "Years, days, I don't know."

My brain feels like it's been tossed off a steep cliff.

"So, what is sickle cell, exactly?"

"My red blood cells don't stay neat red circles. Instead, they sickle, which means they're not as flexible as normal cells. And

251

sometimes if too many of them clump together, they can block oxygen from making it to the rest of my body. And, well, you go long enough without oxygen and . . ."

A beat where neither of us says a word, where I am hyper-aware of every sound coming from Kate's body—the flit of her eyelashes, her breathing, her heartbeat, her teeth grazing her bottom lip.

"There's no cure?" I ask, my voice cracking.

"They're starting to do these stem cell transplants, but you need a donor match. Thing is, less than ten percent of us have a match, so—"

She looks away. "So, for now, there's no surefire cure. For now, you manage. Try to avoid the crises, try to control the onset. But there's no secret formula, no magic potion. You eat painkillers like they're trail mix, which make your head feel like a helium balloon floating away from your body, and you wear oxygen twenty-four hours a day, and your best friends are your nurses because, if you're like me, with *recurring episodes*, you spend more time in a hospital bed than your actual bed. And you sit there, waiting, watching enough reruns to write a *Fresh Prince* dissertation, and you wait and wait to feel better, and sometimes you do in a few days, and sometimes it's weeks. Because you hurt all over." Her face turns back to me. "Your body's at war against itself so, no matter what, you always lose."

"Someone has to be working on something else, some-where."

252

"They are, but . . ." Her voice trails off.

"What?"

"Nothing."

"Tell me."

"There is this one doctor," she begins. "But—"

"But what?"

"He costs more than what my parents make in a year combined."

And I haven't the slightest idea what to say. But I wonder if I could (peacefully) rob a bank or somehow rig the lottery. Or—

"You know, the crazy thing is, at the hospital, they're always asking you to rate your pain, one to ten. Except no one's asking about the pain in here." Kate points to her head. "Or here." She moves her finger to her chest, left of center. "Because there's no rating for that. Numbers don't go high enough."

I wipe away her tears.

I pull her into me.

I feel her nose burrow into my shoulder.

I'm happy she's told me. I am.

But mostly, I'm afraid.

"Listen, Kate," I say. "If we're gonna do this thing, you and me, then you've gotta promise me one thing."

"What?"

"You've gotta stop running away."

"I think I can do that."

"It's just that, well, you're too fast for me."

She laughs.

I keep going. "I can barely keep up, I'm telling you. I mean, you really move."

"Jack?"

"Yeah?"

"You've gotta promise me something, too."

"What's that?"

She grins. "Promise me that you'll kiss me again within the next four seconds. One ... two ... three ..."

And I promise her. Over and over again.

*   *   *

I Google everything I can find on sickle cell when I get home.

I'm so focused I don't even hear Mom come into my room.

"Sickle cell, huh," she says. "What made you think of that?"

"Oh, uh, Kate, it turns out, she has it. I didn't realize how serious it is."

Mom pulls the chair out from my desk, sits down. "I'm a carrier."

"What?"

"Yeah," she says. "Before we had you, your dad and I got screened. Sickle cell is a big concern, especially in the black community."

"I just read that eighty percent of the people affected are black."

She nods. "Yeah, it's a lot. But honestly, I remember being surprised at how many people from other communities are affected, too. There are quite a few Spanish-speaking regions that are just as impacted. Plus, people in India, the Middle

254

East, and the Mediterranean. One of my best friends in college, Mira Hassan, she lived with sickle cell. She was this amazing sculptor, Jackie. She made this one piece, it was two people embracing, it must've been ten feet tall. She was brilliant. And then . . . I remember visiting her in the hospital, and like you, I had no idea what sickle cell even was. She was so sick. She had to drop out of school."

"What? Why?"

"They kept her admitted for almost two months."

"Two months?"

"She had good days and bad days. On her good days, I'd walk up and down the hall with her. She'd be clutching her IV pole, shuffling her feet. I remember thinking how unfair the whole thing was. Here was someone who was so full of life, normally so energetic, and then suddenly, without warning, she could barely hold up her head."

"What happened to her?"

Mom bites her lip and looks away. "They didn't know as much back then as they know now. You make sure you're there for Kate, okay, Jackie?"

"I will."

She stands up, squeezes my shoulder. "I'll bring your dinner up tonight. You just keep reading."

I nod. "Thanks, Mom."

I Google the doctor Kate mentioned.

Dr. Sowunmi.

I dial his office but it's already closed.

The next morning, I phone again. The appointment scheduler confirms that he's all booked up the rest of the month, do I want to make an appointment for next?

Yes, please, I tell her, hopeful that next month isn't too late.

And I'm not sure what I'm going to do.

If I can do anything.

But that has to be the reason I'm here.

To try.

HE'S GOT NO GAME

The Elytown Panthers come up short in the second playoff round again. Franny plays lights out again. The Coupon's in jail. Again.

"At least when he's locked up, I never have to wonder if he's gonna show or not," Franny says as we climb into Jillian's car. "That's messed up, right? Saying life is easier when my father is behind bars?"

"Baby, that's the least-messed-up thing about all this," Jillian says, taking his hand.

"For half a second, right after they announced the starting lineup, I look up and I swear I see him in the crowd. Like, I woulda put money on it. That somehow he'd found a way to make it. Like, he'd dug a tunnel with his prison spoon just to make it to my game." Franny fiddles with the window button. "But that's stupid. You'd think I'd know better by now, but . . ."

"This isn't on you, Franny," I say from the back seat.

"No?" Franny asks, staring out the window. "Then how come my shoulders feel so heavy?"

GRADUATES

Graduation is a collage of group hugs, no-filter-picture posing, and cap reapplication. Mainly because my cap is sized for a giant and swallows my head.

Meanwhile, Franny's cap sits crisply atop his freshly sculpted curl-fro, looking dope as always.

And Jillian, our super-worthy class valedictorian, looks hella cool *and* destroys us with her speech:

"Go forth and conquer," she concludes, throwing her hand into the air.

Our class goes crazy, hats and tassels leaping into the air.

Afterward, I find Kate.

"Hey," she says, smiling.

"Hey," I say back.

She leans in and I meet her lips and—

Have you ever kissed someone where every kiss feels as magical and as necessary as the very first?

Because I have.

Just now.

NOT THIS TIME

We're an hour into my parents' party and Kate's nowhere to be found.

Which at first isn't alarming. Kate is a lot of things, awesome things, but punctuality is not her bag. Even still, I would've expected her by now.

And I can't help but think the worst.

That last time, on this very day, she was lying in a hospital bed. *But this time, things are different*, I tell myself. *This time things are better.*

I text Kate: *Hey, where are you? Are you okay?*

But she doesn't reply.

I let thirty minutes pass before I try calling her. But it rings and rings.

And now it's safe to say I'm concerned.

A few of my parents' old friends try to make small talk. They ask me about college, if I know what I'm going to study, where I'm going to live, if I'm excited to finally spread my own wings.

I do my best to smile, to nod, to be hospitable.

But there's a feeling spinning in my gut. A dread I can't explain, or place. I call Kate again, but this time it goes straight to voice mail. None of my texts show *delivered*.

I know it's probably nothing. She's turned her phone off. Her battery's died. She's in an area with poor reception. She's driving. A hundred plausible explanations.

But none of them are strong enough to combat the feeling that something's happened. Something's seriously wrong. I consider leaving, hopping in the car, driving to her house.

Then I hear Franny's voice in the microphone.

"It's time, everyone. Jack King, please report to the stage."

The crowd turns stage-side.

I try Kate once more as I walk toward Jillian and Franny, their instruments already in hand. Voice mail.

"Kate, please, please call me as soon as you get this," I say.

I pick up the microphone, tap on it lightly. A shrill of feedback makes everyone turn in my direction.

"Mom and Dad, if you could come and take a seat up front please," I say, waving them over from across the lawn. I have note-cards inside my suit jacket, but I don't reach for them. "It's been thirty years since you two began your journey together. Thirty years since you said *yes* to each other, and *I do* to the future. And you've had your share of valleys, of disappointments, of, dare I say, regrets. And yet here you are. Together still. Happy still. And so here we are, friends and family, to share in this day all these years later. Some of us probably thought you wouldn't make it."

Laughs.

"I mean, not for as long as you have, anyway. But screw those people, right? Because they obviously don't know anything."

More laughs this time, a few whoops, some applause.

"Because in the end, it comes down to what you've told me ever since I could walk. Nothing good in life comes easy, but it's about deciding each day that you will stick with it. You choose to stay, to work hard, to love, and you keep choosing. You are the perfect example of two imperfect people making it work. I thank you for that. For everything. So, if you will, please join in raising your glasses for Nina and Abe, my mom and dad. Thirty years from now, we'll do this again, in this same place, at this same time, hopefully surrounded by these same people. Happy anniversary, Mom and Dad. And if you two wanna sneak away for a bit, the rest of us will pretend not to notice you're missing. But hurry back, okay, this is your party after all. Cheers."

"Cheers," everyone echoes.

Kate's still MIA. I clear my throat, push on. "Now, while we still have your undivided attention, my friends and I have been working really hard on something special for you. So, this is our gift. We hope you enjoy. And if you don't, just do what you've done my entire life whenever you haven't wanted to stifle my creativity: fake it."

Mom blows me a kiss, and Dad gives me a thumbs-up, both of them grinning. I nod to my fellow bandmates—my best friends in the world. They nod back. I pick up my horn, let it settle against my lips, and I blow.

And we play like we invented music.

We are in perfect sync.

We are in perfect measure.

Overhead, the clouds thin and vanish.

The small lanterns strung across the backyard fence glitter like fool's gold.

A hundred people sway.

And life, all in all, has been pretty good to me, yes.

But this moment is perfect. Spectacular.

Maybe it's the wine.

Maybe it's the trumpet in my hands, the cool brass against my fingertips.

Maybe it's the smiles stretched across my parents' faces. The joy that's welling up in their eyes, the happy tears they don't bother to wipe away.

Maybe it's just that kind of night.

Maybe it's goddamn everything.

Everything rolled into one.

And it's hard to imagine better.

That's when I get the call.

SECOND CHANCES
ARE STILL JUST CHANCE

There's nothing but open road as far as I can see.

This time I know what to do.

I won't leave Kate's side.

I'll be right there for as long as it takes, as long as she needs me.

I won't let her go.

The eternal Crunch to her Cap'n.

And then I hear a discombobulating shrill. Up ahead, red flashing lights falling horizontally against the dusk.

A goddamn train!

I swear I can't recall the last time I saw a train on these tracks. These tracks that divide our town into two even halves, like a jacket zipper.

I contemplate going around the wooden arms.

I inch the car forward so I can see just how far away the train is, how much time I have to make it across the tracks.

But then the train blares its *get the hell back* horn again and I have to throw the car in reverse, cursing my luck, cursing every locomotive ever built and every track they've ever railed along, cursing the whole misshapen world.

Because time, there's none to waste.

I lay into my horn like a wild man, because dammit, what else can I do?

The train takes its sweet-ass time.

And the faster I honk the slower it goes.

FML.

I bust an illegal U.

* * *

"I'm looking for Kate Edwards, please," I say to the elderly man at the front desk. And it's a different room number than last time. Ninth floor.

I wonder what that means.

If it means anything.

I can barely breathe by the time I make it to Kate's room.

I stare at her from the doorframe, my lungs too flat, too stuck together for decent air, like when you try to peel open a plastic grocery store bag. She doesn't look *deathly sick* exactly, whatever that means. But she's somehow paler, smaller.

"Hey you," she says, her face perking up.

"Fancy seeing you here," I say, stepping into the room,

closing the door behind me. "Nice outfit, too."

She looks down at her hospital gown. "This ol' thing?" She grins. "Just something I picked up on a business trip to Paris last autumn."

"*Très chic.*"

"*Je vous remercie.*"

"Impressive. You speak Français?"

"Um, no, I just exhausted all of the French I know." She scoots herself up in bed, fluffs her pillow to sit up taller. "I'm not contagious."

"What?"

"You're a million miles away."

"Oh," I say, realizing I'm still barely just inside the door. "Right. Sorry."

"It's okay. I guess I was just hoping for a kiss, or even just a—"

But I don't let her finish. I close the distance between my body and her bed in record time. Plant my lips against hers, and leave them there for what I hope to be forever.

But then she pulls away ever so slightly.

"What's wrong?" I ask.

"Um, I can't breathe."

I look back at the door, panic in my chest. "Should I get a nurse? A doctor?"

"Not that kind of *can't breathe*," she explains, smiling. "The good kind."

"Well, then," I say, leaning in for more. "In that case."

I pull up a chair. The nurse brings us cups of ice, and I open the nonalcoholic champagne I'd snagged as I was leaving the house. There wasn't time to pack up dinner, or even cake, but it's something.

We toast.

We talk.

We even laugh, swapping stories about horrific summer-camp romances and nightmare part-time jobs.

I couldn't tell you when I fall asleep.

Only that I awake to the sound of nurses barking orders to a pair of patient care techs, and that overhead, on the PA system, this announcement shakes the entire hospital:

Rapid response, room 918.

Rapid response, room 918.

Kate's room.

This room.

"Folks, we're going to have to ask you to step outside the room, please."

Which is when I see Kate's mom sitting up in the chair behind me.

"Wait, what's happening? Is she okay?" Kate's mom shouts, jumping to her feet.

"Please, we need you both to clear the room."

I don't feel my legs move, but somehow I'm out in the hallway peering into Kate's room through the blinds, her mom and I stepping aside for a handful of docs, and people with breathing masks dangling from their hands, and a machine on wheels that I think reads heart rhythms.

"Kate, we're still here," I call out to her as another doctor swings open her door. "Kate!"

But my voice shrinks into nothing.

A pissed-off headache erupts between my temples.

An ocean roars in my ears.

My eyes lose focus.

I reach out for the wall to steady myself, only I miss, or the wall's moved, or—

"Kate, I'm not going anywhere," I try to call out, but my words are hostages inside my head. "Kaaaaate!"

It's no use. A million blades corkscrew into my spine and my kneecaps melt into my ankles and my head detaches from my shoulders and—

the charm
of **THIRD**
times

THINGS HAPPEN IN THREES

And I wouldn't believe it if this wasn't the second time.

If I didn't hear the familiar thump of partygoers.

The living room TV blaring the same State basketball game.

V-Neck Sweater Guy (*check!*) chatting up Hello Kitty Neck Tat (*double check!*).

The red Solo cup in my hand.

The pissy, slanted stairs.

Jillian leaning against the kitchen counter, the queen in the middle of an undergraduate swarm, waving at me, smiling—

All that's missing is . . .

"Excuse me, man, but you're sort of damming up the steps."

. . . and there she is.

"Actually," I say, turning my head to look up at her. "I'm doing a mediocre job at best. I could really use some stair-damming backup, if you're up for it."

I don't know why I'm back here.

Why time has once again backed its behemoth ass up.

Chances are, I may never know. The why. Certainly not the how.

But I'm here now.

Probably because whatever it is I'm supposed to be doing, I have yet to do it.

At least not satisfactorily.

So if I have the chance to make even a few things better in this world—for my family, for my friends—

Then I'd be a fool not to try.

And Mama didn't raise no fool.

(She really didn't. All of my many and varied foolishnesses are mine alone.)

Anyway.

Enough talk, guys.

There's some crap with my name on it.

(Okay, that sounded better in my head. Let's try again.)

Enough talk, guys.

We got crap to fix.

(Better.)

THE PLAN TO (HOPEFULLY) SAVE KATE

I need money.

An astronomical amount of money.

Which is a problem in the sense that I don't have money.

But the thing is, the treatments that I've researched with the best shot at curing sickle cell cost a lot of the money that I do not have. And the doctor that Kate, and her parents, believe in most costs the most.

So, the plan is to get a lot of money, fast.

So, I'm going to . . . gamble.

I know, Jack + anything that requires "winning" typically = terrible idea.

Except if I do it just right, if it pans out the way I think it can, it won't really be gambling.

Which, when said out loud, does appear to be hinged to some significant caveats. Maybe I should . . .

Nope, nope, it's going to work. It has to work.

In the history of the world, when has gambling ever *not* worked out?

*   *   *

I take a monetary survey. Which basically involves surveying every nook and cranny for money that I may have overlooked.

This is a very expedient survey.

There is zero overlooked money.

In my checking, I have $204.89.

In my savings, I have $2,019.11. Between installing carpet the last two summers and accrued birthday money, I've done a decent job in maximizing my limited revenue streams.

Still, I barely have enough to cover the consultation visit, let alone the actual treatment. And if my calculations are correct, I need roughly one thousand times the amount of money I have. Maybe if I'm lucky only seven hundred fifty times.

Unfortunately, luck continues to ignore my friend requests.

Anyhow. Here's how I think it'll work: I bet on the games that I can remember. Fortunately for me, March Madness is two weeks away. And I'm confident that I remember the outcome of each game, and at least for a few of the games, how close they were.

Even more fortunate, Mandrake University isn't even expected to make the tourney, let alone win the entire thing.

Which means anyone who bets on them is a fool.

Or a time traveler from the future.

* * *

I approach my plan not without reservation.

What if the tournament outcomes change?

Except I keep thinking about the game that was on when I came back on the stairs—that unbelievable comeback by State that unfolded the same way as before.

Plus, the big things have stayed true.

Franny's dad getting early release.

Meeting Kate on the stairs.

The way I feel about her.

But the thing is, what's the same versus what's different doesn't matter all that much. I don't have any other ideas.

This is it.

So.

Go Mandrake Potbelly Pigs!

FRESH 2 DEATH

At the end of the weekend, as Jillian drives us off the Whittier campus, I'm not sure Kate will go to prom with me (spoiler alert: she does). But I am leaving with a massive desire to Kick Everyone's Ass.

You know, if *Everyone* equals Destiny.

"So, you disappear on me for the entire night, and now you're over there smiling like the damn Cheshire cat. What's up?"

"Nothing," I say. "But let me just say, Whittier rocks."

"*Whittier rocks*, huh? What, are you suddenly on their admissions board? What's that in your hand?" she says, snatching the slip of paper before I can answer. She unfolds the paper and laughs. "Whose info is this?"

I shrug.

"You dog, you," Jillian says, barking loudly. The car windows are down, and the passenger of the car beside us stares over. "I should've known you were up to no good."

"We had a connection," I confess.

"That's what I'm afraid of. You *connecting*. I hope you used protection, man."

"What," I say. "No, I don't mean like that."

Jillian laughs. "Duh, I'm joking with you, Jack. Relax."

"What do you mean, *duh*? You're saying I can't get laid?"

She stops laughing. "You're extremely lay-able. You just don't know it yet. But when you finally figure it out, look out, world."

"Now you're just being cruel."

She shakes her head. "Jack, I love you. But for someone so smart, you're really stupid sometimes."

Before I can ask her what she means she blares the radio and sings like it's the end of the movie and Ursula just gave her her voice back.

I turn the radio back down. "Hey, J?"

"Yeah?"

"How are you?"

"What do you mean, how am I?"

"Like with your dad leaving? How are you doing with that?"

She shrugs. "I mean, he'll probably be back. He's just going through . . . I don't know, like a midlife thing."

"Yeah."

"I think it's just something about getting older and feeling like you haven't done all the things you dreamed of when you were young. Like, you had all these goals, and all these mile markers, and then you realize the only thing that's happening is time is slipping by and you've barely cracked your list."

"But how are *you* doing?"

She smiles at me, a forced grin. "I'm doing, man. I'm doing."

"If you ever wanna talk," I say.

"I know where to find you, Jack."

"Good."

"I worry more about my mom than me. She's so sad."

"I can imagine."

"But at least she's painting again, so there's that."

"You're always worried about everyone but yourself. And I love that about you, how giving you are. But you need to take for yourself, too. Whatever you need, I'm here for you."

"I know," she says, guiding the car off the highway. "Thanks," she says, turning the music back up.

And then we're in my driveway. I hop out and Jillian waves, angles the car back toward the street. But I flag her down.

She pops the car back into park. "What'd you forget?"

"Hey, uh, so my parents had this weird thing happen with their electric bill, where Ely Power was trying to say they hadn't paid and were threatening to turn our lights off."

"What?"

Yeah, *what*, Jack? Is this the best you can do? "So, yeah, just, uh, when you go home, make sure your bill is okay, 'cause I wouldn't want that to happen to you and your mom, okay?"

She laughs.

"I'm serious, J. Don't forget."

She laughs again. "Uh, okay, Jack. Thanks for the hot tip."

And then she's zooming down the street and I'm dropping my bags inside the foyer, my parents swarming me with questions. I'm up in my bedroom when I get Franny's text.

FRANNY: I heard you got some ass.

ME: Yes . . . if ass is code for a phone number.

FRANNY: Hey, you gotta start somewhere, bro.

It's definitely a start. A fresh one.

FRANNY: So, I have the craziest news ever . . .

And I have a pretty decent guess what it is, but I text:

ME: They found a cure for your back hair?!

FRANNY: You're stupid af

ME: I know

ME: So you going to tell me or keep me in suspect

ME: *Suspense

FRANNY: *drumrolls*

FRANNY: THE COUPON GETS OUT END OF THE WEEK!

* * *

My birthday is in the first week of September, two weeks after school usually starts, which meant I didn't get to go to kindergarten until I was nearly seven. Mom tried to stem the disappointment of waiting another entire year to start school by telling me that I'd have the distinct advantage of experiencing everything so much earlier than my fellow classmates. *Just think, Jack*, she'd reasoned, *you'll get your license first, you'll get to vote first, and one day you'll get to drink first—legally of course.*

Understandably, she failed to mention another distinct advantage. It probably never even crossed her mind. I get to gamble first, too.

*　*　*

News flash: the internet is awesome.

I post pics of my collectibles and within an hour I make $200. By the end of the day I'm up to $345. And by the weekend I've hit $800. But a quick sweep of the attic confirms my worst fear: I've run out of things to sell.

Or have I?

The girl who answers my ad is a sophomore at State.

"So, what are you going to do with her?" I email her back.

She replies, mainly to get her around campus and the occasional weekend visit back home.

"So, why are you selling her?" she asks, when she comes to pick her up.

"Oh," I say, feeling the slightest trepidation in telling her the truth. "For my girlfriend."

"That's cool."

"Well," I confess, "she's not quite my girlfriend yet."

She smiles as I hand over the keys. "Well, she sounds lucky, Jack."

I wave goodbye as she backs the car out, and I keep waving until the blue sedan turns right into its next life. How I'll explain my latest sale to my parents is a worry for another time.

The important thing is I have a real chance.

Now all I need is a bookie willing to accept a sizable bet from an eighteen-year-old high school senior. The bad news is I know exactly zero bookies.

The good news: I know a guy who may know a guy.

282

WE DON'T ACCEPT COUPONS AT THIS ESTABLISHMENT

I'm rambling while simultaneously uncasing my trumpet.

"... you think we should get stickers made? For JoyToy? I'm thinking maybe we should have some sorta merch, you know, just in case ..."

We'd planned on putting in a lot of work today, but then a few minutes ago Jillian took a phone call, disappearing inside her house.

"... I mean, we probably won't sell a ..."

"So, The Coupon is going to crash elsewhere for a while," Franny interjects.

I set down my horn. "Did you talk to Abuela?"

"I had decided not to. That if she wanted him around, it's her house, you know. But now it's a moot point because once

283

again he's choosing to be somewhere where I'm not."

"Maybe he thinks he's doing what you want."

"When has The Coupon ever done anything for anyone other than himself?"

"Okay. Well, maybe he just wants to take things slow."

"He's a fucking glacier already. I don't know why I'm surprised, right. I mean, this is his MO." Franny shrugs. "At least the deadbeat's consistent."

"Maybe you should talk to him."

"And say what?"

"I don't know. How you feel."

"I didn't want to see him anyway. Who needs him? He needs me, if anything. I've been doing hella good without him, why would I want him in my life now?" Franny lowers his voice. "Jack, am I *that* bad?"

"What are you talking about?"

Franny bites his lip, like he wishes he hadn't said anything, like he doesn't want to say more, but then—"I know I'm not the smartest kid alive, or, I don't know, the strongest, or whatever. But no one could deny I'm handsome, right?" Franny says, striking a pose like he's taking a picture on some runway, then flashing me a patented *Franny doesn't give a damn* smile. Only this smile is dead on arrival, because in this moment, not even happy-go-lucky Franny can disguise the pain on his face.

"Franny," I say.

But Franny keeps going. "I just don't get it. I mean, if you were my dad, how much of a disappointment would I be to you? Like, for real, man?"

"What the heck are you even talking about? You wouldn't be. I'd be proud of you. I am proud of you."

"No, there must be something wrong with me."

"There's nothing wrong with you, Franny."

His voice jumps. "Don't lie, man. You can tell me. You'd know. You're supposed to be my boy, right?"

"I *am* your boy."

"So, tell me the truth. What's so wrong with me that my dad would go out of his way to not be around me? How come my dad doesn't want me, man? Why aren't I good enough? How come he doesn't love me back?"

I'm answerless.

I put my arm around his neck. "If he doesn't see how awesome you are, it's *his* loss, Franny. Because it's easy to see. It's so freaking easy to anyone who bothers to look. Hell, you don't even have to look *long*. You can just *glance* at you and tell."

"Whoa, whoa, what are you guys doing out here," Jillian says, teasing-voice, as she steps through the sliding door onto the back patio. "Am I interrupting some man-love or . . ." She stops when she sees our faces, our teary-eyed expressions.

"Oh, damn," she says. "What's wrong?"

Not waiting for an answer, she wraps her arms around both of us. We lock arms, faces touching, not saying anything more. Not having to.

* * *

Later that night at my house, while Franny's upstairs taking a shower, I fill in my parents on the latest episode of Franny's Dad Sucks. Dad swears under his breath, and Mom has tears in her eyes; they've seen this show before. Franny's Dad Sucks only has one episode and it runs on loop.

When we sit down to eat, I can tell my parents want to slide their chairs away from the table and throw their arms around Franny, but they manage to hold off until after our salads. Then Mom is reaching across the table, squeezing Franny's hand, and Franny looks at me and he knows I spilled the beans. But he doesn't look angry. He flashes a fake grin.

"No pity parties, guys," he says, his voice cracking.

Dad stands and walks around the table, pats Franny on his shoulders, and says, "You are an incredible young man. No one gets to decide your worth except you. And you are worth anything and everything, Francisco."

I'm wondering if I did the right thing here, if Franny is hating this, the attention, the mush factor, but then he swivels around in his chair and lunges his head into my dad's stomach and he's sobbing.

"It's okay," my dad says, squeezing Franny's shoulder. "You're a great kid."

"You are," Mom says, walking over, her hand gripping Franny's other shoulder. "We love you. We'll *never* not love you. Right, Jack?"

And I nod although Franny's back is to me.

"Nothing is more right," I say.

So. I have my reservations about the whole bookie thing.

Fortunately for me, I do know a guy who knows a gal who knows a guy—

Which basically comes down to me asking Franny's dad for help. I know, I know—sort of a dick move, right? While I'd understand Franny feeling betrayed if he found out I'd gone behind his back and met with his enemy, I'm hoping that if he knew the stakes he'd offer his support.

Franny's dad laughs when I pitch him my idea. "Let me get this straight, man," he says, scratching his chin like his brain's doing serious heavy lifting, "you want me to put up a few thousand dollars on your behalf with a bookie who will put a cap in both of our asses if you don't pay up? And the money you're putting up is on a team that hasn't made the NCAA tourney since, like, I was a raggedy kid in diapers? AND you wanna bet that these motherfuckers are gonna win it all? Like the whole shebang? Crown those never-won-nothing-in-their-lives cats king?"

I'll be honest, hearing him spell it out like this is not exactly inspirational, but I nod just the same.

"And your parents don't know nothing about this, right?"

"No," I confirm.

"Franny neither?"

"Also no."

"So, when this *plan* goes south—and I'm not saying if, but *when*—I'm the one who's gonna look like First Lieutenant Asshole, huh?"

I repeat my offer of 10 percent of the winnings, but he shakes his head.

"No, no, man," he says. "Your money, your wager. Besides, not to shit on your dreams, son, but were I you, I wouldn't be counting my chips just yet."

"So, you'll do it? You'll make the bet for me?"

"After all you've done for my kid, I hardly see how I can deny you this, stupid as it is. Just don't come crying and pissing when you're broke as shit, okay? Won't be able to do nothing for you just 'cause you're a kid."

"Thank you, thank you, thank you," I repeat.

But Franny's dad just mutters, "I must have a goddamn death wish."

* * *

Or maybe I'm the one with the death wish.

Going behind Franny's back.

Playing nice with The Coupon.

And there's this nagging feeling that I can't ignore.

Namely, what good is a second (or third) chance if I screw everything up?

Not just with Kate.

But with Franny. What if my deal with Franny's dad changes the entire trajectory of their lives? What if Franny and The Coupon would've ended up happily ever after but now because of me they end up wishing the other person never existed?

And what about Jillian? She'd be stuck in the middle— maybe she'd feel like she had to choose a side. What if she chooses the side opposite of me? What if I lose her forever?

Could I live with all of that?

Am I prepared to say goodbye to all the people who mean something, to maybe save Kate?

*   *   *

While I wait for Kate to email back, I kill time watching the Sports Network debate which teams are guaranteed tournament locks and which teams are riding the bubble. The four sportscasters are split, with the most vocal of the quartet unimpressed by Mandrake's strength of schedule.

I just don't see it, he contends, flailing his arms. *Have they played well, yes, they have. They've done what they've needed to do to have a shot at the tournament. But frankly, so have a half dozen other teams with better résumés.*

So.

Looks like I have until Selection Sunday, two days from now, to know if my investment in the Pigs is a complete butcher job—I'm sorry—but seriously, I'm concerned. But I haven't devised another way to get Kate the help she needs/deserves. And this plan, as evidenced by the above analysis, is/was a long shot from the beginning.

So, I ask you, what good is being from the future if you don't get a leg up on the past?

*   *   *

"Hey, Jackie, what's the word, baby?"

There's something about Franny's dad that makes me think he was a god in the 1970s.

"Um, just making sure everything is cool with . . . uh . . . our . . . agreement."

"Oh, the bet? Yeah, it's all good, man."

"Oh, okay. Good."

"That all you wanted?"

"Actually—"

"Yeah, let me get a number six combo but no lettuce and no pickle but with extra mayo, but on the side. And throw in one of those hash browns, too."

"Uh, are you there?"

"Hold on, Jackie . . . what you mean you done serving hash? I thought y'all served it all day. I have my mouth set for some . . . fine. Whatever. I'll take a cherry pie. . . . Sorry, Jack. You was saying?"

"It's about Franny. Francisco."

"What about him?"

"He wants to see you."

"Ha. Funny way of showing it."

"What do you mean?"

"He won't answer my calls or my texts. The other day he walked out on me before I could get out one word."

I can't believe what I'm hearing. Because isn't it the other way around? The Coupon dodging Franny?

"Well, I'm pretty sure he wants . . . I think he's happy you're . . . you know . . . back."

"Hmm."

"I think were you to try again, like really put some effort

into it, he'd see it differently."

"Throw in some extra hot sauce packets, too. And a spork."

"Hello?"

"I heard you, Jack. I'll think on it."

SELECTION SUNDAY

When Sunday comes, I'm too nervous to be alone, so I invite Franny and Jillian over to watch the March Madness selection committee reveal the chosen teams.

Franny laughs at my invitation. "Since when are you Mr. Basketball?"

I pretend to not understand what he means. "I've always liked basketball."

"Name the one NBA team *not* located in the United States," he challenges me.

I shrug. "Sorry, I'm more into the college game."

"Fine." He crosses his arms. "Name three college conferences then."

"Easy! The Big Ten, the Southwestern. No, wait, no, the Southeastern, plus, uh, the Big Southern."

Franny cracks up. If I don't end this charade, he may rupture something.

"Whatever," I say. "I don't have to prove my love for the game to you."

"Right, man," he says. "You have *nothing* to prove."

I know Mom is a lock for All Things Sports, but I'm surprised when Dad joins us in the basement, too. My surprise mostly disappears when he brings refreshments with him, popcorn and soda and a bag of cookies. Mom has Dad watching his middle-aged figure closely these days, so any opportunity for Dad to cheat on his spouse-sponsored diet is seized with gusto.

"Hmmmm," Dad says, smacking his lips. "Feels like something's missing, doesn't it? I know! Anyone want pizza? I just happen to know Pizza Czar has a specialty supreme on sale right now."

"I've already eaten, but thanks, Mr. King," Jillian says.

"You know I'm always game for vittles," Franny says, springing to life on the edge of the sofa.

"Great, that makes two of us," Dad says. "Jack, looks like you're the tiebreaker, my favorite son on this earth. Heck, you're tied for my favorite person period." He looks over at Mom. "Right there with your mother, of course."

Mom is already resigned to the fact that no one can change Dad, we can only hope to contain him. She tosses her hands up. "Whatever you guys want to do, but at least half of it has to be veggie."

"How about half of a half," Dad pitches. Mom's eyebrows

rise. He's pushing his luck. "No, no, you're right, babe. We can have fun *and* be healthy, too."

Dad slips upstairs to order the food as the program starts.

My stomach is nauseous.

And my heart, although I'm sitting on the floor doing absolutely nothing physically demanding, is pumping hard enough to power a triathlon.

I have no idea how real gamblers cope.

We suffer through an agonizing thirty minutes of sports talk before the reveal starts.

. . . And Mandrake makes the cut, the committee rewarding their conference tournament runner-up finish with a fifteenth seed slotting . . .

I explode into the air in a manic flurry of fist-pumping and chest-bumping, although the chest-bumping is just me bumping my chest against random inanimate things, such as the wall or the basement support beam or the arm of the sofa, because no one else is willing to chest-bump me, probably because they aren't willing to risk a concussion.

But I can't help it.

Because maybe this thing will work after all.

THE GOOD DOCTOR

"I only took this meeting because I received your letters, and your emails, and your repeated phone calls to the office and to the lab, and I must admit, curiosity won out."

"My parents preach perseverance."

"You're certainly younger than I imagined."

"I intend to make a sizable contribution," I interject for no reason other than I'm uncertain what to say.

Dr. Sowunmi peers at me over the tops of his glasses. "How old are you? Nineteen? Twenty maybe?"

"I'm eighteen. Not that it should matter, Doctor. I mean, you're only, what, thirty-two, thirty-three? When you decided you were going to cure sickle cell, how did you feel when people made assumptions purely based on your age?"

Dr. Sowunmi pushes his glasses up his nose, but says nothing.

"Look," I continue. "I'm here because I believe in you. In your research. In your medicine. And because I'm in love."

"Ah." The doctor clears his throat, leans back in his beat-up leather chair. He puts his hands to his mouth in a way that reminds me of someone smoking a pipe, except he doesn't have a pipe, and I doubt he smokes. "It's best not to mix medicine with emotion."

"From what I understand, you have family members who've battled with sickle cell, Doctor . . ."

"Yes." He nods. "Which is why I know it's not wise to mix the two. The only way for it to end, Jack, is badly."

"But Doctor, aren't both things tied to the heart?"

Dr. Sowunmi smiles, and it's like I can see his guard go down, his face relax into what it probably looks like when he's eating his favorite bowl of cereal or rewatching his favorite movie. "How old are you again?"

"Eighteen," I repeat, smiling back. "And did I mention I have money?"

"I can't promise you anything. We're still in the early clinical stages."

"I understand."

"And I'd like to meet with the patient first. To evaluate their current health, their labs. To discuss with her or him, were we to proceed, what our course of treatment would involve."

"Of course, Doctor," I say, standing up to shake his hand. "Thank you so much. Thank you so so so much."

"I can't promise anything," he repeats, smile gone.

"Right," I confirm. "No promises."

On the way out the doctor's office, my cell phone rings and I imagine it's Kate and I think, *Wow, perfect timing.* But it's not her.

"Hey, man, did you forget?" Franny asks, his voice borderline panicked. "Please, tell me you didn't forget and that you're on your way."

"I didn't forget," I assure him, although I did lose track of time. "I'll be there."

"When?"

"Soon."

"But *soon* soon, right? Like you're already on your way?"

"Yes, *soon* soon," I say.

"Tell me everything's going to be okay, Jack."

"Franny," I say with all of the hope and faith that I can muster. "Everything is going to be okay."

I really want to believe it will.

WAIT. WHAT?!

Franny's nerves are more jumbled than the tangle of cords behind our television. But he's doing his best to hide it.

Under normal circumstances, Franny's the epitome of clutch. Take, for instance, his last regular season must-win road game: he was cool, calm, collected on his way to a team-high twenty-four points, sinking the go-ahead free throw with time expired to ice the victory and advance to the playoffs.

But this current Franny isn't all smiles and laughs and joke after joke after joke.

On the way home from school yesterday, he insisted on stopping to get a haircut. Made Jillian pull over in the middle of horn-honking traffic so he could double back up the street and catch a bus (even though Jillian said it was no problem to drive him) over to his cousin's house, who moonlights as a barber.

Crazy thing is, Franny hasn't cut his hair in, like—forever. A while back we started calling him the *Puerto Rican Questlove*. But as of yesterday afternoon his scalp is low and clean, sparkling, too, like he's an executive preparing to lead an important board meeting. *No big deal*, he said when he opened the door to his house, my mouth falling open as I pointed to his dome. *It was just time, you know*, he said in a way that I knew meant he didn't want to keep talking about it.

Even now, he's pacing the floor, pretending like he's exercising, as if all the back-and-forth down the narrow hallway is part of his big-game preparation.

"Franny, it's going to be okay, man," I say not for the first time today.

"Why wouldn't it be?" He walks into the kitchen and I don't move from my spot on the living room sofa. "Gotta make sure these chops don't burn or Abuela will beat my ass."

"*I'll* beat your ass if they burn," I shout.

"Right!" He laughs.

The front door locks turn and Franny emerges from the kitchen, eyes wide. "Wait, what do I do?" he says to me, to the room, to no one. "What do I do?"

"You don't have to do anything, Franny," I say. "This is on him. Not you."

We stand there, waiting for the door to open, for the earth to split.

"Francisco," Franny's dad says. His voice is rich, like it's wrapped in a husk. The Coupon steps inside the threshold,

Abuela standing quietly beside him. Franny doesn't move. I don't know if he's frozen in place or if it's by choice. But then his dad is rushing forward, wrapping his arms around Franny until Franny's all but disappeared in the man's broad chest and arms. The Coupon makes Franny, tall and muscular in his own right, seem small, like a marionette version of himself.

"You probably thought you'd never see me again, huh?"

Franny shrugs at the question, sheds the man's arms from his shoulders. "Never thought about it, really."

He examines Franny's eyes, the way my dad looks at me when he's about to make some important point and he wants to make sure I'm listening. "Well, I'm back now, son. For good this time."

Franny laughs. "What, you want some sort of medal in advance?" He turns to Abuela, kisses her on the cheek. "Food's ready." He walks back into the kitchen.

Franny's dad looks at me, like he's just noticed me standing there, his face morphed into surprise, or maybe embarrassment. He forces a smile and in his face I see Franny's—Franny's light-brown lips and slim nose, the way Franny's eyes seem to glow at the edges, the same oval chin.

I wonder if he's going to give me away to Franny. If this is the part where Franny finds out I went behind his back and have been conducting business with his dad.

"No way this is my man Jack. Last time I saw you you were about yea high, and now just look at you." He extends his hand, his fingers chapped, like he wields an ax for a living. "My man

300

Jack. Long time, brother."

"Long time," I parrot. "So, how was it?" I ask, because I'm stupid.

"What? You mean the joint? Pretty awful, man. Do yourself a favor. Never get locked up."

"Okay." I stuff my hands in my pockets. "I'll try not to."

"You still doing the poetry thing?"

"Not really. I'm more into prose these days."

"*Prose*. Right on," he says.

A pan clatters in the kitchen. And then another.

Abuela points down the hall. "Baby, you go clean up. I washed some clothes, laid them out on your bed. Jack and I are gonna get in this kitchen before your son burns down my house."

"Yes, Mama," he says, stooping down to kiss her on her forehead. "For the last two weeks I've fantasized about your pork chops. You don't know the hurting I'm about to put down." He lets loose a low whistle and strolls down the hall.

*　*　*

Franny's dad wasn't exaggerating. He devours pork chop after pork chop, to the delight of Abuela, who feels infinite joy when people like her food. Meanwhile, Franny barely touches his plate.

"Francisco, you see that State game the other day? That comeback was wild, right? I mean, those cats were all the way in the grave, and then lightning came down from the sky and they couldn't miss."

"I didn't see it," Franny says. Which is a lie. He couldn't stop talking about that game.

"Well, they'll probably replay it on ESPN Classic, that's how good it was," Franny's dad says, leaning back in his chair, his face electric. "I put some money on that game *at halftime*. When they were *down* by twenty points. Don't ask me how I knew, but I just had this feeling that game wasn't over. Like, deep in my gut, you know." He squeezes his stomach, as if to emphasize just how deep.

"Francisco, you know I don't approve of gambling," Abuela pipes up.

"Aww, Mama, it was twenty dollars. It was nothing."

"Still," she says. "Twenty dollars is not nothing."

Franny's dad smiles big. "When you're locked up, you do whatever you can to help pass the time. A little gambling keeps things interesting is all."

"Well, you're out now. And that's all behind you," Abuela says firmly.

"Yes, Mama." Franny's dad leans over, kisses his mom on her cheek. "So, Mama told me you guys are getting ready for prom."

Franny doesn't bother looking up, but the silence is too much, so I mumble a feeble "Yeah."

"I met your mom at prom, Francisco, I tell you that? She went to the high school across town and she came with this other guy. I had a date, too. But soon as I saw her . . ." He pauses, a smile spreading on his lips, stares off like he can see the memory projected on the wall. "Soon as I saw her I knew. I knew.

302

What about you, man? You got somebody special you taking?"

Franny doesn't bite. "Come on, man."

"C'mon on what," his dad says. "Where we going?"

"You don't gotta pretend to be interested."

"I'm not pretending anything."

"Let's just eat, yeah?"

"You gotta come to one of Francisco's games. He's taking them to the playoffs. They're gonna win, too," Abuela interjects. "People always ask Francisco where he got his ball-playing skills from. What they don't know is I was a pretty good dancer in my day. Good dancing and good ball-playing, they're the same."

I clap my agreement, but Franny isn't in a charitable mood.

The Coupon chuckles. "You forget I used to ball pretty hard, too. Ball is in our blood, ain't no surprise that—"

Franny pushes his chair hard away from the table, its feet scraping the linoleum. "Can I be excused, please?"

"But I have pie in the fridge. Made it this morning. Ice cream, too."

"Lost my appetite."

She clicks her tongue. "Francisco, your father just got here. You should—"

"Mama," Franny's dad interrupts. "The boy says he's not hungry, no sense in making him stick around." He winks at Franny but Franny looks away.

"Fine." Abuela sighs. "But your homework better be done right, Francisco. Check and double-check."

Franny squeezes her hand. "Triple-check," he promises, clearing his plate. He gives me a look like, *let's go*. But it feels rude to bail.

"Thanks for dinner, Abuela. It was delicious, as usual."

She pinches my cheek. "You're always welcome here, Jack. You're family."

*   *   *

The rest of the evening Franny's in one of his *I'd rather not talk* moods. Which I try to respect, although there's so much to talk about. Down the hall, his father's voice booms and Abuela laughs in a way I can't ever remember her laughing, like her laughter had been locked away for years. It makes me happy to hear her happy. But the more she bellows the sharper Franny's silence gets.

"We should stay at your house tonight," he says.

"That's cool with me. Whatever you want to do."

"It's what I want to do."

"Okay," I reply, trying to remove any edge from my voice. Were my voice a color it would be white, and were it an object it would be a flag. *The most important thing you can do for Franny*, Mom said earlier this morning, *is just be there, Jack. You two don't know it yet, but one day that'll be the only thing that matters.* So, that's what I've made up my mind to do. Be there. Be here.

"Okay," he repeats.

Franny's bedroom is a hodgepodge of familiar comforts. The beanbag chair I'm slouched in is the same one I've slouched in for nearly a decade. Franny still has posters of bands taped up that he doesn't listen to anymore. His bookshelf is sagging with heaps of comics still in their slipcovers; the latest *Black Panther* sits atop. On his desk, where he's sitting now, is what we've started calling The Stack. The Stack is as precarious as the last few moves in Jenga. A steadily growing pile of scholarship offers to schools all over the country; letters and packets boasting about each school's advantages, falling over themselves to recruit one of the nation's top athletes. You can feel The Stack's desperation. *Look at me, yoo-hoo, please, please, pick me!*

It's odd, though. So many schools ready to hand him the keys to their kingdom, but he wants to be here, forty miles away, with us—Jillian and me. That State is not even one of the top ten schools recruiting him, and yet he's willing to go there because he doesn't want to be away from Jillian, from me. Of course, he'd never say that, but it's understood. Jillian and I have both tried to push him to do what's right for him, but he won't even entertain a different path. *I know what's best for me, man. Trust.*

Franny sees me eyeing The Stack and he smiles. His first grin tonight.

"How many more since last week?"

"Half a dozen maybe," he says. "But still no word from our beloved Whittier."

I shrug. "If they're too stupid to accept you, then maybe I shouldn't go either."

"You're crazy, son," he says, grinning harder. "I tell you that today? How crazy you are? First of all, your moms would go upside your head if you turned down Whittier. And then she'd probably come after me next."

"Probably," I concede, laughing.

"Uh-uh, no probably about it. True story."

"I'm saying, though. Who wouldn't want Francisco Hogan at their school? Who wouldn't want Francisco Hogan, period?"

"I tell you this much, man." Franny wags his head, stares in the direction of the kitchen, of the rolling laughter, of the best peach cobbler known to man. "Either you want me or you don't. But I don't want anything that doesn't want me back."

*   *   *

JILLIAN: Hey, how did it go? He's not answering my texts or calls.

ME: Not great. He's in quiet mode.

JILLIAN: Damn. Too late for me to come over?

ME: Never.

*   *   *

Twenty minutes later, Jillian descends the basement steps, her long legs taking the stairs two at a time. We always joke that she's 90 percent legs, 8 percent head and shoulders, and only 2 percent torso.

"Hey, boys," she says.

Franny looks at her, then at me. "You two texting behind my back?"

Jillian walks over, kisses the top of Franny's head. He looks up at her, his big brown eyes ready for whatever she has to give. She cups his face.

"Baby," she whispers. She sits on the sofa beside him, pulls his head into her lap. He doesn't resist. "Baby," she repeats.

And I can't tell you what we watch, only that we sit there for hours, and that at one point I increase the volume because there's something inside of me, the part that loves these two people, that knows Franny doesn't want me to hear his sobs.

MIGHTY MAGICAL

Mighty Moat is even better the second time.

And it's no secret why. Kate. Even Jillian and Franny seem to have a better time.

"Is it just me, or do you feel like the band is playing just to us right now?" Franny shouts at one point.

"It's not just you," I shout back.

After the show, Kate takes me by the hand, leads our foursome backstage, and it's like she knows everybody, everyone stops doing whatever to wave or say *what's up*, but honestly, I'm pretty sure she doesn't know any of these people; that's just her, she has that *take notice* thing going on and you can't help but to, well, *take notice*.

We stop at a red door covered in black Magic Marker stick-figure people. Kate knocks and someone yells *come on in*, and we go right in. And it's freaking *Mighty Moat*! In their freaking grungy-T-shirt-wearing flesh!

"Katieeeeee," sings the guitarist. "Get your ass in here."

Franny and Jillian look at me in equal disbelief. "This is real, right?" Franny asks. "This is happening?"

"Hey, you guys want champagne?" the lead singer yells, as a cork pops and sails across the room. And then another cork fires. And another. And soon the band's spraying everyone in a champagne shower. And then Franny shouts a war cry, covers his eyes, and dives into the fray.

"What are we waiting for?" I say to Jillian.

But she's already leaping in, her hair damp with celebration.

I take Kate's hands and we dive into the middle, laughing.

"This is what it's all about, *this* is what it's all about," Franny says, dancing in a circle around us.

"We gotta get a pic before we go," Kate tells the guitarist.

"Say 'live foreverrrrrrrr,'" the lead singer croons, as we all crowd into the selfie.

Back at the car, we huddle around a bottle of sparkling cider. *It's not cool to drink and drive. Plus Kira would kill me if I let her baby sis get wasted*, the guitarist had chided us. *Take this*, he said, handing us the faux champagne.

"To Kate," Franny says, holding up a cup of the cider. "Easily the best night of our young, young lives."

"To many, many more," Jillian adds.

"Hear, hear," I chime, cup raised.

Kate shakes her head, like she's embarrassed by the attention, and when she looks up at us she's covering her face with her fingers, but they're parted just enough that I can tell she's beaming.

"Is it possible that you guys rock harder than Mighty Moat?" she asks, dropping her hands to her sides. Jillian smiles. In that moment, it's like the next three decades of our lives together are revealed—that if there was ever any doubt that we'd always be friends, even after we went on to become busy lawyers and never-a-free-moment doctors and volunteers at our kids' schools—all doubt is erased right then, expelled forever in that moment.

Franny covers the top of his cup with his hand and gives it a generous shake, which prompts me to deliver the stern but polite warning, "Uh, don't even think about it, man."

But Franny ignores me, shaking even more vigorously, before releasing his hand and letting it go in a surprisingly generous spray. And it's nice to see Franny happy, even for just a night.

"No one rocks harder," he yells, chasing after us. "No one rocks harder," we all yell, running for our lives.

* * *

We wave goodbye to Jillian and Franny as they back out of my driveway. Kate and I tiptoe through the kitchen and down into the basement.

I turn on the TV, and we lie side by side on the couch, which is trickier than it sounds, because there's really only room for one person, but where there's a will . . .

"Jack," Kate says. "I need to tell you something."

And this is it, I think. This is where she tells me.

"Sometimes . . . I," she starts and stops.

"It's okay, Kate."

"Sometimes . . . I get really sick. Like *really* sick."

I turn my face so that she has my undivided attention. I turn off the TV. "How so? What do you mean?"

"I was born with the sickle cell gene. Both of my parents have the trait. Have you ever heard of it?"

"I have. I've read some things, but I'm not sure I entirely understand."

"Essentially, my red blood cells stiffen, which means they struggle to deliver oxygen to other parts of my body. And most people's red blood cells last a few months, but in people with sickle cell, maybe they last a couple of weeks, so our oxygen supply can't keep up with the demand. So, there are days, weeks, a few times even a couple of months, where I'm pretty weak."

"And does it hurt?"

"I like to think I have a high threshold for pain, but, uh, yeah, it hurts pretty bad."

"I'm so sorry."

Kate puts her fingers against my lips. "Shhh," she says. "I wasn't telling you because I want you to feel sorry. I don't want pity, not from you, not from anyone. I just . . . I want you to know because . . . for some reason I feel like telling you everything. Like, there's nothing about me that I don't want you to know. Does that sound weird?" She pulls back so she can see more of my face. "That's creepy, right? I didn't mean it like . . ."

Now it's my turn to press my fingers to her lips. And this

feels like our new thing, fingers to each other's lips, letting each other know it's okay, that you're safe here.

"It's not creepy at all, Kate. It's beautiful," I say. "The most beautiful thing ever. And I feel the same way. I want you to know everything. Like everything, everything." I fix my eyes on hers and hold them there, because I want her to know that it's true, that we're true, and then I exchange my fingers for my lips, our lips coming together, opening and closing in sync, and I hear her gasp, feel her shudder.

Or maybe it's my gasp, my shudder.

Not that it matters.

Nothing matters.

How could anything?

"I really like you, Kate," I say because I'm afraid to say the other thing. The stronger thing.

"I don't want you to just like me. Save your *likes* for Twitter. I want you, Jack," she whispers into my ear, her voice traveling into my brain, down through my chest. I feel her words in my toes.

And maybe it's that my blood flow is currently being rerouted from my brain. Or the way her face is gorgeously cast in fluorescent basement light. Maybe it's because I was given another chance for this reason. But the fact is this: there's nothing *I* want more than Kate Edwards.

Nothing.

*   *   *

So the earth rotates around the sun, right? And it would be super weird for it to start happening the other way around, right? Like, suddenly the sun starts revolving around the earth—

Except that's sorta like what *loving* someone is all about—

You're moving along life, doing your thing, managing your priorities and commitments—

And then suddenly you meet THE ONE.

And you fall completely out of the orbit you've been spinning in.

And now you're doing laps around this new world.

And you're hoping gravity can sustain you.

But there's no way of knowing if it can until you realize it can't.

Guess it's all an orbit of faith.

MANDRAKE MOOLAH

I'm nearly too nervous to watch.

I'm confident that Mandrake is going to win. I mean, I've lived the goddamned future. But still. There's a beaver-colony-level gnawing happening in my stomach that I can't shake. It's as though my stomach is made of the most tender *whatever wood that beavers love most*. The choicest wood that male beavers send to the female beavers of their affection. And these beavers are going to town in my stomach, because they haven't seen this amount of sweet-ass lumber in a long time and they are taking full advantage of this new haul before it disappears.

At halftime Mandrake is down by double digits and the commentators are saying Mandrake should be happy to have made it so far, that no matter what happens they should be proud, and, hey, even Cinderella had to face midnight, there's

314

no shame in losing this game.

The second half is harder to watch. The first four minutes Mandrake looks like an elementary school team playing an NBA team; it's ugly, but an ugly you want to keep watching. And I do, with my hands over my face.

But then the incredible happens. Mandrake gets hot. They can't miss. They drill shots from all over the court. Mandrake's defense is smothering, the other team struggles to even get the ball across half-court, and that insurmountable lead shrinks. You can see their opponents fading, their poise dissolving. They finger-point. They argue with the refs, with each other. They wave off their coaches. They can't *buy* a basket.

The Mandrake point guard shimmies past his defender, dances into the paint, and launches a midrange floater that kisses off the top of the backboard square before falling cleanly into the nylon. The announcers flip out.

. . . And Mandrake takes their first lead of the game with twenty seconds left! This is the greatest comeback in the history of sports, people! You are witnessing history . . . the fifteenth-seeded Mandrake Pigs have battled all the way back and are now poised to secure their first ever national championship . . . this is beyond words . . . this is what sports is all about!

Me? I can't say what sports is about. Or what this means to the Mandrake players. But I know what it means to me, what I hope it'll mean for Kate.

I jump to my feet and I'm ugly-dancing-screaming around the basement, and Mom is thoroughly confused because a) she didn't realize I was *this* into basketball and b) we have absolutely zero connection to the Pigs.

"It's the classic underdog story, Mom," I assure her, pumping my fists with an intensity that nearly dislocates my shoulders.

She high-fives me. "It is pretty amazing."

My phone buzzes.

FRANNY'S DAD: How did you know?!

ME: What?

FD: You knew they would win.

ME: It was the longest shot ever. I just figured what the heck, why not them?

FD: I'm not buying it, but it doesn't matter. Congratulations! You're now a rich kid—let's just hope you're not a dead one after we try to collect your winnings.

ME (for five minutes, not knowing how to respond): . . .

ME (five minutes later): Is death seriously something we should be concerned about here?

FD: Not WE. I'll text you a time and place to meet tomorrow.

ME: You're joking, right? About the death thing . . . I mean, I KNOW you're joking, but I'd just like some confirmation I guess, because honestly I'm new to all of this gambling stuff and . . .

But I don't hit Send on this last text because I don't want to be an idiot even though I'm having idiotic thoughts. Of course he's joking.

Right?

I don't sleep, just in case.

*　　*　　*

The place: Elytown Public Library. The time: four p.m. I park Mom's car and head inside.

Franny's dad slides in ten minutes late and he looks freaking happy. Or maybe he's pretending because the people who are going to kill me for winning so much money have told him not to tip me off to the danger that I'm in—*stall him, Franny's dad*, they said, *while the assassin sets up his sniper rifle between the bookshelves.*

"Hey," I say, standing up when he gets to the table.

"Hey, killer," he says. He tosses me a duffel bag. "I'd find someplace to hide that were I you."

"Right," I say, surprised by how light $200K feels.

"Count it in the bathroom if you want. I'll wait."

"I trust you. Did you take out your cut yet?"

He smiles in a way that reminds me of Franny. "Told you, it's your money."

"Well, thanks," I say. "A whole lot. I hope it wasn't too much trouble."

"Collecting two hundred Gs? Trouble? Naw," he says, with a dismissive wave, and I'm at a loss if he's being serious or sarcastic. I settle on serious, because there's something about Franny's dad that makes me think he's walked around with a lot more money than $200K before. "So, listen, where to now?"

"What do you mean?"

317

"To celebrate, man. Drinks on you."

"Uh, okay."

He clasps his hands together, like he's finalizing some mega deal. "But listen, first we drop off that money. Walk around with that kind of cash, get your ass killed for real."

*   *   *

Franny's dad heads to the bar while I detour to my house. I'm more nervous than I expected, driving around with a bundle of money. What if I get pulled over? What if they search the car? What if—

I obey all the posted signs: speed limit, stop signs, yield signs. I signal my turns extra early. I make it home without incident.

After a quick sweep of my bedroom, I realize I have no clue where to keep a duffel of cash. This is my first duffel-full-of-money experience.

My desk and dresser *seem* too obvious.

Under my pillow *is* too obvious.

So I stash it under my bed.

Flipping original, I know. No one would ever look there.

*   *   *

"You wouldn't understand, man," Franny's dad says, as the surly-looking bartender sets down another set of shots in front of us.

"Why wouldn't I?"

"When you look at your pops, what do you see? A strong man, right? Someone to look up to. Someone you respect. Even when he's done something to piss you off, you still love him. That's never a question, right?"

I'm not sure if I'm supposed to answer. But he tilts his head to the side as if to say, *Well?*

"Me and my dad are close, yeah."

"Francisco looks at me and he sees none of that. Hell, most days, he barely looks at me. And why should he? What can I give him? What do I have that he needs?"

"He never wanted money, sir. He—"

Franny's dad waves his hand, his drink sloshing but not spilling. "Cut that *sir* shit."

"Sorry," I say.

"S'okay. Go on."

"I'm just saying, Franny never wanted things. He only wanted you. That's what you have to give. That's the only thing he ever wanted. You."

Franny's dad lifts his glass, waits for me to lift mine, and we clink and toss back the shots, or to be clear, he tosses back his shot while I sorta hard-gulp mine down in three or four semi-painful baby swallows.

"I'm not the fearful type, you know," he continues, signaling the bartender for another round. I try to make eye contact with the bartender to signal that he should *not* bring us another round but he's already pouring. "Where I grew up, if you were afraid of anything, you got fucked with a quickness. But you know something? The truth, Jack? I'm afraid, man. I'm afraid it's too late. It's no secret I've screwed up. And not just my own life. His, too. I know that. Shit, I *know* that. But that's not how I want to leave things. I can't fix everything that's happened, but I can make sure it doesn't go that way again. I'm here now.

I can make sure I stay here."

"He needs to believe that you'll keep showing up."

Franny's dad nods. "I'm going to be there. You watch."

* * *

I slip into my bedroom undetected, which given my slightly inebriated state feels like a win. Plus, a quick under-the-bed check confirms that I haven't been robbed. And all is well with the world (with my stomach and my head not so much) because Franny's dad is going to show up at the game this time. No, all the times he wasn't there won't be magically forgotten, but it's a start. Everything, good or bad, starts somewhere.

Meanwhile, my brain decides to torture me with questions about Franny and the money that I'm literally sleeping on, as in, *Just how pissed would Franny be if he knew I worked with his father behind his back?*

Would he understand that I have good intentions?

That I'm trying to save Kate?

Would it matter to Franny that I'd tried to use the time I'd spent with his father to improve their relationship?

I drift to sleep largely answerless, but with one happy thought running Olympic-speed laps in my brain—

Franny's dad is finally going to be there.

PANTS ON FIRE

Except he's not here.

Not when Franny's big game begins.

Not at halftime.

Not when it's over.

When the final buzzer sounds and our school has been defeated, Jillian, Kate, and I race onto the court to wrap Franny into a Friendship Circle of Unconditional Love and Support, and even though he grits his teeth into a smile, it's clear he's not into it. Franny, who's the most competitive person I know, doesn't even seem to be taking our team's butt-kicking that hard.

It's the other thing.

That the person he wanted there isn't.

Abuela tries to cover for him. "Franny, your dad, he wanted . . ."

"My father, not my dad," Franny corrects her.

Abuela takes his hand. "Listen to me, mijo, it's better to forgive. You can't hate him forever, Francisco. I understand . . ."

But Franny cuts her off. "You have to forgive him, Abuela, because he's your son. You're supposed to be there for him. I understand why you can't turn your back on him. But I'm *his* son. He's supposed to be here for me. He's supposed to show up for me. He doesn't want my forgiveness. He has to be sorry first."

"Mijo, listen . . ."

"I'm sorry. I love you. More than anything. The only good thing that man ever gave me was you, but right now, I can't stay here any longer. I gotta get outta here, okay? I'm sorry. I'll call you."

Abuela nods, her eyes glassy. "The best thing he gave me was you."

Franny walks into Abuela, his body twice her size, and she disappears in his embrace. He kisses her gray curls, squeezes her tighter, before letting go.

"You okay to get home?" Franny asks her.

"You go have fun, Francisco," she says. "Have fun with your friends."

He nods. "Make sure you text me, let me know you made it, okay?"

"You know nobody messes with your abuela," she says, smiling.

"They better not," Franny says, raising his fists in the air. He turns to Jillian, to me. "You guys ready?"

"Let's get out of here," Jillian says.

"Where we going?" I ask.

Franny gives the gym one final look as we step into the night. "Anywhere but here."

*   *   *

After pillaging two bottles of wine from Jillian's mom's stash, Jillian drives us to her grandparents' summer cottage out on Lake Erie. Inside it smells stale and the electricity isn't on because Jillian's grandparents are a couple weeks away from opening it up for the season, but it feels good to unwind together.

Jillian and Kate light candles all around and I turn on music on my phone and along the walls our shadows dance. Even Franny, sad and angry, eventually peels himself off the couch, lets us drag him into our *Soul Train* oblong.

He dips his shoulders. "Let me show you guys how this is *supposed* to look." And he's right. His way looks infinitely better.

We wind up on the back deck, and although it's too dark to see the water, we hear it sloshing, clapping below us.

"We still have a chance. With the tourney," I say when a silence settles.

"The consolation bracket?" Franny shrugs. "Long shot."

"But a shot."

Franny pulls a slip of paper from his pocket. "Guess you're right. If this could happen, anything can."

"What's that?" Jillian asks.

"See for yourself," he says. She takes it from his hands, uses her cell-phone flashlight to illuminate the letter.

"Oh my God," she whispers, shaking the paper like it's on fire.

"What?" I ask.

"What is it?" Kate chimes.

"You got in," Jillian screams, jumping up and down. "You fucking did it, Franny!"

"Got in where?" Kate asks.

But I don't need the letter to know what's happened.

"Whittier," Franny says. "I get to be with you guys!"

"That's awesome," Kate exclaims, throwing herself into Franny and Jillian's Jump Party.

"Friends forever," I say in my cheesiest voice.

Only I really mean it.

"Okay, I don't know about you guys, but this wine is squeezing my bladder like a lemon," I say, already headed out of the room.

"That's Jack's super-elegant way of saying he has to pee," Franny interprets for Kate. "He's an awesome kid, but he's a lightweight."

"Am not," I yell.

"Just don't miss the toilet, Romeo," he calls after me.

"No promises."

I set one hand against the wall for balance and, I don't know, maybe it's that my bladder's feeling relieved, or maybe it's the moonlight falling through the small window beside me, everything a swirly yellow glow, but I know everything's going to be okay.

Kate will live.

Franny's going to Whittier with Jillian and me.

Maybe the four of us will get an apartment together. Make our own reality show called *Four Stupid Smart Kids Take on College*. I laugh. At how good I feel. At how lucky I am.

The only thing that's still broken is Franny and his dad.

But there's time to fix that, too.

I can make that right. I'll try until I do.

"Hey, Jack, your phone's ringing out here, man," Franny calls through the door.

"Probably my parents. I'll call them back when I'm finished."

"No, it's not their number."

"Okay, well, just let it go to voice mail then."

"Too late," Franny says, laughing. "Jack's Answering Service, how can I help you?" He's still laughing.

Then he stops, and I can't hear him anymore. Only the girls singing in the distance.

"Franny, who was it?" I say, unsure if he's even still by the door. "Listen, we need more wine now. I'm ready to fill up again."

I flush and stumble to the sink, turn on the water, wash my hands, slap water against my face. Smile to my reflection. My reflection smiling back, harder, happier.

That's when the bathroom door explodes open, the door flung with so much force that it slaps the wall and springs back.

"What the—" I manage to get out. Before I can say another

word, before I can turn the water off, or dry my hands, I'm bulldozed into the rear shower wall.

"What the hell were you thinking?" Franny screams.

I can barely breathe, Franny's hands not exactly on my throat, but close enough to make breathing difficult.

"Franny," I stammer. "What. Are. You. Talking. About?"

"You're supposed to be my boy! What, you're not happy enough with your own TWO perfect parents, you gotta steal my pops, too?"

"That's not what happened. I was trying to make things—"

"No one asked you to try anything!"

He raises his fist, and I squeeze my eyes tight.

But the blow never comes. Not to my face. Franny punches the wallpaper beside my jaw, his hand going through the drywall, a mini cloud of dust and plaster that coats both of our noses, the side of my cheek. Like that time we tried to make a cake for his abuela and got more flour on our faces than in the bowl.

"I can't even get the man to call me back, not once. To show up for my game. To show up for any game, not once. And what, he's calling you in the middle of the goddamn night like you two are best buds?"

"Franny, I'm sorry."

"Sorry? You're sorry? Why is he calling you?"

I wag my head. "Franny . . ."

"Just tell me why he's calling you, Jack. Don't say shit else to me."

"I don't know why," I mumble. Because how do I explain the truth?

"Not only are you a backstabbing punk, you're a goddamn liar, too."

He lets me go, and I slide down into the shower stall, gasping for air.

"We're done, man. In case that wasn't clear," he says in a voice I've only heard him use to curse The Coupon. "You even look at me, or at Jillian, and I'll finish you for good. You got that?"

"Guys, what's going on? It sounds like a zoo in here," Jillian says, her voice light, happy. "Oh my God, what happened?" she says, peering into the bathroom, looking at me sitting in the shower, at the hole in the wall, then up at Franny.

"Jack, are you okay?" Jillian says. She tries to come to me, but Franny stops her.

"Did you know about this?" Franny asks her.

"Franny, she has nothing to—" I start.

But Franny takes a big step toward me, his face sharp teeth and venom. "I told you to shut up."

Jillian pulls him back. "Did I know what, Franny?" she asks. "Look at me, Franny. Look at me! Did I know what?" She cradles his head in her hands, forces his face toward hers.

"About him and my pops. No wonder my pops doesn't want me. Not when he has Super Jack in his life. What would he want with me when he can have the kid who has it all, right?" Franny laughs, but even from the shower floor, I see the tears in his eyes.

"Baby," Jillian says, wiping his eyes for him. "Baby," she repeats. She takes his hands in hers. "I need you."

Franny's face softens some.

"I need you," Jillian repeats. "I WANT you."

Franny pulls her into his arms. "I promise you I'll never let you down. Never," he says, through tears, through anger.

"You don't have to promise me. I know you won't. I know," Jillian says, barely loud enough for me to hear. "Now let's go home, okay? Take us home, baby."

Franny nods. Lets Jillian lead him out of the bathroom. But not before they look back at me, one last time.

Franny, with rage spinning deep in his eyes.

Jillian, with hurt, with sadness. A face like goodbye.

*   *   *

And this is the thing I never truly considered.

What if I save Kate but lose everyone else?

Am I prepared to live out the rest of my days As Is?

With these consequences—

No more Franny.

No Jillian.

Knowing that because of me, Franny and his dad may never figure things out.

I'll be honest with you.

I love Kate. More than nearly anything.

But more than all of those things combined?

I'm not sure.

A CURE FOR BAD BLOOD

It's been four days since I've talked to my friends.

Kate keeps saying they just need time, which everyone says about everything—*just give it time.*

They wouldn't think that about Time—that its passage makes everything better—if they knew what I knew. That more Time mostly screws things up worse.

That's why when I get the call, I'm more than relieved to think about something else. I tell Kate it's a surprise, but at every mile marker she still asks me *where are we going?*

"So, where's your car?" Kate asks for the second time this morning. The first time I ignored her, changed the subject. But I doubt that'll work a second time.

"I sold her."

"What?" she asks, turning in her seat toward me. "Why?"

"She had a few problems going on. Figured I'd sell her while she was still worth something."

"That seems random."

"If everything works out, it'll sorta be like she's still with us," I say.

Confusion contorts her face, her black curls wiggling around her ears. "You're being so weird this morning. You've been weird the last few days actually."

She's right. I have been weird. But you would be, too, if you were counting down the hours until you could take your girlfriend to the doctor's appointment meant to save her life.

"Sorry," I say.

"Yeah, yeah, tell me anything," she says. We ride the next mile in silence before she speaks again. "You may actually have a shot with my brother, you know?"

"Now who's being random," I say. "And no chance. He already hates me."

I'll be honest, it's intimidating to think that in just a couple of days I'm going to be sitting at Kate's dinner table, eating dinner with her parents, with her siblings.

But something about it is pretty cool, too.

When Kate falls asleep, we're still forty minutes away. She wakes up as I pull into the lot. She stares at the squat, gray building. "What are we doing here?"

We spend the entire waiting-room period with Kate bombarding me with questions. If I was a hostile enemy territory and Kate's questions were drone-guided explosives, by the end of the twenty-minute wait I would've been a barren wasteland.

Here's a brief snapshot:

Why am I filling this out, Jack?

No, really, why are we here?

I don't think you realize how much this guy costs?

How much is this appointment going to cost?

You realize it's not covered by insurance, his treatment?

That even if it was, the copay would be astronomical, right?

I just don't get why we're here. There's no way we can afford this, you know that, right? I've told you this before, Jack.

We're wasting our time. We're wasting the doctor's time.

I mean, what's the point?

Oh my God, Jack, please don't tell me this is why you sold your car?

Somehow I keep my lips sealed during the entire episode, despite my mouth being full of Good Supportive Boyfriend material, like: *Who cares how much it costs, we're talking about your life. And, yes, this is why I sold my car, but I would've sold my parents' house, too, if it were possible.*

Only I'm learning that sometimes it's not what you say that matters most. Or not even what you *don't* say. Those things are cool, helpful even. But it's about doing. Do something. Do anything. Do what you can and then when it feels like you've done all you could, do more.

A nurse calls Kate's name.

I hesitate to stand, because I don't want to be presumptuous, though I'd really like to go in with her. Kate stands. "I want you to come with me," she says.

I stand beside her.

A NUTSHELL: WHAT SICKLE CELL IS & WHAT DR. SOWUNMI INTENDS TO DO ABOUT IT

So, Kate's oxygen-carrying cells tend to sickle.

Meaning, they're too hard. Too rodlike. And sometimes they get wedged in her arteries, which means her tissues don't get the oxygen they need. Tissues without oxygen means it's hard for the body to do anything, like move or breathe, means intense pain, and other symptoms I don't fully comprehend.

But Dr. Sowunmi and his team can use these, uh, enzymes, called zinc-finger nucleases, which they'll zap into her genes, and with any luck they'll correct the mutation that causes Kate's cells to sickle. The hope is that they'll also replicate the healthy cells in her body.

The whole process involves two carefully engineered injections.

"Kate will need both injections," Dr. Sowunmi explains. "This is critical."

"How soon after the first can she receive the second?"

Dr. Sowunmi smiles. "Shortly after. We'll monitor her progress closely and if all goes well, it'll be only about six or seven months."

Of course this isn't a big deal to the doctor. But six or seven months is a death sentence. Because, if this whole thing resets like last time, we only have three months left.

"What would happen if she were to receive the second injection sooner?" I ask.

"Her body wouldn't be ready. She could go into shock."

"Meaning?"

"She could die."

OPERATION: TRY NOT TO MAKE A TOTAL FOOL OF YOURSELF

KATE: Just don't mind Reggie, okay? He's acting extra today.

I get this warning text from Kate on my way to meet Reggie and the rest of the Edwards clan. Kate's text does the opposite of its intent, because it makes me *already* mind Reggie.

But Reggie, it turns out, is rather difficult to *not* mind. Reggie has made it his mission on earth to be *minded* by me.

"Jack, this is Reggie," Kate says. "My baby bro."

I extend my hand. "Hey, Reggie, nice to meet . . ."

But Reggie just stares at me and my outstretched hand as though he caught me scratching my butt. "You break my sister's heart, *Jack*"—he says *Jack* really hard, makes it pop—"and I'll break your face. Bet."

Granted, Reggie is three years younger than me, and a good four inches shorter, but still his threat really resonates.

The rest of the Edwards family is far nicer.

Even her dad, which is surprising, because I assumed all dads *loathed* the idea of anyone dating their daughters.

Maybe Mr. Edwards doesn't have to waste his time loathing anyone, though. What with Reggie so able and eager.

"Don't even think about touching my sister under the table, either, *Jack*," Reggie says as we sit down for dinner. "Keep your hands *and* feet where we can see them."

"Uh, not sure how to keep my feet visible, but I'll do my best," I say, trying to laugh him off.

"Reggie," Mrs. Edwards says. "Keep it up and you'll get a close-up view of *my* hands and feet."

"Are we waiting for Kira before we start eating?" Mr. Edwards asks in a way that would seem to suggest he'd rather *not* wait.

Mrs. Edwards shrugs. "Whatever Kate wants to do."

"Let's give her a few more minutes, maybe," Kate suggests, and Mr. Edwards's face drops a little.

Reggie, on the other hand, decides to use this downtime to play a round of Ask Jack Loads of Potentially Uncomfortable Questions.

He begins each question with his hard-hitting pronunciation of *Jack*, too.

"So, *Jack*, how many girlfriends have you had, man?"

"Uh, I'm sorry," I say, looking at Kate for help.

"Reggie," Kate says.

Reggie is undeterred. "Don't be sorry, Jack. Just answer the question."

"Umm," I stammer. "Well . . ."

"Reggie, leave Jack alone already," Mrs. Edwards says.

Reggie shoots me a wicked smile. "I'm just making conversation, Mama."

"I haven't dated very much. I've been mainly focused on school," I offer.

Mr. Edwards grins. "Kate tells us you're quite the student, Jack. We take academics very seriously in this house."

My internal thermostat kicks on the heat despite my already sweaty forehead. "I do okay. I enjoy learning," I say. I'm a nerd.

"I enjoy learning, too, *Jack*. For instance, I believe we'd all be interested in learning if you're trying to smash my sister," Reggie says, smirking across the table.

"Reggie," Mrs. Edwards shouts. "Unless you want me to reach across this table and embarrass you, I suggest you get ahold of yourself with a quickness."

In spite of Mrs. Edwards's threats to maim Reggie, the way the Edwards family looks over at me after this last question makes me feel as if they *wouldn't mind* an answer from me.

Which is awkward.

And definitely not going to happen, because ew, gross, who talks about intimacy with their girlfriend's parents and baby bro at the dinner table?

"So, Reg, how was Amber Rae last night?" Kate says, eyeing

Reggie as if they were having a private conversation telepathically. Which is a downside to only-childship; you don't get to speak in sibling code.

Reggie sinks in his chair, shakes his head almost imperceptibly, as if to say, *Don't do this, don't.*

"Reggie didn't see Amber Rae last night. He was studying biology with Quentin and Johnny," Mrs. Edwards says.

"Oh," Kate says, her smile like a dare, her eyes still locked on Reggie's like two nuclear warheads. "My mistake."

"Maybe we need to have a chat after dinner, Reggie," Mr. Edwards says, not missing a beat. "About *biology.*"

"Ha ha," Reggie says, squirming in his chair. "Nah, Pop, I'm good."

Mr. Edwards glares at Reggie. "That may have sounded optional, but it's not."

Reggie shoots Kate a *thanks a lot* look and Kate squeezes my hand, my heroine. And maybe I don't know the code, but apparently, all's fair in brother-sister warfare.

"Sorry, I'm late, guys. So sorry," Kira exclaims, bursting into the dining room in a flurry of apologies and forehead kissing. She even kisses me on my forehead.

We say grace and everyone holds hands, and even Reggie manages to put aside his hatred for a thirty-second shout-out to God, taking my hand into his without squeezing the heck out of it.

After dinner, Kira, Kate, and I sit on the front porch, eating ice cream and chocolate cake that Mrs. Edwards made.

I can't help but remember this is the porch where I once stood in the rain thinking Kate and I were over.

"So, you two are pretty cute," Kira says.

"You think so?" Kate asks, eyebrows raised.

"Has your big sis ever been wrong?"

Before Kate can answer, the door swings open and Reggie emerges, bowl in hand.

"Don't even come out here starting mess, Reginald," Kira commands.

Reggie grumbles but takes a seat on the stairs by himself and starts in on his cake. The three of us get back to laughing and talking, and eventually, when we reach the subject of who's the next Will Smith, Reggie can no longer pretend not to care.

"It's gotta be Jaden," Reggie says. "It only makes sense."

Mr. and Mrs. Edwards join us with their bowls and Mr. Edwards asks what we're talking about, and says, "What's wrong with you kids? Hell, the question should've been, who's the next Denzel? Now, that boy can act."

Gradually, one by one, the Edwards clan retreats into the house, leaving Kate and me alone on the stairs, the lamppost anchored in her front yard throwing an amber haze into our conversation. "It means a lot that you came here," she says, looking straight ahead at the empty street.

I scoot closer until our legs touch, and I take her hand in mine, her fingers still cool from the ice cream, a firefly burning near her nose. "I'd go anywhere for you."

She leans into me, her lips brushing against my cheek, and I consider a look over my shoulder for any sign of her family, but in the end I just go with it, our lips opening and closing, pressing tighter, then tighter still, like the surest promise.

* * *

Kate leans into my (mom's) car, and we kiss again, apparently so intensely we don't hear her father sneak up behind us.

"Ahem," Mr. Edwards says, clearing his throat.

Kate straightens up, and I accidentally tap the gas, revving the engine. Thank God I'm still in park.

"Daddy," Kate says. "Everything okay?"

"You mind if I have a word with Jack?"

Turns out having a word with Jack means me vacating my car and walking down the dark sidewalk with my girlfriend's dad.

"Jack, I figured you and I should have a chat about you and my daughter."

I nod.

Mr. Edwards continues. "Yeah, well, as you probably know, she's been through a lot."

"Yes, sir."

"The long and short is this: my daughter likes you, and you seem like a nice kid. I'd hate for her to have her heart broken on top of everything else. Stress is the last thing she needs. Stress could kill her."

"I don't want her to be stressed. Definitely not because of me."

"Right," Mr. Edwards says, coming to a stop a block from

their house. "Which is why I think you should break up with her now."

"I'm sorry. I'm not following."

"Oh, I think you're following just fine. You're a smart kid. You can have every good intention in the world, but this thing with you and Kate isn't going anywhere good. You're not even out of high school, Jack. Now the best decision you can make, if you really want to see her well, is leave her be."

"I can't say that I agree, sir," I stammer. "I mean, with all due respect, this thing, as you say with Kate and me, I think it's good, for both of us."

Mr. Edwards frowns. "You think you know more about my daughter than I do?"

"No, I mean. I just . . ."

"You think you know more about love than me, kid?"

"That's not what . . ."

"If you love Kate, let her go, Jack. If you want her to live the best life she can, you need to let her go."

We walk back in silence, and Kate hops off the porch steps, runs into my arms. "Were you nice to Jack, Daddy?" she asks.

Mr. Edwards smiles. "Just a little heart-to-heart between men. Nothing to worry about, baby." He turns to me, clamps his hand on my shoulder. "Jack, it was nice meeting you."

I nod because I can't process another response. Mr. Edwards walks into the house.

"So, tonight went really well," Kate says, her arms over my shoulders, her eyes wide, joyful.

"Yeah." I try to smile. "Really well."

"What's wrong?" she says, seeing through me.

"Are you sure this is okay, you and me?"

Kate dips her head. "What do you mean?"

"I don't want to be a bad thing for you. I don't want to be the reason you don't feel your best."

"What did my dad say to you?"

"Nothing," I lie. "I just . . . I care about you so much and . . ."

"Everyone thinks they know what's best for me. When did *my* opinion stop mattering?"

I pull her closer, and I see the curtain move in the front window behind us. We have an audience. "I don't care what anyone else says. If you want me here, Kate, I'll never leave."

She kisses me. "I want," she says.

I kiss her back. With all that I have, all that I am, I kiss her back.

*   *   *

It's not quite seven in the morning when I get her text message.

Be outside in ten.

I climb out of bed, skip the socks and shoes. She's already on the porch. I sit beside her.

"You really screwed things up this time, huh," Jillian says.

I grit my teeth. "Guilty as charged."

"What did you think would happen? When Franny found out?"

"Honestly? I hoped he never would."

"It's like all you care about is Kate. *Kate's* feelings. Protecting

341

Kate. But what about us, Jack? Your friends? The people who've been there for you? The people you have history with? What about me?"

"Jillian, this wasn't how it was supposed to happen."

"You got that right. Because you promised me that you'd always be there. And we're a very long way from *always* and you're already breaking your promise."

"I was trying to help Franny. I still want to help him."

"You can't help people the way you think they need help, Jack. Good intentions don't grant you license to be an idiot."

First Kate's dad and now Jillian. This is the second time in twelve hours that someone's declared good intentions not good enough.

"What can I do? Franny won't return my calls. My emails. My texts."

"He needs time. Probably a lot."

I used to think time was all I needed. But now—

"What if time isn't enough?"

Jillian frowns. "It has to be enough."

* * *

Since Franny's in an understandable I Hate Jack's Guts phase in his life, a phase that I'm desperate to help him end, I decide to ignore his warning of serious bodily injury and try to talk to him anyway.

Except he's nowhere to be found.

He's not at his house.

Or at the gym.

Or at Jillian's.

It crosses my irrational mind that in the seventy-two hours since he spared my life maybe he's found a new best friend to hang with.

When I finally locate Franny, it's less a question of *what's he doing here?* than *why didn't I think of this place earlier?*

The Wood. The old treehouse we built in the patch of woods behind my house so many summers ago. The outside walls weathered and moss-covered. The roof leaking rainwater and sunshine.

"Yo, I thought I told you I didn't want anything to do with you," Franny says the moment I stick my head through the floor. For a second I think he's going to play whack-a-mole with my face, but instead he turns his body toward the treehouse's sole window, away from me. I pull myself up, lean against the wall opposite Franny.

"I never should have gone behind your back with your dad. I'm wrong for that. And I'm sorry I hurt you. You never would've done anything like that to me."

"You're right about that. I wouldn't have."

"All I can say is that I got caught up. With Kate. She's sick. Really sick. And I had this idea on how to get some money for her to get this treatment, but I needed help. I thought of your dad. But I should've been thinking about you, too. I didn't think about what that might mean for you, for Jillian. I was selfish. And I'm really sorry. All I can say is that if you give me another chance, I'll do my best to be better. To do better."

Franny turns to me and shakes his head. "What? This supposed to be the part where I forgive you? Where I say something like *yo, man, we all make mistakes* and then dap you up and pull you into a bro hug? Because that's not going to happen. I'm not ready for all of that. Not even close."

I nod my head. "Right. Okay."

"Damn, man, you ain't gotta look like somebody just shot your black ass. I'm just saying, give me some time. Then we'll see."

And it's like all anyone ever talks about anymore is time.

MAKEUP TEXTS

And apparently *some time* is two days.

> GROUP TEXT to ME and JILLIAN, from FRANNY—
>
> FRANNY: We practicing tonight, or y'all wanna show up to this party and make damn fools of ourselves?
>
> ME: Uh, I definitely choose A). When and where? 😊
>
> JILLIAN: My house! Now! 😀

I wrap my arms around Franny's neck like we're in a slow dance.

"I missed you, big man," I say in the middle of Jillian's garage.

He tries not to laugh, cups my head like a basketball he's about to dunk.

"Yo," he says to Jillian. "What's wrong with your boy?" But then he smiles and the world is instantly less scary.

345

Jillian grins, races toward us, leaps onto my back, knocking Franny and me onto the old orange sofa. The three of us once again a tangled knot. And it feels right.

We try and throw each other off the sofa, an old game where we pretend the sofa is a lifeboat that can only save one of us; the other two have to be forced overboard. As usual Jillian wins, jumping up and down on the cushions.

Franny and me lying side by side on the paint-splattered concrete floor, he turns to me and says, "So we're cool, but the next time you pull some crazy—"

I put my hands up to stop him. "There won't be a next time."

He nods. "Good."

We give each other the *cool, let's do this then* look. And then we're springing back onto the orange sofa, fighting for our watery survival.

CAPS & GOWNS

Graduation rolls around and Dad is in full Capture This Memory Forever mode.

Last night he sat at the kitchen island cleaning his fourteen different lenses with his specially designed cloths, checking and rechecking his apertures, much the way a hunter inspects his rifle before a hunt.

Dad is a hunter. And special occasions are his prey.

Today Dad has me dead in his sights.

But I don't complain. I get why this is important to parents, a shiny, metallic mile marker on the road to their kid's hopeful success. Mom's eyes have been leaking since last night, and she's still dabbing at her tears with her hanky.

"Mom, are you okay?" I ask. Even when you know the tears are happy, something about seeing your mom cry slays you.

"My baby," she says, as if this says it all.

As for me, I can't help but feel proud.

Loved.

Afraid.

All I can think is, now what? What's next?

The answer is partly college. But the answer is mostly, I don't know.

I look at myself, capped and gowned. I say to my reflection, *Good luck, man.* To which he replies, *You're gonna need it.* And I don't disagree.

I look around my room. Already it's starting to feel like I don't belong here anymore. Like these aren't my things. Not my crappy paint on the walls from back when neon blue seemed genius. Not my collection of various drink stains blotted in the carpet like alien animal print. Not my posters puttied to the closet. Not my favorite comforter, ratty and worn, stained with my sweat and smell. My bookshelf sagging from too many books. Who does this stuff belong to? Whose memories are catalogued in my head? And I feel full. And I wonder, how could I ever fit anything, anyone, else into all of this? Into all of me?

I take in the doorframe, the dark pencil marks where I stood with my back pressed against the wood as Dad ticked off my height, scribbling my age beside each measurement. And I laugh because, shit, I'm short.

I turn off the lights as the doorbell rings.

Mom calls up, "Jackie, Kate's here."

I jump down the stairs, all twelve steps in a single leap, like I used to do as a kid, except this time I stumble and nearly break my neck. Which makes me think about that time I *did* break my neck. The moment that started all of this . . . whatever this is.

But I don't care. Because right now it feels like I'll never break anything again. I'm unbreakable. The world spinning so beautifully.

*   *   *

Kate is radiant. Which is cliché-ridden and easy come. But still—

Look at her.

She is an explosion of light that never stops erupting.

"You came," I say to Kate, my parents looking on behind me. I can sense them, their *I can't believe our son has a bona fide girlfriend in our house right now* energy.

But I only see Kate. I only feel Kate.

Kate, in a white, flowy dress and blue heels, a blue clutch in her right hand. She smiles and we're in that awkward dance, the limbo of deciding if we should just hug or if a quick peck on the lips is okay, too. And we only narrowly miss bumping into each other's heads. I kiss her cheek, and I feel her face warm. Or maybe it's me who's warm. She reaches up and fixes my cap.

"Happy graduation day, Jack Attack," she says.

I shrug. "It's just high school."

But with Kate here, everything's so much more.

I don't even mind the photo shoot Dad puts us through.

THIRTIETH

Twenty minutes before JoyToy takes the stage (also known as the backyard patio), Mom calls me to the front door. I set down a platter of fancy cracker thingies, and get there in time to see Mom hugging someone with bone-crushing exuberance.

"Hey," Kate says, with a slight wave, as Mom releases her from her bear clutch.

"Hey yourself," I say.

My mom steps back, alternates her gaze between Kate and me, like she's a spectator at a tennis match.

"You made it," I finally say. I step past Mom and usher Kate outside onto the relative privacy of the porch. "And wow, you look . . . *wow*. Actually, the word *stunning* comes to mind, only I don't want to sound like your great-grandfather."

She smiles. "Don't worry. My great-grandfather wouldn't

have said that. He was a lot cooler than you."

"Bang. You got me." I clutch my chest. "But then again, being cooler than me isn't anything to hang your hat on. I mean, you'd have to be spectacularly uncool if you wanted any chance at dethroning me, because . . ."

She kisses my cheek.

"What did I do to deserve that?" I ask. "I'm asking because I want you to do it again."

"Where do I start?"

"I'm really glad you're here," I say, nearly adding *this time*, but catching myself.

"Thanks for inviting me. So . . . where is this party?"

"Oh yeah. The party. You didn't just come here so we could stand on my porch and stare at each other?"

"I thought that was *next* week," she says.

"Oh, you're right, it is next week," I agree. "Sorry, I keep getting my days mixed up."

I take her hand and lead her to the backyard.

"Wow, you guys did a great job. It's so elegant."

"It was all Mom's design. She pointed and Dad and I basically moved things back and forth around the yard until she got frustrated and said it was good enough."

"Well, she has very good taste."

"I feel like I have better," I say, running my fingers along her shoulder.

She pushes me, playfully. "Gross, not at your parents' anniversary."

"Why not? You know, if you play your cards right, it could be *our* anniversary, too."

"Okay, that was easily the creepiest thing that's ever come out of your mouth."

"I told you I wasn't cool."

"How many times must I tell you? *That's* why I like you." She kisses me again, on the same cheek, and I temporarily lose muscular control.

"There she is! The woman who's making my best friend a better man," Franny shouts from across the lawn.

He and Jillian are wearing matching sunglasses, except Jillian's are black whereas Franny's are hot pink. "Nice glasses, man," Kate tells him.

"C'mon, Kate, now you've done it," I complain.

"*Thank you*, Kate. As I've already told this Neanderthal, it takes a real man to pull off something so bold, so inspiring," Franny says, sliding up the glasses so he can apparently big-wink at us.

"You guys ready to rock?" Jillian asks, motioning toward the stage.

"Born to," I say, sticking my hand out, which Franny promptly slaps onto with his palm.

"My middle name is Rock," Franny says, somehow curling his lip in a way I've never seen him do before.

"So, then your last name should be Hard," Jillian says, high-fiving Kate before adding her hand to our hand pile.

Kate laughs.

"Well, what are you waiting for, Kate," I say. "You better get in on this."

"But I'm not in the band," she protests.

"But you definitely rock, right?" Jillian says.

"Hard, right?" Franny adds.

And Kate, still laughing, puts her hand into our huddle.

"Oh yeah, now we're ready," I say.

"Rock hard on three," Franny shouts, his eyebrows arched intensely. "One-two-three . . ."

*　　*　　*

And the day's so perfect it's hard to believe that today also marked another anniversary.

That this is the night that everything's gone black.

Except this time Kate isn't in any hospital.

Her treatment's working. Even better than we could've hoped for, according to Dr. Sowunmi. There are a dozen reasons to be optimistic. To be happy.

So, the question is, why am I so afraid?

"Maybe you can stay tonight," I suggest to Kate.

She laughs. "You mean, as in at your house, with your parents' consent?"

"Why not?" And no, I'm not entirely sure my parents would be excited about a Jack-Kate sleepover, but tonight I don't want to let her out of my sight.

Despite my best efforts, Kate's not having it. "I have plans with Kira in the morning, and you should be with your folks tonight," she insists.

There's no changing her mind, either.

She won't even let me give her a ride back to her parents' house.

"Go back inside and get drunk with your parents," she says, smiling.

"Don't worry, Jack," Jillian assures me, starting up her car. "I'll get her home safe."

* * *

My parents and I share a bottle of wine and I listen to them reminisce about their courtship and the first years of their marriage and I wonder what it would've been like to have known them back then, the younger versions of my parents. Would I have thought they were cool? Might we have been friends? What if I had *Back to the Future*'d it and had traveled back far enough to go to prom with my mom? It's disturbing to contemplate (that last question, anyway).

Before I climb into bed, I set my phone ringer to deafening, just in case.

I call Kate, but she doesn't answer. I text her to call me whenever.

Franny, Jillian, and I group-text into the wee hours; I'm determined to stay awake all night, like maybe that could be the difference.

I wake up, in what I think is the middle of the night, to my alarm.

I shake the sleep from my brain, reach for my phone.

Only it's not an alarm.

"Jack, I don't know what's happening to me," Kate screeches into the phone.

"Wait, what do you mean? What's going on?"

"I think I'm going into crisis," she says.

"But you can't. The treatment. Dr. Sowunmi said—"

"Jack, I'm scared . . . it feels different this time. Worse than before . . . I don't know what to do."

"Where are you?"

Kate's breathing is jagged.

"Kate, where are you? I'll come to you. I'll call an ambulance. Just tell me where you are . . ."

I race to the top of the stairs. I can't believe it. This is happening again.

"Jack . . . ," she says, faintly. I hear a thud, like maybe she's dropped her phone.

"I'm coming," I swear to her, though I don't know where she is.

I tear down the stairs, careful to hit each step. I make it to the bottom without falling. No cosmic trips. No black-hole surprises.

Twenty seconds later I'm backing Dad's car out of the driveway.

The other injection, I think. Kate needs the second injection.

*   *   *

In the car I dial. The phone rings so long I expect voice mail, but then—

"Hello?"

355

"You lied," I say to him.

"What? Who is this?"

"You told me you could save her."

"Jack?"

"She's still going to die, though, isn't she?"

"Jack," he says, and I can hear someone say something in the background, hear his hand cover the speaker, everything muffled. "Jack, listen to me," he starts again.

"Just tell me the truth, Doc."

"The only truth about medicine is—there is no truth. We don't know. We practice at it and we don't always get it right. That's why we say *practicing medicine*. Sometimes we get it really wrong."

"But you're different. Kate, her family, they all believe in you. Everyone says you're the best."

A long pause, a deep sigh. "I wish I was better."

". . ."

"Jack? Jack? You there?"

"Night, Doc." I toss my phone onto the passenger seat.

I stand on the gas and the car lurches forward.

I can't help but wonder what I'm doing. Is there a chance that none of this is real? Maybe I'm in a coma and this is all a byproduct of narcotics and my own screwed-up subconscious. Or maybe my entire life is an elaborately staged production, some medium-budget reality television show, and everyone I know is a paid actor, like that *Truman Show* flick. What if Mom and Dad aren't even my real parents? What if Jillian and

Franny were hired to be my best friends? And Kate. What if she's . . . what if we're not really in lo—

Then a bomb explodes.

Rather, that's what I think at first, what the impact is like. The nose of the car crinkles shut, folding in on itself like a construction-paper fan, metal bending, tearing. I feel heat and fire. Smell smoke. Someone, something screams. But from where? And then I realize it's me. I'm screaming. And I can't stop. I can't. But it doesn't matter, the screaming, because I start thinking of it less as a sign of weakness, of fear. It's my battle cry. Because I'm going to make it to Kate even if I have to crawl on all fours, or hobble on one leg. I don't care.

Maybe, in the end, none of this turns out to be real.

But it's real to me.

"Kid, kid, are you okay?" a lady is yelling into my window. "Oh my God, oh my God, I didn't see you. I swear, I looked both ways and everything but you just came out of nowhere . . ."

I try and push my door open but it doesn't budge. "Get back," I tell the lady. I kick out the remaining broken glass and climb out the driver's side window. But my legs give out and I collapse to the ground.

Her hand touches my shoulder. "You need to stay still. I've already called 9-1-1."

But I stand up anyway. My legs are wobbly but I'm okay. I'll be okay.

"Oh my God, what are you doing? You shouldn't move. You might make things worse. Maybe you have a concussion.

Maybe some broken bones, or—"

I move past her and start down the road.

"My girlfriend," I tell her. "I have to get to her. She's dying."

I hear sirens a few streets away and I pick up the pace, which still isn't fast, considering my lungs are on fire and I think my right kneecap's broken. It never occurred to me that you could break a knee. I've never heard someone say *yeah, I'll be okay, just a broken knee.*

"Oh, God, was there someone else in the car? Your girlfriend? The ambulance is coming. The paramedics will . . ."

Only I don't hear another word she says.

All I can think is, I tried. I tried so hard to do everything right. But I failed.

A bright light flares behind my pupils. My brain spins in my skull. My teeth play musical chairs in my gums. And it's as though my heart's plugged into an exposed electrical socket in the middle of a typhoon.

In other words, it happens.

Again, it happens.

four YOU
& me

I CAN'T EVEN

The only thing worse than losing someone you love is losing them again.

People say *I'd do anything to see them again, to hear their voice just once more*, but what they don't consider is losing them all over again. That it doesn't get easier. If anything, it's harder. So much harder.

"Excuse me, man, but you're sort of damming up the steps," Kate says.

"Sorry. I'll get out of your way." And I do. I get the hell out of her way, out of her path, out of her stratosphere.

Because even after all that we've been through together, even though I'm so very happy to see her alive once more, I can't do it again.

I'm sorry. I just can't.

*　*　*

Don't hate me, but I'm going to say something ridiculously, exceptionally *hole in the head* stupid. As in, I'm going to invoke cliché to explain my running away from Kate.

Three strikes and you're out.

You see, it's just occurred to me (well, it occurred to me before but I promptly shoved the thought into the dankest, most cobwebbed corner of my brain) that maybe I'm not supposed to save Kate. That maybe we aren't even supposed to meet. Suppose the way I save her is that I leave her alone altogether.

I had my three swings, and I missed—badly, wildly.

Now I'm out.

And I do the one thing I should've done in the first place. I storm the kitchen, slicing through the crowd, pausing long enough to tell the group huddled around the TV to stay tuned because State is about to make a huge comeback, *no way, man*, they say dismissively, but I don't argue. I weave through the dancers and drinkers until I'm right behind her.

She turns around, like she knows what happens next. Like she's been waiting for me.

"Jack," Jillian says, "what are you doing?"

"What I should've ages ago."

I pull her close and peer into her eyes and I press my lips against hers and I wait for her to push me away. But she doesn't move, except to open her mouth, her warm tongue slips between my lips, her fingers cradling my head, and this isn't how I imagined things, but it'll be okay.

Everything's okay.

HOW TO BETRAY EVERYTHING YOU'VE KNOWN

The only thing I'm surprised about is that Franny hasn't beaten my ass . . . yet.

He's shoved me, bumped into me, given me the Franny Disintegrating Stare of Excruciatingly Uncomfortable Death plenty of times up and down the school hallway, but so far he hasn't decided to kill me.

I know I deserve any pain he chooses to dish out.

Franny's being nice to Jillian. Maybe even nicer to her now, if that makes sense. Perhaps it's true, about not appreciating what you have until it's gone.

I don't need to be without Kate to appreciate her.

But I'm still without her, just the same.

It's hard being an asshole, or at least it's hard knowing your former best friend thinks you're the World's Biggest Asshole, and that you can't really disagree with him.

And maybe there's not exactly the happiness circus going crazy in my stomach, but I'm pretty happy with Jillian. She gets me. And she really knows me. There's something to be said for spending the last four years of your life growing up with someone. She's been there. And she's still here.

THE DISAPPOINTMENT OF ANCESTORS

I hold out as long as I can before telling my parents.

Of course, they've asked and asked, *Where's Franny? Is he okay? Are you two okay?*

I pick my fork back up, spear some brussels sprouts. Why are brussels sprouts the universal vegetable for tension? Every time there is unease over dinner, brussels sprouts are likely on the table. I feel bad for brussels sprouts. What a thankless gig. Everyone hates you because 1) no one prepares you properly, or because 2) you remind them of some awful dinner where they received terrible news. Poor brussels sprouts. I'm actually a fan, myself. Because normally Mom nails them.

But tonight they don't taste the same.

And it's safe to say that I've never seen my parents so angry. Especially with me.

For your convenience, I've prepared a table of the ~~high~~low-lights for you.

Mom and Dad's Table of Supreme Sadness & Major Disappointment

MOM	DAD
I just can't believe you would do that to Franny! He's your best friend, Jack! You guys have taken baths together!	How many times has he spent the night over here? A thousand? Three thousand? I feel like a thousand is a very realistic estimate.
I just can't emphasize enough how thoroughly disappointed I am in you right now. I wish there was a way I could emphasize it, but I don't think there is.	Your mom and I have done our best to raise you right. All of our friends are constantly remarking on how good a kid you are. Now what are they gonna think?
Okay, maybe a Disappointment Scale. On a scale of 1 to 10, with 10 being disappointment of the worst kind, like say you were a murderer or something. I'd say this is a solid 8.5.	Franny hasn't had a lot of good things happen in his life and now he can add Betrayed by His Supposed Best Friend to the list. Awesome!
Jillian over Franny, Jack? You never choose a ho over your bro. Even I know that. Haven't you heard that before?	I just don't understand. Did we not teach you the value of friendship?
I go to all of Franny's games. I've literally never missed any of his games. Do you know how awkward that's going to be for me to keep going even though he and my son are no longer friends? Did you ever think about that, Jack?	Who are you right now? Because you're not the Jack I know. Where's my son Jack? My friend Jack? That's what I want to know.
I buy extra groceries each week just because I know Franny is going to be here. And now what? Am I supposed to just rethink my entire grocery-shopping strategy?	No, seriously, who are you?

JACK, YOU SUCK, MAN

And I get it, of course.

I'm mad at me, too.

But tell me, what was I supposed to do?

Keep trying the same thing over and over again?

It wasn't working, guys.

I'm sorry.

I tried and I failed.

And then I tried and I failed more.

What choice did I have?

No, seriously, help me figure it out. I'll wait.

*   *   *

Lesson number *whatever*: Keep your replays straight.

When you've experienced the same, or at least very similar, moments multiple times over, it's easy for your brain to splice them together to make one scene.

The problem is you say things that the other person doesn't understand because things—small, micro things—don't happen exactly the same.

JILLIAN: Hey, where are you?

ME: Look up

She looks up from the mound of pizza dough she's kneading, only to see me doing some weird impromptu jig in the storefront window, beside the giant Pizza Pauper decal. I open the door, the wind pushing its way inside behind me, the door chimes rattling.

"You're late, Jack King," Jillian says, folding her arms.

"Better late than—" but I don't finish my sentence. I step behind the counter and kiss her instead, her nose wrinkling against my own.

How many times did I dream this?

Kissing Jillian.

Jillian kissing me back.

And now it's here.

We stop kissing, and she grins, puts a hand on her hip. "So, you gonna help me with my French or did you just come here to eat my face?"

"Hmmm," I say, tapping my chin. "Definitely the latter." I lean over to kiss her and she playfully moves away.

"Babe, come on, please," she pleads. "I'm bombing French."

"You're not bombing French. Your idea of bombing is an A-minus."

"Well, if I'm going to study abroad at Whittier then I need

to learn the language, don't you think? Otherwise, how am I going to order us room service?"

My throat tightens, because honestly whenever I think seriously about the future, it's still hard to imagine mine without Kate.

And it's like Jillian can read my mind because she asks, "You think we did the right thing? Deciding to be together?"

This isn't the first time we've wondered this aloud. Each time I answer the same way. "The way things happened, it felt like the only decision we could make."

"Yeah," she says, not super convincingly. "You still coming for dinner tonight? Mom's making your favorite."

"White bean sausage chili?"

"You're so spoiled."

"How is your mom doing anyway?"

Jillian shakes her head. "We got into it again."

"About your dad?"

"The thing I dislike most about this situation, in which there are plenty of things to dislike, is not the sight of my mom, but what the sight of her does to me. Which I know sounds selfish, but."

"It's not selfish, J. You get to feel things, too."

"You should never have to pity your parents. I mean, not this way." She stops rolling the dough. "I mean, every time I come into the house, I feel like she's just waiting for me, ready to pounce. Like she's just rechanneling all of the energy she used on Dad into me. And I love my mom, but . . . it's just too much sometimes. And she's all over the place. Happy and sad and laughing and angry and . . . it's a lot. Not to mention, she's rearranged everything in the house."

"Like, the furniture? She's always done that, though, right?"

"Not just the furniture. All the furniture. And yesterday, I came home to all our dishes, pots and pans, all our food, like the entire pantry, spread out across the kitchen table, the counter, and on the kitchen floor."

"What? Why?"

"Because she felt like things could be better organized."

"Wow."

"Yeah."

"That makes me sad."

Jillian nods. "Part of me wants Dad to come back and make amends so Mom can go back to being Mom again. But also, part of me wants to never see him again, too. And depending on when you ask me, the ratio of see him versus never see him is always in flux. I mean, this is his mess, and he's just gone. How could he just leave, Jack?"

"I don't know. I'm sure he misses you. I'm sure he's somewhere sad and regretful."

"I hope so," Jillian says. "But whenever I imagine him, I picture him somewhere really happy. I see him laughing, tossing his head back like a wolf. Ha."

"You think Franny feels like your mom?"

Jillian shrugs. "Mom lost her love and her best friend. Franny lost love and two best friends. You do the math."

"I hate math."

Jillian wipes her doughy hands onto her apron. "I heard The Coupon got released."

I raise my eyebrows. "Oh yeah?"

But I already know this.

I'm meeting Franny's dad tomorrow.

WHY I ALREADY KNOW

"Mr. Hogan," I say, extending my hand.

But Franny's dad laughs, grabs me by my shoulders. "Ha, look at you, a full-grown man now. Peach fuzz and everything."

And I nearly say *well, it has been eight years*. But I smile instead.

"It's good to see you, sir."

"You either call me Francisco or you call me nothing. And don't even think about calling me *sir* again."

"Okay," I say, deciding in my brain to not refer to Franny's dad as anything. "So, the reason I wanted to see you was—"

"Hold on," Franny's dad says, motioning for the waitress. "You guys have anything good on tap?"

The waitress rattles off the list. "I'll take a tall of that last one, honey," he says, flashing her a smile that makes her blush,

372

proving that million-watt smiles are highly genetic. He turns back to me. "Now, why are we here?"

He laughs for three minutes straight when I tell him. But he agrees to help.

"There is one other thing, though, Mr. Hogan."

Just because Franny despises me doesn't mean I don't care about what happens to him. Or to Kate. Although I'm making different choices this time, I still want them to be happy, to have what they need.

"Told you to cut that *mister* crap."

"Sorry. The thing is, sir, I mean, uh . . . the thing is I don't think you understand how much Franny's missed you."

Franny's dad chews on a toothpick. We're at a bar and grill he chose. He claimed they have the best corned beef, though he's mainly feasting on beer.

I wait until he takes a big bite from his sandwich before I tell him things that Franny probably wouldn't want him to know.

"On Franny's twelfth birthday he waited in the window for you to come for like three hours. He did that even though Abuela told him you weren't coming. Even though in his heart, he knew you weren't coming. That you couldn't come. It was the only time I remember Franny crying when we were kids."

"Franny? Crying? Hard to believe he cares enough about what I do to cry behind it."

"Did you know he wrote you a hundred emails while you were locked up?"

He stares at me. "I never got a single one."

"Because he never hit Send."

"Why would he do that? Why would he write emails he never sent?"

"Because he was afraid you wouldn't write back. I suppose not hearing from you at all was easier to take than reaching out to you and you not reaching back."

"That's stupid," he says, but I can tell by the way he says *stupid* he doesn't mean it.

"Did you know Franny chose basketball even though he's better at football because he remembers growing up watching you play at the park?"

"He remembers that?"

"Franny still has this Post-it note from you. You probably don't even remember it, but you scribbled a few words on a green note and stuck it onto Franny's brown bag lunch before school. Franny still has it. It's in his sock drawer."

"No way."

"It's true. He brings it out when he thinks I'm not looking."

And I know I'm betraying Franny all over again, revealing his deepest truths.

But sometimes you're wrong for the right reasons.

DOCTOR, DOCTOR, GIVE ME THE NEWS

"What exactly are these injections, anyway?"

"Zinc-finger nucleases."

"And she needs both injections?"

Dr. Sowunmi nods. "Without both, she'd eventually regress back to her original condition, yes."

"I see."

"Is that a problem, Jack? Kate receiving both doses?"

"No," I say. "No problem."

"Because it's the third or fourth time you've brought it up. If you're worried about payment, I've already told you that you'll—"

"It's not the money. It's just that, you're certain there's no way to speed up the second injection?"

"Not without considerable risk, Jack."

"You know this because you've tried it?"

"I haven't tried it, no," he admits. "But based on the research . . ."

I lean forward. "Doctor, whatever happened to leaving room for miracles?"

"Excuse me?"

"I mean, science is obviously what you do here, right, but, like, don't you need faith, too? Some hope?"

"Faith and hope play their part, certainly, Jack, but if you . . ." He stops himself. "Faith and hope are important, sure."

"I have faith in you, Doc."

Dr. Sowunmi studies me across his desk.

I press on. "So, you'll take her on as a patient?"

"I'd like to meet her first. Get to know her before we even consider treatment."

"Fair enough," I tell him. "But let me warn you. If you get to know her, then you're definitely going to treat her. There's no way you know Kate and don't want to help her."

Dr. Sowunmi folds his hands across the front of his desk. "How long have you known Kate?"

Well, Doc, we've technically known each other for over a year now but at this moment in our history I'm a complete stranger to Kate because I seem to be caught in a time-traveling loop and rather than stick things out all over again, like the coward that I am, I opted to run the other way, so . . .

"Actually, we don't exactly . . . uh, the thing is . . . it's sort of a weird situation but . . . I mean it makes sense because sometimes you don't have to actually know someone to *know* them, you know what I mean?"

"Jack, are you telling me that Kate has no idea who you are?"

"I wouldn't say *no* idea. Not exactly."

"Really," the doctor says. "Then how would you describe your relationship with Kate?"

"Complicated."

"Complicated," Dr. Sowunmi repeats, smiling for the first time since I stepped into his office. "I wish I could tell you it gets easier when you're older, but as a doctor I've sworn to do no harm."

"Glad to know I'm not the only one who sucks at love."

"So," he says, his face already back to its *take crap from no one* expression. "If Kate doesn't *know* you, how will you convince her to see me? And to let you, a stranger, pay for it?"

"I have a plan."

No, I don't.

*   *   *

But then I do have a plan.

Just remember, I never claimed it was a good plan.

"Hello, is this Mrs. Edwards?"

"Who's calling?"

"My apologies. My name is . . . uh . . . Thurgood Marshall Thomas the second. I'm on the Whittier board of trustees. But we can get into all of my, uh, credentials later."

"Is something wrong with Kate?"

"Huh? I mean, uh, how do you mean, Mrs. Edwards?"

"I know her grades have slipped a bit. She's been in and out of the hospital more this past semester, but I can assure you she's fully dedicated to her studies."

"No assurance necessary, ma'am. That's actually why I'm calling you today. It is my aim to help ensure Kate continues to benefit from her education here at Whittier."

"I'm not sure I follow."

"Her illness, Mrs. Edwards. We want to help get her well."

"You want to . . . I don't think I understand."

"We're prepared to make a rather large donation on Kate's behalf to one of the best hematology doctors in the world. Our hope is that, at the very least, he can get her sickle cell under control."

"There's no way we can afford that. Her father and I don't have—"

"It's already taken care of, Mrs. Edwards. You and your family will not have to make a single payment."

A long beat.

Did I lose her? "Mrs. Edwards, are you still there?"

"Yes . . . I'm here . . . Mr., uh?"

"Thomas."

"Mr. Thomas, may I ask you a rather rude question, sir?"

I try my hand at how I think a wealthy benefactor might chuckle, a cross between *don't be ridiculous* and *I wipe my butt cheeks with fifty-dollar bills just because.* "Ask away, Mrs. Edwards."

"Are you and my daughter . . . are the two of you . . . are you sleeping with my daughter? Is that why you want to help her?"

"Mrs. Edwards, to tell you the truth, I have not even been formally introduced to your daughter. But I can assure you there is no impropriety here. Every year the board reviews dozens of applications for candidates who may be in need of some form of assistance. This is at the bequest of several of our rather, to be perfectly blunt, financially able alumni who are eager to give back to the school that they love. Your daughter is this year's chosen applicant."

"So, this is something she applied for? Kate filled out some application?"

"No, we work on a nomination basis. Kate was nominated by one of her peers."

"Can you tell me who? Who nominated Kate?"

"I'm afraid I can't. But what I can say is, with your and Kate's blessing, we are anxious to get started. I'd like to verify your mailing address and best point of contact, so that we can be in touch, Mrs. Edwards?"

More silence.

"Mrs. Edwards . . ."

"I just can't believe this is happening. I'm grateful. I am. But . . . well, pardon my cynicism, but . . ."

"I'm going to send you over the official paperwork, dear. You'll see. Everything's already in motion."

"I don't know what to say."

"Say nothing, my dear. You've raised an exceptional child. It is this school who wishes to thank you." I clear my throat, feeling my voice aching to crack. "So, shall we get this ball rolling?"

DILEMMAS, DILEMMAS

Even after my Thurgood Marshall Thomas II routine (or maybe *directly because of*), it's safe to say Kate's mom is still (understandably) skeptical, but eventually, once I've forwarded her all of the appointment information, along with a letter of explanation printed on Whittier letterhead (the miracle of Photoshop) indicating the evaluation fee payment is already pending and with a phone number directing her to Whittier's impossible-to-navigate alumni directory with any questions, she slowly starts believing.

I do my best to keep tabs on Kate from a distance.

Which sucks because trying to watch someone from a distance is exactly the way it sounds—like observing someone through a telescope. Sure, you're zoomed in on them and you get to see everything that they do up close and magnified. But could you really claim to know them, when you miss out on all the details, on what's happening around them, what they're really feeling, what they're going through?

And it blows because the best part about my life lately has been Kate. Only in this life, I don't get to know her at all. She's not my girlfriend. She's not my friend. She's not even an acquaintance. I'm nothing to her, and she's supposedly nothing to me.

And yet—

That's the one thing she could never be.

Sometimes it feels like I'm cheating on Jillian. So much of my time is spent arranging things and monitoring Kate's progress and talking to Dr. Sowunmi, who informed me, given that Kate hasn't given written consent, he can't actually discuss with me any specifics regarding her treatment, that he shouldn't even discuss it in the very broad strokes that he's thus far spoken in.

Today he's carved out three minutes between his patient appointments to talk to me.

"I don't want to get you into any trouble. If you don't feel comfortable talking to me about your work, I understand. I don't want you to feel obligated."

"I guess I feel like you deserve to know *something*. I don't know, Jack. It's complicated."

I laugh.

"So, why this girl, Jack?"

I shrug. "Just paying it forward."

He rolls his eyes. "C'mon, Jack. You can do better than that."

"Because she's one of these people who go through life caring about everyone else, doing for everyone else. She deserves for someone to do for her. She's so smart and funny, and this planet needs her here for as long as it can have her."

"So, you love her."

"I don't *not* love her."

*　　*　　*

Jillian is harder to convince, though.

She wants to know why I'm making the trip to Dr. Sowunmi's hospital.

Or why I'm suddenly so interested in sickle cell disease.

Or what we're going to do if Franny actually gets into Whittier.

And who's going to take his place in the band?

All of which are very good questions.

All of which I have a hard time answering.

THE TALK

We're driving to school when Jillian tells me.

"Franny says he needs to talk to me."

"When?"

"After school."

"Today?"

"Today."

"Good."

"Yeah."

"Should I be there, too?"

"I'm thinking no."

"Yeah."

"I mean, I wouldn't want to aggravate the situation any more than it has to be, you know?"

"No, yeah, of course. That makes sense."

"So, you okay finding a ride home? After school?"

"Sure."

I spend the rest of the day going to class but learning nothing, except how to be good at thinking about Jillian talking to Franny about the fact that we betrayed his trust and got together behind his back.

*　*　*

"How did it go?" I ask as soon as she descends my basement stairs.

"We hurt him, Jack."

"Yeah."

"No," she says, picking up a throw pillow from the couch, sitting down in its place. "We really hurt him."

"What did he say?"

"Not much actually. It was mostly me apologizing. And then at the end he looked at me and said, *I don't think you'll ever understand how much I loved you both.*"

That's not what I expected. I feel like I've been stabbed all over. "Damn," I say. "And what did you say to that?"

Jillian shakes her head. "Nothing. I just sat there hating myself. And then he took my hand in his and said, *All I ever wanted was for you to be happy. And I still want that.*"

"I feel like this is the part where I should be led out in front of the firing squad."

"You and me both," Jillian agrees. "And we'd still get off easy."

AN EXPLODING APPENDIX

Jillian and I are at the hospital together, visiting her cousin, whose appendix nearly ruptured, when The Most Random Person I'd Ever Expect to See Anywhere on Earth steps right onto the elevator and commands, "Sixth floor, bro."

Normally, I'm not big on elevator eye contact. The premise of an elevator is uncomfortable enough—standing silent and motionless in a cramped rectangular box centimeters away from random strangers?

But also this guy's voice. The way he says *bro* instead of *please*, like it's my job to do his bidding, like I'm *working* this elevator and I've been sitting here with my button-pressing finger extended, eagerly waiting for an asshole to order a floor.

I recognize him right away, but of course he has no reason to know me. And even if he did know me, he strikes me as the kind of dude who goes around being recognized but can't be bothered to remember your name, or even how he knows you. So instead he *bros* you.

But I admit I'm biased.

I snap my fingers. "Hey, aren't you . . ." and I start to say *Flanders* or *Sanders* as *bro* payback, but I'm actually so happy to see this guy I can't even bring myself to be petty. "You go to Whittier, right?" I say.

And Xander looks up at me from his phone.

"Do I know you?" Xander asks.

"No, I've seen you around campus is all."

Without a word, Xander goes back to swiping his phone screen.

"So, what, uh, brings you here?" I ask.

"What?"

"What brings you to the hospital? Everything okay?"

"Yeah, everything's great. I'm here for the fish tacos."

I scrunch my face. "Wait, what?"

"Screwing with you, dude, relax. My girlfriend is sick, so."

"Oh, she's admitted here?"

"Yep."

"Is she going to be okay?"

Xander shrugs. "This is nothing new for her. She's practically lived in hospitals her entire life. I think she's used to it now."

"I feel like that's something you'd never be used to."

"I guess." Xander buries his face back into his phone. "I need

386

to be studying right now, but I have to be here. Gotta be the doting, supportive boyfriend."

"You don't."

"What?"

"You don't have to be anything to her. No one's forcing you to be here."

"Ha. You try dumping the sick girl."

And by now you guys know I'm not a fighter.

But I promise you it takes every ounce of restraint that I have ever accumulated past, present, and future to not dump Xander on his fish-taco-joking ass.

But then I remember: I have also dumped the sick girl.

* * *

So, plan B.

First, I secure her room number from the information desk.

Then I race to the gift shop and buy ALL THE FLOW-ERS. The volunteer cashier loans me a cart to transport my flowers. I barely clear the elevator, flowers blooming in every direction. But I make it inside, petals largely intact. The car starts to climb and my stomach churns, only it's not the elevator motion.

I pause outside her door, my stomach queasy now. *What are you doing here, Jack?* But then, without my consent, my hand knocks.

"Come in," Kate calls.

I push the cart inside. I can't see her and I imagine she can't see me, the botanical wall separating us.

"I think you have the wrong room," she says.

I step around the cart and there she is, lying in bed, a book open on her lap, and although she's staring right at me, it's clear she doesn't know me. Which, while expected, is still brutal on a level I'm incapable of articulating.

"You're not Kate Edwards?"

"Yes, that's me," she confirms.

"No mistake then."

I gather as many bouquets as I can hold, arranging the flowers around the room.

"Who are these from?" she asks.

I set a vase filled with yellow and red tulips on the windowsill. There's a stack of books there, and movies, too. *Short Term 12*. We'd watched it together. Well, more like I'd watched it and she'd watched me at all her favorite parts. *What are you doing?* I'd asked, blushing at her staring. *I just want to see your reaction*, she'd said. *If it hits you the same. Do you want me to stop? I'm creeping you out, right? No*, I'd said, *don't stop*.

"Is there a card?" she asks.

"Uh, no, ma'am. Not that I see."

She laughs. "Please never call me ma'am again."

"Oh, right, sorry."

"It's okay." She points to the cart. "I don't understand who'd do this."

"Your boyfriend," I suggest.

"You obviously haven't met my boyfriend."

Okay, I admit, this makes me happy. But also not happy,

because she deserves a boyfriend who'd fill her room with flowers. Although, she deserves a boyfriend who wouldn't abandon her just because things got hard, so I shouldn't toot my own horn too enthusiastically, either.

"Parents maybe? Siblings?"

"Not their style."

I study her eyes. I can't help but wonder if on some deep-down, hard-to-retrieve level she still knows me. Like if she burrowed far enough into her subconscious she might find traces of us. That maybe with the right combination of words, if I moved a certain way, she might remember. But she grabs her phone, taps the screen.

"You figured it out?" I ask.

She glances up, smiles. "Unless someone steps forward and takes responsibility for this flower assault, I think it's likely to remain a mystery."

I nod. "Right."

She goes back to her phone.

"Well, that's all of them," I say, purposely saving the last flower arrangement for the table beside her.

"Thanks," she says, not looking up.

"Sure. My pleasure." I'm lingering; I don't want to leave. But if I stay any longer, it's going to be creepy. Maybe she'll call security. I stop in the doorway. "Well, you take care. I hope you feel better soon."

In the hallway, my heart thumps so hard I have to lean against the wall to steady myself.

"Hey, wait," she calls out. "Hey!"

Could it be? She feels something? Somehow remembers?

I step back in. "Yeah?"

"*Phalaenopsis* Blume. How did you know?"

"I'm sorry?"

"*Phalaenopsis* Blume, also known as moth orchids."

"Oh. Right. The phalen . . . phalanges . . . what you said."

She laughs. "So, how'd you know these are my favorite?"

"What do you mean?"

She grins. "Out of all these flowers, you put the orchid next to my bed. Who are you, really? Do we know each other? Someone put you up to this?"

"I'm just a hospital volunteer."

"Oh yeah? Then where's your red volunteer vest?"

Good point. "Dry cleaner's," I say. It takes everything in my power not to slap myself across the forehead.

She stares at me like she doesn't believe me. "Well, thanks, anyway. You made my day."

"Glad I could help," I say, wishing I could say more. That I could pull up a chair beside her. Find out how's she's been. Apologize for abandoning her.

But I can't.

I shuffle out into the hallway, pulling the door behind me. As it closes, I take her in one final time. Kate brings the tiger lily to her nose and her eyes drift toward the window, the smell triggering a memory.

The door clicks shut.

* * *

Jillian's in the waiting room outside her cousin's room, munching dried cranberries.

"There you are," Jillian says.

"Is everything okay?" I touch her arm. "Is your cousin all right?"

"Nothing's wrong. I was just worried about you. You vanished. And you weren't answering your phone."

I fish my phone out. I've missed nine calls, a slew of texts. All but one text is from Jillian. The other one from Mom asking if I'll be home for dinner. "Sorry, J."

She leans into me. "I missed you, baby."

I wrap my arms around her. And she feels so good. So warm and comfy.

"Jack?"

"Yeah?"

"Have you been in a nursery?"

"Why?" I ask, glancing down at the top of her head. "Don't tell me someone's baby spit up on me without me noticing."

"Not that kind of nursery. I mean a *plant* nursery. You smell like you've been rolling around in a flower bed."

* * *

You know how in the movies the two people who are in love and who will inevitably wind up together by the end have all these artificial obstacles thrown in front of them? How as we, the audience, watch the two lovers fight through these obstacles in the name of true love, we can't help but want them to be

391

together at all costs; no matter what, they *have* to be together, right?

Except at least one of them, if not both of them, are already in semiserious relationships. And everyone knows your two main characters need to be somewhat likable, so you can't just have them be complete assholes and dump their SOs. And so, to make the inevitable happy ending more plausible, the writers decide to make their SOs complete assholes—that way we *hate* the people that they're with and have no problem rooting for our two lovebirds to kick their crappy relationships to the curb, and to run into the waiting arms of their true, always-meant-to-be loves—

And boom, our Hollywood happy ending. Everyone wins.

Except I don't have an awful relationship with Jillian. She's pretty much perfect. The only fault I can possibly attribute to her, you know, other than the minor transgressions, like how she squeezes from the bottom of the toothpaste tube (uh, *weird*) or how she leaves the toilet seat down after she's finished (the nerve!), is that she's not Kate.

She's not Kate.

But of course she's not.

She's Jillian.

And Jillian is incredibly awesome in her own right.

And we're happy together, right?

Right.

Then how come it feels like I've made a mistake?

LIKE THIS

"There was a time," Jillian admits, "when I thought you and I would end up together."

By now, after all that's happened, I've mostly cobbled this sentiment together, but it's different to hear her say it, to echo what I'd always thought, too.

"Really?"

She cocks her head to the side like she's considering this even as she says it. "Maybe not in the *near* future. Certainly not like . . ."

We both know the word she's omitting.

Not like *this*.

But that word never materializes. It hangs, a ghost in the room.

"But still," she continues. "I thought maybe something

would happen at college, you know. And if not at college, then after we'd graduated, and gone off to different grad schools."

"Yeah."

"When you were this great writer and I'm a pretty decent entertainment lawyer ..."

"*The best* entertainment lawyer," I interject.

"... and we show up at the same work meeting and we're all grown up and single and finally ready. Or something like that."

"Yeah," I agree. "Something like that."

But maybe not like *this*.

DUFFEL BAG BAGGAGE

He hands me a black duffel bag, disbelief frozen on his face. "C'mon, don't do me like that. You gotta tell me how in the hell you knew."

I don't look inside the bag. I've only held $200K in my hands one other time before, but this is roughly the same weight.

"I got lucky."

"Stop. This wasn't luck. Somehow you knew. You knew. And now you don't wanna tell the man who helped you make it happen."

"What do you want me to say?"

"How about the truth, Jack?"

"I'm from six months into the future and I already knew that Mandrake was going to win."

Franny's dad waves me off. "Fine, don't tell me. But this is the last bet I make for you. I had a hard time collecting. You pull another rabbit out of your hat and we'll both be floating in Lake Erie."

"I'm done with gambling."

"Good," he says, folding his arms.

"But there is one more thing."

"Fine, you can tell me at the bar. Drinks on you. But first, we drop this money off. I'm not the nervous type, but damn."

*   *   *

The bar's a ghost town.

There's a couple sitting at the end, their faces twisted, the woman picking up her drink every so often and sloshing its melting ice.

After Franny's dad orders, he turns to me, says, "So, what'd you want to talk about?"

I opt not to mince words. "You haven't seen Franny."

He slumps forward on his bar stool, pulls from his beer. "Yeah, well, I've been busy. I'll get to it, when the time's right."

"You've been busy. You're going to get around to it," I say. "You've been out of prison for weeks and you can't manage one phone call? To your only son?"

"How do you know what I've done?" he asks.

The truth is I don't one hundred percent know. But it seemed like a safe bet.

"Jack, I did you a favor because you're my kid's friend, but that's where our business begins and ends. Don't think for a second you and me are friends now. That we're gonna discuss how I deal with my son. Our relationship is none of your business."

"Relationship? Are you kidding? What relationship?"

Franny's dad jumps, his stool skittering behind him, his fist raised at me. "Don't make this go sideways, kid."

"Look, I'm sorry if—"

"You stay here another second, you'll be more than sorry."

"Fine." I pull a twenty from my pocket, toss the money onto the bar.

"Drinks on me," I say. "Bullshit on you."

* * *

I call out to Mom and Dad but no one's home.

I kick off my shoes, grab water from the kitchen. I collapse on my unmade bed and commence a lengthy Pointless Ceiling Stare session.

That's when I remember:

The duffel.

I reach under my bed, grabbing for the strap. Nothing. I reach again, still nothing. I drop to my knees to get a better look, my stomach dropping.

Because I know without looking.

The bag is gone.

I freak the fuck out. Checking under my pillows, tossing my sheets, doing ridiculous things like pulling out all my desk drawers and checking under the rug—as if $200K could fit in an envelope-size drawer or somehow slip under a square of commercial-grade carpet.

I race around the house that way.

I check every nook, cranny, and then recheck. All while screaming wholly original curses. *I just lost $200,000* type curses.

Nothing cool, mind you.

Mostly nonsensical. Definitely irrational.

Mother-squeezing-tiger-lily-having-crappy-poop-pants.

Stuff like that.

But in the end, for all my destroy-the-house efforts, all I have is shortness of breath and my crying, trembling face.

I call my mom's phone. Voice mail. I nearly hurl my phone against the wall, but I stop myself. Try Dad's.

"Dad, did you, uh, find . . . ," I say, stammering, my voice an avalanche of panic and dread.

"Jack, are you okay, son? What's wrong?"

"No, I'm not okay. I need to know if you found something."

"Found what? What are you talking about?"

"A bag, Dad," I blurt out, even though at this point I'm confident he has no idea what I'm talking about.

"What bag? Are you in some kind of trouble, Jack? Do you need—"

But I don't hear the rest of his sentence because I take the phone away from my ear and glance at the screen.

A text pops up.

I have something that belongs to you.

Be at The Wood in 20.

*   *   *

I can't tell you why we call it The Wood. I guess because it's in the woods, except the exact location is in a large clearing in the least woodsy part of the woods.

Anyway—

When I stick my head up through the floor, Franny's leaning against the wall, arms folded, the duffel bag at his feet.

"Hey," I say.

"Why the hell do you have this money?"

"I robbed a bank?"

"The truth. Now, Jack."

What is it with everyone demanding the truth?

The truth? The truth? You can't handle the truth! No, really, you can't. I know the truth and I can barely deal with it.

"I won a bet."

Franny's eyebrows rise. "You won a bet? That's the best you've got?"

"It's the truth."

"You're a real piece of work, King, you know that?"

"I bet that Mandrake would win the tourney."

"You did what? Only a fool would make that bet."

"I sold my car, used all of my savings, and I made the bet."

"Even if that was true, you wouldn't know how to place a bet this size."

"I got someone else to do it for me."

Franny laughs. "I know for damn sure Mama or Papa King didn't place any wagers for you."

I shake my head. "It wasn't them."

"Then who?"

"It doesn't matter, Franny."

"No, I think it does. It matters to me. I want to know."

"What were you even doing at my house, anyway? You think you can just drop by anytime, unannounced? Just take a shower or grab a bite or steal someone's money from under their bed?"

Franny shrugs. "I left some clothes at your house. And my phone charger. I knocked, but no one was home, which actually seemed better. I didn't want to have to see . . . it was just better. I grabbed the spare key from the rock."

Damn you, fake, spare-key-holding, save-Kate-plan-foiling rock!

"Just give me my money and I'll—"

"You'll what, Jack?"

"I'll forget about the whole breaking and entering thing."

"To be so smart, sometimes you're so stupid. Where'd the money come from? Huh, Jack? Tell me so we can be done here."

"It was your dad, okay! There! Now you know! Are you happy now?"

But Franny's shaking his head. "I already knew, man. I just wanted to hear you say it." He kicks the bag toward me, and it zips across the uneven planks. "Take your money and stay the fuck away from me."

"Franny . . ."

"I promise you on Abuela's life that if you don't climb down that ladder right now, I'm going to throw your lying, backstabbing, trifling ass down myself."

I believe him.

But part of me wants to hang out on that ladder just long enough to antagonize Franny and get the ass beating I've deserved for far too long, the one that he has no business sparing me.

"What? You think I'm lying? That I won't do it?" he spits. His face and fists squeezed in fury.

"No," I say. "I believe you."

Say what you want, but Franny's a man of his word.

Which is far more than anyone could say about me.

I drop the duffel to the ground. I let go of the ladder.

*   *   *

Prom and graduation fly by in the senior-year whirlwind.

Prom with Jillian is fun. We dance the night away. But I spend a lot of the evening wondering what'll happen once Franny shows up. He never does.

I take my Avoid Franny at All Costs tactics to new heights. He's playing the same game. And we rarely see each other.

The Panthers advance deeper into the playoffs than before, and I wonder what the Franny-Jack rift has to do with that. Of course, maybe the answer is nothing at all.

Jillian and I go to their third playoff game, and Jillian waves at Franny from up in the stands during warm-ups, and he flashes her a small smile. Rita Marquez, who rumor has it is his new girlfriend, is three rows below us, holding up a poster that she's adorned in Magic Marker swirls and happy faces and that has a massive hot-pink arrow that points down at her head, and the poster says *Cisco's Cheerleader*. She waves the poster around like she's fanning the crowd, as though she's attempting to single-handedly cool down the entire gymnasium.

Franny's a madman on the court. There's not a rebound he doesn't snag, a shot he doesn't contest on defense. As usual, he's an offensive stat-stuffer, scoring twenty-eight points and racking up five assists.

This time his play spells victory for Elytown High.

Our classmates and his teammates mob him at center court.

I consider congratulating him, but I decide not to press my luck. But then he bursts through the crowd, runs up the stands, and squeezes Rita, and it's weird not to say *something*.

"Good game, man," I offer.

He shakes his head. "*Good?*"

"*Great* game," I correct myself.

"My baby is unstoppable, right," Rita coos. She cups his face and they kiss, and I wonder if this is the cue for Jillian and me to leave.

But then Franny says, "You guys are coming to the celebration, right?"

"I hope it's cool. I mean, it's in the bougie part of town, so you never know," Rita says. "Oh, wait, don't you live over there, Jack?"

I'm not quite sure how to take her question. "A few blocks over actually," I reply.

Jillian smiles. "I'm sure you'd have more fun, you know, without us around. But thanks, Franny. That's really sweet of you."

402

Franny leers at me. "Time heals all wounds. Isn't that what they say, Jack?"

"Right," I say.

Although I know Time is as likely to inflict wounds.

* * *

Jillian decides that Franny's invitation is a peace offering.

"After everything, how can we not go," she reasons.

So I hop into my dad's car, surprised when Franny slides into the passenger seat, fastens his seat belt.

"Rita drove here, too. So I asked Jill if she'd mind riding over with her. Figured the girls ride with the girls and the guys with the guys."

"Uh, okay," I say.

"Besides, figured we should probably talk."

"Yeah. Okay. Talking is good."

We drive the first minutes in silence. Then Franny raps his knuckles against the window, tapping a made-up beat.

"How's the band?" he asks finally.

I fiddle with the radio buttons but I don't turn it on. I try to think of the right words. "Not the same without you."

"Hmm," he says.

"Listen, Franny . . . you . . . I—I'm sure this doesn't come as a surprise, but I've always been jealous of you."

"Say what?" Franny laughs.

"I'm serious. Before you and Jillian got together, I spent a month working up the courage to ask her out."

"You never said anything."

403

"What was I supposed to say? 'Hey, Franny, you stole my girlfriend'?"

"You should've said something. You know, *before* I got super into her."

"Maybe," I admit. "I guess I was hoping I'd just get over it."

"But then you didn't. Instead you pull a punk-ass move and betray your supposed best friend."

"I couldn't even figure out why you wanted Jillian. You could have anyone."

"If you couldn't figure that out, then maybe *you're* the one who doesn't deserve her."

He's right. Here I am pretending as though I'm the only one in the world who can see how awesome of a person Jillian is, as if I have the Jillian Is a Spectacular Human Being patent, never once considering that Franny sees it just as clearly. The whole time I've told myself no one understands the connection that Jillian and I have, how we click. But maybe Franny felt the same.

"And as if the Jillian thing isn't bad enough, then you start hanging out with The Coupon behind my back. What's that about, man? Other than using him to make you money?"

"Uh, just, you know, I heard he'd gotten released and, uh, I don't know, I guess I was hoping to help you—"

"You mean help yourself. Everything you do is for you, man. Stop lying to yourself."

"I wanted him to know how awesome you are, in spite of him. That he was crazy to waste time away from you all these years. That you deserve so much better, Franny."

"Just stay away from my family."

"Franny, I wasn't trying to . . ." And I don't know how to finish that sentence. What is it that I wasn't trying to do? Ruin our friendship? Make him miserable? Because I probably could have done a lot better job of *not* doing that stuff.

"And you can kill all the *Franny* talk, okay. It's Francisco to you, man."

"I'm sorry."

"I could've killed you, after the stunt you pulled, man. But I didn't. I should've at least messed you up a bit. But . . . I don't know . . . I guess I'm a sucker for loyalty. So I gave you a pass on that. But you're out of passes, kid. You keep screwing with business that doesn't have anything to do with you and I'm going to have to do what I have to do, you get me?"

I nod. "I understand."

"You better."

"I'm sorry, Frann . . . Francisco. I'm really sorry."

"No, you're not. You feel guilty. Learn the difference."

"I *am* sorry. Guilty, too, I guess."

"The whole basketball team wanted to jump your punk ass, but I put a stop to that."

"I don't know what you want me to say." I pause longer than normal at a stop sign, so I can face him. So I can really hear him.

"Nothing you can say." He unlocks his door, slides out into the cool night.

"Where are you going, man? We still have another five or six blocks."

Franny shrugs. "Feel like walking. Only so much bullshit I can stomach in one night."

"Franny, why did you even get in the car if you hate me so much?"

Franny shrugs. "I thought maybe we had something worth salvaging, you know, after a lifetime of friendship, but I was wrong, clearly."

"Come on. I get it. And everything you've said is true. Just let me drive you to this party and then . . . if you never want to talk to me again . . . okay . . . I wish . . . I just have to accept that."

Franny leans into the open passenger door and makes a face that I've seen before, usually right before he punches someone into the next galaxy. "You say you were jealous of *me*, Jack. *You* jealous of *me*? When you have, like, literally *everything*. Parents who actually care about you, and who have been around your whole life, a nice house in a safe neighborhood, food on the table that you didn't have to figure out how to scrape together, more clothes than you can count. Literally, a bag full of money. And I have, what? Man, I don't even know. But at least I had you. A best friend who made the world a little less cold, you know. And then I get lucky, and I get someone else good in my life . . . Jillian . . . and she makes everything bearable, everything better . . . and you took her from me the same way everyone has taken every good thing away from me . . . and the worst part is . . . I never would've done that to you. *Never*. Far as I was concerned, you and me were brothers, man. But I guess that was a lie, because brothers wouldn't do that to each other."

And I sit there at the stop sign, waiting for him to turn around, waiting for him to reconsider, but he's not coming back. He pulls his hoodie over his head and keeps walking.

* * *

I take my time getting to the party. Figure it's best to give Franny time to cool off. Figure if I drive around long enough maybe I'll come up with a way to make him not hate me so much. Only when I get there, he hasn't made it yet.

"Where's Franny?" I ask Rita.

"I was going to ask you the same thing," she says. "He's not answering his phone." I can see the worry in her face. Jillian's, too.

I want to say something comforting, but in the end I don't remember if I even say anything at all. Which is just as well, because I probably would've said something stupid like, *I'm sure he's okay.*

Which isn't true.

Franny never shows up to the party.

Turns out he took a shortcut that, in the end, wasn't so short.

WORST THING EVER

We get the news as the party is fading.

This kid Mike Whitney turns down the music, stands on a couch, and tells everyone to shut the hell up, before he makes the announcement.

"Francisco's been shot!"

*   *   *

The emergency room waiting area is full of sad people, but it feels like we're the saddest. Abuela comes bounding through the sliding doors, out of breath and hysterical, and the three of us do our best to settle her down. My parents show up a little later and talk to the police about what happened.

Apparently, some suspicious neighborhood-watcher spotted Franny cutting through her gated community and called the police. She decided to follow him in her slippers and housecoat.

"I called the police," she called out to Franny. (And this is according to what she told the police, so, of course, it may or may not reflect what actually happened.)

Franny shrugged, or shook his head, or something else that rubbed her the wrong way. "Whatever, lady. Let them come," he'd said.

"Take your hands out of your pockets, and sit on the curb."

"Fuck you. I'm going home."

"Put your hands up where I can see them."

"You're not the police. Give it a break."

And then he *made a sudden move for his pocket* and removed something shiny. *I was afraid for my life. I just reacted. I didn't have time to think*, she'd said. So, she shot him. *Bang.* Square in his chest. Watched him crumple to the ground, a weird smile on his face, she'd said. She said it was only afterward that she heard the music playing, that she thinks maybe she'd heard it before, but it was only after she'd fired that she registered the sound. It was the Bee Gees that she was hearing, a twenty-second ringtone coming from the shiny phone Franny held in his hand.

"The Bee Gees," I ask the officer. "You're sure?"

"Yeah," the officer said, referring to his notes. "That's what she said, anyway."

I nod because I know why Franny was so anxious to answer that call. "That's his dad's ringtone."

* * *

We're not allowed to see him.

But we're told he's out of surgery and resting in the recovery room. If everything goes okay, they'll move him to critical care.

Abuela hasn't stopped sobbing.

Franny's dad finally shows up and his eyes are a deep pink, like he's been drinking, or maybe crying. Or both.

"How's my boy?" he says from across the waiting room.

I stand. "He's in recovery. We're waiting to see him."

The Coupon nods, hugs his mom, then steps away. "I need coffee."

"I'll walk with you," I volunteer.

It's a short walk to the vending machine, but I'm not interested in the eighty-five-cent lattes.

"Where were you tonight?" I ask him when we're out of earshot from the others.

"Excuse me," he says.

"You missed his game."

"I called him."

"Yeah, afterward," I say, when what I want to say is *yeah you did, which is partly why he's in the hospital recovering from a gunshot wound*, but the other responsible party stares back at me from the shiny vending machine glass, so.

"Easy, Oprah," The Coupon says. "What I do with my son isn't your concern."

My voice leaps out of my body, even surprising me. "What happens to the people I love *is* my concern. And this is the worst. You popping in and out of his life like a jack-in-the-box, it's tired, man. It's selfish and it's old and it's hurtful. You don't even realize how awesome your son is. But you don't want to know, do you? Because then you might have to be a real dad for

410

the first time in seventeen years."

The Coupon shoves me hard against the vending machine. I wait for someone to intervene, except the hallway's clear.

"I suck as a father, that what you wanna hear? Huh? There, I said it. Now we can all go back to the business of living, right? Secret's out." The Coupon relaxes his grip on my chest, lets my shirt go. Starts to walk away but stops. "Do you have any idea how it feels to walk around the world knowing you ain't shit? That nothing you've done means anything? When you look out at the sky and you don't see a limitless horizon, when the sky doesn't shine for you how it does for everyone else, when you know . . . when you KNOW that there's nothing to look forward to because you've already lost all the good things that you were supposed to take care of? I haven't woken up happy in forever, Jack. I don't even know if happy is a real thing anymore. You think I'm cold? Hard? You goddamn right I am! That's the only way I can go about my day. That's how I got through prison, how I got through being a shitty dad, a shitty son, once upon a time a shitty husband. That's how I get through."

I swallow hard. "Maybe if you told Franny all of that. Maybe if you . . ."

He jumps toward me, a red cyclone of anger and hurt in his eyes. "Tell him what? You don't think he knows his pop is a failure? That that's some kinda news flash for him. He been knowing that about me. All his damn life."

"It's not too late."

"It's been too late. It's the bottom of the ninth, two outs,

411

two strikes, and I'm in that batter box, man. And that pitcher on the mound, I ain't never got a hit off him, I'm zero for a million against him, and he's throwing heat that I can't even see, let alone catch up to. And I know what you thinking, 'cause I've thought the same. Maybe if you just swing one more time, maybe you finally get that hit that's long overdue. But I don't ever get on base, Jack. You looking at the strikeout king, my friend."

He laughs. Slaps me on my shoulder like he's just delivered a punch line, except his eyes are wet. "Hell, that's not even true. In reality, you gotta be in the game to strike out. When it comes to that boy, I've never even been in the stadium. I was never there. So, you don't have to tell me how much it would mean to my son. I lived with that disappointment every day of my life. And the sun ain't never gonna set on that. Never."

Before I can get a word out, Franny's dad walks away, thumping his shoulder into the automatic door before it can fully open, turning the next corner.

I walk back to the waiting room, my face buzzing with anger and sadness. I think of my friend lying there, hurting, just hurting, with no one in the room that loves him.

I want to be in the stadium.

I want back in the box.

Hit or miss, I need to swing.

* * *

The cafeteria is closed, so Mom hands out snacks from the vending machine.

412

Every half hour Dad checks in with the front desk for updates, but they keep telling him there's nothing new to report.

"No news is good news," Franny's dad says. Which somehow seems typical of him, that he'd equate nothing with something good.

Jillian sips on a coffee. Her hands are shaky and she keeps spilling it down her arm and on her chair.

Rita's on her phone, talking to her parents, and then her sister.

You can't save everyone. I know that. Believe me, I get that. But forget about *everyone*, I can't save *anyone*.

*   *   *

They finally let us in to see him. Only one at a time, though, the nurse tells us. And ten minutes at the most. He needs rest.

I stand in the doorway, just watching his eyes flutter in his sleep. I probably waste two or three of my minutes just watching.

"Go play," he says, softly.

I step into the room, walk beside his bed. His legs are nearly too long, his feet glancing the footboard.

"Play what," I say. "What do you want me to play?"

Franny's chest is wrapped tightly in gauze, and there's a long skinny tube snaking out from the dressing, feeding what looks like blood down into a clear, fist-size bulb; must be the collection drain the surgeon mentioned. Franny shakes his head, groans like it hurts.

"Not play," he says. "Go away."

He doesn't open his eyes.

Of course he doesn't want me here. He wouldn't be here if not for me. I stand there, my brain scrolling for the right words to say, but *no search results found*.

"I'll leave, Franny," I say. "But I promise you, I'm not going away."

BREAK IT UP, EVERYBODY. PARTY'S OVER.

Mom and Dad decide to reschedule their anniversary party, because *how can you celebrate when you don't have all your family there*, Mom reasons.

I don't mention that Franny might not have come, anyway.

I decide not to remind everyone that he hates my guts. Because that's inconsequential. I just want him to be okay, whether he hates me forever or not.

We still open our bottle of wine.

And it's easy to tell that we're all distracted. But we push through. We put on semibrave faces. "It's just not the same, you know," Dad says, pouring another glass.

And he's right.

We all know.

And more than anything, I want another chance.

One more reset to undo this tragedy.

Only I can't count on some magic that I don't even understand.

Not this time.

Not when this could be the last time.

And what if this is what I have to live with, for the rest of my life?

Knowing that because of me, maybe Kate lives, but Franny dies?

What if I traded Franny for Kate, without even knowing?

How could I live with that?

So I excuse myself, head up to my room, and close the door. I bring the alarm clock that's on my desk and set it on the foot of my bed and I stare and I stare and I stare.

And I wait.

Just before one o'clock in the morning I dial into my phone.

The operator tells me that Kate is indeed in the hospital, only it's after-hours and she cannot transfer me to her room.

"It's okay," I assure her. "I'll try her again later."

I slip out the back stairs, around the house, and into my dad's car.

The highway's deserted. It feels like I'm the only one awake tonight. I pull into the parking lot and try the front door. Locked, of course. But it doesn't matter. Not tonight. I walk around to the side of the building where the office is. I toss a rock through the window. Alarms sound like crazy, but I ignore them. I climb into the window and walk into the cooler. There are boxes upon boxes, and I'm not sure which one to grab, so I take them all, setting them one by one out the broken window. I pull Dad's car closer and load them into the trunk.

Two minutes later I'm turning onto the highway as three police cars, sirens screaming, lights pounding against the foggy night, zoom past me.

* * *

A cruiser's parked beside the door, but I don't care.

I hurry through the door and crash into a human wall.

"I got him," the officer mumbles into the walkie holstered on his shoulder. "Back outside, you," he orders me, pushing open the door, his other hand hugging his gun grip. "Come on. Let's go."

And I've failed.

It doesn't matter what I do, what I try—definitely not what I want—everything is doomed from the start.

Franny's hurt.

Kate's dying.

I broke into Dr. Sowunmi's office, and for what?

To come up short, again. Again.

I try to push past the officer and bolt for the stairs but his grip just tightens. "Don't make me lay you out," he barks.

"Maybe that's for the best," I tell him.

They order my legs spread apart, my cheek mashed against the back of their cruiser.

"Please," I beg them, "my girlfriend's dying. Please. Just five minutes. Please. A heart, have a heart. Just let me see her for five minutes and then you can haul me away to prison, throw away the key, whatever. Please. *Please.*"

I try dropping to my knees to beg, but that's tricky when you're physically restrained. The officer who put the cuffs on me looks over to the other officer, a dirty-blond woman with bloodshot eyes, and she sighs but nods.

The cuffs come off.

The elevator turtles its way to Kate's floor.

We detour because the floor's wet.

And then Kate's nurse tells us visiting hours are over, but the woman officer intervenes, and the nurse rolls her eyes but steps aside.

It's almost too late. Kate's barely there.

"Kate," I say softly.

She opens her eyes, a flash of panic. "Who are you? What are you doing here?"

"Hopefully saving you this time," I say. "I've never told you this, but I love you, Kate."

"What are you—"

But before she can finish I reach into my shoe, pull out the syringe, and fire it into her thigh. Her body quivers, like I've just hit her with a million amps.

The police tackle me, shouting curses into my ear, into the room.

As I fall to the ground, my nose crunching against the

418

linoleum in a way that I know it's broken, lots of feet dash into the room. There's more shouting and people keep shaking me, blood dripping from my nostrils, asking me what I injected her with, what was in the syringe, and the truth is I couldn't explain it if I wanted to.

This is the only thing that I could do. The only thing left.

I shut my eyes and I wait.

FIVE-ever

WHAT WOULD BILL MURRAY DO?

"Excuse me, man, but you're sort of damming up the steps."

I turn to Kate and smile my heart out.

Because seeing her here on these steps means I have failed yet again.

But more importantly it means I get another chance.

*   *   *

I watch *Groundhog Day* for what I believe to be two sound reasons: 1) Bill Murray and 2) because while we are not exactly in the same shoes, I figure there is something to learn from watching a man relive the same day.

And I do learn. What not to do. How not to live.

I don't want to spend my time perfecting myself in the eyes of other people. I'm not out to be the wittiest, the coolest, the most brilliant. Some Jack 5.0. Sure, if I can avoid some costly mistakes along the way, specifically on how to avoid hurting the people I love, then yes, absolutely sign me up. But I'm not going to use my power (or whatever you wanna call it) to study the right combination of words and memories to make Kate fall helplessly in love with me.

Because I believe our love is the only thing that's for certain in these rewinds.

That no matter what happens, we are destined to love each other.

Maybe I'm a romantic. Maybe I'm a fool.

But I don't need to wake up on the same day a thousand times to know that I love Kate and that I would do anything to wake up beside her for the rest of our days.

No matter how many. And no matter how few.

Whatever put me on these goddamn stairs is bigger than me, bigger than anything I've ever known. I'm *supposed* to be here. With Kate. Nowhere else. I'm going to keep showing up on these stairs, waiting for her to say *excuse me* for as many times as it takes.

SOME GOOD ADVICE AMID GROCERY STORE GROSSNESS

I tell Dad that maybe instead of a writer, I'll be a scientist, a researcher, and dedicate myself to finding cures to especially crappy diseases.

Dad appears genuinely happy at this possibility. This is confirmed when he launches a throat-clearing monologue. Which I don't mind, even though we're in the grocery store, an endless row of milk cartons and jugs stretching before us.

"Is it safe to presume this has something to do with Kate?" he asks.

I nod. "Meeting her has made me reexamine a lot of things, I guess."

"Jack, I happen to think it's a great thing you're considering. Sometimes you have to reinvent yourself. Decide what you really want to do in life. People always say you have to be happy with yourself first before you can find happiness with someone else. There's truth to that, Jackie. But honestly, there's something to be said for finding that person who reminds you how happy life can be. You find that person, boy or girl, and you never let them go. Your mom has opinions for days, and it can get tiring . . . for other people . . . me, it doesn't bother me. That's who she is, that's who she was when I met her. But she's also the person who makes me better. So if I have to choose between someone opining about which cereal actually has the most beneficial fiber and being some miserable fecally impacted poor lonely bastard, guess what I'm choosing—I'm choosing to crap regularly and be happy, Jackie boy. Every damn time, and each day I wake up new, I choose your mom."

Which is when Mom, who apparently is *not* back in the car looking for coupons but instead eavesdropping around the corner, coos, "Oooooh, Abe, I choose you, too!"

"Kiss me, dollface," Dad says.

"Oh, come on, guys. In the dairy section? This is a bit *cheesy.*" But I don't really mean it. Because if there's one thing I appreciate after all this time, it's expressing your love while you can. Never take time, or love, for granted.

But Mom ignores me anyway, planting a sloppy wet kiss onto Dad's face. "You haven't lost a step, Abe."

Dad grins. "You keep me young, baby. Jackie boy, we're gonna need cleanup in aisle five."

And I watch in semihorror as they press against the milk fridge in a blur of middle-aged body parts.

ALL THE THINGS

I ask Franny if it's okay to talk to his dad.

"About what?"

"Honestly, I need him to do me a favor."

"A favor? From The Coupon?" Franny shrugs. "Knock yourself out, if you like disappointment."

"You sure it's okay?"

"What's it for?"

"I'm betting."

"Betting on what?"

"On love."

"Jack?"

"Yeah?"

"How are you so corny?"

I put all my money on Mandrake—

"You sure about this, Jack?" Franny's dad asks. "This is a lot of money to lose. I won't be able to get it back. It'll be out of my hands, kid."

And Mandrake—

... Oh my goodness, are you kidding me? Mandrake has just taken their first lead of the game with twenty seconds left ... This is the greatest comeback in the history of sports, people ... You are witnessing history tonight ... History, with a capital H!—

Well, the Potbelly Pigs come through yet again.

I schedule the evaluation with Dr. Sowunmi—

"Jack, there are no promises. This treatment may not work for Kate. Do you understand that?"

"I believe in you, Doctor," I assure him.

"Well, then, I hope to God I don't let you down," he says, reaching across the desk to shake my hand.

Kate gets the first injection.

She's sick for a few days, mostly nauseous, but she starts to rebound by week's end. "I don't know if it's working, or if it's just in my head," she says, beaming. "But I feel better, Jack. Better than I can remember feeling in a long, long time."

Band practice is better than ever.

Kate and I go to prom together. We kiss. The kiss is as magical as our *first* first time. And we dance our ugly dances with unrelenting gusto, as if we've just discovered that ugly dancing saves lives, and we are determined to save every life that we can.

Leave no life behind, we say, doing our best-worst Runaway Rodeo Bull in a China Shop dance.

"Please, please, tell me you guys are high," Franny pleads.

"Off life, my friend," Kate yells, jumping higher still. "Off life!"

I lay the guilt trip on extra-thick, and then, just to make sure, I drive over to Franny's house and pick his dad up.

"You're sure about this, Jack," he says. "Because I'm sure as hell not."

"Franny knows you're coming. He wants to see you. He's *been* wanting to see you. All this time he's just been waiting for you to finally show up."

Franny pretends like he's only mildly excited, but anyone who knows him knows he's ecstatic. I've known him since sandbox days and I can't remember him smiling so hard, so much.

"You came," Franny says.

His dad nods. "I never want to miss another game. I just hope it's not too late."

I graduate high school, high-five all the on-stage faculty as I dance across the stage. Dad makes the family take lots of pictures, Kate included.

Jillian delivers The Mic-Drop Commencement Speech of All Time. "And so when all's said and done, the time we've spent here at Elytown High is not about the number of hours we've spent in class, or *not* in class."

The audience chuckles.

"It's not how many touchdowns we've scored, or free throws we've missed," Jillian continues. "It's not even about this school, really. Not the building, anyway. These last four years, if we lived them right, are about growing up, about learning to battle, about trying our best and still failing, about picking ourselves up again and again. These years were picking each other up. About friendship. The type of friends that show up when you need them the most. That text you and call you when you don't want to talk. That show up and keep showing up, day in and day out, every week, every semester, again and again. The type of friendship that doesn't end with graduation. The type of friendship, like the very best type of love, that never ends."

When she's finished, we erupt in applause, Franny and I exploding out of our seats, several aisles apart, pumping our fists, whooping and hollering Jillian's name. She blows kisses to us, then takes a bow.

Kate's baby brother Reggie still gives me a hard time—

Except this time around I don't meet him at family dinner, where his parents can rein him in, if necessary. Nope. This time he goes with Kate and me to the movies and proceeds to 1) sit between us, 2) hog the popcorn that I bought, and 3) spoil virtually every scene, which initially I thought made him some sort of plot-guessing film savant, only to later learn, no, he'd already seen the movie and was just being a grade-A asshole.

"So, uh, Jack, tell me what your intentions are toward my sister."

"Easy," I say. "I intend to be with her for a long, long time."

And this doesn't come close to shutting him up. He piles on the *I don't like you liking my sister* routine, but it doesn't bother me so much, because that's what little brothers are for. I respect him for it.

Franny scores a gazillion points in the playoff game and leads Elytown to victory. He gives his dad his game jersey, and his dad pulls off the T-shirt he's wearing and slips Franny's jersey on, half a size too small and sweat-drenched, but he doesn't take it off or make a face. He struts around the gym, singing, *That's right, that's my boy* to anyone who looks at him. Abuela even shows up on time.

"What," she says, incredulously. "I've been on time before."

But none of us can remember when.

We all go out to eat to celebrate and somewhere between appetizers and entrees, Franny clinks his glass.

"Attention, family and friends. I have an announcement to make," he says, standing up. We all look over.

"You are now looking at a Whittier enrollee," he says, his smile with extra Franny wattage.

Jillian jumps from her seat, throwing her arms around his neck and nearly taking out our appetizers in the process. "Oh my God, are you serious? Baby, I knew you'd get in. I knew it!"

Franny doesn't get shot, unless you count from Jillian, courtesy of Cupid's pointy arrow. (I know, I know, so achingly cheesy, but give me a pass here. I'm happy.)

Turns out Kate's sister Kira is pregnant, which excites Franny the most because he envisions lifetime front-row seats at every Mighty Moat concert.

Meanwhile, *our* band keeps practicing.

My parents' anniversary party is killer. Kate, Jillian, Franny, and I barely leave each other's sides. After four summers of practice (condensed into one), I still find a way to flub a few notes in the beginning, but no one seems to notice.

"Mom, are you crying?" I ask, not because it's not obvious that she is, but to distract everyone from the fact that *I'm* crying, too.

We share a bottle of wine. We all clean up.

"We're going to take off now," Franny says, taking my hand into his and pulling me into a bro hug. Jillian wraps her arms around Kate, and then turns to kiss me on my cheek. "Love you, man," she says.

"Love you more," I say.

Kate and I walk them to the driveway, to their car, and we watch them drive off into the starry night.

"You wanna take off, too, or," I say, letting the *or* hang there.

"Or," she says, taking my hand. "Definitely or."

*   *   *

Kate leans into me on the basement couch, her body warm perfection. We kiss, but she pulls away.

"What's wrong?" she asks.

"Huh?"

"Earth to Jack," she sings. "Where are you right now?"

I kiss her cheek and hop off the couch.

"Come on," I say, extending my hand to her. "We've gotta go."

"Where are we going?"

"We don't have a lot of time."

"Why are we at the hospital?"

"Because you're sick, Kate."

She shakes her head. "I feel fine. Actually, no. I feel better than fine. I feel better than I can remember ever feeling. The treatment is working, Jack."

"Do you trust me?"

She scrunches her face.

"Just trust me, please."

The nurse in the ER makes the same *what are you talking about* face when I explain to her that even though Kate isn't showing outward signs just yet, she's going to have a crisis. The nurses and the doctor on duty aren't buying it. They won't even run tests.

"We appreciate your concern, young man," they all say, and you can hear the *but* coming from a mile away.

"I don't think that you do. If you truly appreciated my concern, you'd run the tests. You'd keep her here and you'd—"

"Jack, I'm okay," Kate says not for the first time. "Really, I am."

But I'm not above pleading. I'm not too proud to beg. "Please, please, just run the tests. That's all I'm asking."

"Young man—"

"Please! I have money."

"That's not what this is about—"

"I can pay for the tests. I can write you a check right now. I just need a pen."

"We're going to have to ask you to leave now."

"You're not hearing me! She's going to die! If you don't do something, she will die. It's not a question. It's not a possibility. It's reality! It will happen!"

They turn to Kate. "Is your boyfriend currently undergoing any treatment? Are there any medications that he's been prescribed that he's stopped taking?"

"He's not crazy," Kate insists.

"No one's saying anyone's crazy, but—"

"I'm not crazy. I just know because . . ." This is the part where I can tell the truth. I can say I know because I'm from the future. I know because I've already lived this. But I know that I can't tell the truth without landing an overnight suite on the psych ward.

"Jack," Kate says, turning to me, her hand clasping mine, her body turned to walk us both out from behind the exam room curtain, back through the ER waiting room, and back out into the cold, dark night. "Let's go."

Now there are tears in my eyes that I can't do anything about, least of all stop them. "I can't go. We can't go, Kate. Please. Listen to me. I'm *not* crazy."

"I know you aren't. But I don't understand any of this."

"I wish I could explain how I know . . ."

"How do you know?"

I look over, the nurse's face as hard as rock, her arms still crossed. "I can't say . . . I'm sorry . . . But I can't."

"Well, then I'm afraid you're out of time, young man," the nurse says, calling out into the hallway for help.

And I'm going to fail again.

I've exhausted every option.

Maybe I just have to accept the truth. That there's nothing I can do to change anything.

Except I refuse to believe that.

"Jack, what are you doing?" Kate asks.

"Whatever I have to," I tell her.

"Security, security," the nurse yells into the corridor.

I won't be stopped.

"Jack, what are you doing?" Kate asks again. "I don't understand."

"Trust me, I don't either. But we've got to try anyway."

By the time two security guards show up, I'm barricading the exam room with all the hospital equipment that I can move: IV poles, cardiac monitors, an ultrasound machine. But the larger of the two guards forces his way inside, lifts me off my feet, and carries me out into the hallway. I reach for the curtain. "Let go of that," he says, trying to bat away my hand.

His partner, a wiry, gray-haired man, seems less eager to engage me. He instead talks into his radio and remains on the sidelines. Maybe because at this point I have officially lost all my *I'm not crazy* credibility, I scream, "They're trying to kill me!" and flail and karate chop and contort my body into pretzel-like configurations. Because I don't care what people think of me. What happens to me. I'll do anything to keep Kate here, to keep Kate safe.

By the time Laird (I have an awesome up-close view of

435

his name badge as he bear-hugs me into submission) wrestles me into the waiting room hallway, Kate starts having trouble breathing. They stick an IV in her, hook her up to fluids and oxygen, check her vitals again, get labs drawn. They march me into the waiting area. An hour later the doctor comes out, shaking his head. "I don't know how you knew, but you might've saved her life."

I glance at the waiting area clock.

"Not yet I haven't," I say. "Not yet."

The doctor frowns. "Well, we've moved her into an observation room. We want to keep her overnight. Make sure her hemoglobin remains stable. We'll draw some more blood in the morning. You can see her now."

I thank the doctor, resist the urge to check out the time again, and head back to Kate's room. She looks over at me, standing in the doorway, and grins.

"Hey, Incredible Hulk," she says, pushing the button on her bed to make her raise her head. "Or are you back to Bruce Banner now?"

I laugh. "How are you?"

"Mmm. Better now. I think. But then again, I didn't even know I *wasn't* okay before. But somehow you did."

"Lucky guess."

"It didn't seem like a guess."

"You want to know the truth?"

"That would be pretty cool."

"I'm from the future and I knew the exact time when you

were going to get sick."

"Okay, this is definitely a lie."

"It's not."

"You want to know how I know it's a lie?"

"Okay, but it's not a lie."

"Because who would care about what happens to me enough to send you back in time? Like, what's so special about me? Am I going to be president of the United States? Or cure cancer? Or, I don't know . . . do anything important?"

I shrug again. "Honestly, I never made it *that* far into the future. So I guess we'll have to find out together."

She wiggles her fingers, holds out her arms, and I step into them.

"Promise?" she asks.

"Depends. What am I promising?"

"That we'll find out. Together."

"Either that, or I'll keep coming back in time until I get it right."

"You'd do that for me?"

I grin. "Maybe."

She sticks out her tongue at me. "Well, I'd build a time machine for you, mister. Now get in bed and cuddle me."

"This bed is barely big enough for one person," I complain, but I'm already climbing in. "You know the nurse is going to curse me out as soon as she comes into the room, right? I'm pretty sure everyone that works here hates me now."

"Ask me if I care."

I smile.

"No, really, ask me," she insists.

"Kate, do you care?"

"Hell no. Now ask me if I hate you."

"Do you hate me, Kate?"

"No. I'm incapable."

And I can't even begin to tell you how good it feels to hear those words.

"Kate?"

"Yeah?"

"If you had a choice, I mean—to live the same four months over and over again with me, or live the rest of your life without me, which would you choose?"

"That's a weird question. You're really playing up this time-traveling thing, huh?"

"C'mon, just play along."

"So, explain it to me. We'd just be like on this never-ending loop then?"

"Yes."

"Is it a good four-month loop at least?"

"It's pretty amazing. The best, I'd say."

She nods. "I like the sound of a Jack and Kate loop."

I kiss her cheek.

"So, let me ask you something now."

"Shoot."

"This is going to sound strange, but I've always wanted to be one of those couples whose names get mushed together in a symbol of achingly beautiful love—like Bennifer or Kimye," she says, a goofy smile on her face.

"Wait, you're joking, right?" I say.

"Nope. And I've been giving this a lot of thought. I've come up with a few ideas, if you care to hear them."

"Bring 'em."

"Okay," she says, leaning her head back against the pillow. I join her, so that our cheeks touch. "First up, Kack."

"Hmmmm. I don't know."

"I think it's sort of cool. Sounds like someone just got karate-chopped in the chest."

"Ouch, I didn't realize you were so violent."

She slices through the air with the side of her hand. "You better be careful, King."

"I think you were supposed to tell me this *before* I fell for you."

"Yeah, well, better late than never, right? Okay, you ready for the next one?"

"Hit me."

"I think you're going to love this one . . ."

"Look at you, selling me. Just tell me already."

"Okay, brace yourself . . ."

"I'm braced."

"Jate."

"That's what I was bracing myself for?"

She punches me. "Our names are too short for anything cool. Let's see you do better."

I think of the possibilities. "You're right. Those two are it."

"I told you."

"You did."

"Next time you should just listen to your girlfriend, Jack Attack."

"Next time," I repeat. "Next time."

THE AGONY, THE HORROR

.

I wake up in terror, fumbling with the blankets, the sheets. I look over at the clock on the wall, but it's too dim in the room, the only light coming from her IV pump, and I can't make out the time. Kate's beside me, her back to me. And I can't explain it, but something feels different. Like I'm on new ground. In an unfamiliar place.

"Kate," I say softly.

Nothing. Just the buzz of the IV, the chug of fluids flowing into her arm.

"Kate," I repeat, bringing my hand slowly to her shoulder. Her skin is cool.

"Kate," I whisper into her ear, shaking her gently.

I listen for her breathing, but I can't hear anything over my own.

"Kate," I say once more.

I sit up.

I take a breath.

And that's when I see it.

A shiny box of Cap'n Crunch sitting atop the hospital tray.

And then I'm crying.

And then I'm laughing.

And then it finally happens—

I'm craughing.

I'm craughing.

ALMOST THE END

Okay.

So now that you know Kate and Jack survive, I'll be honest.

These four replays weren't the only ones.

They're more like a composite of a lot of other replays.

I lost count after three dozen.

I still can't tell you why any of this happened. And even if I knew, it probably wouldn't be satisfying. It's like that Sesame Street story, *The Monster at the End of This Book*. When you read it for a second, third, and fourth time, when you already know it's only Grover at the end, the journey isn't any less real, you know?

But what I can tell you is that I tried *everything*. Some things I tried thrice.

A few times I tried nothing at all.

Sometimes I was too tired, too late, too sad.

It was like enduring the worst hangover ever. Except no matter how much you closed your eyes, or drank water, or begged God to make the world stop spinning, it was still there.

The head-splitting doubt.

The dread slugging me in the gut.

Everything sloshing inside me, sick.

I didn't think I was going to make it.

And I just couldn't put you through all of that.

Watching me fail time and time again.

Watching her die over and over.

No one should have to.

But mostly I was just thankful for the time I got to be with her, wondering if and when it (whatever it was) finally stopped, if it would be the end of me, too.

I guess the reason I'm telling you all of this is because I don't want you to misunderstand this story. Because it's important for you to understand that I'm no hero.

I didn't save Kate.

She didn't need saving.

If anything, she saved me.

She taught me that *almost* doesn't have to be a bad thing.

You can try your hardest to change something—exhaust every possibility—and sometimes it's still not enough.

But *almost* means you were there. You did all you could.

In the end, it's the smallest decisions that matter most.

The seemingly insignificant choices we make every day—

To be honest with the people we love and with ourselves—

To let go of the things we can't control, and appreciate the things we can.

Sometimes it's hard to see how much these things mean.

But they add up.

They mean everything.

Take it from someone who's seen the future.

FIN, FOR REAL THIS TIME

"You sure your parents are okay with me being here? In their house? In your bedroom?" I ask.

"A little late for that." Kate smiles. "But yeah. I think they're just happy I'm happy."

Kate's childhood sheets are weaved between us, covering her stomach, her legs, my feet, joining us at our hips. Her eyes not letting mine go. Her breath so close, I taste spearmint. I blink, but only for a second. I don't want to miss anything.

"Did you ever think we'd be here?" she asks.

"I dreamed we would. But I'd be lying to say I thought it could ever happen," I say.

"I think that's what scared me. I think I did know."

"I think you're beautiful, Kate. That's what I know."

"Stop. You're making me blush."

I trace her shoulder blade. "Black people don't blush."

And she laughs. A beautiful laugh that comes rolling up from her feet, makes the bed quiver. "Why wouldn't we?"

My own cheeks go warm; maybe we do blush. "I meant, like, visibly."

She shakes her head. Sits up on her elbows, her eyes still on mine. "I know what you meant, silly. I just like to see you sweat sometimes."

"Uh, mission accomplished." I run my finger across her cheek. We lie there, quiet. I hear the clock tick a new minute on the far wall. And then another. "So? Are you going to tell me?"

"Tell you what?"

"Do we blush?"

"You're looking right at me, Jack King. You tell me. Do we?"

I study her for another moment. And then when I can no longer wait another, I lean in, kiss the space beneath her forehead, between her eyes. Her eyelids twitch against my chin.

She closes her eyes tight, like a fist, like she's trying to get back a dream.

She says, "I think blushing isn't something you see. It's something you feel."

And though she can't see me, I nod. "I feel it, Kate. Every bit of it. I feel."

"Come here," she says, eyes open now, holding her arms out wide.

"I don't think I can get any closer," I say, even though I want to, even though closer is all I want.

"You can," she says, pulling my head into her face. "See."

She's right.

And I see.

"You know what I love about the end of black family movies?" I ask Kate.

"Coming from anyone else, that would be an interestingly racist way to begin a conversation, but you've stoked my curiosity anyway. Please proceed," she says.

"The dancing. There's like almost always some large party—like a wedding reception, or family reunion, or whatever—and after everyone has finally settled whatever differences that need settling, when everyone is feeling the love, they end with some massive aerial shot of people doing the Electric Slide or a *Soul Train* line—like, I love the idea of everything ending that way. With people happy and smiling and dancing their asses off."

She shakes her head in that disapproving way you'd look at your puppy who's done something charmingly destructive. She laughs. "Me too," she says. "Me too."

She taps on her phone, fires up her Bluetooth speaker. She pulls me out of bed, and we clear off a spot in the middle of her floor, kicking away crumpled clothes and schoolbooks and whatever. We join hands and we shake our heads at each other.

"Will you do me the honor?" I ask her.

She bows and I curtsy and we dance.

"Hey, just so you know, I so don't love you. Not at all," Kate says, rather breathily because we can't stop dancing. Not for anything. Even weird, awkward proclamations from our hearts.

I grin. "I don't love you, either. Just so you know, too."

"Cool," she says, doing some dance that looks as though she is fishing but has suddenly hooked a killer whale. "I was hoping you felt the same way."

"Cool," I repeat, doing a dance I like to call *cleaning windows on scaffolding fifty-six floors up*. Okay, I just made that up. The name, not the dance. That move happens to be a staple in my repertoire.

And we keep on dancing, Kate and I. Our bodies twisting in ways they are not meant to twist, a lot of robot dancing, some old-school Cabbage Patch with a few pathetic Running Man interpretations thrown in for good measure.

So, no, not *good* dancing.

Not even halfway decent.

Nothing you'd be impressed by.

We're not turning heads at any party—not in a good way, anyway.

But give us our freaking aerial shot, please.

Because, fuck, we dance.

ACKNOWLEDGMENTS

Thank you to the two most amazing people on this planet and elsewhere, Brooklyn and Kennedy. Brooklyn—you're so funny and artistic. But most importantly, you have the biggest heart I've ever known. Never stop feeling. Kennedy, you're never gonna be taller than me, I don't care what the doctors say. But I know you'll definitely pass me in all the best ways. You both inspire me each and every day to be better than yesterday. Thank you for loving me, for teaching me what it means to love someone else, unconditionally, eternally.

Thank you to Pam. Whew. So many crazy times, but still we've always come out the other side (*It's been colder*). We've shared lots of laughs, tears, and memories. Thanks for holding me down and for your unwavering love. For falling asleep during every movie. For all our period-piece TV show binges and our *House Hunters–Project Runway–Top Chef* marathons. I wouldn't change a thing. I hope you wouldn't either. Always and forever, P.

Thank you to the best sibling anyone could ever ask for, Allisyn. We've been through so much, but we've been through it all together. Thanks for telling on me when I tried to run away. Also, I'm sorry you never get to have a mini–license plate with your name on it because Mom chose to spell your name funky, but hey, silly memorabilia isn't everything, right? Seriously though, I just want you to know, when I finally leave this place, you get: NOTHING! (Hahaha.) Until then, let's keep plotting our global takeover.

Greyson, you'll get those waves eventually, keep brushing; I believe in you, haha. Thanks for being the best big cousin ever, for being patient and kind and protective. You're great. Keep banging those drums, man.

To Mom and Dad, it all started with you. Mom, thank you for instilling in me a love for words, for guiding book after book into my hands, for reading to me, for reading all my stories, for talking me through life. This book doesn't exist without you (hey, just like me!). Dad, thanks for being pragmatic and making me think about things like supporting myself, and for reminding me from an early age that kids can go bankrupt, too, without sound financial planning. Also, thanks for letting me root for Michael Jordan and the Bulls at all the Cavs games. I love you both, always.

Beth Phelan, the best agent ever. Sometimes the stars align, but other times, entire galaxies. Thank you for believing in me from the *beginning* beginning. For all our talks, book-related and otherwise. For knowing when to push and pull. For your steady hand, and your wise (and funny) words. Out of all the Twitter pitches, in all the Twitterverse, I'm glad you walked into mine. Seriously, thank you for masterminding #DVPit and championing diversity. Let's keep this thing going; we've got a lot more work to do. No pressure! But PRESSURE, haha! ☺

Ben Rosenthal. What can I say? You're a brilliant editor, but an even better person. Always positive, constantly encouraging. Thank you for believing in this book from the start. Maybe it's because we're two Midwest kids, or because we both have a love affair with sports franchises that perpetually let us down, but I think we get each other, on and off the page. In your excellent editorial-speak: let's keep it *authentic*, haha.

Special thank-you to Mabel Hsu, for your insight, spot-on notes, and willingness to answer ALL the questions. And for understanding that texting drama is the WORST, haha.

Thank you so much to Katherine Tegen—I can't imagine publishing my first book anywhere else. Shout-out to Erin Fitzsimmons for your fantastic design work; thanks for pushing and pushing! Thank you to Allison Brown, Emily Rader, Gina Rizzo, Audrey Diestelkamp, and copy editor Megan Gendell—your contributions were so crucial.

Thank you to Rachel Petty for understanding this story and for being so awesome in general. Also, thanks for letting me think I could name your twins, haha. Thanks to the incredible

UK Macmillan team; you rock!

Thanks to Gemma Cooper for your enthusiasm and tireless support, for talking me through all the things, and for figuring out overseas three-way calls like a champ.

Many thanks to everyone at the Bent Agency for their hard work, and their incredible sub-agents who pushed to ensure more than just my mom reads this book. And a special shout-out to Victoria Cappello for her diligence and behind-the-scenes heroics.

Thank you to Stephanie Singleton; they say you shouldn't judge a book by its cover, but if it's your dope artistry on the jacket, I'd wholeheartedly disagree.

Thank you to the incredible team at Gallt and Zacker for your enthusiastic support and for making me feel at home.

So much love to my original crew and hometown friends, who always hold me down: Tony—man, our sitcom is still funny, I don't care what anyone says. *You're so . . . tall.* Des—few people understand me like you do, which should scare everyone else, haha. Drew—I don't care what Des says, keep shooting. Scales—my "little brother" through and through; thanks for bringing me cookies and relaying messages, no matter the content, verbatim. Anthony—man, I can't imagine nursing school without you; let's keep working smarter not harder, haha. Ariana—you were there when this story was just an idea. If I ever need killer makeup, you know where I'm coming. Thanks for the laughs and the best TV recommendations. *I hate it,* hahaha.

Thank you to Tiffany J, for all the long talks, pep and otherwise, for having my back, always; you know I've got yours the same. LB4L.

Thank you to Angie T, for all your sage advice and bottomless encouragement, for always being real, for casting the best movies, haha; you deserve all that you've gotten.

Super thanks to the Stupid Smart Kids: we met at NASA and took off from there (oh snap, that subtle pun-work). Drew—I don't know anyone who'd want to read through all my awful half-baked stories, except you. Thanks for all the chats, for letting me crash, for telling me I was a writer. Jesse—you could grow a full beard since we were fifteen (jealous), but you never let that go to your head, haha. Thanks for all the jokes, brother, and for the belief. Khadijah, my sister in words, few people understand the power of the written word more than you; hold on to your fire. We, and this world, need it. Karen, always so direct but also so genuine, and hella caring; thanks for working to keep the crew together; Rhode Island is blessed! And Amma, my sister and eternal homie, thanks for listening to all my literary scheming and for insisting that all of it was not only possible but eventual. You're my favorite artist by a landslide. Life's a dash . . . dancing around the living room to "Little Boxes" . . . all of that, always. By the way, Kwame, I'll read you the same stories over and over again any day, little man.

Big ups to the Trash Can Writers Crew: Ashley (it's fitting we're agent sibs because we're also twins!), Mark, Patrice, Kwame, Zoraida, Jalissa, and Saraciea. You guys are the best, and I *meme* it! Wakanda forever! And special Trash Can honorary shout-out to Nic and Dhonielle, who know all the things and share accordingly.

Thanks to my Beoples family for all your support and humor. I'm in awe of your talent and generosity.

To the following teachers, thank you for your near-irrational belief in my potential. It started with Mrs. Bennett in third grade (also the year I found out I needed glasses) who assured my mom I had *it*; Ms. Johnson in junior high, who guided me to Power of the Pen; Bruce Weigl, who saw something in me I didn't even recognize and who told me over and over through the years; Dr. Rachel Carnell, who wrote one of the best recommendation letters ever (that letter got me through some hard times), thank you; and to Sheila Schwartz, possibly the greatest teacher Cleveland State University has ever seen, but certainly the most inspirational. You got me my first fellowship despite reading some of the crappiest things I've ever written, all with graciousness and style; rest in peace.

Thank you to Mojo's for the best coffee (medium miel) in NE Ohio but also for never kicking me out. I drove past many a café to make it to you. You guys are awesome.

Thank you to libraries everywhere for giving me refuge and hope.

Thank you to the city of Cleveland, for nurturing me, for pushing me, for giving me a place to call home. We take a lot of crap, but we keep it moving. Cleveland versus the World, always.

Thank you to Love. Damn if we don't need more of you. Please stick around.

Thank you to Life. Maybe we didn't get here conventionally, but to heck with convention, right?! We made it, anyway.

Thank you to all the friends and family that I didn't mention expressly by name; you're not forgotten. I carry you in my heart.

Thank you to Papo and Aunt Elaine, I would gladly trade this story for another moment with you both, but between these pages, you live on.

And to Jack, Kate, Franny, and Jillian—thank you for all your words. But mostly, thank you for reminding me no one ever really dies.

TURN THE PAGE FOR AN EXCLUSIVE PEEK
AT AN ALTERNATE ENDING FOR

OPPOSITE
OF
ALWAYS

Dear Reader,

By now you know there are no easy endings to Kate and Jack's story.

Their love is hard-fought.

Their love is earned over and over.

So I thought it would be fun to imagine a different ending to their story; one where the roles are essentially reversed. Kate hovering over Jack, panicked, worried he won't survive, not sure what to do but ready to do everything, anything. And Jack on the opposite end of the spectrum, this time uncertain what's happening to him, what, if anything, awaits in the next moment.

After everything I put them through, Kate and Jack deserve multiple happy endings.

And from the *beginning* beginning I loved the idea of Kate, even just once, recognizing Jack on those well-traveled stairs.

Possibly sensing all their history. Absolutely feeling all their potential.

Both of them already madly in love, wanting, wanting.

So, here they are, one more time, moving through Time, hopefully, inevitably, hurtling straight into each other's open arms.

Hope you enjoy!

Justin

WOOD YOU BE MINE

Kate leans into me on the basement couch, her body warm perfection. We kiss, but she pulls away.

"What's wrong?" she asks.

"Huh?"

"Earth to Jack," she sings. "Where are you right now?"

"The only place I want to be." I kiss her cheek. "Right here. With you."

"You're so the-last-ten-minutes-of-a-cheesy-rom-com right now." She grins. Our noses brush.

"Yeah?"

"Definitely. And I love it."

My turn to grin. I touch her chin and she tilts it so, and we kiss again. And this is something I could get used to—kissing, a few happy lines of dialogue, and then kissing, kissing.

"Jack?"

"Yeah?"

"I want to be alone."

"Huh? Oh. Okay," I say, barely able to mask my disappointment. "I can drive you home."

She laughs. Kisses my nose. "Uh, no. I want to be alone. With you."

And right then, all of me liquefies. "Like *alone* alone?"

She nods. "*Alone* alone."

"So, this is the infamous Wood," she says, glancing up at the fort, the two of us standing below the ladder hatch.

"This is it."

"Are you gonna show me in?" she asks, laughing.

"I will. But first you have to give me a sec alone up there, okay?"

She laughs more. "Uhhh, what exactly are you going to do?"

"It's a surprise," I say. My backpack slung on my shoulder, I'm already climbing the rope. "Just give me five minutes tops."

"Okay, but hurry. It's kinda creepy. I feel like this is the opening five minutes of a horror movie. And you know the black kid always dies first, so."

"I'll hurry, I promise," I call back down. I unzip my backpack, pull out about a dozen candles of all shapes, sizes, and colors. A quick whiff of my bag confirms that some of the scents may not be super compatible, but it was the best I could do on short notice, running around the house, collecting as

462

many of Mom's candles as my backpack could hold.

I place them all around the perimeter, lighting them as I go—and for a moment, I consider the possibility that maybe I'll somehow burn the place down. But if I'm gonna go, at least it's on a night like this, on a night with me, Kate, and the moon.

"Has it been five minutes yet," Kate yells.

"Almost," I say. "Forty more seconds." I remove the Bluetooth speaker from my bag, set it on the small TV tray table in the corner. Prop my phone beside it, cue up a playlist I started for me and Kate to curate together. The first track is our favorite Mighty Moat love song—"As You Are."

"Is that my song you're playing up there?"

I look down at her through the open hatch. "Come see."

And she grabs the rope.

"But watch your step," I say. "The rope's a little damp."

She takes a deep breath and then scales the ladder. She scans the candlelit space. And then she punches me.

"Owww! What was that for?"

"What do you think is about to happen up here, Jack Ellison King?"

And my cheeks go warm, because clearly, embarrassingly, I've misread the entire situation. "Oh, ummm, I didn't mean to . . . I'm sorry if . . . I'm really sorry."

"Jack. Stop." She smiles. "This is beautiful. Absolutely perfect."

"It wasn't perfect, but then you got here, and . . ."

She pulls me into her. "We could do this all night, exchange witty banter, and that would be cool, but how about we both shut up so you can kiss me already."

And I agree. And I oblige. And when we finally pull away, my lips feel incomplete without hers pressed against them, and where her lips met mine there is an ache and a longing.

We dance until the song ends, kissing—and also doing that thing you think is really corny when you see other people do it, especially when you're single, that stare-deep-into-someone's-eyes-and-sing-to-them-the-perfect-love-song thing.

When the music stops, we keep moving, her heart knocking against my chest, or maybe that's my heart; it's hard to say. And then her body stops moving, and she pulls me down onto the rug. Takes my face between her hands. "As you are," she says softly.

"As you are," I repeat.

THE AGONY, THE HORROR

I wake up in terror, fumbling with the heavy sleeping bag draped around us, the candles still twitching, the moon lower in the sky now. I reach for my phone, tap the screen, but it's dead and there's no power in The Wood.

Which means I have no idea what time it is.

Which means I have no idea if . . . if . . .

Kate has her back to me, her shoulder blades arched, two perfect parentheses. And I can't explain it, but something's different. The air thicker, buzzier.

"Kate," I say softly.

Nothing.

"Kate," I repeat, bringing my hand slowly to her shoulder. Her skin is cool.

"Kate," I whisper into her ear, shaking her gently.

I listen for her breathing, but I can't hear anything over my own.

"Kate," I say once more.

I sit up.

I take a breath.

"Kate, we have to go. We have to go now."

She stirs, just barely. "What's wrong," she says, reaching back and stroking my bare arm.

"Please, just get dressed. We have to go."

"But where?"

And that's when I see it.

A small, shiny box of Cap'n Crunch poking out of the top of her purse.

And then I'm crying.

And then I'm laughing.

Because we're gonna be okay.

And then it finally happens—

I'm craughing.

I'm craughing.

FENDER-BENDING TIME

We pick our way through the woods and slip into the car.

Kate looks across the seat at me, concern all over her face. "Should I be worried about you?"

"No," I say, shaking my head. "Everything's going to be okay. I know what we have to do."

She looks skeptical. "Oh, really? Are you thinking of clueing me in, too, or . . . ?"

"We have to get to the hospital."

"For what?"

"So that . . ." But I don't have a good answer for her. Because how could I?

"For what, Jack?"

"I don't know how to explain it, but . . ."

"Just tell me."

"You want the truth?"

"Uh, yes."

"It's wild."

"I can do wild."

"Okay," I say with a shrug. "I've fallen in love with you so many times now, only to watch you fade away. But for whatever reason, I think because I'm supposed to somehow fix things, I keep coming back to you, on the stairs, on these old college-house-party stairs, and . . ."

If she was skeptical before, she's at least five levels beyond that now. "Okay, if you don't want to really tell me what's going on . . ."

"This is the truth. I know how it sounds, and I know I just did a terrible job of explaining things. I know I've only confused you even more, but you have to trust me. You trust me, right?"

She nods.

"Kate, you're not going to survive the night if we don't get you to the hospital right now. That's the one thing I know."

"But . . ." Her voice tapers, and she falls back into her seat. "I feel fine."

I reach across the seat. Place my hand on her knee. "I know," I assure her. "I know."

There's possibly a million cars on the road right now, all of them content to tortoise along—except we don't have time to mosey. I mash the pedal, yank the wheel sharply to the right, the car jumping into the oncoming lane—I pass one car, then a van, then some hybrid. I just need to get around two more cars and we'll be in good shape, we'll be cruising.

That's when I see it.

But it's too late to avoid it. To swerve.

A cargo van headed straight for us, its headlights illuminating our entire car.

"Jaaaack," Kate screams as she reaches over and throws the steering wheel in the opposite direction. The car lurches, slips into a tailspin, and we narrowly miss the cargo van, which screeched the other way.

But we can't miss the light pole, the back bumper of the car snapping against it.

We don't miss the car parked along the street, my side of the car careening full speed into its side. A high-velocity aluminum sandwich, me in the middle.

And I feel something happening, but I don't think it's that. This is different.

"Jack," Kate says. "You're bleeding. Don't move. Oh my God, don't move. I'm calling 9-1-1. You're gonna be o . . ."

But her voice muffles, or my ears stop being ears—either way her lips are moving but I can't hear what she's saying. And then the edges around Kate start to blur. I blink, but the world only gets fuzzier.

I can't be sure whether I actually say these words out loud, but I try.

I try.

"Kate," I say. "I'm sorry. I'm so sorry, Kate. I love . . . I luhhh . . ."

I see her face once last time, her eyes larger than I've ever seen them, larger and wilder, her mouth wide, then wider still, like she's howling.

And then nothing.

A whole lot of—

Nothing.

STAIRING THE FUTURE IN HER SWEET, SWEET FACE

My head is throbbing, my ears buzzing, my jaw tight, but at this point that feels like victory. At this point, any bodily feeling is a triumph.

I hear music.

I open my eyes.

My ass hurts, which means, yep, same ol' stairs.

"Excuse me, man, but you're sort of damming up the steps," Kate says.

"Oh, my bad," I say, sliding over to let her pass, because I'm currently out of ideas. Because this time-traveling love affair is exhausting.

But she drops down, slides onto the stairs next to me. In fact, she's sitting rather close, our legs touching. "So," she says.

"Sooo," I say, not knowing where this is going, but willing to go with it.

"I guess you decided not to get me a drink then," she says, elbowing me in the side of my ribs.

"Huh?" I turn to face her, which is hard, because, you know, small stairs, two grown bodies.

She smiles. "You said you were gonna get me a drink while I went to tinkle. I mean, if you didn't want to, you could've just told me. I could've drunk from the bathroom faucet."

What is she talking about? And wait—WAIT—does she know me?

No no no no no no. This isn't happening. I'm asleep. I'm dead. I'm . . . I don't know what I am.

"Oh, uh, my bad?"

"It's okay. I'm almost ready to go anyway."

"Oh, you have big plans?"

She looks at me like I'm crazy. "First no drink, and now you're trying to renege on hamburgers, too?"

"I don't understand. Please explain to me what's happening."

"What don't you understand."

"Do you know me? Like, you know who I am?"

"Of course I do."

"Who am I?"

"What?"

"Say my name. If you know me, say my name."

"What is wrong with you?"

"Just . . . please . . . say my name."

She shakes her head. "Fine. Whatever. Your name is Kyle."

"What? You just said . . . did you just say . . . ?"

"I said your name, Kyle. Kyle."

"But . . ."

"Oh my God, I see someone's been drinking without me, ha ha ha."

"Kate . . ."

"Jack . . ."

"But you just said Kyle . . ."

"Right. I was just messing with you. Which is clearly not the best idea right now. Are you okay, man? Like, for real?"

She knows me.

Somehow, she really knows me.

Yes, I'm okay. For real.

"Hello? Jack? Are you there?" She taps on my head.

But I smile. Like, my face might explode, that's how big I smile.

"Will you dance with me?" I ask her.

"I thought you'd never ask."

I stand up, hold out my hand, and she takes it in hers.

This must be how it feels to be shocked (you know, if being shocked was a good thing). A million unexpected volts bounding through my body, end to end.

You could hand me a lamp and together we would light up this room.

And we descend those sweet-ass stairs, one by one, hand in hand, until there are no steps left to take.